LAST DAY
IN PARADISE

Thanks Kat
the best
R.K. Swish

Other books from Sunstone Press
by Robert K. Swisher Jr.

THE LAND
THE LAST NARROW GAUGE TRAIN RPBBERY
LOVE LIES BLEEDING
FATAL DESTINY
ONLY MAGIC

Also by Robert K. Swisher

THE MAN FROM THE MOUNTAIN
AN AMERICAN LOVE STORY
THE WEAVER

LAST DAY IN PARADISE

by
Robert K. Swisher Jr.

SUNSTONE PRESS
SANTA FE

Cover photograph by Carl Condit

© 2004 by Robert K. Swisher Jr.
All rights reserved.
No part of this book may be reproduced in any form or by any electronic or mechanical means including information storage and retrieval systems without permission in writing from the publisher, except by a reviewer who may quote brief passages in a review.

Sunstone books may be purchased for educational, business, or sales promotional use. For information please write: Special Markets Department, Sunstone Press, P.O. Box 2321, Santa Fe, New Mexico 87501-2321.

Library of Congress Cataloging -in-Publication Data:

Swisher, Robert K., 1947-
   Last day in paradise / by Robert K. Swisher, Jr.
      p. cm.
   ISBN 0-86534-394-2 (pbk.)
   1. Difference (Psychology)—Fiction. I. Title.
PS3569.W574 L36 2004
813'.54—dc22
                              2003022295

Published in Santa Fe
WWW.SUNSTONEPRESS.COM
SUNSTONE PRESS / POST OFFICE BOX 2321 / SANTA FE, NM 87504-2321 / USA
(505) 988-4418 / *ORDERS ONLY* (800) 243-5644 / FAX (505) 988-1025

for the lady and the horse
killed in a moment of freedom
a small blessing
before the end
once I was a cowboy.

for the lady and the horse
killed in a moment of freedom
a small blessing
before the end
once I was a cowboy.

ONE

Banjo Ortega was sitting beneath the gnarled limbs of an ancient pinon tree that perched on the edge of a steep bluff like a hungry hawk. Banjo put the 30/30 rifle against his shoulder and scanned the horizon through the sights. "Ride to me gringo," he muttered in a sinister prayer.

But nobody appeared and Banjo dejectedly lowered the rifle. "You are lucky this day. I do not miss," he said with a wry toothless smile.

He scanned a dry parched hillside to his right and started counting. "Uno, douse, three, four, quatro, sinco, seven," but the bright New Mexico sun glared in his eyes and he had to stop. Several of his sheep were missing, but because of the sun and his poor eyesight Banjo knew he could do nothing about it and he decided to roll a smoke. With stiff fumbling fingers he reached into his faded blue denim shirt pocket for his tin of Prince Albert tobacco. Because he was missing the middle two fingers on his right hand it was difficult to roll cigarettes and, spilling enough tobacco for another smoke, he managed to roll a sad excuse for a cigarette. With difficulty Banjo pulled a stick match from his other pocket. When the fire touched the excess paper at the end of the cigarette, a flame shot up almost catching his scraggly moustache on fire. "No good gringo match," he swore, blowing out the flame.

He took a deep drag on the smoke. Another drag and the cigarette burnt down to his arthritic fingers. He tossed the butt onto the dusty, dry ground and smashed it with his boot heel.

The sun was higher in the sky and once again Banjo tried to count his sheep. He could see several lying under a stubby cedar tree while others lay in and around pinon trees and bleached red sandstone rocks. Turning dejectedly from the hillside and his sheep, he gazed south away from the bluff. The land from the base of the bluff was a seemingly endless hilly and eroded arid plain that was dotted by tumbleweeds, tenacious cedar trees and rocks in various shapes and sizes that had to be in agony. There was a small stream, no more than a foot across, fifty yards from the base of the bluff that Banjo used to drive his sheep to. This tiny river was now cut off by a fence the new owner of the Last Day In Paradise Ranch had ordered built. The fence bordered the entire west side of Banjo's land and was constructed without a gate.

"Pendaho gringo," Banjo grunted, struggling to his feet. "You have so much money you do not need friends."

It was not easy for Banjo to stand up. At eighty-five years old, nothing was easy. Banjo had lived outdoors his whole life and looked like a shriveled up piece of over dried beef jerky. His white hair was bushy and uncombed. He had a blotchy short white beard and a few long hairs under his nose that he called a moustache. His eyes were mountain sky blue and even clouded with cataracts were bold and proud. He was only five feet four inches tall and his faded Levi's and shirt had more patches on them than the original material. His boots should have been thrown away and he did not wear a hat. Banjo dreamed of owning a big black cowboy hat. One with a brim so big he could sleep in its shade. And a pair of tall black boots with riding heels that had eagles sewn on their sides. But they were a luxury he could not afford.

Once again Banjo tried to count the sheep on the hillside but gave up and shuffled to his bay mare, who was tied to a pinon tree a short distance away and had a swarm of flies buzzing around her head.

Banjo whistled softly as he got close to the horse. Although she was gentle, he knew she did not like to be snuck up on. She had kicked him more than once during their twenty-year relationship when Banjo had forgotten and run up to her while she dozed. The old mare opened her eyes, looked at Banjo, and took a deep breath as though lamenting her fate.

He put his 30/30 in the scabbard and led the mare to a rock. He stood on the rock to mount the horse. As he did, Banjo caught his right leg on the back of the saddle and almost fell off. "No good gringo saddle," Banjo grunted, catching himself and pulling himself with difficulty the rest of the way into the saddle.

Banjo gently nudged the mare with his knees to get her to move. When she balked, he kicked her as hard as he could and she began walking as slowly as possible. In earlier years this would have made Banjo extremely angry, but now it was not worth the energy it took to get mad.

Banjo rode down the rock-strewn hillside, away from the arid plain, and into a valley dotted with stands of straw colored gamma grass growing between the rocks. At the end of the valley he bowed his head as he passed a series of rock headstones. The dates and names on the stones were beat in with a chisel but there were no statements of love. Here at rest were three generations of his people who had lived on the land. He looked at the red and pink plastic flowers Angelena had put on the graves. A prickly pear cactus had taken root next to the bouquet on his father's grave. "One day soon I will be laying there," Banjo said to the horse, "and my no good son will sell my land to the rich gringo who owns the Last Day in Paradise Ranch."

Banjo pictured the man and some of his friends riding by the graves. "Mexicans who used to own this place are buried there," the gringo would say, as though dead Mexicans were just another possession.

Banjo spit on the ground. "Gringo bastard," he cursed.

The old horse ignored him and plodded along with her head down.

"If I cut the fence between every post it would give him something to think about," Banjo grinned.

"It would be better for me to do that than shoot him in his stupid head and have to go to jail for doing this country some good," he decided.

A fire was blazing under a washtub by the woodpile and Angelena was hanging wash on the line when Banjo rode in to his small homesite. Angelena did not wave at him. Banjo unsaddled the horse and put the tack in a log shed that most of the mud chinking had fallen out of years earlier. Taking the rifle with him he led the horse to a dilapidated corral and tossed her a wedge of hay and then walked over and washed his hands and face in the laundry water.

Angelena went to the house. She was seventy-five years old and exactly five feet tall. She wore a brown sack dress and a faded blue apron with yellow flowers on it. She had on brown army shoes, with green wool socks pulled up to her knees. Her dark face was etched like the side of a storm beaten cliff. Her once coal dark hair was now grey and grew to the center of her back and she kept it out of her eyes with a blue bandanna wrapped tightly around her forehead. Her hands were rough and chapped from years of doing laundry in a tub and splitting and carrying firewood. But she walked upright and proud, arthritis not claiming any of her bones, and her eyes were midnight black and filled with fire. Unlike Banjo she had all her teeth and her smile lit up her aged face like a young girl going to a dance for the first time. She reminded Banjo of a small Banti hen that all the big chickens were afraid off.

Banjo went behind the three room adobe house and took a leak behind a shriveled up cedar tree. He did not like to go into the outhouse in the summer. Besides the smell, he had the fear of being bitten on the rear by a black widow spider, an incident that happened to his father when Banjo was a boy and left a lasting impression in his mind.

Banjo went into the house without brushing the dust off himself. This used to bother Angelena, but she did not waste her time complaining about it anymore.

Banjo put the 30/30 in his bedroom and sat down in the kitchen. A wood-burning cook stove took up most of the north wall. On the east wall, was a twenty year old freezer and, opposite it, a cheap, wooden table with two chairs, one blue and the other red. On the table were several statues of The Virgin Mary, a set of yellow plastic salt and pepper shakers, and a Folger's coffee can filled with sugar. The other two rooms of the house were bedrooms, one Banjo's and the other Angelena's. They had not slept together in years. The floor of the entire house was red and white checked linoleum with brightly colored throw rugs by the beds and door.

"How are the sheep?" Angelena asked, putting a bowl of menudo and a cup of coffee in front of Banjo.

"Sheep are fine," Banjo answered, "but they do not have water." He did not feel like telling Angelena some of the sheep were missing, he did not want to worry her.

"Something will happen," Angelena said calmly.

Angelena being calm angered Banjo but he did not say anything. They had already argued when he told her he wanted to cut the fence. "It will do no good to do anything rash," she had told him.

Angelena brought Banjo a warm tortilla. Banjo loved his wife's tortillas. Angelena made better tortillas than anybody in the world. They were not the little flat ones that sold in Santa Fe for a dollar a half dozen. Angelena's were large and thick like pancakes and made from scratch. Even though they were hard for Banjo to eat with only a few teeth they were always delicious—a day without a tortilla was a sad day for Banjo.

After finishing his meal, Banjo sat in an old wooden kitchen chair on the covered front porch and put his feet up on the rail. Along with the rest of the adobe house the porch had long ago fallen into disrepair. He watched a half molted rooster grab a fleeting scorpion that made the mistake of coming out of hiding before the sun went down.

Banjo was beginning to relax when he remembered the pig. The pig grunted when he saw Banjo and Banjo scratched the pig's head. The pig's pen was only four feet wide. When the pig was big enough and had trouble turning around in the pen, he would go into the freezer. Banjo went to the shed, filled several coffee cans with pig pellets and took them over and fed the pig. He checked the water dish, which was full enough, and went back to the porch.

Angelena was sitting in her own chair, placed as far away from Banjo's chair as it could possibly be and still be on the porch. She was smoking a hand rolled cigarette bigger than Banjo's finger. Banjo, being proud, did not ask his wife to roll him a smoke. He fumbled around and managed to roll one, as usual spilling enough tobacco to roll another cigarette. He tried to hide the sorry excuse for a cigarette, but Angelena watched him out of the corner of her eye and Banjo knew she was laughing inside. Banjo lit the cigarette and dodged the flame that shot from its end, giving his wife a look like he rolled his cigarettes on purpose so they would flame. He tossed the match into the front yard where it was quickly attacked by two competing chickens, one of which grabbed it and ran off with the other in quick pursuit. Angelena butted her smoke and placed the butt in a Prince Albert can.

"Guess we'll have to go to Santa Fe soon and buy supplies." Banjo said.

Angelena did not answer, since the only answer would be, "I suppose," and I suppose was really no answer.

The sun set and Banjo and Angelena listened to the crickets start their nightly chorus. After it was dark, as Angelena walked by Banjo, she leaned over and kissed him on the cheek, then went into the house to go to bed. She smelled like flour and for a moment Banjo was hungry for another tortilla.

Banjo looked into the darkness. He pictured the white man who owned The Last Day in Paradise—all 160,000 acres—sitting in his tri-level, adobe house built next to his air strip. Banjo wondered what he was doing, besides scheming to get Banjo's 80 acres of rock, cedar and pinon trees? He had never met Mr. Cook and had only seen him from a distance. Banjo sighted his 30/30 at the man and pondered if he could hit him in the head from over a quarter of a mile away. But he knew he could not, even if he had one of those new 7 m.m. magnums he had seen in a sporting goods store in Santa Fe.

Banjo went to his bedroom. Angelena's light was still on and he knew his wife was reading one of those trashy romance novels, one with a white man and woman on the cover, both nearly naked and gazing at each other like they were the other's only thought in life. "Stupid gringos," Banjo said.

Banjo sat in his rocking chair and while looking at the green plastic crucifix nailed over the head of his bed, he took off his boots. With the aroma of socks filling the room, he knelt down by the bed and crossed himself. "God, please let me find my sheep," he said. "And let there be rain so my sheep can drink. Bless my wife. And let the bastard gringo with the big house and an airplane die in his sleep from a heart attack so I do not have to shoot him and go to jail. Thank you."

Banjo recrossed himself, got up, turned off the light and fell fully dressed on the bed. As he was about to doze off he thought about throwing his socks out on the front porch but was too tired to move. As sleep overcame him he mumbled, "No wonder my wife does not sleep with me."

Banjo woke with a start. His chest hurt and he could barely breathe. He peered into the coal darkness of his room and listened to Angelena's snoring. He sat up slowly and swung his legs over the edge of the bed. Sitting for a few minutes the pain subsided and his eyes adjusted to the darkness. He took a deep breath, stood and went outside, shutting the door quietly behind him. Even standing on the porch, he could still hear his wife's snoring. He sat down heavily in his chair and looked at the night stars. The stars were his friends. After years of sleeping under them while tending his sheep he should have known all the constellations by name, yet he only knew them as something that made him wonder. Stars were not to be named; they were too grand and mysterious to have names.

Banjo heard the pig snort and the mare plodding around in the corral. He had never named the horse; she was simply the bay mare. He wondered if the old horse ever looked at him and saw him for the old man he was—an old Mexican man with white hair and scraggly beard and moustache, whose shirts and Levis seemed to hang on him like ancient folds of skin.

"Mother of God," Banjo uttered.

Everything was old now. The house was old. The adobe bricks his father and his father's father had slaved over and plastered with mud and straw were beginning to crumble. It did not matter that it would take at least another two hundred years for the house to fall to ruin, it was old. Young hands could re-mud the walls and paint the interior, but Banjo did not have the strength or maybe he no longer had the desire. He thought about Angelena in her bed and he was sad he had not done better for her. She only owned two dresses and her room consisted of a bed and a cedar trunk they had hauled in by wagon years ago. He did not remember getting her the mirror that hung on the wall surrounded by pictures of Jesus and Mary.

Banjo could see Angelena when she arrived from Mexico. The thought made him smile. She was nineteen, short and thin, as delicate as a new shoot on a tree. Now, like him, she was old and wrinkled like the land around them.

Banjo knew nothing about the world. Only his 80 acres of dry alkali land had any meaning in the realm of the universe. He knew every rock and cactus and cedar tree on his land. He knew where the coyotes lived and where he could shoot a deer. He also knew all the crooks and crannies of the Last Day In Paradise Ranch, which was now fenced off from him. The old owner had been an understanding man who let Banjo water his sheep.

Everything had changed so much during Banjo's life. Banjo was never one to worry about making money, stealing sheep had always made enough to buy beans and flour and pigs and goats. When it was really lean, there was always a deer to shoot. Now, he constantly worried about money and dying.

His family was dead, his wife's family long ago forgotten in Mexico. His only son was an up and coming painter in Santa Fe, but, to Banjo, his son was nothing but a sell out to his race. A man who lived in town and dated white women and went to fancy parties. His son was a turncoat, a traitor to his heritage, a man who had forsaken the land for the white man's world.

Banjo did not like white people. He had never talked to many white people but he did not like them. It was because of them his people lived how they did. He hated the new owner of the Last Day in Paradise. There were millions of miles of fence in the west and it was all built by white people.

Banjo remembered when he was a young man. He and his father and his father's brother would ride horses all the way to Colorado and steal sheep and drive them back to the ranch. They would never cross a fence.

The next year, the people from Colorado would ride down and steal their sheep. On and on the exchange went—until the fences. The fences ruined a good situation.

Banjo remembered when he was six years old he and his uncle had ridden to the mountains that loomed like constant shadows to the west. For the first time he saw tall pine trees and large green meadows filled with streams. He marveled at the green and the beauty and wondered why his family lived so far from the mountains, in a part of the country where there were rocks and stubby cedar and pinon trees and very little water and grass. Sitting by the fire eating trout he asked his uncle, "Why do we live in the desert when we could live here?"

His uncle laughed. "Beauty is only for the rich," he said without sounding bitter.

When they returned from the mountains Banjo thought the mud house and the rocks and dried cedar fence posts that made up the sheep pens and corrals were ugly. It took him several years to find beauty in his home once again. But he never forgot his uncle's words.

Now, rich white people thought the high desert with its brown rocks and dusty trees was beautiful. Land that once could not be given away was now going for $3,000.00 an acre. The rich man who had built the fence had offered Banjo over $200,000.00 for his 80 acres, but Banjo would not sell—there was not enough money in the world to buy his land or the ghosts of his ancestors.

He knew Angelena and his son wanted him to sell. For his son he did not care. For Angelena he felt sad. She deserved a finer life. A warm house in town, a washer and dryer, maybe a T.V. and a phone. Banjo inquired about getting a phone once. But the cost of having the cable run to his house was more than he could afford. His son offered to bring them one of the new phones that did not need wires but Banjo would take nothing from his son nor would he buy one himself since his son had recommended it.

Banjo rubbed his forehead. "Maybe in the morning I will find my lost sheep," he said.

He hoped he would, he needed to sell a few of them. They needed some supplies and he needed tobacco. He might even buy some of those already rolled cigarettes. Spilling his tobacco was a waste, or maybe he would buy a pipe. With a pipe, he would not always have to worry about lighting his face on fire.

Banjo carefully shut the door. His wife was still snoring loudly. "Maybe it is those trashy white man's books that make her snore," Banjo said.

Laying down and shutting his eyes, he sighed deeply. "I wish I could ride all the way to Colorado and steal some sheep." he said. "Ride and ride and ride. I miss stealing sheep."

Banjo visualized the new fence. "I do not want to kill you gringo, but I will," he swore.

Two

Rodney Slugger had problems he knew the beer would not help. He had been lucky getting a ride out of Montana but now he was worried about getting out of Santa Fe. Getting to Texas was a lot harder than he figured it would be. The fact he was almost broke would not have bothered him back home, a cowboy was always broke, but on the road and down to $50.00 he needed to find a part time job or go hungry.

Cowboys on the ranch where he had worked in Montana had told him about Santa Fe. How Santa Fe had crept into bunkhouse conversation he did not remember? "It's a town where people sit around and talk about paintings and pottery while reciting bad poetry," Moose said.

"Everything costs three times more than it should because only rich people can afford to live there," Bull said.

"There isn't a woman in the town who isn't pretty," Riley said.

How any of the men had known about Santa Fe, Rodney did not ask. Most conversations to Rodney were only spoken for the ears of the speaker and as useless as flies.

Rodney was in a bar on the northern edge of Santa Fe. In the bar were long hairs, good looking women wearing diamond rings the size of his eyeball, an Arab, several Indians covered with enough turquoise jewelry to open their own jewelry store and men and women who looked like bankers or lawyers.

Rodney, wearing well worn Levi's, a snap cotton western shirt, a dirty off white cowboy hat and scuffed brown cowboy boots, felt as out of place as a canary at a cat show.

"You want another beer?" the bartender asked.

"I want a job," Rodney said truthfully.

"You might be in luck," the bartender said surprising Rodney. "I read the paper everyday for jobs. I saw an ad yesterday that the Last Day In Paradise Ranch is looking for a cowboy. It was strange. I didn't think people advertised for cowboys."

"We're in short supply," Rodney said dryly, and added with a bit of hope. "Where is the ranch?"

"Go to where highway 64 enters town and then it's about ten miles to Lamy. The next road to the right will take you to Galisteo. The road to the ranch headquarters is on the other side of town," the bartender said.

"You wouldn't be putting me on would you?" Rodney asked, trying not to sound desperate.

"I sure as hell don't want to work on any ranch?"

Rodney straightened his cowboy hat, picked up the suitcase that contained all his worldly possessions and had his sleeping bag strapped to it. "Thanks," he told the bartender as he left. It took two hours for Rodney to get through town and reach Highway 64.

"Please, a few weeks work," he said looking down the two lane black top road that led out into the country.

After walking for an hour, and not getting a ride, the sun began to set and Rodney knew he was still a long way from Galisteo. He spotted a large cedar tree about fifty yards from the road, luckily there were enough dead branches in the tree for a fire. He started a fire and heated a can of Campbell's Chicken and Noodle soup. The stars came out, almost as vivid as Montana. Drinking his soup he wondered if Hazel was happy with her world famous bull rider? He spread his sleeping bag out and tried to keep the thought of Hazel out of his mind.

Rodney lay underneath the tree and listened to a diesel truck drive by.

Rodney thought being a trucker was much like being a cowboy. It took a certain type of man, a restless man, to want to be either. There were a lot more truckers now than there were cowboys. It took an idiot to want to be kicked by cattle and work all day for lousy wages but he supposed it took an idiot to want to drive a truck all over the country—both jobs only led to hemorrhoids and the poor house. Rodney rolled over on his sleeping bag. "Life is a bunch of forgetting," Rodney said to the night.

Rodney looked up through the branches of the tree. "Hazel," he muttered. "You could have told me. All you had to say was I fell in love with another man. You should have told me and not run off to Vegas to watch him at the finals. Then at least I'd still be in Montana on the ranch with my friends and not running from my shame."

He knew the kidding he got from the men after Hazel took off was not intended to hurt him. But he still had to leave. A man did not have anything unless he had pride.

Rodney got up before sunrise and was headed down the highway by dawn. The land rolled like gentle waves and here and there a cedar tree or pinon dotted the brown landscape, but the land seemed lifeless. To his right, at least ten miles away, was a low ridge of rock hills devoid of any vegetation except small cactus. Distant mountains, looking like pale shadows, loomed on the horizon. The mountains reminded Rodney of vultures waiting patiently to devour his flesh.

During the four hours it took Rodney to reach Galisteo, three cars sped by his outstretched thumb without so much as a wave.

A bullet hole riddled sign informed Rodney that Galisteo had a population of sixty-seven people. To his left and right were several expensive adobe homes with tall adobe walls. The remaining houses were run down adobes—their yards cluttered by the junk and debris from many years of poverty—the haunts of a few goats and chickens. Directly across the street from an adobe church, with boarded up windows, was a small house with a gas pump in front and a vintage Coca Cola sign nailed over the door. Rodney saw an open sign on the door. A bell rang as he entered. The store was the size of a jail cell and all the canned goods were covered with dust. In the corner was a cooler, half filled with Cokes and 7-Ups and V-8 juice. In the window sill, a large, cast iron pot sat on a hot plate with a sign written in pink crayon—TAMALES. A stack of plastic bowls was beside it. A short, stocky, Mexican lady, came into the tiny room through a hanging curtain. She smiled at Rodney but said nothing.

Rodney looked at her, put three tamales in a bowl and set them on the counter along with a 7-Up. Rodney could hear a baby crying from the back of the house. He paid for the tamales and the lady put the money in a cigar box. "Señora, how far is it to the Last Day in Paradise Ranch?" he asked.

"Only a mile to the dirt road but seven miles more down the road," she answered shyly.

Rodney went outside. He sat on a crumbling rock wall and ate the tamales and guzzled the 7-Up. A scruffy black and white dog eyed him suspiciously from across the street. Rodney looked up and down the street for a trash barrel, but noticing there were empty cans and paper everywhere, he tossed his trash next to the wall and headed out of town.

Within fifteen minutes, Rodney saw the hand carved, wooden sign, hanging over the entrance to the ranch. As he read the sign, Last Day In Paradise, he felt apprehensive, like the day he joined the army, but he shrugged it off and started down the red, brick dry, dirt road.

Sizing up the land he knew the ranch could never make any money. The grass could not feed enough cattle to pay the taxes. But, even being lifeless brown and filled with gullies and dry canyons, there were no houses to be seen, or cars speeding by. "Maybe paradise is anywhere there aren't people," Rodney said.

Rodney crossed a cattle guard where at one time there had been a gate and fence running off in either direction. Now there was no gate and no wire on the dried and cracked cedar posts. The sun made the cedar posts look like shriveled up men who had been staked out to dry. Rodney made a sour face. If he did get a job, the boss would probably want him to mend fence and Rodney hated mending fence. He would rather cut it than fix it.

Rodney was getting tired and thirsty as he crested a hill. Below him, about a half mile away, was the headquarters to the Last Day In Paradise Ranch. The road sloped gently down into a flat valley that had to encompass at least a hundred acres. In the center of the valley was a large, steel, Quonset hut that Rodney presumed was a barn. Next to the Quonset hut was parked two bulldozers, a road maintainer and several tractors. A hundred yards from the barn was a series of corrals attached to horse stalls. A little farther down the road was a rust colored brick house and not far from it was a small tan colored adobe house. Set apart from these two houses was a house an oil tycoon could not afford. All of the houses were surrounded by huge cottonwood trees that were so magnificent they seemed out of place.

Rodney noticed there were no horses or livestock in the corrals. As Rodney started down the hill he saw an air strip about a half mile from the houses and a twin engine airplane setting by an aluminum hanger. "This boy has it all," Rodney muttered, wondering how he could be without a truck and on foot and this guy own the whole state?

Rodney crossed another cattle guard at the bottom of the hill and noticed all the headquarters was surrounded by five strand barb wire fence. He hoped that if the owner did not give him a job he would at least drive him back to the highway. He heard classical music coming from the adobe house.

The adobe house had a chain link fence around it. Rodney sat his suitcase by the gate and looked in the yard to make sure there was no ranch dog waiting to ambush him. Every ranch Rodney had worked on seemed to have one dog that did not bark or make a ruckus, but was a champion at running and biting a person without warning or provocation. Satisfied there was no dog, Rodney went through the gate. There were four cow skulls nailed to the trunk of a cottonwood tree and a hummingbird feeder hanging from a lower branch. The screen door was closed but the door was open. Rodney knocked on the door and for some reason he felt like a salesman. He waited but there was no answer. He knocked on the door harder and a woman hollered from the back of the house, "Where do you think you are? Chicago. Come on in. It isn't locked."

Rodney left his suitcase by the door and went into a kitchen and did not know why but he felt self-conscious. Rodney took off his hat and looked at an assortment of magnets stuck to the refrigerator. There were bears, and cats, and a green frog with his tongue sticking out, one that said, "NOT ON MY TIME", an elephant, one of two monkeys and at least a dozen red hearts of various sizes. There were no photographs.

"I like magnets," a woman said as she turned off the radio. Rodney looked at a lady that had entered the kitchen from the back of the house and felt like he had been run over by a horse. In a few seconds he knew she was blond, blue-eyed, long-legged and beautiful. She was wearing a cropped white T-shirt, a pair of very short, cut off Levi's, the toes of her bare feet had pink nail polish, and she was in her thirties. But it was not her good looks that snowballed him—it was something else—a feeling he had experienced only one other time in his life. A feeling that although wonderful was also frightening.

"Quickest going over I've ever had in my life," the lady said, but not angrily.

"Sorry," Rodney apologized nervously, trying to stop the feeling he had in his chest.

"Looking is free, everything else is extra," the lady said and winked playfully.

Rodney did not know what to say. He felt like a ten year old boy who had fallen in love with his math teacher.

"Do you want something to drink, or do you want to stand there and let your tongue dry out?" the lady asked.

"Please, anything," he said, his lips feeling like rubber. "Can I sit down? My feet aren't used to walking."

She pointed at the table and went outside, returning with a jar of sun tea. Rodney sat at the kitchen table. The lady placed a glass of tea in front of him, poured herself one and took several swallows of hers. Rodney watched the way the muscles in her stomach flexed as she swallowed. Rodney picked up his glass and drank all the tea without stopping. The lady refilled his glass and sat down.

"My name is Karen, I'm divorced, no kids, I am trying to be an artist, I tried decorating cattle skulls but the market is glutted and now I am going to be a painter but I have not started a painting yet. I rent this house much to the pain and agony of my family and, I'm thirty-eight years old," Karen rattled off with no tone of good or bad or importance.

Rodney was lost in her smile. "I'm Rodney, forty-seven years old, drifter, cowboy, no good, lost, hopeless, tired and out of work."

"Well Rodney, welcome to the Last Day In Paradise Ranch. I suppose you're looking for the job that was advertised."

"I didn't walk all this way for my health," Rodney said truthfully.

"Mr. Cook needs somebody around here. He doesn't know a damn thing about ranches except that he has the money to buy them," Karen said with a trace of contempt in her voice.

"That's how most ranch owners are," Rodney said.

"Mr. Cook and his wife will be back in an hour or so," Karen said. "They went for a horse back ride. You can sit here or walk around if you like. I'm doing laundry and cleaning the house."

As Karen walked out of the room, Rodney admired the backs of her tanned legs and took several deep breaths. "Dear God," he mumbled as he put his hat on and went outside.

Sitting under the cottonwood tree, he tried to relax and quell the feeling inside of him from meeting Karen. "It's impossible," he said. "I'm too damn old for that kind of stuff."

Rodney gazed at the brown, seemingly lifeless land around him. This was different country than the waving grass of Montana. But, it was still the West, and this was a ranch and he was a cowboy. Even if being a cowboy was not much, it was better than being a banker.

Karen folded her silk underpants and matching bras and put them in the dresser. On the walls were several pictures of San Francisco and one of Yosemite Park. Sitting in the corner was a purple vase filled with cattails and in another corner lay a cow skull, half covered with turquoise. She had stopped working on it when she saw about a hundred of them for sale in Santa Fe. She started to go into the living room when she looked out her window and saw Rodney sitting under the cottonwood tree. For the past several years she had avoided men. They all seemed so childish or fumbling or insecure. But there was something about the cowboy that interested her. A feeling she had not felt in years stirred in her the moment she saw him. She did not want to run out and rip his clothes off, she did not want to invite him to dinner, but, there was something about him that attracted her. She looked closely at the stranger. He was not tall, maybe 5'10". He weighed about 175 pounds. He had sandy short hair. His beard was scruffy but she could tell he shaved daily when he could. She knew from talking to him his eyes were a light green. He had a weathered tough looking face but he did not seem mean or ill tempered. His hands were rough and his fingers crooked and she bet he did not wear gloves when he worked. She liked his Levi's and western shirt and boots. She felt he was probably dumber than a rock but he reminded her of a mean mutt dog that people were afraid of, that in truth was gentle natured and only needed a pat.

Karen went to the living room to do her vacuuming and dusting. "Dear God, please, I know it's been a long time, but not a cowboy," she said and made a perplexed face as she turned on the vacuum.

Three

Mr. William Cook, Bill to his few friends, dismounted the Arabian gelding he had recently purchased for $48,000. The thrill of buying the horse was gone after riding over two miles for the first time in his life. The insides of his legs ached and he knew, if he stepped too quickly, he might get a cramp in his calf.

Even in his discomfort, Mr. Cook felt elated looking at the miles of brand new fence that stretched before him. The fence marked a portion of his western boundary and would be the back part of his sub-division. The fence also cut off Banjo Ortega from the river and hopefully would force the Mexican to sell his land to him. It cost Mr. Cook $8,000 to have the fence built but it was worth every dime.

Several hundred yards behind him, Mr. Cook watched his beautiful wife leading a sorrel mare over a stretch of exposed rock. She looked hot and tired and completely out of her element, which for the past nine months had been the high society of Phoenix, Arizona. Mr. Cook figured it would take time for her to grow accustomed to the ranch but the expansive house he had built for her should help. Although the house was not one he had pictured all the years he was gaining a fortune and dreaming about owning a large ranch, he knew a woman must be accommodated.

Gloria caught up to him. She plopped wearily on the ground and held the horse's reins loosely. The horse drooled on her new Casper Tweed cowboy hat, making Mr. Cook wince thinking about the $450 price tag. "This is what life is all about," he said proudly, "land."

"No, life is a country club and pools and shopping. No dirt, horses, flies, scorpions, and rocks," she thought, but she replied, "I'm glad you love it."

"Toughen up," Mr. Cook said, going into his fatherly tone, which at times he felt he needed as he was 56 and she was 32.

"In a few months you will start to discover things about yourself you never knew. We are embarking on a new phase of our lives. A return to man's true nature. A kinship with the outdoors. Life as it is meant to be lived," he preached.

"Yes," Gloria thought, "Rich and steeped in luxury and maids."

Mr. Cook mounted the Arabian, trying not to let on how he ached, secretly wishing he was back at the ranch house, sitting in the Jacuzzi and sipping on a gin and tonic.

Gloria, with a stiff upper lip, mounted her sorrel and dutifully fell in behind her husband as he, thank God, started back toward the house. More than anything, she wanted to take a shower and get in the Jacuzzi.

"Can you imagine our ancestors coming across this land a hundred years ago," Mr. Cook said. "It was nothing but fear—fear of the Indians, fear of no water, fear of no food, trusting to fate and the gods. Day after dreary day and the endless sea of land still before them."

"Poor wretched things," Gloria said. "Nobody who had anything going for them would have come west. Only thieves and outlaws and idiots."

"It was a test of the true human spirit," Mr. Cook went on. "Something us poor modern souls have never had to face."

"Here comes the dissatisfied rich man's speech again," Gloria thought.

She had discovered in her months of marriage that more times than not, it was easier for her to think her own thoughts and keep silent when Bill talked.

Mr. Cook watched two coyotes scamper over a hill. It was beyond belief how good it felt not to be sitting in some board room bickering with the directors of one of his companies.

Within thirty minutes, they were back at the headquarters and Mr. Cook unsaddled the horses. He watched Gloria walking toward the house and she reminded him briefly of his third wife. They both were 5'4" tall and had black hair and intoxicating slate gray eyes. Gloria entered a room with a sensuous air that immediately turned men's heads. She was the type of woman men looked at and wanted, knowing deep in their heart she would only cause them trouble. The type that men spent fortunes on and were always afraid she would run off with one of their many suitors.

Gloria was Mr. Cook's fifth wife and he did not worry about it anymore. If Gloria ran off he would give her a nice check, like all the others, and have another one within a few months. Women came easily to Mr. Cook. Love was something Mr. Cook had given up on years earlier. Impression and power were all that really mattered.

Finished putting the saddles in the tack room, Mr. Cook turned the horses out into the corral, checked their water and put two slivers of timothy in the feed bin. The sorrel immediately kicked the Arabian when it tried to eat beside her. Envisioning Gloria in the Jacuzzi Mr. Cook headed quickly for the house.

He could hear the water churning in the Jacuzzi when he got to the enclosed swimming pool. Gloria smiled and pointed at the two gin and tonics sitting on a silver tray beside the Jacuzzi. Mr. Cook returned her smile, undressed and got into the wonderfully soothing water.

Rodney could hear Karen inside the house running the vacuum cleaner. It seemed as though he was the man of the house—the little lady was doing all her domestic chores, while he napped in the shade before getting up and trudging once more out into the world to bring home the money. In Rodney's case, it would not be enough money to cover the bills for lipstick, eyeliner or pantyhose, not to mention food.

At the moment he did not feel pressured, nor worried about getting a job. He forgot he only had $50 to his name and a suitcase with a few odds and ends in it. The brown land lay lazily before him and he did not have to eat, or sleep, or drink, or love, or fight wars.

When Rodney saw the two figures riding toward the ranch headquarters, it did not register in his mind they were people. They were more like a dream, something distant and beyond reach. But, after watching the two bobbing riders for a few minutes, he knew they were people who were not good riders and were both probably in great pain—if not in pain, numb, with the pain coming later.

Rodney figured the man must be the owner. The man was round and soft looking, a man used to having things done for him. He also knew by the way the man handled himself he was secure in his life. Even though he bobbed and jostled with the horses, he had the air of a minor king or at least, a prince. His wife, Rodney presumed it was his wife, was obviously wishing she was anywhere but riding a horse. Even in the distance, Rodney could see her twisted smile, a smile Hazel had been good at. A smile put on like a plaster cast. Even with the distance he noticed she was beautiful.

When they rode within two hundred yards of him and headed for the horse stalls, Rodney was once again back in the real world—worried about not getting a job, remembering he only had 50 bucks, and it was along way to Texas in cowboy boots and riding ones' thumb.

The screen door banged shut behind Karen and she sat down underneath the tree, but not close enough for Rodney to take it as a flirtation. He tried not to stare at her shapely legs and bare midriff.

"There went the owner and his young love," Karen said.

"I gathered," Rodney answered.

"If I was you, I'd wait until they got out of the Jacuzzi before I went and asked for a job," Karen said.

"I imagine that's a good idea," Rodney replied.

"I'll fix us a light lunch and then call over and tell him you'd like to see him," Karen said.

"You don't have to do that," Rodney said.

"I don't have to do anything," Karen said letting Rodney know that independence was important to her.

In a few minutes, Karen whistled through the kitchen door. Rodney went inside to a tuna fish sandwich, cottage cheese and cut up tomatoes. Rodney wished he had a beer but drank his iced tea not wanting to overplay his welcome.

While they ate Karen eyed Rodney closely. Rodney, feeling her gaze, felt uneasy.

"I do hope he hires you," Karen said, "I'd like to know you better. I've never known a real cowboy."

Rodney gave Karen a shy look and could think of nothing to say but he wondered why he felt like he knew Karen.

Karen looked at a clock on the wall that had a small poster on top of it that said, 'Art Sucks.' "I'll call Mr. Cook now," she said as she went to the other room.

Karen came back. "He says come on up, he'll be by the pool."

"There's a pool here?" Rodney said, surprised.

"Behind the brick house and his house is an enclosed pool and a Jacuzzi," Karen answered.

Behind the main house Rodney saw what looked like a greenhouse and he knew it covered the pool.

"Hell of a ranch," Rodney said shaking his head.

Mr. Cook was sitting by the pool in a pair of red and orange bathing trunks, drinking his fourth gin and tonic. Mr. Cook was not tall, and shaped like a pear. He was bald on top of his head and dyed what hair he had brown. His eyebrows were bushy and reminded Rodney of a squirrel. His muscles were soft and had no definition. He wore a gold watch on his left wrist and a gold bracelet on his right wrist and had a diamond pinky ring large enough to make the Queen of England envious. Around his neck he had a large gold chain with a gold coin, surrounded by diamonds, hanging from it.

Mr. Cook stood up as Rodney approached and he knew that here was a real cowboy. He was even bowlegged and stupid looking.

"My name is Rodney Slugger, I'm looking for work," Rodney said simply while trying not to show his amazement at the pool and the numerous potted plants that made the area seem like a small jungle.

Mr. Cook, having never been around many true cowboys in his life, had always heard cowboys were not impressed by what one owned but by what one did. Roping, riding and cussing were high priorities in life—not how big your car and house were. Seeing Rodney up close, his first impression of stupidity vanished and he was left feeling slightly intimidated, which was a feeling he did not relish. Mr. Cook was fumbling for what to say to the cowboy, besides, "Have you worked on a ranch before?" which he knew the man had done just by his look, or "Do you ride?" which sounded dumber yet.

Gloria climbed out of the pool wearing a skimpy bright yellow bikini. Rodney gave her a sideways glance and looked back at Mr. Cook.

"You've got the job," Mr. Cook said, impressed that Rodney had shown no alarm over his almost naked wife.

"I'm a good hand," Rodney said simply. "Point me to the bunk house and I'll stow my gear and you can show me around the place."

"Your house is the brick one, it's nicely furnished and it has a washer and dryer. Take it easy this afternoon. If you need to go to town, there's a Ford pickup up in the garage you can use. Comes with the job. Gas pump is by the Quonset hut. I pay $600 a month cash. You file taxes if you want. No insurance. You buy your own food. Rent is free, truck is free. I pay all the bills."

Rodney felt like he had died and gone to heaven. Montana had paid $450 a month. He had never made $600 a month in his life. And he had never had a truck to use. He felt like jumping up and down but he did not want to look like he was excited. It was against a cowboy's code to really look too excited or happy, toughing out life unsmiling was more to the mettle.

Rodney put out his hand and shook hands with Mr. Cook, which was like shaking hands with raw liver.

"Thank you, Mr. Cook."

"Aren't you going to introduce us," Gloria said as she walked over to the men.

Rodney took off his hat and with great effort looked Gloria in the eyes. "This is my wife, Gloria," Mr. Cook said.

Rodney nervously shook hands with Gloria. "Glad to meet you ma'am," he said.

Gloria smiled at him with a smile that could melt rock but did not say anything.

Gloria watched Rodney leave. "Nice," she thought. "I'd like to try a little of that one."

Rodney went to Karen's house to get his suitcase but could not get the image of the almost naked Gloria out of his mind. "There's one you have to stay away from," he told himself.

Karen was standing by the fence. "I bet you got the job," she said.

"He didn't ask me anything, just hired me," Rodney said cracking a big grin. "I get to live in the brick house."

"I'm happy for you. How about I fix us dinner to celebrate? Say around seven," Karen said but had no sooner uttered the words than she wondered what in the world she was doing—she could get to know Rodney without having him over to dinner.

Rodney picked up his suitcase. "You bet," he said. "I'd like that a lot."

But, walking to his new house Rodney wondered why he accepted Karen's invitation. He did not want to get involved even with the feelings she stirred inside of him.

Rodney soaked in the bathtub and listened to the sound of the washing machine on its rinse cycle. The house was nicer than anything he had ever lived in. There was a room to remove dirty clothes and boots that led into a living room with a fireplace. The living room opened to a dining room which led to a kitchen that the shelves were stocked with canned goods and every type of utensil he could think of. Behind the kitchen was the laundry room and a door to a small back yard shaded by two sprawling cottonwood trees. The two bedrooms each had a bed. There was a radio in the kitchen and no T.V., which suited Rodney fine as he hated T.V.. The house had gas heat. In Montana they spent half the winter chopping wood to feed the pot belly stove.

"Life sure has a way of going from bad to good and good to bad," Rodney said outloud, adding, "Hazel, leaving me might have been the best thing you ever did."

But the ache in his heart told him his statement was not true.

Rodney put on new Levi's, a white western shirt and his most prized possession, a pair of black lizard boots. He was both excited and apprehensive about dinner. He had felt the same shock wave when he first met Hazel and Hazel had dumped him. "I will never let myself get hurt again," he said.

Karen was dressed in a light blue summer dress with spaghetti straps that stopped several inches above her knees and was not wearing shoes. She reminded Rodney of springtime. There were yellow black-eyed susans in a mason jar in the center of the table, with a lit candle on either side of them and the lights were turned off. Rodney did not know what to think. The only time he had ever eaten by candlelight was when the lights went out in Montana. Candlelight dinners were for rich people in fancy restaurants, but, he supposed he was rich now.

Karen poured his glass of wine before hers. Bathed in the golden candlelight she made Rodney feel warm and safe. He wanted more than anything to say something, anything about how she looked, but 'you're pretty' did not seem enough and, 'you look like a summer morning with the golden rays of dawn dancing off of your face' seemed too much like a sissy. So he sat and smiled and felt inadequate.

"Here's to your new job, Rodney," Karen said picking up her wine glass. They clicked glasses and he took a drink of wine.

"Boy, this is good," Rodney said.

"It should be," Karen said, "It's a bottle of 1966 Saint Emillion."

Seeing the look of confusion on his face Karen realized Rodney did not know the difference between Ripple and Saint Emillion.

"It would be easier if things were good and bad and not labeled, I suppose," Karen said, "Then you could enjoy what was good and not try and impress people with fancy names."

"When I get my first check, I'll take you to dinner in town," Rodney said and quickly wondered why he would say such a thing.

"That would be nice," Karen smiled then went to the stove.

Karen brought a baked chicken sizzling in a light mushroom sauce over to the table. She felt happy seeing Rodney's face brighten as he looked at the food. He seemed so simple and unpretentious. The last man she had dated felt like he knew everything. She wondered if Rodney knew much at all? But then, being a cowboy, he really did not have to know too much. But, Karen could tell there was a far deeper side to Rodney that did not show in his eyes, or his easiness, or his shyness—a side that was not a cowboy or simple—a side she perhaps did not want to know.

They ate in silence. She filled the wine glasses when they were empty and opened another bottle of "that good wine", as Rodney called it, having forgotten the name. She did not tell him it cost $48 a bottle in fear he might not drink anymore.

When Rodney was full, he pushed himself away from the table.

"That's the best feed I've had in years," he said, beaming like a small boy who has just eaten a watermelon all by himself.

Karen refilled his wine glass enjoying his simple enthusiasm.

"This wine gets better and better," Rodney said picking up the glass and taking a big drink. "You could really grow to like this stuff."

Karen cleared away the plates and put them in the sink. She sat down and crossed her legs. She caught Rodney taking a quick glance at her legs, which strangely made her tingle and did not bother her. They sat in silence but both were content with the quiet. Outside, a slight breeze rustled the leaves of the cottonwood tree and several crickets chirped. Rodney emptied his glass.

"Would you like to go for a walk, Rodney?" she asked.

Rodney did not answer immediately and Karen saw a moment of hurt in his eyes. "I'd like that," he said as if he had to force the words out of his mouth.

Karen went and put shoes on and wondered why she had asked Rodney to go for a walk. "I feel like a little girl who is falling into puppy love," she said.

They strolled, several feet a part, down the dirt road that Rodney had walked in on earlier in the day. Karen had her arms folded in front of her. Rodney had his hands in his pockets and felt uneasy. The moon was half full and their shadows stretched out in front of them like stick people. Several charcoal colored clouds drifted between the stars.

"I suppose you've spent a lot of your life alone?" Karen asked, breaking the silence.

"I like being alone," Rodney answered and Karen could feel a seriousness in his voice.

"Nobody likes being alone," Karen said.

"You're alone," Rodney answered.

She did not answer for awhile and Rodney did not pursue the statement. Several minutes later she said, "Why do you like being alone?"

"Guess because I've always been alone," Rodney said without hesitation. "Seems to work out that way for me. Always seem to be on the side of the river that doesn't have the people on it. Probably why I fell into ranch work. A lot of time to be alone."

Karen looked at his shadow next to hers on the dry, dark ground. "A shadow is all one ever really sees of another person," she thought sadly.

"I've never met a real cowboy," Karen said.

Rodney laughed. "Karen," he said, "Cowboys are people like everybody else. Every black, red, green, blue, yellow, white, orange and grey one of us are people."

"No, I don't think you're like most people," Karen said.

Rodney stopped. "We should head back. It's been a long couple of weeks for me and sleeping in a bed in my own house is very inviting."

Karen did not know why, but she knew if Rodney would make the slightest come on, she would end up in bed with him, but, standing by her gate he looked her in the eyes and smiled his homeless dog smile and she could feel a deep sadness that rested in his heart.

"Next time I'll buy some of that good wine," he said. "Thanks for dinner."

Karen watched Rodney walk into his house before going inside. She poured the last drop of wine into her glass. Sipping it slowly she watched the shadows the candle flame made on the wall. "He didn't even try to kiss me. Can you believe that?" she said both pleasantly surprised and slightly sad.

Rodney woke as the sky was beginning to turn red. He carefully made his bed, stretching out a small crease in the middle. After shaving and brushing his teeth he put on a pot of coffee and turned on the radio sitting on top of the refrigerator. He found a country station and sat down at the table. Rodney had never had a house by himself. After the Army, for his misspent year in college, he had shared a small house with four other boys. College had seemed like a waste after twelve months of killing—the thrill of going to football games and getting in the spirit never materialized.

He really could not remember how he ended up going to Montana. He knew he had to get away and the highway from California took him there like it was predestined. Being raised a factory worker's son in a medium sized town in California, he never dreamed about being a cowboy. Once in Montana, he found himself working on a ranch. A real ranch, a ranch where the owner lived in a modest frame house and worked everyday with the men. The men lived in a bunkhouse. When Rodney applied for the job he told Mr. Jacobs the truth, "I was in Vietnam and afterwards I flunked out of college. I've never been on a horse but I can learn."

Mr. Jacobs looked him straight in the eye, spit a large gob of tobacco on the ground and hired him. Starting pay was 50 bucks cash a week and meals. A man was expected to work six days a week, dark to dark, and often seven days.

At first Rodney mucked out stalls and cleaned tack. Then he cooked and then he drove back and forth to town for supplies. Slowly the cowboys taught him to ride and rope and tie knots, until three years later nobody could remember him not being a cowboy. He was there for twenty years, long enough for Mr. Jacobs to die and his son to take over. And then Hazel and his broken heart and his shame.

Rodney stood up, poured himself a cup of coffee and put a pot of water on the stove to boil for oatmeal. It was light now, but through his back window he could see no sign of life in the big house where Mr. Cook and his wife lived. Through the side window of the kitchen he saw Karen's house, but it also showed no signs of life. He pictured Karen curled up in bed with one of her luscious legs sticking out from underneath the covers and thought about how good Hazel used to look in the morning. He hoped Hazel was not like the war—an ache that never really seemed to go away and he wondered if Karen was like Hazel. For a reason he did not understand he hoped not.

Rodney drank his coffee, poured himself another cup and made the oatmeal. He felt guilty, back in Montana he and the men would already be outside. There was always something to do on a ranch. Eating his oatmeal, Rodney wondered if he would have to do anything on the ranch or if he was the token cowboy, something for Mr. Cook to laugh about behind his back?

After eating, Rodney went outside and looked at the deserted corrals and cattle pens. The ranch was set up to be a big operation. At one time the owner must have made his money by wintering cattle from up north. Rodney had always dreamed about owning a small cabin up in the mountains on a few acres. Owning something this big would be like running for President of the United States. Rodney was about to turn and go back inside when Karen pranced out of her backyard in a pair of pink running shorts, a white T-shirt and pink tennis shoes. She did not see him as she bent over and did some toe touches, pushing the fabric of the thin shorts tightly against her rear.

"Jesus," Rodney said out loud.

Karen ran in place for a few moments before jogging down the dirt road. Rodney watched her disappear into the distance.

By 9 o'clock Rodney was bored stiff sitting in the house. He had watched Karen jog back to her house and seeing her had made him smile, but he then sat in the living room and looked at the walls until he was fit to be tied.

It was not until 10 o'clock that Mr. Cook knocked on the back door. He looked like he had been up all night drinking or, Rodney figured, trying to keep up with his young wife, neither one being good for him.

"Come on," Mr. Cook half ordered. "Let's go up and I'll show you my place."

Rodney followed Mr. Cook over to the big house where they got into a brand new blue Suburban with leather seats and power windows, tilt wheel, tape deck, CB and air conditioning. They drove toward the air strip and the twin engine airplane. Rodney tried to quell the butterflies in his stomach, but it did no good.

"I can tell you don't like to fly," Mr. Cook said as they got out of the Suburban.

"A helicopter I was in got shot down in Nam," Rodney said.

"Don't worry son, I've been flying for years. I've limped them in on one engine but never crashed."

The information did not make Rodney feel relieved, but, he climbed into the front of the twin engine Beech and fastened his seat belt. Mr. Cook cranked up the engines, checked the gauges and before Rodney knew it they were up in the air. Mr. Cook banked the plane east towards the highway. "I'll fly you around the perimeter," he said.

Rodney was impressed by the vastness of the ranch. From the headquarters to the pavement were seven miles of rolling hills covered with pinon and cedar and pockets of scrub oak. A small river cut off to the left and went within a half a mile of the headquarters before angling off behind a large rock mountain.

"Land runs past the river for a few miles and then the river goes into the MaKee Ranch," Mr. Cook said.

Mr. Cook turned the plane back west and flew directly over the top of the headquarters, dipping his wings as he did so. Going west, the land climbed up into small rolling rock studded mountains with cedar and pinon trees clinging precariously to their sides.

"Big deer back in here," Mr. Cook said.

Rodney saw two roads zigzagging up the face of the mountains.

"Gold miners tried a few shafts back there but didn't find enough gold to make a living," Mr. Cook said.

He turned the plane and went over the tops of the mountains. On the other side the land leveled off into a large bowl at least five miles by five miles. Windmills were scattered in the bowl. Rodney figured an old rancher used to winter his cows here.

"This place is 167,000 acres," Mr. Cook said. "It's got Indian ruins on it, old Mexican homestead shacks that are over two hundred years old and thousands of pottery shards and arrow heads. I like to go out and hunt them, my wife doesn't, it chips the nail polish on her fingernails."

Rodney did not know whether to laugh or not. Mr. Cook turned the plane, they flew over a large cactus covered tract of land that dropped into a small depression of at least one thousand acres. There was a brand new fence that stretched into the horizon and running parallel to the fence for a short distance was a trickle of water. Tucked back in a small hollow, less than a mile from the fence, Rodney saw an adobe house with smoke coming out of a stove pipe.

"Old Mexican named Banjo Ortega and his wife live there," Mr. Cook said in a tone that Mr. Cook considered Ortega an enemy. "I've never met him, but my lawyer offered him $200,000 for his 80 acres. He runs a few sheep. Wouldn't sell, the dumb old sheep lover, guess he likes to sit back there and scratch out a living. But I fixed his ass—he doesn't have any water for his sheep and I fenced my river. That new fence goes the entire length of my land and their isn't a gate in it. I need his land for my plans and I will get it."

Rodney did not like the tone in Mr. Cook's voice.

As the plane banked to the right, Rodney saw beside the fence a grizzled old Mexican man riding a bay horse. As they flew over, the old man stopped his horse and shook his fist at the plane. Mr. Cook laughed, "See there, bull headed old geezer, he'll sell," he said. "He'll have to sell."

Rodney got one more quick glimpse of Banjo before Mr. Cook turned the plane. The old man's horse was bucking and he was trying to get a rifle out of a scabbard. Rodney felt strange. The old man reminded Rodney of himself.

Rodney was relieved when the plane landed, even though seeing the ranch from the air was impressive. He now knew the general layout and which roads would lead him to different parts of the ranch.

"I stole this ranch," Mr. Cook explained as they drove back toward the houses. "The man who owned this place went under and needed money badly and I bailed him out. Funny thing, when I moved in he was already gone. Never shook my hand for saving him from bankruptcy."

Rodney felt a deep empathy for the unknown man.

Mr. Cook stopped the car by his house. "There's a Ford truck in the garage, it's yours to use," Mr. Cook said. "I suppose you need some stuff from town. Why don't you take the day off and tomorrow I can go over what I want you to do."

Mr. Cook stuck his hand in his pocket and pulled out a wad of cash he could barely put his fist around. He peeled off two hundred dollar bills and gave them to Rodney. "Hiring on bonus," he said. "You draw full wages the end of each month."

"Thanks," Rodney said, shocked over the cash.

"One more thing. Don't you ever help that old Mexican. You understand?" Mr. Cook said with a cold edge to his voice.

Rodney nodded and felt a feeling of foreboding.

Rodney got the pickup. The pickup was new and had a CB, air

conditioner and tape deck. It was automatic, telling Rodney that Mr. Cook did not know what he was doing. A good ranch truck needed a standard transmission with a good granny gear. Rodney parked the truck in front of his house. Karen waved at him through her kitchen window. He waved back and smiled.

He went into his house and thought about the old Mexican man trying to get his rifle. For some reason he could picture details of the old man's face—the defiant set of his jaw and the way his white whiskers grew in all directions. The old Mexican reminded him of old Vietnamese men he had seen. Old men who were made to be servants in their own land. Old men who hated him for being there when all he really wanted to do was help them. Rodney knew he would meet the old Mexican man. What he did not know was whether it would be good or bad?

Four

Banjo Ortega was riding to try and find his missing sheep when the blue and white twin engine plane flew over him. He shook his fist at the plane. "Gringo puta breath," he cursed. "You are not worth the dirt on the bottom of my boot."

Banjo reached for his rifle, but the mare, frightened by the noise from the plane, started bucking after the plane passed over. Banjo held on with all his might. "You no good gringo, you thief, you stupid old horse," he hollered.

When Banjo finally got the mare settled down it was too late to shoot. "If you fly over my land again I will shoot your noisy gringo plane out of the sky," he swore breathlessly.

"That is if you hold still long enough for him to get the rifle out of the scabbard," he scowled to the horse.

"You're like my wife," Banjo continued to the horse. "You must like white people."

The horse ignored Banjo and stretched out its neck to nip at a tuft of dry grass. When he was younger, Banjo would not let the horse eat as they rode, but now he was almost too weak to stop her, and he figured the more the horse ate on the trail, the less he had to feed it.

When Banjo reached the hillside where his sheep had been the previous day they were gone. He saw two sets of coyote tracks and a trail where the sheep had run with a coyote on either side of them. Banjo took his rifle out of the scabbard and tried to make the mare trot, but she would not and Banjo had to kick her as hard as he could to make her break into a fast walk.

On the other side of the hill Banjo found the sheep milling around a cedar tree. They were nervous, but they were all there, even the ones he had not seen the day before. He whistled softly and started driving the sheep toward the valley where his ancestors were buried. He could not pen the sheep by his house and feed them. It would be too expensive. And he could not water them by his house as his shallow well would go dry. As Banjo crested the hill he looked once more at the new fence. Taking his rifle from the scabbard he aimed at the fence and fired. The mare did not look sideways or jolt at the sudden noise. She had never been afraid of guns, which had always surprised Banjo. She was afraid of everything else, but not guns. His son had told Banjo everything was a reincarnation of something else. Banjo scoffed at the idea but maybe the old mare was a reincarnated bandit, afraid of everything except guns. Guns were something she could understand.

Banjo patted his shirt pocket for his tobacco and then remembered he was out. He also remembered his futile attempt this morning, before his wife woke up, to find Angelena's Prince Albert can holding her cigarette butts.

"You'd think once in all these years I'd find the thing," he said to the horse. "Women only let you think you are the boss."

The sheep walked quickly, a mindless blob of white against the dry brown land. Banjo remembered as a boy and when he and his father would drive the sheep to Santa Fe once a year. They had several hundred then. His father would sell the sheep, give Banjo a few cents to spend on himself and go and get drunk. Banjo would make his way past drunk Indians and the few white people in town and get an ice cream cone at a store on the plaza. There was still a place to buy ice cream cones on the plaza but a cone was

$4.95 and all the drunk Indians were gone. Now there were only tourists, jewelry stores, travel agents, expensive restaurants and realtors. Banjo patted his shirt pocket once again but there still was no tobacco. He would have to beg a few cigarettes from his wife which meant he would have to watch her roll them for him, she not wanting him to spill any of her tobacco.

"The whole world is against a poor man," he lamented to his horse, "even a poor man's wife."

The horse ignored him.

When Banjo reached the valley, the sheep parted like a small white cloud and let him pass. In the old days, Banjo had a dog to work the sheep, but his dog had died and he did not get another one. He thought about it, but every time he came close to getting one he did not. He liked his last dog so much there would never be another one that could replace him. He knew if the horse died he would have to get another horse, but dogs were different than horses. "All horses are stupid like you," he said to the horse.

The horse twitched its ears.

Banjo rode into the yard and looked at his wife who was sitting on the porch plucking a chicken and smoking a large cigarette. She looked ancient. The years of living outdoors were etched on her dry face like brown lines on a road map. "How can you love me?" he asked himself, feeling a deep and warm love for Angelena.

The cigarette smoke drifted seductively over to Banjo. Angelena smiled warmly at him, but he only scowled at her as he led the horse to the corral.

Standing by the porch, Banjo watched the last feathers come off the chicken and the last puffs come out of the cigarette before Angelena carefully took the butt and put it in the Prince Albert can. Angelena looked seriously at Banjo, and then pulled from the folds of her apron a large hand rolled cigarette and handed it to him. Banjo took it, rolled it between his fingers, sat down and took a match from his pocket and lit it. A flame did not shoot up in the air off of the end of the cigarette like the ones he rolled. He looked over at his wife, looked at the dry brittle boards on the floor of the porch, looked back at his wife, and clearing his throat said meekly, "gracias."

Angelena smiled at him, and took the chicken into the house, proving once again, it was only in his mind that he was the boss.

Banjo was in his room and Angelena sat on the porch enjoying the night. Angelena was a woman truly at peace with herself. Her belief in Jesus and Our Lady had sustained her throughout her entire life. She accepted all that was and what she was. She took each day as another day, and each task as another thorn that must be endured until death would take her to heaven. Life was not difficult, it was a process of bearing grief and laughing when possible.

Angelena had known little in her life except this portion of land in New Mexico. She could barely remember being young in Mexico. She could remember being barefoot and sleeping in a flea infested bed, but Mexico was too far in the past to have a bearing on her life. When she rode out of Mexico with her brother she was only fifteen. She did not dream at the time she would spend her life married to a man who raised sheep and spent a large portion of his life stealing them.

Life in all of Angelena's years had changed very little, except they now had electricity. Life was nice with a light bulb in each room and a freezer. They still cooked on a wood stove and heated the house with wood, and she still did the laundry in a wash tub and they had no inside toilet, although she had running water. During the summer they bathed under the windmill and in the winter in a washtub in front of the wood stove. She did wish for a phone. She knew Banjo was not well, even though he did not tell her, and it would be good to be able to call for help. But Banjo, with his foolish pride, would not get a phone. But life was good. She was not hungry and she was not cold.

With no T.V. or radio she did not know what the rest of the world was doing and really did not care. Her only touch with the world were the romance novels she loved to read. At night, in her bed, she would read and wonder about the lavish homes and dresses and cars the books told about. But, she had no desire to live a life like in the novels. They went to Santa Fe enough to see the houses and the finely dressed people. She knew she was just a poor

Mexican, like the majority of the people in Santa Fe, and to dream of what was not possible was not God's will.

Angelena worried about Banjo. He was overly preoccupied with his problems. He had never before been bothered about being poor. Proud of his sheep and his home and his gun and horse, he said more than once—"all a man needed was a horse and a gun and sheep and a good woman."

But now he was preoccupied. It started when their son left the land and went to Santa Fe to live and try to become a successful painter. She knew this had broken Banjo's heart. From that day on, Banjo seemed to do nothing but go through the motions of living and grow weary and then, to compound his grief, there was the new fence cutting his sheep off from water. Banjo did not sing at night like he used to. He only sat and looked at the land as though it was no longer there. He did not help her in the garden. Angelena grew chilies and corn and beans in the dry soil. Enough to get them through winters with very few supplies from town.

Angelena took her can of Prince Albert out of her skirt pocket and deftly rolled a cigarette. She lit it and put the can back in her pocket.

"We've grown old and time has passed us by, my husband," she said. "There is no room for the land anymore. Now, one can no longer simply live. I am glad I am old."

Angelena butted her cigarette and put it in the Prince Albert can. She thought about when she first saw Banjo. She was in Santa Fe living with her aunt. Her brother had gone off to Colorado to work on a ranch. Banjo drove a wagon into town and was standing in front of a cantina drinking a beer. He looked so strong, so filled with life, brave and fearless, with his wagon beside him and his rifle resting on the buckboard seat. She did not know it, but Banjo saw her as she was watching him and, a month after much inquiring to find out her name and where she lived, he rode into town on a fine gray horse. They sat on the porch while her aunt sat with them. After two months of porch sitting, they were married. On their honeymoon, Banjo brought her to the ranch with the adobe house and horse stalls and sheep corrals. There was no electricity then, only candles and kerosene lamps for the rooms. But

Angelena felt immediately at home. Once her crucifixes were on the walls she knew she would live and die in this dry and crusty corner of the world.

She had been a good wife, Angelena knew she had, she had never complained or shrugged off her duties. Although, once, when Banjo had returned from Colorado after stealing sheep, she did not sleep with him for a week. "But, men were not supposed to be close to God like women," she told herself the night she lay naked in his arms when her punishment grew weaker than her desires. And even God could not condemn a man to hell eternal for a few measly sheep that the people in Colorado would steal back in a year.

Angelena went to her bedroom. Banjo's light was still on and she heard him cough several times. She wished he would read like she did. Maybe then he would find a way to use some of his time besides thinking about what he had no control over. She undressed and put on a flannel dark blue nightgown with many patches. Kneeling, she reverently said her prayers and then climbed into bed to read the newest Harlequin romance that her son had brought her. Before she opened the book she looked at her crucifix and said, "You know my husband is more dear to me than You."

Five

Rodney started to drive to town when he saw Karen walk out of her house and he pulled up next to her. "Would you like to go to town?" he asked. "I have to do some shopping."

"I'd love to," Karen said. "Give me a few minutes."

"You are falling for this guy," Karen told herself as she changed clothes.

The thought of Karen going with him made Rodney feel good. But, they were no sooner on the paved road when Rodney felt one of his moods coming over him. It happened ever since the Army. A cold hand would reach into his heart and drive Rodney deep within himself. He tried to fight it, to drive the hand away, but it never completely worked until Hazel, and now Hazel was gone. He wished it had not come over him now and he tried harder to stop the icy feeling. "I have a good paying job," he told himself. "It is a nice sunny day. I am with a woman who makes me feel good and I am driving a truck that is mine to use without all the headaches of insurance or bills or worrying about buying gas."

Rodney turned on the radio and found a country western station although he did not enjoy listening to music when he drove. Karen gazed out of the window looking both beautiful and at peace with the world.

Rodney took off his cowboy hat and set it down on the seat. "Funny how life just kind of takes you and puts you in different places without you really having any control," Karen said.

"I suppose," Rodney said, but in truth he believed what Karen said.

Rodney had never found anything in life that made sense, but he did not want to admit life was a befuddling thing to him. The most enjoyable times of his life were sitting on a horse and riding. It was then, if there was a direction to Rodney's life, there was a moment of tranquility. His mind seemed to go into automatic and control his body without him having to think. The world seemed to be a wonderful, secure, and ordered place on a horse.

"Is that all you have to say is, 'I suppose'?," Karen asked.

"Haven't thought about it much," Rodney lied, knowing in truth he thought about it all the time.

"No, you think," Karen said. "You can't fool me, you think a lot. You're not one of those cowboys who only knows cows and horses, there's more to you than that."

Rodney chuckled and turned off the radio. "Let's talk about you, Karen. Then maybe one day we can sit down and try to figure out Rodney Slugger," Rodney said, thankful that he was winning the battle within himself—at least for the moment.

"Okay, what do you want to know?" Karen said matter-of-factly.

"Everything," Rodney said.

"I've always had everything," Karen said. "Good clothes, nice cars, private schools, the best. Then one day I was sitting in my nice brownstone, waiting for my lawyer husband to come home and I was overwhelmed by the knowledge that I was going to die. And all the good wine and clothes and high society people with their picky phobias and minuscule problems would not mean a thing. I didn't know anything about life. I was simply a rich kid who had married for money and not love."

"Only poor people truly understand life?" Rodney said, trying not to sound sarcastic.

Karen ignored his remark. "I was tired of being a sex object, maided and bedded I called it. I would sit at luncheons and hope that when all the ladies died, they would go to heaven and have to go to a luncheon that went on forever. All they talked about was their vacations, new fur coats and where they were going skiing during the winter. After my divorce I rented a small apartment in the city. Then one afternoon, I was sitting and looking out over the city when I had this urge to go west. Go to where there were few people, fewer cars, where the night was still covered with stars and not the glow of fluorescent lamps. I put a few clothes in my car and headed west and ended up in Santa Fe."

Rodney was impressed.

"In Santa Fe," Karen continued, "I worked at a café for minimum wage. I worked at an art gallery, for less than minimum wage. But I was supposed to feel I was being blessed for being able to work around art gallery owners. Then I was a bar maid. I did all the Santa Fe things. I went to the galleries. I looked in awe at all the bad art hanging on the walls. I ate sushi and drank red wine. I went to the opera. Then, after six months, I knew I wanted to be an artist. There was nothing stopping me. Anyone can be an artist, look at the art around town. All it takes to be an artist is have a little paint on you, look at life strangely and brag a lot."

Rodney laughed.

"One day I decided to take a walk in the mountains, Karen said. "For the first time in my life I was where there were no people. For the first time I truly saw birds, and trees, and rocks, and dirt, and grasshoppers, and stink bugs, and flies, and ants. I discovered I didn't know who I was but I also found out I could be alone. Little old me, little rich girl, the pampered one could really take a breath without a bombardment of how good my life should be, or how rich I was or what I owned. My life changed. I wasn't afraid. A few weeks later I found this house on the Last Day In Paradise and rented it."

"Besides being pretty you have guts," Rodney said.

Karen smiled. "A day at a time, cowboy. I try to take it one day at a time."

Rodney drove into the outskirts of Santa Fe. He looked at the many large, adobe homes scattered over the pinon-studded hillsides and wondered how people ever made that kind of money.

Karen directed him to the Sears store and he bought several pairs of new Levi's.

They then went to a grocery store. "Where's your list?" Karen asked.

"Don't have one," Rodney said.

"You'll forget something," Karen said.

"Part of it," Rodney answered.

Rodney bought milk, and cheese, and coffee, and cokes, and 7-up, and cookies, peanut butter, crackers, sardines, canned ham, canned Spam, eggs, bacon, beans, ten cans of Hearty Man's Soup, and four pairs of white socks that were on special.

"Great food," Karen said looking at the array of junk. "Enough chemicals there to starch your pants."

"Food's food," Rodney said. "Chemicals don't mean a thing."

Karen made a face at him. He might be a thinker, but he was still a cowboy. "It's a good thing you're cute," she said and walked out of the store.

Rodney pushed the cart to the truck. Karen watched several women look at him as he passed. "Apple pie and home," she thought. "The last remaining role model for America is the cowboy."

Rodney put the groceries behind the seat of the truck and returned the cart to the store.

Back in the truck he said to Karen. "Alright, where do you want to eat?...my treat."

She almost said Chinese, but she had heard men say that to her so often she stopped. "How about some good old down home greasy stuff?" she said. "Steak and potatoes."

"I haven't had a good steak in ages," Rodney said.

They sat at a small, wobbly, corner table. Rodney ordered a T-bone, rare, with hash browns and a beer. Karen, thinking about fat and carcinogens and cholesterol, ordered a tossed salad.

The waitress muttered to herself as she walked away, "Another vegetarian ruining the cattle industry."

Karen watched Rodney inhale the steak and potatoes. She pictured the little globs of fat as they swam up Rodney's blood stream and formed tiny stalagmites around the openings to his heart.

Rodney watched her nibble on her salad and wondered how she could possibly live eating only a salad.

After eating Rodney stopped at a liquor store and bought two cases of beer while Karen picked out several bottles of red wine with names that Rodney could not pronounce.

The sun was setting over the mountains and a pale purple settled over the land as they drove through the gate to the ranch. Karen had a vision of a large painting all done in pale purple, while Rodney wondered if the refrigerator would hold all the beer.

"I'm glad you went with me," Rodney said as he unloaded the truck. He wanted to ask her over but he felt nervous and did not.

"It was fun," Karen replied, hesitated a moment, not wanting to leave, but then went to her house.

Rodney put the groceries in the cupboards and loaded the refrigerator as full as he could with beer, putting several cans in the freezer. He felt tense from the afternoon in town, there was something about being around a group of humanity that made him nervous. Life seemed to lose all meaning, he felt like another number, another person caught in the trap. Although he knew he was caught like everybody else, there was something about being out in the country that took the gut-wrenching truth away. He could always dream—dream that he was an old time cowboy—a man who came out west before social security numbers, mandatory insurance, and income tax—in a time when there was truly freedom, not a far distant definition mankind had been force fed until they believed the myth.

Rodney took a can of beer out of the freezer, even though he knew it would still be hot and went to the back yard. Sitting on the porch step, he drank the warm beer. It felt good going down his throat. The slight burn of the foam made him long for a cigarette, even though he had stopped smoking over a year earlier—something Hazel wanted him to do. "Two things you did good for me," he said softly, "you made me feel for awhile and you made me quit smoking."

When the beer was finished, he got another one, and went back outside. Sipping it slowly, he thought about Karen and wondered what it was like to be rich—to be able to buy what you wanted, when you wanted it. But not having money did not bother him. He had always done what he wanted ever since he got out of the Army. There had always been enough money to buy a saddle, boots, clothes, spurs, chaps, lassoes and enough money to get drunk.

"Maybe I should feel like a failure since I don't own anything," he said out loud.

"No, you shouldn't."

Rodney jumped up, startled by the voice. Karen smiled at him and it seemed her smile was a star in the night sky. For a moment he did not know whether to be embarrassed or mad or both for being snuck up on. Karen looked lovely in her short pants, cropped t-shirt and bare feet.

"It's not polite to walk up on people," he said, "Especially in the dark."

"You always talk to yourself?" Karen asked.

"A lot," Rodney answered truthfully. "At least I always listen to myself."

Karen laughed and sat down beside him on the step.

Rodney could smell her lilac perfume.

"You have another beer?" Karen asked.

Rodney went into the house and brought out two cans. He handed one to Karen who popped the top and took a large swallow.

"Ugh," she said. "It's lukewarm."

"You didn't ask if it was cold," Rodney said.

"You ever want a wife?" Karen asked. "Ever want to settle down?"

"You come right to the point, don't you?" Rodney said.

"Life's too short not to," Karen answered, sipping her beer.

Rodney chugged his and opened the other one, taking a long swallow. "I suppose every man wants to find a good wife and settle down," Rodney said, thinking about Hazel. Then he added, "I don't know if I could though, guess I don't have much to offer when it comes right down to it."

"Maybe not having much to offer lets you offer only yourself," Karen said.

"Maybe offering yourself only gets you hurt," he said.

"It doesn't mean a person gives up," Karen said feeling an undertone of sadness in Rodney's words.

Rodney looked at the cottonwood tree and at the stars that peeked between the branches. The tree reminded Rodney of a certain spot on the ranch in Montana where they would camp as they drove cattle in for the winter. The nights would be cool. The stars would twinkle and look so close he felt he could reach out and pick a few and put them in his pocket to look at on some cloudy night.

"If I told you I came over here because I wanted you to seduce me what would you say?" Karen asked.

Rodney looked at the tree, looked at the stars, and then looked at Karen. "I would say I am flattered but I don't think right at the moment it's proper," Rodney said.

Karen was amazed and she laughed. "I could get to really like you," she said as she stood up.

After Karen left Rodney stayed on the porch. "I could get to like you too," he said. "But it would do neither of us any good."

But, he knew he already liked her.

Karen lay in bed. "It shouldn't happen to a woman my age. Meet a broke cowboy and know as soon as you see him you want to be with him. Dear lord," she said.

Rodney lay in bed and all he could think about was Karen.

In the morning Rodney went to see Mr. Cook. Mr. Cook was sitting on the front porch drinking a cup of coffee. "Want some?" he asked.

"Please," Rodney answered. He normally drank four or five cups of coffee in the morning.

"Bring Rodney a cup of coffee," Mr. Cook called.

Gloria came out of the house and handed Rodney a cup of coffee. She had on an orange, terry-cloth bathrobe and there were dark circles under her eyes. "She's allergic to the clean air," Mr. Cook said.

"I'm allergic to this whole ranch," Gloria said, trying to give Rodney a half smile, but failing.

Even bags under her eyes Gloria was a beautiful woman. Not clean pretty like Karen, but sophisticated. The stuck-out little pinky, with the diamond ring on the finger type, pretty. "Rattlesnake pretty," his friend Toad Face used to call them. "They'll take everythin' ya got, and spit ya to the dawgs," he would say and then wink at whoever was listening.

No one ever figured out how Toad Face knew so much about women since he had to be the most un-handsome man that was ever born, but, he spoke with such conviction and faith that everybody believed him.

"That Karen is one gorgeous lady," Mr. Cook said.

"She sure is," Rodney said.

"I've had me more than one pretty one," Mr. Cook went on. "Slept with them in airplanes and boats and under bridges and in cars. Nailed one once at Gilly's in the bathroom. Pretty women are worth all the pain and misfortune they can hand out."

Rodney sipped his coffee and knew he would not grow to like Mr. Cook. He wished he was saddling his horse for a few days of looking for strays and trying to get his mind back in order. Life was good, but it was also getting a little confusing. Rodney knew that most of the time when life seemed to be on the up swing and everything was going well, there was always a haymaker that crashed one back down to earth with no teeth and a bloody nose.

"I suppose you've wondered why I need a cowboy around here?" Mr. Cook stated. "What with no livestock or horses or anything else."

"I've wondered," Rodney replied.

"I travel a lot and I need a man to watch over the houses. New Mexico is still a rough state. Indians don't like white people, Mexicans don't like white people, Mexicans don't like Indians and nobody likes tourists or Texans.

There's nothing up in the northern part of the state for people to do to make a living, especially the poor people, so they steal. If you don't tie it down, it will disappear."

Rodney felt disappointed.

"I've thought about buying some llamas," Mr. Cook went on. "It might make my wife like the place a little better."

To Rodney, llamas were no higher on the pecking order than chickens.

"I also want you to ride around the ranch for two reasons," Mr. Cook said. "You can use my horse or the wife's or take the truck. I want a report on what you think of the ranch and how I might be able to generate some income from the land. I also have an offer from a movie company to let them build a western movie set on the place. They will pay me each time they shoot a movie. I want you to pick out a good location for a movie set. And I bet I can even get you a part in any movie that they shoot."

"When do you want me to start?" Rodney asked, feeling a little excitement. He had not been on a horse in over a month and the thought of getting out and riding made him miss Montana. He did not know about being in a movie although he felt like all he had been was an actor in his own life.

"Take off anytime you want. Gloria and I will be flying out soon. When I come back, give me a report on the ranch and a place you think might be a good spot to build a movie set."

"I don't know what a good movie site should be," Rodney said.

"Think about all the western movies you've been to and pick one out," Mr. Cook said, adding, "that little town, Galisteo, watch out for the people. I've heard it's full of nothing but thieves."

"I saw several really nice houses," Rodney said.

"Those belong to rich artists who like the feel of the high desert," Mr. Cook informed him. "Some Indian who paints fat ladies and a guy who paints highways."

Rodney walked away thinking maybe he should become an artist, make things out of barb wire or tumbleweeds or rocks or scorpion tails. Being an artist seemed to be a good job to have in New Mexico.

Thirty minutes later Rodney was trotting away from the houses on Gloria's horse. He could tell an inexperienced rider had been riding the horse. He pointed the horse west toward the rock mountain in the distance.

He rode for about a mile and then stopped and dismounted. There were no fences in sight, no buildings, and, for the moment, no jet vapor trails in the sky. Darting among the scattered trees were sparrows and high over head, two crows flew in lazy circles. Rodney felt at home. He was away—far away from it all. He stroked the silky neck of the horse and smelled the salt earth fragrance of her.

"Wish I could ride forever," he said aloud. "Point you west and ride until there was no place left to ride, and then head north and do the same thing. Spend my life chasing the directions of the compass."

Rodney started to laugh. "A damn movie set," he said to the horse. "Can you imagine? And me maybe being in a movie."

Rodney rode on and he thought about Karen. Feelings were stirring in his heart he really did not want to have. The thought of opening his heart to a woman frightened him. He had done it with Hazel and Hazel had used his trust. But Karen seemed different. How, he didn't know? But it was a good difference.

It was dark when Rodney got back to the headquarters. He groomed the horse, fed her and let her out in her own corral away from the Arabian.

He saw Karen's light on and he wanted to tell her about Mr. Cook's plans for a movie set.

"That is really exciting," Karen said, after hearing the news. "I bet you would make a wonderful western actor. All the women in the country would fall for you."

"I doubt it," Rodney said and wanted to say. "I want you to like me."

"You be sure if you meet any big Hollywood people you tell them you want a job," Karen instructed him.

"Mr. Cook said he would do that for me," Rodney said.

Talking to Karen, Rodney felt good. There was something about her that made him feel safe. Hazel never made him feel safe. With Hazel he was always on edge. After telling Karen goodnight, he wished he could have sat with her and talked all night.

Laying in bed, Rodney looked at the ceiling and daydreamed about being in a movie. Hundreds of Indians were riding madly around a burning cabin, shooting their bows. Inside the cabin a young pretty woman was cringing in the corner. Rodney rode, unscathed through the Indians, not holding onto the reins but shooting from each hand a silver six shooter. The lady, hearing the shots, ran outside the cabin. Rodney swooped her off her feet and onto the horse and escaped. As sleep was about to overtake him, he had a good happy thought about Karen and then a stabbing feeling in his heart as he visualized Hazel kissing her new boyfriend.

It was still dark as Rodney packed himself a lunch and slurped down several cups of coffee. The sun was rising as he mounted the mare and rode north toward the new fence. The air was fresh and had a touch of fall to it. Neither Karen nor the Cook's were up.

He passed several old homestead houses. All that remained were the crumbling rock and mud walls. He wondered how the people had managed to eke out a living in the barren land around him and what had become of them and their dreams?

Rodney was riding in a sand wash and happened to look down. Half buried in the sand was a black obsidian arrowhead and he stopped and picked it up. He examined the arrowhead and put the arrowhead in his pocket.

The mare, now used to him, was proving to be a fine and worthy mount. Rodney wished he could try her out heading a few cows.

Rodney rode until he ran into the new fence at the base of a red sandstone cliff. Etched into the face of the cliff were many round circles, some with eyes and mouths, others with nothing. Indians had scratched them into the face of the cliff hundreds of years earlier and he wondered what now dead god they represented? The fence stretched in either direction as far as Rodney could see. Running parallel with the fence, for about three hundred yards was a ribbon of green grass. The green ribbon was a stream no more than a foot wide and a few inches deep. Small bugs skimmed over the surface of the water. Rodney followed the stream and saw deer tracks, coyote tracks, what he believed to be a fox track and several skunk prints. The stream suddenly vanished under the ground. He rode back to where the stream trickled out. With a little work, the spring fed stream could be dug out to form pools, then there would be more than enough water for a few cattle or horses. In the thousands of acres around him, there was ample gamma and other tenacious grasses to sustain enough cattle or horses to at least pay a few of the bills around the place. He made a mental note to mention this to Mr. Cook. He might let Rodney run a few head. Rodney had never had the opportunity to have his own cattle. It was a dream he had given up on when he discovered the only way most people ever got a ranch was through the womb or the tomb.

Rodney thought about the old Mexican man he had seen from the airplane and felt uneasy and he wondered why Mr. Cook wanted the man's land. What could another 80 acres mean to a man who owned 167,000 acres?

Rodney followed the fence for a short distance. It was a good fence, cedar posts were set fifteen feet apart with a metal post in between and five strands of tightly strung barb wire. Twanging the wire, he knew it was good American wire, not the cheap stuff from Belgium that would break or rust out in several years.

He turned the horse around and headed back the way he came. At the base of a steep hill he stopped to eat. He wondered if the Indian who had made the arrowhead in his pocket had ever sat where he was and looked at the vastness around him. He knew one thing, the Indian never had to worry about a fence blocking his way.

Banjo watched the cowboy riding beside the stream his sheep used to drink from. Banjo knew the man was not the owner. The owner was a bouncing blob of jelly when he rode, but this man sat in the saddle like he lived on a horse. He had a steady graceful flow with his horse. The man looked at the river and then rode back and followed the fence further south. Banjo did not want to but he felt respect and kinship with the stranger. The man was somehow like Banjo.

Banjo took his 30/30 out of the scabbard, got off his horse and sat down with his back up against a rock. He sighted the 30/30 several feet over the cowboy's head and held it there for several seconds. "It would be easy to kill you," he said.

He lowered the rifle.

Banjo sighed and felt as though he was no longer part of anything. He reached out and touched the grey muzzle of his horse. He liked the softness of a horse's nose, it was like it really did not belong to the horse but was a living thing all its own.

Banjo wondered how long he could manage to hold out and live on his land? He knew he could not make it much longer. Cutting wood, filling the stove, butchering a pig or sheep would soon become too hard for him. But then what? He knew nothing of town, he had never lived in Santa Fe, or even Galisteo. A man who ran a store or worked for somebody else was an unpleasant thought to Banjo.

He wondered if Angelena knew how much he loved her? Banjo wished he had the money to take Angelena to Albuquerque for a weekend and let her go to Sear's or Penney's and buy herself a few dresses or a new pair of shoes or one of those fancy machines that rolled your cigarettes for you. Maybe, after all these years, a small gold wedding ring.

Banjo was thinking about his turn coat son when Rodney dismounted not more than fifty yards away and started eating. Banjo wondered what he was eating. He knew he was not eating one of Angelena's big thick tortillas with butter and honey and he smiled at the thought.

Rodney's mare whinnied and a horse answered from behind him. Rodney jumped to his feet and saw a brown mare tied to a cedar tree and an old Mexican man sitting in the shade of the tree cradling a rifle. At first he was afraid, but after a moment he called. "Mr. Ortega, I'm the new man at the Last Day in Paradise," and he waved.

Banjo started to wave, but then caught himself and glared at the white man. Rodney felt the man's hate boring into him. "My name is Rodney Slugger. It would help if you and I could get to know each other," he called.

Banjo did not respond.

Rodney mounted his horse, looked at Banjo again, tipped his hat to him, and started back toward the headquarters.

Banjo set the sights of the rifle in the middle of the cowboy's back. He took a deep breath to settle his nerves and put slight pressure on the trigger, hesitated, and lowered the rifle.

Rodney was far off in the distance before Banjo stood up and painfully mounted his horse, sliding the 30/30 into the scabbard as he did. Nudging the mare he grunted, "damn gringo."

Rodney felt ill at ease and edgy like he did in Vietnam. He could not get the image of the old man out of his mind. It was as though he had been looking at himself forty years down the road. Some old, rusty relic, weary beyond imagination, but still tough. Tough and enduring like the unforgiving land around him, but something isolated and so alone that the loneliness called out.

Rodney remembered Mr. Cook's words, "I don't want you doing anything for that old Mexican."

Rodney put the mare up and made sure she had fresh water before feeding her and going to his house. Rodney realized he had not once thought of Hazel during the day, either in a good way or a hateful way. When he walked into the kitchen, he smelled food. On the table was a bottle of wine and two place settings. Karen was by the stove wearing Levi's with a white tank top and cowboy boots. Her hair was pulled back into a pony-tail. Rodney wanted to walk over and hug her, but he only smiled at her as she smiled back.

"Mr. Cook and Gloria flew out today and I felt like being domestic," Karen said. "So I came over and made us a little dinner. It won't be long."

"I'm glad you're here," he said and he sat at the table.

Watching Karen cook Rodney smiled to himself. "You and I are about as opposite as two people can get," he said.

"Yes, you are a man and I am a women," Karen said and gave him an impish smile.

Karen brought out stuffed pork chops and a fresh salad.

"I had a craving for pork chops," Karen said.

They ate in silence but Karen felt something was bothering Rodney.

"You seem distant, like you don't want company," Karen said.

Rodney took a deep breath. "I feel as though I'm a million miles away from everything. Life goes on and on and I'm stuck on a highway that I can't get off."

For some reason he did not want to tell her about the Mexican.

"Let's sit out back," Karen said.

The sun had been down for over thirty minutes, but a pale red still tinted the sky. They sat on the step, but Karen got up right away and went back inside, returning with the bottle of wine. Sitting beside Rodney, she could feel nothing emitting from him. Not a spark of life or even a low sound of breathing. She sipped the wine and then held out the bottle for him to take, which he did slowly, as though something besides his muscles and his mind moved his hand to reach out and touch the bottle. He did not take a swallow of the wine, but let the bottle hang between his legs.

"Just because you won't sleep with me doesn't mean you can't talk to me," Karen said and playfully nudged him with her shoulder.

Rodney laughed, a low sigh of resignation. "You ever wonder how people end up being together?"

"No," Karen said, taking the bottle back from Rodney's unprotesting hand.

"Sometimes it's love, sometimes it's needing to be touched, sometimes it's talking and sometimes pity," Rodney said.

"Sometimes it's being drunk," Karen smiled.

Rodney chuckled.

"How come you wanted to work on ranches?" Karen asked.

Rodney sat up straight, took the wine bottle and took a large swallow. "First time I've ever drank anything that really tasted good is with you," he said and smiled a far away smile.

"That grin won't get you out of answering the question," Karen said.

"Same reason you want to be an artist, I suppose," Rodney answered. "Have to be something."

"You still don't want to sleep with me, do you?" Karen asked.

"It's not that I don't want to," Rodney answered, giving Karen a sad far away smile. He wanted to tell her, "Yes I do. I need your warmth." But he didn't.

Karen stood up and took several steps toward her house before stopping and saying, "I know why you cowboys are heart breakers."

Rodney did not watch her as she walked to her house. He hoped he had not hurt Karen's feelings. "Life's nothing but a war," he mumbled.

Karen sat on her sofa. She felt like getting up, taking her clothes off and walking over to Rodney's and crawling in bed with him whether he liked it or not. She wanted to be touched, even if the feelings that were inside of her for Rodney could not be returned she could pretend. "Even cowboys need kisses," she said as she went to her bedroom.

Rodney stood by the window and looked at Karen's house. He pictured her curled in bed and he wanted to knock on her door and say. "I need a hug."

Six

Rodney turned the truck onto a rutted dirt road that led to Banjo Ortega's house. The road twisted in and around scrub oak and cedar trees until it reached the top of a hill. At the bottom of the hill Rodney saw Banjo's crumbling adobe house. There was an outhouse behind it, a log out-building, a pole corral that was held together with rusting bailing wire, a pen that Rodney figured might hold a goat or a pig, a large pile of firewood and a tiny garden. By the out-building was a dilapidated pickup from the early sixties. Skinny chickens patrolled around the buildings searching for bugs. There were no horses in the corral and Rodney figured Banjo was gone. Smoke came out of the stove pipe from the house and lay like a thin fog over the meadow. Feeling like a spy, Rodney drove toward the house. He really did not know what he wanted to say to Banjo and he felt like he was being pulled by a force that was beyond his control.

An old Mexican lady came out of the house as Rodney got out of the truck. Seeing Rodney, she showed no fear but smiled warmly at him and stepped off the porch. Rodney was amazed at the deep cracks on her brown face and the years of toil etched like tattoos on her hands. "Are you thirsty?" the lady asked in faulty English when Rodney walked up to her.

Rodney, who was not, answered, "Yes ma'am, I am."

"I will bring you some water."

Angelena brought him a Mason jar filled with water and inspected him as he drank.

"You must be the new man at the ranch," Angelena said.

"Yes, ma'am."

"I am Angelena Ortega," she said proudly and held out her hand.

Rodney shook her hand and was both impressed and surprised at the firmness of her grip. "Rodney Slugger," he replied.

Rodney felt ill-at-ease. He had never been this close to a person so poor. Why did Mr. Cook want this piece of dried-up land?

"Sit down, please," Angelena said pointing to the porch.

She pulled Banjo's chair closer to hers and they both sat down.

Angelena began to roll a cigarette. Rodney watched in fascination as the bony, dried fingers deftly rolled the tobacco in the paper and then lit the end with a stick match. The look of satisfaction that covered her face as she smoked the cigarette made him smile. He felt as though he was sitting by his mother and, even though he was a grown man who had fought in a war, he was still a child waiting to be taught life.

Angelena took a deep drag off the cigarette and exhaled loudly.

"My husband does not like white people," she said with a tinge of sadness in her voice. "I try to tell him we are all the same, but it does no good."

She took another drag off the cigarette.

"I might not like him," Rodney said truthfully. "But not because he is brown."

Angelena carefully butted her smoke and placed the butt in the can.

"You might like him. He is just another man, he can be broken."

Angelena went into the house and Rodney heard the sound of wood being forced into the firebox of a wood stove. Soon, the scent of browning flour drifted to the porch.

Angelena brought Rodney a thick tortilla covered with butter and honey. She stuck the tortilla in his face with more of an order than asking if he was hungry. "You may wait for Banjo. He should be back soon. I have work to do," Angelena said.

As Rodney was about to take a bite Angelena went to the garden.

Rodney ate the delicious tortilla and thought that maybe he should not have invaded Banjo's space. He knew Banjo would be riding in soon and they would meet, but maybe their meeting should have stayed a hateful stare and an unreturned wave.

Banjo saw the new truck as soon as he dismounted from his horse. He had not seen it when he rode in as he had been watching Angelena working in the garden. Then he saw the cowboy sitting in his chair, which was close to his wife's chair, and a deep rage filled him. If he were younger, he would run over and tear into the cowboy, but he knew he was too old. Banjo looked over at his wife, who was staring at him as he led his horse to the corral. He unsaddled and fed the animal, watered her and then, with his wife still watching, took his 30/30 and walked menacingly toward the cowboy.

Rodney stepped off the porch as Banjo approached and held out his hand to shake but kept his eye warily on the 30/30. Banjo did not extend his hand but kept the 30/30 pointed at the ground. Rodney noticed Banjo was missing the middle two fingers from his right hand.

After a moment of icy silence, Banjo asked gruffly, "Why are you here?"

"Came over to meet my neighbors," Rodney said, putting his hand back down by his side.

Rodney felt like leaving and forgetting the whole matter. But, under the circumstances, that would be running, and he was not a coward.

"You should not have wasted your time, gringo," Banjo said. "You are on my land and I want you out of here."

Rodney looked deeply into Banjo's eyes. He could see nothing but hate. Rodney adjusted his cowboy hat and walked briskly away. As he got in the truck he waved at Angelena who returned his wave with a sad look on her weather-beaten face.

Angelena stood by Banjo who defiantly watched the truck until it crested the hill. "You cannot change time, my husband," she said to him and went into the house.

Banjo sat down on the porch and tried to relax. He saw the crumbs from Rodney's tortilla, which had attracted several red and black ants that were fighting over the spoils.

Banjo wanted to yell at his wife for feeding a gringo the best tortillas in the world, but knew she would only ignore him and maybe not fix him tortillas for several days. It was her punishment and one that she used every time she felt wronged. Once Banjo had ridden into town and bought her real cigarettes and a new hoe after an argument so she would fix tortillas again. "They fenced off the water," he hollered at the door.

Angelena let his cry fall on deaf ears as she looked at her tiny crucifix nailed to her bedroom wall and sadly wondered why men were such foolish creatures.

Banjo stewed in his anger. But after a few minutes he started thinking about the cowboy. The cowboy only came over to try and be a friend and Banjo could sense that the cowboy was a loner like himself. "I wonder if he has ever been a bandit?" Banjo asked himself.

But, he did not answer the question. If Rodney had been a bandit Banjo would have to like him. Banjo went into the house to apologize to Angelena for losing his temper. She would not believe him but it was at least worth a try.

Rodney was not angry but felt confused. He had never been the brunt of racial prejudice. But, Rodney knew Banjo did not like him simply because he was white.

Rodney's thoughts darted from Hazel to Banjo, to Angelena, to the wonderful tortilla, and then to Karen. Each in their own way confusing, but Karen was both confusing and perplexing.

"My life might have been better if I would have kept going to Texas," he said.

Rodney knocked on Karen's door. He wanted to talk or merely see her smile. When she opened the door her smile made him feel like a teenager.

"Dinner at your place or mine, stranger?" Karen asked before he could say a word.

"Yours," Rodney answered, "in about an hour."

Rodney was taking a shower when he wondered, if in reality, the last several weeks were nothing more than a dream. He might wake up sitting in the bar back in Montana feeling jealous as everybody looked at Hazel.

Rodney was drinking a glass of wine while Karen was cooking. "You know, being an artist is just sitting down and doing something. You don't have to have a degree in art to be an artist," she said.

"The only artist I know except you is a man in Montana who paints animals on old boards and sells them at the gas station in town," Rodney said.

Rodney was enchanted with the way Karen's hair seemed to flow around her face like a golden halo when he suddenly felt a deep wave of feeling roll over him. He had never felt this way with Hazel. With Hazel, love had been either a constant fight or the tight feeling of jealousy over other men looking at her all the time. Rodney took a gulp of wine and fought the feeling. "I cannot love," he told himself.

Karen placed two bowls of strange looking food on the table.

"Seaweed and tofu," she told. "Eat it, you'll live longer."

Rodney ate the food and told Karen it was good even though it tasted like salty paste.

After eating, Karen picked up the bottle of wine and taking Rodney by the hand, led him to the living room and pointed at a overstuffed sofa for Rodney to sit. She put an album of soft music on, lit a candle and turned off the light.

Karen, bathed in the flickering light, surrounded with the slight aroma of paraffin and the music made Rodney want to lay out his soul at her feet.

Karen sensed his feelings. "My poor, poor cowboy," she said, leaning over and kissing him lightly on the forehead. "For all your rough outside I know you are as confused and lost as the rest of the world. The only problem is, there are no sunsets to ride off into anymore."

"Fences tore us all up," Rodney said feeling intimidated by Karen's kiss.

"Do you think people can love anymore, Rodney?" she asked. "Or is it too late?"

"I hope not," he answered truthfully.

He looked deep into her eyes and smiled.

"Sit here with me," Karen said. "We don't have to talk."

Sitting by Karen and the silence made Rodney comfortable. He thought about Angelena and pictured her hand-rolled cigarette hanging out of her mouth. Even with her skin as hard as shoe leather, her eyes were soft and kind and forgiving.

"Banjo, you bastard, you don't know how lucky you are," Rodney blurted.

"Do you mean Banjo Ortega? The old Mexican man that lives next to the ranch," Karen asked slightly puzzled.

"How do you know his name?" Rodney asked in surprise.

"I met his son in town at an art opening, he's a painter. One of the up and rising Mexican American painters in the area. We had a few drinks, and he told me all about his early life with his family. It was quite a coincidence that I happened to be living here."

"What did he say about his father?" Rodney asked.

"He said he was a head strong bandit who had lived so long on this God forsaken land he couldn't change. He won't let his son help him because he thinks Armondo has copped out and has turned white."

Rodney thought back to a dried-up cowboy he had known in Montana called Pete. Pete had squatted in the national forest for so long the government gave up trying to kick him off. Pete was one of the last men alive to feel it was man's right to just live—to be alive and to breathe and fish and hunt and live and let the world go on its way.

"Damn fences," Rodney muttered again.

"Fences aren't the only problem in life," Karen said.

"Fences are the source of all problems in life," Rodney said.

"Only the ones we build around ourselves," Karen said.

Rodney smiled sadly at Karen. "How can a person tear a fence down when they have built it so strong," he asked.

"With the help of a friend," Karen said almost sadly.

Seven

*B*anjo, as usual, woke up thirty minutes before dawn. He could count on one hand the days in his life he had not seen the dawn, three of which had been spent in jail, and two sick in bed. Banjo liked the early morning—the world was at peace and filled with hope. He went to the porch and sat heavily in his chair. He coughed several times and a sharp pain shot through his chest that almost took his breath away. So far he had been able to hide the cough from Angelena and when they were together he forced himself not to cough. If she knew he was not well she would make him go to the doctor.

"I wish it was five hundred years from now," Banjo said. "Then this house and all of my people's graves would be so deep beneath the earth we would be like an Indian ruin. Five hundred years would surely be enough time to wipe out the longing of our ghosts."

The eastern sky began to turn a deep blood purple. It was as if the night sky had finally bled to death and the blood would have to be pealed off of the horizon. It was the blood of the past, centuries and centuries of losing and growing old.

"Dear God," Banjo said, "it is so difficult."

Banjo thought about his son the famous Mexican painter. Banjo loved Armondo, a man had to love his son, and deep inside he was proud of him. He could not expect him to want to live like he and Angelena—poor for their entire life. But, the land had been his life for so long he could not bear the thought of passing it on to a son who did not believe like he did.

He knew that he could not force himself to tell his son he was proud of him. There were too many stolen sheep and too many harsh winters, too many hungry nights with not even a tortilla. Life was not soft, life was a battle, a battle with the sun and the wind, and the snakes, and scorpions and the white ranchers who wanted to take it all away. It was a battle that could not be stopped, even if the battle itself could not be won. "I know I cannot win," Banjo said. "But it does not mean I cannot fight."

Banjo heard Angelena putting kindling in the stove and he thought of all the women in Santa Fe turning on the burners to their gas stoves and he felt sorry for his wife. Sorry she had not married a rich man in town, a storekeeper or a bar owner. As beautiful as she was she could have married any man she wished. He knew his life would have been empty without her. He would have been alone and unloved. Banjo, if nothing else, knew he needed love even if he was too proud to tell his own son he loved him.

Armondo Ortega stopped his new four door Saab, got out and opened the gate to his parents land. At one time he hated this place. He hated chopping wood and hauling water for his mother. He did not like sheep or hunting or riding horses. He remembered waiting for the school bus and dreading going to school in town. Dressed in faded and patched Levi's, with worn shirts and jacket, he felt as though the whole school looked at him and felt sorry for him because he was a poor Mexican. He would eye the clothes of the white boys enviously and dream of a day he too could wear new clothes. School had been nothing but a time of embarrassment to Armondo and his group of friends. There were the Mexicans and then there were the whites and the two worlds did not meet. Now, many of those old friends were drug addicts and thieves, who spent their lives lost in unreachable dreams and blaming the world for their lot in life.

Through art Armondo had managed to make a break. He no longer felt the pangs of being poor and he no longer envied white people because they were white. He grew out of his prejudices—there were good and bad people in all races. But, now, at forty years old he was filled with a strange longing and looking back on his young life he knew it had taught him a lot.

Armondo wished with all his heart his father would talk to him but he held little hope. If his father would only understand that an artist could make more of a statement about his culture than any man who was poor, no matter how proud a man he was.

Armondo parked the car by the woodpile. He saw his father's horse was gone and he felt relieved even though he wanted to talk to him.

His mother was carrying an armful of kindling for the wood stove. Armondo's heart bled for her. How he wished she would move to town. He could rent her an apartment and she could spend her last days doing something besides working. He knew that as long as Banjo was alive she would stay with him. Angelena dropped the kindling on the ground and hugged her son warmly, kissing him on the cheek. "I am happy to see you," she said with a tear of happiness in her eye.

She started to bend over and pick up the kindling. "No mother. I will get it," Armondo told her.

Armondo put the wood away in the house and got a sack from the car. His mother was fixing coffee. When she turned around there were four tins of tobacco and five novels on the table.

Angelena's eyes lit up. Armondo loved to see his mother smile. It took so little to make her happy.

"One of the cans is for father, you can tell him you have been saving it for him," Armondo said.

"Your father is a strong-headed, old goat who one day will wake up and see the world for what it is, and not for what it was," she said.

"I do not think so," Armondo said sadly.

Angelena looked at the novels. "You know," she said with a twinkle in her eye, "These are really naughty. But I like them."

She took everything to her room, came back, and poured them a cup of coffee and they sat at the table.

"Such nice clothes you wear," Angelena said. "You have become a handsome man."

Armondo was close to six feet tall and had black wavy hair that touched the back of his collar. His facial features were almost Indian and he had happy eyes. He chose his clothes carefully and wore the best that he could buy. Unlike his father, he was quick to smile and made friends easily.

"At times now I miss this place," Armondo said quietly. "But I would not want to live here."

"You will miss it more as you grow old and the world carries you along," Angelena said.

"Why do you live this way?" Armondo pleaded.

"My life is my own business. Not the business of my son," Angelena said firmly but not with any anger in her voice.

Armondo patted her hand. "My dear mother, I love you so."

Angelena smiled. "You have been a good son," and changed the subject. "Your father's sheep need water. The new owner of the Last Day In Paradise Ranch fenced off the river and I fear Banjo will do something that will get him in bad trouble."

"He should sell the land and move to town. You both are too old to live this way," Armondo said trying not to sound like he was pleading.

"People get too old to live in any way," Angelena said with finality in her voice.

Armondo was about to speak when the door swung open and Banjo walked into the kitchen. He looked at Armondo and a small smile crossed his grizzled face, then quickly vanished.

"The famous painter," he said sarcastically and sat down at the table as Angelena stood up to bring him a cup of coffee.

"What brings you here?" Banjo said harshly. "Do you wish to remember how real people live?"

Armondo looked troubled. "No," he answered carefully. "I wanted to see you both."

Banjo, started to cough, but held it and did not show the pain that raced through his chest.

Armondo noticed how tired his father looked and he seemed to be loosing weight.

"Mother says the new owner of the ranch has fenced off the river," Armondo said.

"Something else for the white man to use to push those weaker than him further and further into the ground," Banjo answered.

Banjo sipped his coffee and watched Angelena begin to roll a cigarette. Angelena noticed the glance, finished rolling the smoke, and handed it to Banjo. He seemed to visibly soften as he took the cigarette. "Gracias," he said.

Armondo had to force himself not to smile seeing the simple pleasure on his father's face.

"Why don't you talk to the rancher and see if he will let you use the water?" Armondo said.

"He won't," Banjo answered gruffly. "He only wants to buy me out and then he will own all the land that can be bought for miles around. But, if I see him I will tell him not to worry because my son will sell it too him."

Armondo did not reply, not wanting to cause an argument, but when the time came the money he could get for the land would ensure him years of being able to paint without worrying about placing his works in galleries.

"I can talk to the owner for you," Armondo said.

"Even though I am old no man will speak for me," Banjo said.

"Will you ever accept me?" Armondo asked with a heavy heart.

"I do not think so," Banjo said and looked away from his son.

"Are you staying for dinner?" Angelena asked Armondo and gave Banjo a scornful look. Armondo shook his head. "There is a party for gallery owners I was invited to."

73

"Are you taking a white woman?" Banjo asked with a trace of disdain in his voice.

"I'm not taking any woman," Armondo lied.

How could he tell his father about the white woman he felt he was in love with. Armondo stood up and he wanted to hug his father, but Banjo did not stand or say good-bye. Angelena went with him to the car.

"It is a pretty car," she said looking at the new car. "But it would not haul any sheep or wood."

Armondo kissed her lightly on the forehead. "No mother," he said, "it would not haul any sheep or wood."

Angelena smiled at him with understanding.

"Have you talked father into getting a cell phone or letting me get one for you?" Armondo asked.

"His pride is in the way, as usual," Angelena said. "One day when he is about to die he will see how stupid he has been."

Armondo waved at his mother as he drove away, then looked toward the porch to see if his father had come out of the house. Banjo had not. "I still love you father," he said to the empty porch.

Armondo thought of all the old Mexican people still living in the mountains and corners of the state who were not members of the modern world. "Maybe they are the truly fortunate ones," he said.

Angelena watched her son drive away until she could see only a dust cloud on the horizon. She was happy he had been able to get away from the land, but she was also sad. It seemed the young people were so alone with everything they had. They possessed no peace, only a drive for more, a drive that could never be satisfied.

Banjo was looking in awe at the full can of Prince Albert tobacco on the table. Angelena got a can of tobacco from her bedroom. "From your son," she said simply and held it out for Banjo.

Banjo looked at her and for moment his eyes softened as he reached for the tobacco, but then he put his hand down refusing to take it. Angelena put it in his shirt pocket. "Pride is for your son, but not for your wife," she said and went outside.

"My sheep will die," Banjo hollered at the closed door, "and my son will paint pictures."

The door flew open and Angelena glared at Banjo. "Those pictures will live for years and years," she yelled, "long past your sheep, long past even your son," and she let the door slam shut.

Banjo sat as the silence settled around him like a heavy frost. He opened the new can of tobacco and with great difficulty rolled himself a large cigarette. He lit the cigarette, dodged the flame that shot from the end and savored the burn as the smoke entered his lungs but he could not get his wife's words out of his mind or the sadness that rested in his heart over Armondo. "Is pride such a bad thing to have," he asked himself. "And if it is not bad why does it cause so much grief?"

Eight

Karen woke up and it was only 5 a.m.. She did not try to go back to sleep but got up and went to the kitchen. Instead of turning on a light, she lit a candle and sat at the table feeling as though she was intimidating the dark. She heard a lone bird begin to chirp and saw a faint splash of red in the sky signaling the new born dawn. While she was making a cup of tea, she saw Rodney leaving his house and head toward the corral. He looked like an old cowboy from a western movie—tall and lean with his hat pulled low over his eyes—all that was missing was a pistol and holster. Karen was filled with the same warm feeling she got the day she saw him sitting under the tree. She knew he was different than most men and not simply because he was a cowboy. Rodney was not surly, nor was he a male ego freak and Karen knew, there was a deep side to his heart. She realized she did not know much about him, only small fragments of conversation, but she knew she loved him. She had loved him from the moment she saw him. But he always seemed to be guarded when he was around her, as if he was afraid to tell her anything that might lead to an insight into himself. It was as though he was afraid to be close to another human being.

"He's the kind that will hurt you and not even try," she said outloud as Rodney walked into the corral.

She watched as he caught the mare and led her into the stable.

A few minutes later, Rodney rode away from the headquarters. Karen wanted to run to him and hug him. She wanted to tell him she loved him and tell him she would marry him and buy him a ranch and they could live as far from people as he wanted to. All she needed was him.

She suddenly felt alone and lost, as though her strength had gone from her and life was too overbearing and too unpredictable for her to go on. She walked outside and stood by the tree with its decoration of skulls. "I'll love you and you'll leave me, as sure as the sun is rising, you'll leave me," she said as Rodney rode over a hill.

She heard the lone bird begin singing once again. "The sad thing is I won't even be able to hate him after he goes," she sighed and went back into the house.

Rodney did not really know what to look for in an ideal movie site. He tried to picture all the western towns he had seen as a kid when John Wayne was saving the world from villains in black hats.

He remembered the black arrowhead he had found a few days earlier. Feeling in his pocket and finding it still there, he felt a sense of relief knowing he had not lost it. It would be a shame to find something that had lain on the ground for hundreds of years only to lose it to time once again.

Rodney saw the new fence about half a mile away. "If this was my ranch old-timer, I'd let you run all the damned sheep you wanted to on this place. You couldn't afford to buy enough sheep to hurt this place," Rodney muttered.

Rodney suddenly had a great dislike for Mr. Cook. "Maybe if you had to work a ranch and see what it was like, you might grow to respect your land," Rodney said aloud. "Maybe then it would be more than just another trinket to add to your collection of things."

In disgust, Rodney started to turn his horse back toward the house, but as he did, he saw Banjo on the opposite side of the fence. He stopped his horse and watched as Banjo dismounted his horse and began to cut the fence. Even though he felt empathy for the man, what he was doing was wrong.

Rodney kicked his horse and took off at a gallop toward Banjo. Banjo saw him, finished cutting the fence and rode away. By the time Rodney had covered the half mile all that remained was a hole in the fence. Five sheep had already darted through the cut and were running as fast as they could toward the tiny river. Rodney remembered a summer in Montana when there had been no rain and the cows stood with their tongues hanging out of their mouths. He turned his horse and started back toward the ranch house. He could wait a few days before coming out to fix the fence.

Banjo lowered the rifle sights off of the cowboy. He could hear his heart pounding in his ears and his hands were sweaty. Watching the cowboy he was confused. Why did Rodney not fix the hole? "It would be a shame to have to kill you, gringo. You must be a good man," Banjo said, getting back on his horse. "But I am only doing what I have to do. An old man has no tomorrow, only today."

Rodney did not look back at the fence as he topped the hill. He knew he would see fifteen or twenty sheep filling their parched bellies and he also knew that Banjo was somewhere on the hillside watching him. He figured Banjo was armed. He would have to tell Mr. Cook he needed a rifle in case the crazy old coot decided to take a shot at him.

Not far from the headquarters Rodney veered east and rode where he had never been. He came to a large, rolling hill, covered with small, yellow flowers. From the top of the hill a large plain spread out before him. Behind the plain, looming in the distant horizon were the Rocky Mountains. The mountains formed a back drop and it dawned on him here was a good site for a western town. It was dry and dusty, but on the horizon was the promise of mountain air and water. A dream, the symbol of the old west, always the dream on the horizon. A dream that modern man had wiped out. There were no dreams anymore, only the movies, and movies were a far cry from filling the gap of no dreams.

"Maybe besides fences, it was the damn movies that ruined us," he said to the horse who was busy shaking its head trying to scare away a sweat bee buzzing around its ears.

Rodney looked at the area once again. Here, Mr. Cowboy could save the fair maiden and the town and could chase away all the outlaws.

Rodney turned his horse back toward the houses. He wondered if Banjo would really and truly shoot him over his motley herd of sheep and he came to the conclusion that he would. Rodney laughed a laugh like he was in the army. "You'd kill me, you dried up piece of jerky, but I can still feel for you. You aren't any different than any of us cowboys. Just something that houses and condos and time shares and social security haven't wiped out yet. We're just hanging on by a thread old pard', if the government doesn't get us, then old age surely will."

After unsaddling and watering the horse, Rodney noticed Karen was in her backyard working on a painting. Looking at her lost in her work he tried to cover up the way she made him feel but it did not work. He wanted to walk over and see what she was painting, but he felt he should not disturb her. He had read somewhere how artists needed quiet and solitude and would jump on anybody that bothered them at the wrong time.

He walked to his house, got a cold beer out of the refrigerator, and sat on the steps in the backyard. Drinking the beer, he wondered what Hazel was doing right at this exact moment and wondered if she was happy with her new man? He wondered if he had really ridden bulls on T.V. or if that was just a ploy to get in Hazel's pants? His started to get up and get another beer when Karen came around the corner.

"You didn't even walk over to see what I was painting," she said looking hurt.

Rodney also had heard artists were temperamental.

"Didn't want to disturb you," he answered.

"Bring me a beer, would you? I've lost the feeling," Karen said.

Rodney brought out two beers and Karen plopped down beside him on the step. He handed her the beer and reached into his pocket for the obsidian arrowhead. "I found this and thought you might like it," he said.

Karen took the black arrowhead and held it up to the light and then leaned over and kissed Rodney lightly on the cheek.

"It's so pretty, thank you," she said.

"Not as pretty as you," Rodney said, speaking before he thought.

Karen gave Rodney a puzzled look.

"I found a spot for a movie set," Rodney said.

"Good," Karen replied but still looked puzzled.

She smiled at Rodney. "I'm going to paint," she said.

Rodney contemplated the growing feelings he was having for Karen. Life was much simpler alone but he did not want to lose the feelings.

Karen sat the small arrowhead on the edge of her stretched canvas and smiled as she picked up her paintbrush and started to paint once again.

Nine

*M*r. Cook set the airplane on automatic pilot and looked at his wife. Gloria was not in a good mood, but at least she was not talking. He knew she hated to leave Phoenix for the ranch. And now Mr. Cook wished he had left her at home. He could not see his marriage to Gloria lasting much longer. He learned early in life to calculate all the possibilities and be ready for any eventuality. Except for several mistakes, one which cost him several million, he had been very adept at this practice.

Mr. Cook was in a hurry to get to New Mexico. For the last several days he had been in meetings with representatives from the Pyramid Motion Picture Company and felt the movie site deal was in the bag. The deal would mean great sums of money, which he did not need, but more importantly, he would be able to hob-knob with the producers and actors which meant he would meet some of the young beauties that graced the screen.

Gloria gazed vacantly at the ground. At first she did not want to come back to the ranch, but as her fate was sealed, she began to think about Rodney. Unbeknownst to Rodney or Mr. Cook, Gloria amused herself by watching Rodney as he worked around the ranch. What intrigued her the most was the fact that Rodney did not seem to notice she was alive. Even the first time, when she was in her bikini, Rodney had barely given her a second glance. Most men could not keep their eyes off her. She looked over at her husband who was fiddling with a dial on the instrument panel and started to speak, but then decided she would just as soon make the trip in silence.

Rodney was in the corral working with the mare when the plane circled low over the ranch and dipped its wings. Within a few minutes, the plane was on final. Rodney drove the Suburban to the airstrip. Gloria smiled at him as he opened the door for her and Rodney tipped his hat. Mr. Cook and he shook hands.

"Great to be back," Mr. Cook said. "The big city was about to get me down."

Rodney could not remember the last time he had been in a big city. He had been to Missoula a few times with several of the boys to get drunk and raise a little hell. But in the way of cities, Missoula could not really be considered a city of much importance.

"How's the ranch been?" Mr. Cook asked.

"Fence was cut," Rodney answered. "I'm going out this afternoon and fix it."

Mr. Cook looked agitated but did not say anything for a few minutes. "I'd like to ride out with you," he said, as Rodney stopped the Suburban by the house. "You can show me the fence and the movie site. Saddle the horses up for us in about an hour."

Gloria got out of the Suburban and smiled at Rodney in a way that made him feel uneasy.

Rodney decided he would eat lunch before getting the horses ready. He wondered what it would be like to ride with the boss and decided it would be like taking a dude on a trail ride.

Much to Rodney's surprise, Karen was sitting in the kitchen. She had blotches of purple paint on her face and blouse and she was excited.

"It's one of the best things I have ever gotten into Rodney," she said. "It's as though my mind is bleeding and coming out of my fingertips and forming the painting."

Rodney opened the refrigerator and took out a ring of bologna and a beer and sat down at the table.

"Lunch?" he asked.

Looking at the bologna, Karen made a face.

"I've dreamed at night about what it would feel like to really get into a painting, feel like Picasso or Van Gogh, or Andy Warhol. So wrapped up that life seems to stop and the universe within comes into order."

Rodney took a pocket knife out of his pocket, cut off a large chunk of the bologna, took a bite, and gulped his beer. Swallowing hard, he cleared his throat, "Show me after I eat."

"Can't," Karen said. "Not now, not until it's done."

"Fine," Rodney said. "I can understand that."

Karen took the arrowhead Rodney had given her out of her back pocket. "It's because of this, Rodney, this timeless gift, this piece of history, this heart of the desert." She leaned over and kissed Rodney on the forehead and went back to her house.

Rodney tried to think of the last time in his life he had felt truly excited about anything, but there was nothing he could remember. He thought about Karen with the purple paint all over her, how exuberant she was, and he smiled.

Mr. Cook was putting on his cowboy boots. There was something about wearing cowboy boots that made a man feel like a man. Something about the curve of the toes and the high heel that made a man feel brave and tough.

Gloria sat in an overstuffed chair in the living room looking out upon the vastness of the land around her. There were no buildings, no parks filled with flowers or people. It was a desolate, lonely place.

"Going to go for a ride," Mr. Cook said.

"Have fun," Gloria said halfheartedly.

Rodney had saddled the two horses and tied them to the corral. Mr. Cook walked up to him. Rodney handed Mr. Cook the reins to his Arabian and swung up on the mare. Mr. Cook mounted carefully under Rodney's scrutinizing stare.

"Not a bad mount," Rodney wanted to say, but knowing Mr. Cook was the boss, decided to keep his mouth shut.

"Now where's that cut, Rodney?" Mr. Cook said, fighting to keep the Arabian from prancing around in small little circles.

"Couple of miles," Rodney answered.

"Damn Mexican," Cook snarled so vehemently it caught Rodney off guard.

"I have the stuff to fix the fence," Rodney said, remembering poor Vietnamese farmers walking around in rags after their small farms had been bombed into nothingness. It's all power, he thought, nothing but power.

Rodney led and Mr. Cook followed, having difficulty controlling his horse. Rodney was not a big fan of Arabians. They reminded him of bankers, for what reason he really did not know, since he had never really had enough money to come in contact with a banker.

Karen was in her yard busy with her painting and did not notice the two men riding away. She was torn between the color purple and the color red.

Gloria was sitting by the large picture window. She had to smile as she saw Rodney riding by, looking as though he and the horse were one, while Mr. Cook bounced in the saddle. She wondered what it would be like to sleep with Rodney? She pondered if he was what she figured a cowboy would be like, a quick wham-bam and thank-you ma'am? After the past months with Cook, she enjoyed tinkering with the idea of a real man on top of her.

"You ever want a ranch Rodney?" Mr. Cook asked.

"Yes sir," Rodney answered.

"It's a great feeling to know that everything around you belongs to you," Mr. Cook continued. "Every rock and bush and tree and lizard and deer. It's all yours. I didn't have a thing when I was young. My dad worked as a tailor and raised six kids on spaghetti. I hated it, being poor. But after I got out of the Air Force, I went for the money. What I did wasn't always pretty, but now I've got it and it was worth everything I ever had to do to get it."

Rodney thought he heard Mr. Cook chuckle and wondered what it took to go out and get it. He knew you had to know about law and corporations and boards and stock and interest and CD notes and bonds, none of which Rodney knew much about. He knew you had to know about taxes which Rodney definitely did not know, having never filed in his life. He drew cash, and if the government wanted some of his cash, they would have to find him. In Rodney's mind, he paid his share of taxes with every dime he spent. He also figured if the government needed to come after him and his measly amount of cash, they must be harder up than he figured.

"What would you do if you had a ranch, Rodney?" Mr. Cook asked.

Rodney was silent for a moment, wondering where to begin. Dreaming about a ranch had been a past time of his for over twenty years. Where some people dreamed about gold, houses and pretty women, Rodney dreamed about land. There was nothing in life worth more. Money had always eluded him, the one time he was in love hurt him, but land was something he could see and dream about.

"I'd have a place like an old time ranch," Rodney started. "I'd have a parking lot by the main gate where people would have to leave their vehicles and ride a horse into the headquarters. I'd raise beef and good cutting horses and, if I was lucky, I'd guide deer hunters in the fall for extra cash. I'd have cook wagons for the cattle drives and nothing but real cowboys working my spread and I'd pay cash. A man could work for a season and quit and hire on the next season as long as he was willing."

"Damn, son," Mr. Cook said. "It's a hell of a dream but I wonder if a person could pull it off."

"Don't know," Rodney answered. "Might be the system has everything so tight you couldn't do it."

"System is what made me rich," Mr. Cook said seriously.

Rodney thought to himself, "That's what I mean."

As Mr. Cook and Rodney topped the hill that overlooked the fence Rodney saw twenty or so sheep scattered over a small area by the river.

"Hole is right over there," Rodney said pointing his finger. "In the old days we'd just go over and hang that Mexican for cutting my fence. Hang him up on a cedar tree and let the buzzards pick his bones," Mr. Cook snarled. "But now days," Mr. Cook went on, "you hang a man by the laws. You get a good lawyer and you make a man wish he was dead."

"There's only a few sheep," Rodney said.

"It's not the sheep," Mr. Cook said coldly. "It's the idea. I don't want sheep on my place and I don't want that Mexican thinking he can do whatever he wants on my land. I offered him more money than he has ever seen in his life for his little piece of dried up nothing."

"There isn't enough money for everything a man has," Rodney wanted to say, but he knew it would only enrage his boss. Being broke, Rodney was in no position to say what he felt.

"We'd better drive the sheep back through the hole," Rodney said, nudging his horse into a trot.

He knew sheep were hard to drive because they would only scatter before a horse.

It took Rodney and Mr. Cook over an hour to get the twenty three sheep back on the other side of the fence. An hour in which Mr. Cook almost fell off his horse three times. When they were finally back, Rodney took foot long pieces of wire he had brought in his saddle bags and fixed each strand of fence. Mr. Cook sat on a rock and watched him work, trying to ease the burn in his legs and rear from riding.

While fixing the fence Rodney had no doubt Banjo was watching him and he had his 30/30. He only hoped the sights were on Mr. Cook's head and not his. It would be a shame to be killed for something that was not yours.

For some strange reason, Rodney suddenly had an idea for a painting, and put it in his mind to tell Karen about it. It would be a big landscape with a fence running diagonally across it with a hole cut in the middle of the fence. The painting would be called "Freedom".

"I'll show you where I think would be a good movie site," he told Mr. Cook as they rode back toward the houses.

"We can fly over it," Mr. Cook said wishing they were already back at the house and the horses were put away.

Banjo sat next to the trunk of a sprawling cedar tree that had to be at least two hundred years old. Through a small opening in the branches, he watched as Rodney and Mr. Cook herded the sheep through the hole in the fence. He chuckled at Mr. Cook, but watched with admiration as the cowboy cut and turned his mount skillfully. When the sheep were back on his land, he watched the cowboy fix the fence and the other man sit. While the fence was being fixed, he took turns resting the gun sights of his rifle on each man. It would be so easy, so easy to pull the trigger. Take a deep breath, steady the sights and squeeze. He could see the tiny red blotch on the shirts of the men as the bullets entered their bodies and see them fall to the ground. He wondered if jail was where he should be? Sitting in jail with all the other passed over and destitute men of society.

When Rodney and Mr. Cook rode away, he once again rested the sights on the two men, but as they crested the hill he took a deep breath and wiped his brow. "It is bad to think of killing," he said, thinking about his wife and the crucifix on his wall.

He lay his rifle down and rolled himself a smoke, being extra careful to not spill any of the tobacco. He lit the cigarette, blew out the flame from the excess paper, and took a deep drag. Exhaling, he looked at his sheep who were standing and looking forlornly through the fence at the small sliver of green grass and precious water. When he finished the smoke, he butted the stub and put it back in the can. He would show his wife that he, too, could save. He walked to his horse and put the rifle back in the scabbard and got a set of wire cutters out of his saddle bags. "Do not worry. I will help you," he said to his sheep.

With a twang, Banjo once again cut the fence in exactly the same spot he had cut it before. The sheep dashed through the hole and headed straight for the tiny stream. Banjo smiled and got back on his horse and rode toward his house. Angelena was having tacos tonight with refried beans. It was a lot of work to convince oneself to not kill two gringos and then cut a fence and it made him extremely hungry.

As he rode, he felt the tin of tobacco in his pocket and thought of his son and the words of his wife ringing in his ears about paintings lasting longer than life. Although his sheep would eat and have water for a few more days he was troubled and ill-at-ease knowing this was only the beginning. He coughed several times and a sharp pain shot through his chest.

🐏 🐏 🐏

Gloria was growing restless. She had spent an hour painting her fingernails and another thirty minutes standing in front of the mirror pulling her hair back in different directions. Bored with this, she clicked the T.V. dial to all the channels but found nothing interesting and turned it off. It was not even noon when she drank her first gin and tonic, then mixed another one. For a moment, she wondered what her friends were doing in Phoenix, but then decided they were really not her friends, but more her rivals. Contenders to see who had the newest dress, the best shoes, or the best tickets to the shows. She thought about going swimming, but swimming alone in the Olympic size pool did not seem like much fun.

Before she was married, living in Phoenix and always out of money, she went for a walk every night. It was on a walk that she decided the way to escape her life was to find a man who had money, then marry him. She saved her pennies, bought good clothes, went to all the right places, and in time, she had her man. Now she was wondering if she had not cheated herself. Her friends, who had married for love, seemed to be much happier than she was, although they did not have half as much. Possessions gave one a good feeling, but it was not a sensation that held much worth when one was alone and not able to show off.

Gloria went outside and saw Karen painting in her backyard. Over the months, the two women had not said more than a few words in passing. When Karen came to the ranch to rent the house, Gloria had shown her the house, but it was Mr. Cook who had okay'd her renting it. Gloria went over and watched Karen painting.

Karen did not notice Gloria, and continued to paint and talk to herself. "There, good...it's flowing...no...no.." Karen said outloud.

Gloria looked at the painting but could not decide if she liked it or not. The more she watched Karen, sensing the labor that was going into the work, the more she liked the painting even though, for her, the color scheme was a little off. Karen was painting a landscape, but the mountains were red and purple and the sky a deep, almost black blue. In the far right corner was the outline of a horse and rider.

Karen stood back from the painting and she noticed Gloria standing there. She felt violated for a moment, but maintaining her composure she put her brush and palette down and smiled at Gloria.

"It's coming, she said. "My first one."

"I like it," Gloria said. "Not at first, but now I like it."

"The cowboy will be riding into the sunset," Karen said. "All you will see is his back."

Gloria smiled. "That's their reputation."

"Would you like to come in for some tea?" Karen asked.

Gloria walked around and came into the backyard while Karen held the back door open for her. Karen poured two large glasses of sun tea.

"Almost time for hot tea," Karen said as she sat down. "Fall is coming. Some of the leaves are starting to turn."

"Lord, I hope we don't stay here for the winter," Gloria lamented.

Karen sipped her tea. "I like the winter," she replied. "It seems so sad and alone, but so filled with hope and courage."

"Winter in the Bahamas would do me," Gloria said. "Lying on the beach and taking in the dance clubs at night. I could dance every night until I dropped dead."

Karen thought about her college days in Europe, remembering evenings with the men all vying to get into some American pants. She had not thought about dancing in a long time. Karen wondered if someday Rodney would take her to a honky tonk.

"I see you and the cowboy have struck it off," Gloria said, eying Karen for some kind of reaction.

Karen thought about the statement for a split second before replying, "He is like no man I have ever met in my life."

"Do they really stay on longer?" Gloria asked, with a sly smile on her face.

Karen ignored the remark wishing she was still in her back-yard lost in her painting and knowing she did not like Gloria. They finished the tea in silence. "Thank you for the tea, I was bored and thought I'd drop over," Gloria said.

By the door, she looked back at Karen. "You never did answer my question."

"He has never tried," Karen said.

"I will try to find out for myself," Gloria told herself.

Karen returned to her painting and, in the distance, she could see Mr. Cook and Rodney riding toward the house. She thought about Boston with its teeming streets and people elbow to elbow, and it was as though Last Day In Paradise Ranch was not a part of the real world. The real world was noise and cars and busses and angry people. Here there was quiet and space and time to think and two men riding horses that only she could see. "Maybe when the big war comes and we have wiped out mankind, there will be a few cowboys left to start it all over," she mused picking up her paintbrush. "A few cowboys and me."

Rodney waved to Karen as he and Mr. Cook rode by on the way to the tack room. She smiled and Rodney felt a wave of good feeling sweep through him.

"She likes you," Mr. Cook said as they rode on. "Nice looker, you could do worse."

Rodney did not answer. They dismounted by the stable and Mr. Cook looked seriously at Rodney. "I want you to ride over and tell that Mexican the next time he cuts my fence, I'm going to cause him big trouble. And tell him my offer to buy is still open."

"Yes sir," Rodney answered as Mr. Cook walked away leaving him to unsaddle the horses.

Rodney brushed the horses and checked their legs for cuts. He put each horse in their own corral, fed them and checked their water. Walking back to his house, Rodney grew angry thinking about having to ride over and deliver Mr. Cook's message to Banjo. It was the boss's job to do his own dirty work.

Rodney got two beers and sat down at the table. He dreaded going over to Banjo's and threatening the old man. When he did go over, he hoped his wife was around and she could talk some sense into the hard headed old goat. He chugged the two beers.

Rodney was deep in thought when there was a knock on the door. To Rodney's surprise a well-dressed Mexican man was at the door. "My name is Armondo Ortega, may I come in?" he said agreeably.

"You must be Banjo's son. I'm Rodney Slugger," Rodney said as they shook hands.

Armondo followed Rodney to the kitchen and Rodney got two beers out of the refrigerator and gave one to Armondo. "I suppose you're here to tell me about your father," Rodney said.

"My cantankerous old father," Armondo replied, immediately liking Rodney.

Rodney guzzled his beer and got another one before speaking. "It's a get drunk night," he said then added. "I've had a few run-ins with your dad. Rode over to the place a few days ago. He isn't the most talkative man a guy wants to meet."

Armondo ran his hand through his hair. "You have to understand my father," he said.

"Oh, I understand," Rodney said. "Strong, self sufficient, never needed anybody, always poor, always stepped on by the whites, there's nothing about him I don't understand. I wish he knew all white people weren't out to get him."

"Wish he knew I wasn't out to get him," Armondo said softly.

"He cut the fence the other day to water his sheep," Rodney said. "Boss flew in and wants me to go tell him not to do it again."

"I came out to see Mr. Cook, I'd like to talk him into letting my father run his sheep on the ranch," Armondo said worriedly.

"Mr. Cook won't let him," Rodney answered flatly. "I haven't been here long, but I guess Mr. Cook wants your father's land and will do everything he can to run him off just to get it."

"Are you sure he won't reconsider?" Armondo said, gazing at his beer can.

Rodney glanced through the screen door at the yellow leaves dotting the cottonwood tree. "Sure as winter's coming," he answered.

"Then I'm afraid you might have to kill my father," Armondo said with no remorse in his voice. "Either that, or he will kill you."

Rodney got two more beers out of the refrigerator. "I figured that," he said. "A man lives his life and it reaches a point where there really isn't much else that can be done to him. He'd rather die than change. Suppose if I was your dad, I'd be the same way."

Armondo opened his beer and took a long drink. "Strange how a man can have so much around him and make it hard for everybody else."

"Story of mankind," Rodney said. "Guess we are mostly a bunch of greedy, self-centered bastards that go through life seeing how many people we can screw over so we can tell the rest of the world what we have."

"Is Karen still out here?" Armondo asked.

"She's working on a painting," Rodney said, feeling jealous that Armondo would ask about Karen.

"I met her at a party and she told me she wanted to be an artist. Everybody disenchanted with life wants to be an artist. She seemed nice enough but I couldn't convince her to give up art and go back east where people were sane."

"I don't think you can tell her anything she doesn't want to hear," Rodney said.

Armondo stood up. "You know, my father will cut the fence again, don't you?" he said. "And he won't sell."

"I know," Rodney said.

Rodney and Armondo smiled wryly at each other.

"Wish you could talk some sense into your boss, let him give the old man a break. He cannot live forever and I'll sell him the land when it's mine."

"I'll try," Rodney said, opening the door for Armondo.

Rodney watched Armondo drive away. He went back to the kitchen and finished his beer, and got another one out of the refrigerator. "Maybe Armondo, if you understood your father, you wouldn't sell the land," he said, taking a long swig of his beer. "And your father could find peace before he died."

After three more beers, Rodney was feeling surly. The more he thought about riding over and seeing Banjo, the angrier he became. Angry at Mr. Cook for not having the strength to do his own dirty work, angry at the Mexican for not seeing he could not win, and angry at himself for being the one caught in the middle. He felt like drinking another beer, but he had not eaten and he knew if he was going to get plastered, he had better get some food in his stomach. But bologna and crackers was not what he was really hungry for. Peering in the refrigerator, he wondered what Banjo was doing right at this moment? He wondered if he too was sitting drinking a few beers and pondering his predicament, or if he even pondered it at all. Maybe his life had been so filled with hardship that this was just another problem that did not cause anxiety or lack of sleep or the need for a few beers. Rodney got another beer out of the refrigerator, writing off dinner. He thought about walking over to Karen's. Maybe with a little luck she would be right in the middle of cooking some great food and there would be enough for two.

Rodney took a deep swig out of the beer and hoped a little magic would happen in his life and he would figure out how to talk to Banjo. "You can't win, Banjo, don't you know?"

Rodney thought about his own life. His life had been a dream, and still was a dream. Once one reached the point where they know dreams are only for dreamers, all that's left is the hope that one dream does come true.

"Hell," Rodney slurred, "A cowboy is nothing but a billboard with a cigarette hanging out of his mouth."

Rodney sat in the kitchen drinking beer until it was dark. He opened another beer and half-fell through the screen door and lurched toward Karen's house. Her kitchen light was like a lighthouse on a rocky point. Karen was sitting in the living room eating a T.V. dinner when she heard her gate open. She hoped it was Rodney. She had been thinking about him all evening, but had sworn to herself she would not throw herself at him again like some dumb teenager. It was his turn.

She heard the loud knocks on the door, and upon opening it, saw Rodney was not in the best of shape. She smiled and opened the door wider.

"Guess they closed the bar," she said as Rodney stepped into the house.

"You're beautiful," Rodney said staggering by her and falling onto the sofa.

"You're drunk," Karen said, "but if it makes you talk like that all the time, you can stay that way."

When Karen sat down on the sofa, Rodney looked at her T.V. dinner and made a face.

"You think you can come over here and ply me for food and favors, cowboy, you've got another thing coming," she told Rodney with a sly smile on her face as she sat down.

"Not exactly," Rodney answered, laughing a deep easy laugh. "But close."

Karen went to the kitchen to put a T.V. dinner into the microwave and came back and sat down.

"I'm tired," Rodney mumbled and rested his head on her shoulder, falling instantly asleep.

Karen ran her hand through his hair and shut her eyes and thought to herself, "Oh God, we both need."

The bell went off on the micro-wave. Karen lifted Rodney's head up and went to get his dinner.

When she got back he was stretched out on the sofa oblivious to the world. Karen got a blanket and covered him. "I know you like me. But you are afraid. Afraid I might hurt you. I won't hurt you, you dumb cowboy."

She kissed him gently.

In her bedroom she scrutinized her painting. The half-painted figure of the cowboy was riding away. "Leaving is the modern answer to it all and I am too old to hold onto hopes for too long," she said.

Karen went to bed and she felt warm and secure with Rodney sleeping in the next room. She desperately hoped the feelings would stay with her every moment of her life.

Ten

*R*odney started to drive to Banjo's when Gloria waved at him from the corral, a wave that Rodney felt duty bound to return. But there was a confident look on Gloria's face that Rodney did not like.

Rodney left Banjo's gate open, hoping he did not have to make a hasty exit. The adobe house came into view and he saw Angelena by the wood pile splitting cedar with a hand axe. Angelena saw Rodney approaching and she picked up an armful of the split wood and started toward the house. By the time Rodney got to the house, Angelena had put the wood in the wood box and was standing on the porch. She smiled at him but Rodney could see a trace of worry around her eyes. He thought about his great grandmother when she was a young pioneer woman in Oklahoma. He figured his grandmother looked much the same as Angelena.

"It is good to see you again," Angelena said.

"It's good to see you," Rodney replied. Then after a moment he added, "Is Banjo around ma'am? I have to talk to him."

Angelena pointed towards the rolling hills to the south. "He is there somewhere, he will not be hard to find. This is not a large place."

Rodney tipped his hat to Angelena and started walking the way her finger had pointed. Passing by the barn, he noticed the pig in its small pen.

Rodney followed the fresh prints of a horse.

Banjo sat under a tree, rolling a smoke, his 30/30 across his legs and watched Rodney approach, but strangely the cowboy did not make Banjo feel angry. Rodney was so intent on following the horse tracks that he did not see Banjo until he was almost on top of him. Rodney jumped and Banjo laughed and finished rolling his smoke before saying, "You would have been easy to shoot. But it would be no fun shooting a cowboy who is not on a horse."

Rodney, feeling foolish, sat down on a small rock a few feet away.

"I cut the fence," Banjo said, eying the younger man. "That is why you are here. Now you can leave."

He lit his cigarette and Rodney watched the flame shoot off the end of the cigarette.

"You have to put more tobacco toward the end," Rodney said.

"How can I roll good cigarettes with this?" Banjo said holding up his right hand with the two missing fingers.

"I knew a cowboy who could roll a smoke with one hand," Rodney said.

Banjo thought for a moment. "He must have been a talented man. I would have liked to seen that."

"How did you loose those fingers?" Rodney asked.

"I won't tell you but it is how I got my name, Banjo," Banjo said.

Rodney looked confused.

"My real name is Henrique. But my old friends named me Banjo because with no fingers I can't play the Banjo," Banjo said with a grin.

"You probably lost those fingers sticking them where they didn't belong," Rodney said with a smile.

Banjo did not really like the statement, but said. "It is true."

Rodney took off his hat and looked at the brim. He ran his hand over his chin and scratched the back of his neck. He knew he had to say something, he knew what he wanted to say, but what he wanted to say and what he was duty bound to say were two different things.

Banjo was eying Rodney carefully, sitting in the middle of nowhere, there really did not seem to be much difference between them.

"Mr. Ortega," Rodney began. "You have to understand that fence and that land doesn't belong to you. You can't keep cutting that fence and letting those sheep of yours go over on Mr. Cook's land without his permission."

"The hell with Mr. Cook," Banjo said. "The hell with his fence, the hell with his land and the hell with his permission."

"Damn it," Rodney exploded, jumping to his feet. "If it was my land I'd let you run your sheep on the place. They could eat every dried up piece of grass they could find and drink every last drop of the damn water, but it isn't mine. And even though I don't like my boss or what he is doing to you I still work for him and I have to do what he says."

As quickly as he had lashed out, Rodney was finished. He stood there, his face flushed, glaring at Banjo. Banjo looked at him calmly, took the last drag off his cigarette, butted it on the ground, and stood up using the rifle like a cane. He walked over to his horse, put the rifle in the scabbard, and mounted. Looking over at Rodney he said simply. "Follow me," and rode off.

Rodney was still shaken by his outburst as he watched Banjo ride off. "Damn," he mumbled, "I hate walking," and quickly followed Banjo.

Banjo rode on a twisting trail that went in and around limestone and sandstone bluffs and ended at a rock bluff with more than a one hundred foot vertical drop to the land below. Here one could see for miles. Banjo dismounted as Rodney puffed up to him. "Now you know how a horse feels," Banjo said with a crooked smile on his face.

Rodney did not see any humor in the comment.

Banjo pulled out his Prince Albert can and started to roll himself another smoke. Finished he asked Rodney, "You want to roll one."

"No thanks. I quit."

"Too bad. It will make you live longer," Banjo said.

Rodney did not laugh when Banjo lit his smoke and the flame from the end of the cigarette almost burnt his face. Banjo took a deep drag on the smoke, exhaled loudly and said looking out at the land. "This is all there is in life gringo...land, endless land, lonely land. I was born here on this land, it is all I know. Cactus and cedar trees, and pinon trees and sheep, there's nothing else. When I was young we rode everywhere, everybody let their sheep run on this land and everybody had sheep. Now look at all the fences that cut the land."

Rodney looked at the miles of fence crisscrossing the brown expanse below them.

"Now people who do not know the land own the land," Banjo said. "Rich people who live in big cities buy the land so they can spend their money on something. I am nothing, but I know it is not right for a big powerful man to step on a little man." Banjo tossed the cigarette to the ground. "I have lived too long, cowboy," he said solemnly, "and you were born too late. We're just as useless as the Indians, but we don't have their faith."

Banjo mounted his horse, looked once more at the vista, and rode back the way he had come. Rodney remained for a few moments and tried to visualize the land years earlier, before all the fences. He could see antelope run, without having to alter their gait to run parallel with fences. He could feel himself galloping his horse for miles and miles. He could see small dots of sheep spread for miles with an occasional darker dot of cattle.

Banjo was on the porch when Rodney got back. "Come on in," Banjo told him, surprising Rodney.

Angelena smiled at Rodney and poured them a cup of coffee. Banjo looked at her hands to see if she was making tortillas, but there was no trace of flour.

Looking at the sparse room, Rodney thought about Mr. Cook's house, and then about the house he was living in. He looked at Angelena wearing men's shoes and sitting in a wooden chair by the stove. He thought about all the women he had ever known worrying their life away about hair color, and styles, and shoes, and lipstick, and lotions and wondered what made life the way it was? It occurred to him that Karen did not wear makeup and as he thought about how full and rich her skin was, a jolt went through his body, and he wished he was with her right now. He wished she had been with him and Banjo on the mesa top and heard the old man's words.

"My son is a painter," Banjo said, bringing Rodney back to reality. "A rich painter," he added. "He drives a fancy car and takes out white women."

"I bet you are proud that he is a painter," Rodney said.

"My son is a traitor and he is not proud of me," Banjo said. "To my son I am only an old man who has wasted his life."

Rodney sipped his coffee.

"I do not blame him," Banjo continued.

"I don't have a son," Rodney said.

"I will give you mine," Banjo grinned.

Angelena started to refill Rodney's cup. "No, thank you," Rodney said standing. "I have to be getting back."

Banjo opened the door and Rodney stuck out his hand to shake. Banjo looked troubled, glanced at his wife, and then shook Rodney's hand. Rodney started toward the truck.

"Hey, gringo," Banjo called to him. "Tell your boss I will cut his fence every time you fix it."

"I know you will," Rodney replied. "I wouldn't expect anything else."

Rodney drove home feeling both perturbed and happy and thinking more about Karen than some useless fence.

When he got back to the headquarters, his stomach was doing flip-flops. He looked toward Karen's, but did not see her working on her painting. He noticed how the leaves on the cottonwood tree in her yard were filtering down to the ground. He wondered how New Mexico winters compared to Montana winters, but decided they could never be as bad as winter in Montana.

Rodney opened a can of chili and beans and poured it in a sauce pan to heat. He ate a piece of plain bread to hold his stomach over, then went to the closet to get his coat. If he laid it out where he could see it, maybe he would remember to put it on when the mornings started to get cold. Back in the kitchen he wondered what the exact date was. His life was regulated by the season and not exact dates. He knew it was early October, he could not recall the exact day of the month. In Montana the boys would be up in the high country driving the cattle down to the flat lands.

Rodney poured the chili into a bowl, sat down, and started to eat. While he ate, he stared through the back door glass and saw Mr. Cook coming toward the house. Rodney remembered Gloria waving to him earlier in the day and it occurred to him that her wave seemed to be a little more than friendly.

Mr. Cook banged on the door. Rodney opened the door and knew immediately Mr. Cook was not in a good mood. He walked in and sat down at the table.

"Movie people will be here late tomorrow afternoon. They'll be flying in a helicopter. I have to go back to Phoenix so you show them around. Show them that site you thought was best, the one we haven't gotten around to looking at yet," Mr. Cook said.

"Want me to tell them anything?" Rodney said.

Mr. Cook shook his head. "What happened with the Mexican?"

"He says he won't cut the fence anymore," Rodney lied.

"Did you tell him if he does I'll get him tossed in jail?" Mr. Cook asked.

"Yes, sir," Rodney said, lying again.

"Good," Mr. Cook said. "I'm going into town to pick up a few things and I'll be flying out later this afternoon. Gloria is staying at the ranch, for some reason she doesn't want to go to Phoenix."

Mr. Cook walked to the door and turned. "Do you think he will sell?" he said.

"Not on your life."

With that Mr. Cook left the house in the same mood as he had arrived. Rodney wondered why he had lied for Banjo? Lying could only lead to trouble.

Rodney did the dishes and went into the living room and sat down. He had never in his life been able to really do much sitting during the day. Being a cowboy on a ranch was not much of a sit down job unless you were sick or had been kicked by a cow or horse.

Rodney thought about his brother and his wife. His brother had two kids, a house, two cars and a camping trailer. He worked every day to pay insurance and taxes. Rodney was still trying to figure out Social Security. He knew it was something you put a lot of money into but got very little in return. He was beginning to feel since most of the people in the country paid into it, maybe he should, even if it was a rip off. Having a little when you were old was better than having nothing. But then, Rodney had the feeling he would never get old, he did not want to get old.

His mother had told him once, "Getting old is not worth a damn," and from everything Rodney had seen about being old, it was true. Old was just old. Old, worn out and discarded. Rodney could not visualize himself sitting in an old folk's home playing checkers with other old men and talking about their lives. Rodney yelled at the wall. "Banjo, you old son of a bitch!!"

Karen was about to knock on the front door when she heard Rodney yell and, instead of knocking, ran into the house. Rodney was walking back and forth like a caged animal when he saw her and his anger immediately disappeared. "It's good to see you," he said like he had not seen her in years.

"Are you okay?" Karen asked him with a worried look on her face.

"I'm okay."

Karen had a feeling he was lying to her.

"Movie people are flying in tomorrow in a helicopter to look at the ranch. Mr. Cook wants me to show then around."

"Wouldn't it be something if they filmed a movie here?" Karen said. "And you were really in it."

Rodney smiled, "It would be different. Nobody would ever believe me."

"They don't anyway, do they?" Karen teased.

They went to the kitchen and sat down. "I think Mr. Cook's wife wants to get you in bed," Karen said.

Rodney shook his head.

"I saw her wave at you this morning, that was a come on wave if I ever saw one."

Rodney did not like the way the conversation was going but was at a loss to say anything. It seemed he had been at a loss to say anything for a lot of his life. Things came and went in his life and he didn't know what to say half the time, or what to do. Right now he wanted to stand up and pick Karen up and carry her to the bedroom, telling her he had been thinking about her all morning while he was trying to figure out how to handle an old Mexican man and not get shot and that he thought he loved her.

Rodney looked at Karen seriously and felt butterflies in his stomach. "I've been thinking a lot about you."

"To tell you the truth," Karen answered, also feeling nervous. "I've been thinking a lot about you."

"What have you been thinking?" Rodney asked.

"I've been wondering, if I let myself fall in love with you if you would ride off into the sunset?" Karen said.

"I might," Rodney answered truthfully, looking back at Karen, "but I wouldn't want to, at least not right now."

Karen smiled, "When then, when I was eight months pregnant and a bitch?"

"No, " Rodney answered. "When I felt you were tired of playing with me and it was time to go."

Karen took a deep breath, "We're both afraid aren't we?"

"Probably," Rodney said.

"Maybe if people didn't fall in love it would be a lot better," Karen said. "Then there would never be any meaningful relationships and nobody would get hurt."

"I don't know," Rodney said. "Maybe getting hurt a few times lets people really enjoy somebody that won't hurt them."

Karen reached across the table and took Rodney's hand and held it between hers. "I don't think it's that simple."

Gloria was relieved when Mr. Cook went to town. He had an important meeting with lawyers in Santa Fe and all that Gloria knew was that it was about Mr. Cook's plan to sub-divide part of the ranch into smaller ranchettes and his fear that the Mexican who owned the eighty acres could somehow ruin the whole deal. Gloria remembered waving to Rodney as he drove away in the morning. It had been deliciously bad of her she knew, but the more she thought about Rodney, the more she wanted to sleep with him. She figured it would not be all that hard to bed him. Getting men into bed with her had never seemed to be much of a problem, the problem was getting them out again.

She walked to the back room and she felt like taking off all her clothes, putting on a bathrobe and walking over to Rodney's house. And then, while they talked, let her robe fall open just to find out what he would do. She went to a window and saw Karen sitting at Rodney's kitchen table. She did not know why she felt threatened by Karen, but there was something about her air and her confidence that did not fit well on a woman who was supposedly divorced and wanting to be a painter. There seemed to be no anxiety in her face nor worries about money that haunted other people in the arts. There was no bowing down, in any form, when the two of them were around each other.

With her daydream about seducing Rodney bashed for the moment, Gloria went back into the kitchen and mixed herself another drink.

"Maybe I should have gone into town with hubby dear," she said outloud. "Gone and looked at all the quaint little shops and bought a few things."

As she walked back toward the living room and the T.V., Gloria smiled to herself. "I'll get you yet, cowboy," she vowed. "And when I do, you'll never be able to be with another woman without thinking of me."

Karen had gone back to her painting and Rodney was sitting in the living room drinking a beer when he heard the engines of Mr. Cook's airplane kick over. He heard the airplane engines rev and the drone of the plane as it took to the air. Rodney felt relaxed, the big bad wolf was leaving.

Karen was in her bedroom, naked, caught up in enraptured bliss—examining her painting. Her cowboy was riding away, but she was contemplating adding a bird of some type to the upper left corner of the canvas flying toward the viewer. She figured it would show hope or promise of return. She thought of all the people who painted hawks and eagles and knew she did not want such a ferocious bird, but she could not decide what type of bird would fit. She knew a robin or a sparrow was definitely out.

As suddenly as the inspiration had come over her, it vanished. Karen was again conscious of her breathing and the steady thump of her heart. She sighed deeply and put her brush down. While she was putting her clothes on, Karen began to feel empty. Her inspiration was gone and she was suddenly a single woman, living in a small house, trying to be a painter, and in her own mind, not doing a good job.

She finished dressing, walked to the living room and sat down on the sofa. For the first time in months, she began to think of her ex-husband and wondered how he was? She wondered if he was still going a hundred miles an hour trying to be the biggest and the best lawyer in the world, or if he understood that once you were in the trap, you could never make enough. She wondered what he would think of her now, living in a small house in the west trying to be a painter. The rich girl trying to make it through life on her own.

She turned her thoughts to Rodney and what he would do if he knew she was worth well over one million dollars. She was certain he would stop seeing her.

She got up from the sofa and stood by the kitchen door and looked through the fading leaves of the cottonwood at the setting sun. "The days just come and go," she said. "One by one and one day everything has been wrung out of you. Dear God, please let me never lose hope."

She saw a light brown night owl diving through the sky. Its path was erratic and jerky, but it cut through the evening air without a sound. "It is a sign," she said, and went back to her painting.

Rodney had not slept well. He spent the night dreaming he was a cowboy movie star. In one dream, he was being whisked from the airport in L.A. in a fancy stretch limo. Karen was sitting beside him, wearing a full-length mink. Every place they stopped, people were clamoring around the limo trying to get his photograph or asking him to sign an autograph.

In another dream, he was sitting in front of a T.V. camera and a shapely lady, with bright red hair and legs that never seemed to end, was telling him how wonderful he had been in his last movie and he was explaining how it had been when he was a real cowboy. He left out the parts about the cold, and hurting, and no money, and made it sound as romantic as he possibly could. The lady's eyes were dripping with the thought of having him in the sack, but he was returning her unspoken come on with his 'I'm a true blue cowboy to my one and only' stare.

Although he had not slept well, he still got out of bed earlier than usual, took a shower, and put on a clean pair of Levi's and one of his good shirts. He put a quick shine on his good boots and cleaned off his cowboy hat. When the movie people came, he wanted to look his best. He scrambled two eggs and washed them down with steaming coffee, then paced around the house waiting for the sound of the helicopter.

By the time 10:30 rolled around, he was tired of pacing. Jacked up from all the coffee he had been drinking, he wished there was something for him to do, but on the Last Day In Paradise Ranch, with no stock, there was nothing to do but wait.

By noon, he was ready to be tied down and was tempted to go over and see Karen. But he figured that Karen was painting and he did not want to disturb her. He walked out of the house, stood in the backyard, and looked over the horizon toward Banjo's land, wondering what the old man was doing today besides cutting the fence.

Lost in thought about Banjo, Rodney heard the sound of a helicopter and for a brief moment he was standing in a small clearing in the jungle firing his M-16 madly into the dense foliage around him. Men ran into the clearing as a helicopter hovered over head with door gunners firing furiously into the jungle.

Rodney took a deep breath and pushed the memory back into his mind, a trait the years had taught him. He walked to the main house and waved at a blue and white Bell helicopter as it flew over the headquarters. Karen had also come out of her house, but, instead of waving at the helicopter, she waved at Rodney. Rodney watched the helicopter land on the airstrip and drove over.

By the time Rodney got to the strip, the helicopter had been shut off and the pilot was taking a leak over by a bush. Two men, both with beards and styled dark hair, were looking around them. Rodney got out of the truck and noticed the men were both wearing designer jeans and western shirts and brand new cowboy boots.

A man wearing lizard boots held out his hand to Rodney. "I'm Irv Abraham," he said, "and this is Saul Heilman."

Saul did not bother to shake hands. Rodney noticed both men wore gold chains the size of a small rope around their necks.

"Mr. Cook wants me to show you all around," Rodney said.

Abraham put his arm around Rodney's shoulder and steered him toward the helicopter. Within minutes they were in the air each wearing a helmet hooked up with a microphone system so they could talk. Rodney directed the pilot where to fly. As the helicopter banked sharp left to head for the site Rodney had chosen, he could see in the distance the white dots of Banjo's sheep grazing along the river and laughed to himself.

The men were talking to each other about lighting and background and seemingly ignoring Rodney. Since Rodney had taken an immediate dislike to both of the men, their rudeness did not really bother him. They reminded him of little boys out from the big city who were going to play cowboy. He wondered people from L.A. could possibly make a western that would be any good?

After flying over the site several times, the helicopter headed back toward the landing strip. Rodney got out and waved as the helicopter took off and disappeared quickly into the distance. He felt slightly disappointed. After all his daydreams about suddenly becoming a big Hollywood western star, he had not been able to talk to the movie men, let alone negotiate a contract. It was not until he was almost back to the house that he remembered the sheep. He decided he would not fix the fence until Mr. Cook was coming back.

When Rodney got out of the truck, Karen walked from her backyard toward him. "I suppose you know who you were just with," she said.

"No," Rodney answered truthfully.

"That was Saul Heilman, the highest paid director in the country," Karen said.

"I'll be damned," Rodney said.

"You haven't seen any of his movies?" Karen asked in surprise.

"I haven't been to a movie in years," Rodney answered.

"Are they going to give you a job?" Karen asked.

Rodney looked away from her. "I didn't ask," he said. "I figured Mr. Cook would do that."

"That's one thing about cowboys. They don't know when opportunity knocks or how to take the initiative," Karen said as she started to walk away.

Rodney did not know if he was angry or not over her comment.

Rodney went to the corrals. In his excitement, he had forgotten to feed the horses. Since this was the number one mortal sin of a cowboy, he imagined all sorts of bad things had happened to the horses. As he stood by the corrals, to his relief, he could see both horses were in good shape. He fetched each of them a wedge of hay and tossed a can of grain into their feed bins. While checking their water, he realized he still had his good boots on, so he walked gingerly around the stalls. With the water tanks full and the horses eating contently, he went to his house.

Rodney made himself a cup of coffee and sat in the kitchen watching the dust particles float through the air. He thought about Karen's statement, "Just like a cowboy to let opportunity slide by." Now the statement made him angry, not so much because it was not true, but because she had the nerve to say it. He got up from the table and poured the remainder of his coffee down the drain and walked over to Karen's, feeling as though he should tell Karen she was out of line.

When Rodney knocked on the door, Karen was in the process of taking off her clothes and starting to paint. She peeked through the window and, seeing it was Rodney, did not bother to put her clothes back on but hollered. "Come on in. I'm naked and painting. You can talk to me from the living room."

Rodney sat down on the sofa while Karen was standing in front of her painting deciding upon the exact spot to paint her night owl. She wondered if it were possible to make the bird look like it was smiling without making it look stupid and ruin the serious tone of her painting. "People don't realize how tough it is to get across the exact mood of a painting," she said loudly to Rodney.

"How come you said it's like a cowboy to pass up opportunity?" Rodney blurted out.

Karen made a wry face. She had made the statement but did not intend it to sound the way it did. In a lot of ways, it was good to find somebody who was not always looking for the angle. But then, if human beings did not look for the break, they were bound to be whatever they were forever, although being a cowboy was a forever job.

"Because it's true," Karen finally said.

"What are you, the absolute authority on cowboys?" Rodney shot back, letting Karen know he was angry.

"Oh Rodney," Karen said. "It seems that cowboys are so simple, and everything so black and white that they don't know when opportunity knocks."

"Simple, what do you mean, simple?" Rodney demanded.

"You know what people say about cowboys, Rodney. You spend your lives on horses, carefree, not thinking about the world, lost in the past, you're all a bunch of dreamers who think the world doesn't exist. All that exists is what you see," Karen said carefully.

She knew all the other men she had ever known would think of a cowboy as being simple in the dumb sense of the word.

Rodney let the words sink in. It had all been simple for a lot of years, and he knew that was why he had become a cowboy. But he was not young anymore. He could not run away from life. There was no future in being a cowboy. Maybe it was Banjo who had shown him the end. An old man, with not enough strength left to do what had to be done—old, with no money, in a young man's world.

"What happens to a cowboy when it isn't simple anymore, Karen?" Rodney asked over his shoulder as he went out of the house.

Karen did not hear Rodney leave, but the question settled around her like a cold fog, chilling her bones. She chewed on the end of her paintbrush. Cowboys were like the last of the cave men to the modern world. She set her paintbrush down, put on a robe and walked into the living room. Finding Rodney gone, she answered his question. "I don't know Rodney, I don't know."

Rodney got his billfold. He still had some money left from the two hundred Mr. Cook gave him. He got in the truck and headed for Santa Fe. Driving through the ranch, he thought about all the men he had worked with over the past years and he could not remember any of them that were old. He wondered where the older ones were? He knew some were driving trucks or tending bar or working in feedlots and none of those jobs were too appealing to Rodney.

As he left the ranch and turned onto the paved road that led to Santa Fe, all Rodney wanted to do was sit in the corner of some bar and have a few drinks and listen to the music. He knew a few drinks were no answer, but drinking was better than no answer at all.

Karen heard the engine to the truck and watched as Rodney drove away from the house. She wanted to run outside and wave at him and tell him to take her along, but something held her back. She turned away from the window and walked back to her painting. Picking up her brush, she started the first lines of her night owl.

"Don't you know, you dumb son of a bitch?" she said. "Don't you know half the people in the world would trade their problems to be a cowboy?"

Eleven

Rodney drove to a gas station and asked where there was a country bar in town. A band, consisting of a drummer, bass, and guitar player were warming up on the stage when Rodney walked in Mr. R's. He headed for the sit-down bar at the far end of the dance hall. An attractive barmaid in her early twenties smiled at him. She was wearing a black skirt that barely covered her rear, fish net stockings with a red garter and a white blouse showing a small amount of cleavage.

"Give me a shot of Jack Daniel's and a Coors," Rodney said, returning her smile.

When she returned with the drinks, she said. "Two bucks. It's time to forget the world. But drink them quick, it's back to a buck and a half each in thirty minutes."

Rodney gave the girl three dollars. "Keep the change," he said.

The girl winked at him.

Rodney took a sip of beer and then drank the Jack Daniel's in one swallow, followed by another swallow of the beer. In Montana, he and the boys drank shots and beer. Wages, being the way they were, it only took a few shots and a couple of beers to get sufficiently pie-eyed. It cured the aches and pains of a week on the ranch and got one in the mood for dancing.

Rodney felt depressed. He could ride, rope, saddle and shoe a horse, head off a calf, and that was about it. If he suddenly broke his leg or arm, he could not do anything to support himself. The way the V.A. was cutting back, they might not even help him. "Damn government," he thought.

The barmaid came back over. "I'll take another one," Rodney told her and handed her the empty shot glass.

Rodney watched her pour him a double shot. Setting it down in front of him, "on the house, you look like you need it," she said.

Gulping the double shot, Rodney made a face and washed it down with another swallow of beer. The band started playing a very bad version of ME AND JESSE ROB TRAINS. Several couples got up from tables and started to dance as several men cruised the bar looking for women to dance with. Rodney felt like dancing and suddenly wished he had not left the ranch in such a huff and had asked Karen to come with him. With the whiskey starting to take effect, he no longer was depressed but felt stupid about getting upset over the remark Karen had made.

The barmaid sat down on a tall stool behind the bar. "You're new in town, aren't you?" she asked.

"Working on the Last Day In Paradise Ranch by Galisteo," Rodney said.

"I'd think that would be the most exciting thing in the world being a real cowboy," she said bending towards him and showing off more cleavage.

"About as exciting as doing laundry," he said.

Rodney wished the girl did not work behind the bar and could dance with him. The band was now playing "LUCKENBACH TEXAS", still doing a bad job, but good enough to dance to.

The barmaid eyed him closely, "Whiskey is getting you, boy."

"When I drink it, that's why I drink it," Rodney said, feeling his lips begin to grow numb.

Several men dressed in suits sat down at the end of the bar. The girl went over to them.

Rodney was sad for the girl. Having to wear some skimpy outfit so a bunch of drunks could ogle over you was no life.

Rodney turned around on his stool and watched a few couples dancing to BLUE EYES CRYING IN THE RAIN. They looked carefree and happy. But looking closer he saw a lost look on their faces. A look as if they knew the music or dancing would not change the world, or their lives. Rodney turned around and saw the barmaid talking to the two suits. He wanted another drink, but he did not want to wave at her.

He began to feel like he did when he got out of the Army. Nothing seemed important, nothing had pertinence. Looking back he knew there had never been anything that had stirred him. The years on the ranch had only been spent killing time, day to day, like in the Army, day to day hoping the sunrise would bring a change. But there never was a difference. He always felt about the same. Outside all of it. There were the trees, and the sky and the cows. But he was not a part of anything. He was just there. Then there was Hazel and for those few short months there was something—love, jealousy, dreaming, anxiety. "We all sold out," Rodney muttered outloud.

"Yeah and we're all just pawns who can't do anything about it, but be whatever life has dished out to us," Rodney heard from behind him.

Rodney turned and looked at Karen in surprise. She was not smiling.

"Boy am I glad to see you," Rodney said standing up and taking her hand, his face exploding into a grin and not wondering how Karen had found him.

"I'm glad to see you," Karen answered, slightly perplexed as Rodney led them to a corner booth.

They sat down and continued to hold hands, neither speaking. Rodney felt himself wanting to hold Karen. Wanting to tell her all about his life. Wanting her to crawl inside of him and feel what he felt. But he could only sit silently with his hand in hers.

"Dance with me," Karen finally said as the band started to play

DESPERADO. Rodney followed her to the dance floor. Leading her into the two step, he was amazed at how warm and good he felt—how his thoughts had cleared and how suddenly things seemed to be better.

Karen looked at his eyes, leaned close to him and kissed him gently on the cheek. "You cowboy, dumb ass," she said. "To keep you from riding away, I'm going to have to put a rope around your neck."

"All I've ever done is ride away," Rodney answered.

"I know," Karen said, "I know."

Karen and Rodney danced through WILL YOU EVER LEAVE ME?, MY HEART'S MADE UP, and BORN TO LOSE. Rodney did not notice the barmaid looking intently at him while they danced. All Rodney could see was Karen's eyes.

Walking back to the table, Rodney asked, "How did you get to town?"

"I keep my car in Mr. Cooks' garage," Karen said. "You've never seen it."

"Guess not," Rodney said.

"It's a blue Cadillac with tinted windows," Karen said.

"I guess you really are a spoiled rich lady," Rodney said. "I always thought you were kidding me."

"All women aren't liars," Karen said.

"This damn New Mexico has been a major turning point in my life," he said. "It's something I will never forget."

"What was the other turning point?" Karen asked.

Rodney smiled at her faintly and answered flatly, "The war, I suppose."

"Are you looking for sympathy, Rodney?" Karen asked in a voice that Rodney knew she was willing to offer some.

Rodney looked away from Karen and saw the barmaid serving drinks to several new customers. He looked from the barmaid to the dance floor where a lone couple was dancing to I WALK THE LINE. Turning back to Karen he answered her. "Not now, maybe a few years ago, but now I suppose I'm old enough to know my life would have been about the same with or without the war."

Karen wanted to say, "That's not true," but there seemed to be no need.

"It's strange," Rodney continued. "I've spent my whole life just going from day to day without ever really formulating any true philosophies about life. All the time my mind was telling me what I felt, I just never realized it until now."

Rodney looked over at the bar. He wanted a drink and no waitress had been to the table.

"You want a drink?" he asked Karen.

"White wine," Karen answered.

Rodney went to the bar. Karen watched Rodney and felt both happy and sad. Happy she had come to town to find him, but sad knowing Rodney had been in a war, and sad also knowing in her heart that cowboys were really nothing one could make heroes out of.

Rodney came back with a white wine and a beer.

Karen picked up her white wine and Rodney clinked her glass with his beer.

"To your painting," he toasted. "May you become the new hot shot of the art scene."

Karen sipped her wine, then held up her glass for Rodney to tap once again. "To the next John Wayne."

They sat and sipped on their drinks while the band played BLUE SKIES.

"Did you eat anything?" Karen asked Rodney.

"Whiskey," Rodney answered.

"I'll take you to eat," Karen said.

"How about a greasy old hamburger and fries?" Rodney said.

"Whatever you want, cowboy," Karen smiled, shaking her head in disbelief while thinking about broiled fish.

Rodney followed the Cadillac down Cerillos Road. He wished he could tell the boys back in Montana about Cadillac's and rich ladies who painted nude, and ranches that did not have cattle on them. They would think he was lying. Rodney sighed at the irony of it all.

Karen pulled into a Lotta Burger. Rodney parked next to her and they walked in together. Inside there were several Mexicans and an Indian couple with three kids. The people behind the counter looked like they had been on speed for the last week. Rodney ordered a double burger, fries and a cup of coffee. Karen, breathing in the grease, ordered a glass of water.

When the order was ready, Karen paid for it and handed the bag of grease to Rodney saying, "Follow me."

Rodney followed Karen down the street where, to Rodney's surprise, she pulled into a small motel with individual bungalows. She went into the office for several minutes, came back out and walked to Rodney's truck.

"My treat," Karen said. "I've always dreamed about picking up some hamburger-eating cowboy at a bar and taking him to a motel."

"Karen, I don't know....." Rodney said before Karen cut him off. "No excuses," she said simply.

Rodney followed her to the room feeling both excited and nervous.

It was the nicest room he had ever been in. It was the only motel room he had ever been in that did not have cockroaches wrestling on the floor and the walls were so thin you could hear the guy next door breath.

Rodney sat his hamburger sack on the table.

"You eat and I'll be back soon," Karen said and left.

Rodney devoured the hamburger and fries. He wiped the grease off his hands and looked around the room. He took his boots off and lay down on the double wide bed. "This is a hell of a note," he said.

Within fifteen minutes, Karen was back with a bottle of Jack Daniel's and two six-packs of Coors. "Kind sir," she said. "This is going to be one of those knock 'em down and tie 'em up kind of nights. For the first time in her life, this city girl is going to learn how to drink like a cowboy and no matter your morals you will sleep with me."

"I want to sleep with you. The only reason I didn't is because I don't want to hurt you, Karen," Rodney said.

"It's too late," Karen said opening the bottle of Jack Daniel's.

"You're going to regret that stuff," Rodney said.

"It won't be the first thing I regret," Karen said slipping off her shoes and sitting down. "And sad to say," she added, "probably not the last."

An hour later, Karen and Rodney were sitting facing each other in the bathtub, their legs intertwined. Karen was reclining in the back of the tub while Rodney had to sit straight up or get jabbed in the back by the water faucet. Karen had a beer in one hand and a water glass half-filled with Jack Daniel's in the other. She was drinking the beer and whiskey like it was Kool-Aid. Rodney was sipping on a beer.

"You said tonight, the war didn't change you," Karen said with a slur to her words. "It had to, don't give me that macho I'm a tough guy garbage."

Rodney looked at her face and then at her breasts bobbing in the water. "I take it you want to talk," he said.

"Talk," Karen answered, "and then play, and play, and play," she giggled. "What were you like as a boy, Rodney?"

Rodney glanced at Karen's breasts and then at the dark shadows of her thighs below the water.

"You like," Karen slurred.

"I've never taken a bath with a woman," Rodney said.

"You lie," Karen answered. "Answer my question."

"I wasn't any different than most boys," Rodney said. "I liked baseball and football. I wanted a nice car. I believed in America and freedom. I thought we were the best nation in the world. I just kind of wasted my young days in California, chasing girls and dreaming about cars."

"Then the war," Karen butted in, a serious tone to her voice.

"Then the war," Rodney answered her.

"What then, cowboy?" Karen asked and drank more whiskey.

Rodney chuckled dryly. "You're a tough one under all that good looking skin."

"I want to know you, Rodney, you're the first man I've ever met in my life that I really want to know."

"To make it short, Karen, I guess the war told me nothing is true. There is no glory, no honor, no heroes. When I got home, I went west, west to where men were men and life was simple, where the last remnants of freedom lived in this land. I found it, I suppose. Found it riding horses far away from highways and laws and presidents, but even that is going away. Big business is killing the rancher. Slowly but surely the old ranches are going under and becoming what Mr. Cook's ranch is, just a place where the wealthy can live and hire a few old broken cowboys to sit around and look useful."

Karen took a big swallow of the Jack Daniel's and slurped her beer. "What's a cowboy to do when there's no more need for cowboys, Rodney?" she asked softly.

"Drink whiskey with a beautiful woman while sitting in a bathtub," Rodney said, giving Karen a little boy grin.

Karen set her whiskey glass on the floor and finished off her beer.

"How come life is so sad that it takes all of one's energy to try and be happy," she slurred and then her head fell forward and she passed out on Rodney's shoulder.

Rodney laughed, feeling both disappointed and relieved. He carried a dripping Karen to the bedroom and lay her on the bed. He dried her limp form off with a towel and pulled the covers up to her shoulders. After drying himself, he put his Levi's on and went outside the room and looked at the night sky. Cars raced down Cerillos and the neon signs outshone the stars. The chill in the night air began to get uncomfortable and he went inside and looked at Karen's peaceful form.

He lay on the bed, turned the lights off and kissed Karen on the cheek.

In the morning, Karen felt like a horse had bucked her off and proceeded to stomp her into the ground.

"Welcome to whiskey," Rodney joked as Karen slowly got dressed.

"Did we do anything?" Karen asked.

"Only in my dreams," Rodney said.

Karen finished dressing and staggered to the door. She stood by the door and tried to smile at Rodney, but what crossed her face was more of a grimace. "Next time, cowboy, I'll show you a better time," she groaned.

"Being with you was good," Rodney said.

"Maybe one day it will be more than good, Rodney," Karen said. "Maybe one day you'll love me."

"Do you love me, Karen?" Rodney asked.

"I don't know why, God knows I should know better, but yes, I think I love you stranger," Karen said.

She walked out, closing the door behind her.

Rodney stood looking at the door and heard the engine of Karen's Cadillac kick over. As she drove away, he walked toward the bathroom. "Maybe I love you Karen," he said. "And I don't know how to say it. But my love is no good for you."

As Rodney drove to the ranch, he could not help but laugh to himself about Karen. He knew she would feel terrible all day and wondered if he should check on her or let her suffer through her whiskey hangover by herself. He knew when he tied one on, the next day he would just as soon be left alone. But, there were some people who liked company when they were in misery.

Driving through the gate to the Last Day In Paradise, Rodney saw Mr. Cook's airplane circle off to the south and he knew Mr. Cook would be looking at the sheep drinking his water. He drove slowly toward the house not really relishing seeing Mr. Cook.

He parked the truck by his house and glanced over at Karen's. All the curtains were closed as if nobody was home. Rodney had no sooner walked into his house when he heard loud banging at his back door.

Rodney opened the door and Mr. Cook stormed in. "That no good Mexican cut the fence and his sheep are running all over my land again," he fumed.

Rodney started to speak but was cut off sharply by Mr. Cook. "And just where in the hell have you been?

Rodney had no time to answer before Mr. Cook continued, "I called the Sheriff and he will be out here this afternoon. The three of us will take a ride over and see Banjo Ortega and tell him just where he stands."

Mr. Cook turned sharply and stomped out of the house letting the door slam behind him.

Rodney went to the bedroom, changed shirts and went to the porch and put on his old boots.

"I hope Banjo puts a hole in your ass, Mr. Cook," he said outloud.

He made a pot of coffee and sat at the table drinking a cup and fuming. Rodney could not remember the last time he felt as angry as he felt now. Losing Hazel, he had not felt angry, only hurt. He had not thought about shooting the bull rider, that would have only caused him trouble. But now he felt angry. Angry at being hollered at. Angry at Mr. Cook for being a jerk and angry at Banjo for cutting the damn fence.

He finished another cup of coffee and decided to walk over and see Karen and maybe help her in some way. At least he could tell her not to drink any water as it would only make her feel worse.

Rodney knocked on Karen's door. To his surprise, the door swung open immediately and Karen stood there dressed in Levi's and a sweater and looking as though she had just come back from a vacation and had the time of her life. Her cheeks were rosy and she was smiling from ear to ear.

"Haven't I met you before," she said to Rodney. "In a bathtub somewhere."

"No, that was some other cowboy," Rodney said walking by her and sitting down at the kitchen table.

He could smell a cake in the oven and noticed dishes from where Karen had just eaten lunch.

"You're sweet," Karen said. "You thought I was dying and decided to come over and see if I needed help."

"You're amazing," Rodney said.

"I saw Mr. Cook outside. I could tell he wasn't in a good mood."

"Mad enough to kill a Mexican," Rodney said. "Banjo cut the fence again."

"I would too," Karen replied.

"Mr. Cook saw the sheep on his ranch while he was flying in and called the Sheriff. Mr. Cook, the Sheriff and I are going over there this afternoon."

Karen took the cake out of the oven and set it down by the sink. "I bet Banjo doesn't have a dime," she said.

Rodney scowled. "He's just an old man with nowhere else to go."

Karen looked at Rodney and knew now why he had been so touchy. "Old Mexican cowboy, huh," she said.

"Old Mexican cowboy," Rodney answered, standing up.

"You don't have to rush off," Karen said, hoping Rodney wouldn't leave.

"I was just checking on you," Rodney said. "But I see you survived whiskey and beer."

"Survived it enough to know I never want to drink it again. I may look decent, but you can't see the inside of my brain right now," Karen smiled.

As Rodney opened the door, Karen said, "Tonight, come over for a piece of cake and ice cream and more than a peep show."

"Best peep show I've ever seen," he smiled.

Rodney looked at the large cottonwood tree, its leaves were a bright yellow. He glanced to the west, where Banjo's house lay hidden by the hills and he knew if he was Banjo he would also cut the fence.

Twelve

Banjo was cold when he woke up. He got out of bed, went into the kitchen and started a fire. Angelena's snores echoed through the house. Banjo felt weak and sat down. For the past several weeks he was having difficulty catching his breath and he had not said anything to Angelena.

He put more wood in the stove and put the coffee pot on to boil. He decided he would ride out and cut the fence as soon as the sun was up. It would give him something enjoyable to do.

He poured a cup of coffee and listened to Angelena snoring. She seemed to sleep so well. He sipped the steaming coffee and remembered the first time he drank coffee with the men of the family. There were many mornings when coffee was all he had for breakfast. Coffee so black and thick it was a meal in itself.

As the sun rose, his scrawny rooster let out a few half-hearted cackles. Banjo went to his room, brought his tobacco back to the table and rolled himself a smoke—dodging the flame as he lit it. Smoking and drinking coffee, he watched the dawn while his wife snored in her room.

When it was fully light outside Banjo went out to feed the horse and the pig. A light frost covered the earth which was not at all beautiful to Banjo. The old horse, as usual, whinnied when he tossed an armful of timothy over the fence and stood contentedly while Banjo rubbed her head as she ate.

He carried a bucket of pig pellets to the pen. Banjo knew that in only a few weeks it would be time to butcher. He did not know why? But, he had begun to feel sorry for the pig. This one was no different from all the other pigs he had bought, fattened in the small pen, and then butchered. There had been hundreds of them, and he had never felt sorry for them. But there was something about this pig that tugged at the corners of Banjo's heart. Something that made him want to open the gate and let the pig go free. The pig grunted at him in anticipation of breakfast. Banjo reached over and scratched the pig's head. The pig closed its eyes and began to rub its right side against the pen. "Stupid pig," Banjo said as he poured the pellets in its trough.

By the time Banjo got back to the house, Angelena was cooking bacon. Banjo liked his bacon thick and chewy, not like the thin strips of fat one bought at the store. Angelena smiled at him but said nothing as she refilled his coffee cup.

They ate breakfast in silence. When Banjo was done he told his wife. "I'm going to check the sheep."

Through the window Angelena watched Banjo walk to the barn. It was sad that the men of her house were divided. There was nothing she could do but hope God would reunite her family.

When Banjo rode away from the house, Angelena was out by the wood pile picking up pieces of kindling for the stove. Banjo waved, but she did not wave back.

The old horse was in a frisky mood.

"Your bones are stiff like mine old friend," Banjo said. "Don't hurt yourself."

The horse tossed her head in a feeble attempt to anger Banjo, who hated it when the horse tossed its head. This was a battle they had fought for years. Once, in anger, Banjo had hit the horse on the side of the head only to break his thumb. Banjo ignored the head tossing and let the horse stop of its own accord.

When Banjo crested the hill that overlooked the spot where he cut the fence, he was surprised to find the fence still down and his sheep contently grazing by the small river.

"The gringo cowboy must be falling in love," Banjo told his horse. "The only thing that ever stops a single man from working is a woman."

Banjo felt glum he would not be able to cut the fence and he turned his horse back toward the house. Suddenly, a twin engine plane, flying no more than two hundred yards off the ground, circled the sheep. Banjo could make out the scowling face of Mr. Cook as he banked the plane hard to the right. Mr. Cook saw the grizzled old Mexican man fighting to keep his horse under control while at the same time trying to get his rifle out of the scabbard and turned the plane sharply toward the landing strip.

The horse settled down with the plane gone and Banjo spit on the ground. "Rich gringo dog," he sneered.

Riding back toward the house Banjo felt much better and started whistling a tune his father used to whistle while he worked.

Banjo stopped whistling when he saw his son's car parked in front of the house. His wife and son were sitting on the porch—it was too late to turn around.

As he rode toward the barn, he could hear Angelena talking to Armondo. Even though he could not make out the words, he knew she was excited. He unsaddled the horse and could hear his son laugh and it was a pleasing sound—a sound he remembered when Armondo was young and playing outside of the house—before he had learned how poor they were and began yearning for the white man's world.

Banjo walked toward the house, feeling a slight pain in his chest. Angelena stood as Banjo stepped up on the porch. "Armondo tells me," she said excitedly, "there is going to be a western movie made on the Last Day In Paradise Ranch and they are looking for extras to play in the movie. They especially need good Mexican men from the area to play bandits. Both he and I think you should go and try to get a job."

"Only Mexican's can be bandits?" Banjo scoffed.

"You're a natural," Armondo said. "They pay $50.00 a day and three meals."

Banjo sat down in his chair. "I wonder, since I have been a bandit, if I could play a Mexican bandit?" he said and grinned devilishly.

Angelena smiled sweetly. "What else could you play, my husband?" she said with a tint of sarcasm in her voice.

Armondo tried not to laugh, but a few chuckles escaped from his mouth.

"How would I do it?" Banjo asked Armondo.

"In two days you have to go to the La Fonda Inn. They are going to pick out extras. I know they would take you."

"Are you going to try?" Banjo asked.

"No," Armondo answered.

"I forgot, you are rich and famous, you don't have to work," Banjo said with more venom in his voice than he really wanted.

Angelena looked at her husband and, for the first time in months, wanted to tell him to shut up. She had enough of her husband bemoaning the fact his son did not want to live like he did. What a man's son wanted to do was up to the son, not the father.

"You are a stubborn old dog, Banjo, " Angelena said softly, hiding her anger. "I only hope before you die you see how selfish you have been in your actions and God can forgive you."

Her comment made Banjo angry but he could think of nothing to say. He went to his room and sat down in his rocking chair. His chest began to hurt and it was hard to breathe. "Please, not now, lord," he prayed.

When the pain subsided he rolled himself a cigarette and wondered if he should really try to be in the movie. Being in a movie would be something. Something he could tell all his friends about. He might even get autographs from some of the big stars that he could give to his wife.

Banjo lit the cigarette, dodged the flame and sat daydreaming, Banjo heard his son start his car and drive away. Within a few minutes Angelena came into the house and he could hear her start to fix lunch. He knew she was mad at him, but he only hoped she did not punish him by not making tortillas.

When the cigarette was finished, Banjo went to the kitchen and sat down. "The sheep are still on the gringo's ranch," he told Angelena.

"You should fix the fence, "Angelena said simply, stirring a pot of beans on the stove.

Banjo, scratched his chin, took a deep breath and wondered how his wife could say such a thing?

Banjo was sitting on the front porch trying to figure out what had happened to the summer. Memories were flashing through his mind and he was trying to decide if these things he was thinking about happened this summer, or last summer, or ten years ago. His chest had not been hurting and he was not having difficulty breathing, but he felt slightly lightheaded.

Christmas was not far away and he wished his son would bring him some already rolled cigarettes for Christmas. He could think of nothing he really needed besides money. Nobody he knew could give him any money so cigarettes seemed to be the logical thing to wish for. With the money he would make from being in the movie he would get Angelena a new dress, new shoes and several sacks of flour for tortillas.

He thought about the delicate flour cookies Angelena made every year for Christmas. He wished he had some now. It was always a sad day, when several weeks after Christmas, the cookies were gone and Banjo knew it would be another year before he ate them again. But now the years were short and it seemed Christmas had been only a few weeks ago and here it was creeping up again. "I'm glad I'm not rich," Banjo decided, "then I would have to worry about what to buy all my useless relatives I have never seen, but who would come to see me because I was rich."

A sharp pain darted across his chest. He sat unmoving for a few moments. He remembered his father growing old and how everybody used to laugh at him and joke in a loving way about how hard it was for him to walk. Banjo now knew there really had been nothing to laugh at. There was nothing good about being old. Even an old dog could die with more dignity than an old Mexican bandit who lived off in the boonies with nothing to show for his life but wrinkles.

Banjo heard a car coming toward the house. He did not stand up or go inside to get his 30/30 like he would have in the old days. He only sat and wondered who would be coming. He knew it was not his son since his son had already come and gone today.

When Banjo saw the red lights on the top of the car and the word SHERIFF written on the door, he wished he had fetched his rifle. To Banjo there was nothing lower in life than a lawman.

Sheriff Mendosa got out of the car first. He hitched up his patent leather pistol belt as he looked at the run down house and buildings around him. Mr. Cook got out of the shotgun side of the car and glared at Banjo. Banjo, looked him straight in the eye and spit on the ground.

Rodney, who was in the back separated from the Sheriff and Mr. Cook by a thick screen wire, had to wait until the Sheriff opened his door, since there were no door handles inside the back.

"Mr. Ortega," the Sheriff called out, "We're not here for any trouble."

Sheriff Mendosa knew there had been more than one policeman killed in the remote corners of New Mexico. New Mexico was still a wild place, a place where most cops were not welcome and he really did not want to be here now. This was not a town with backups available within a few minutes. Looking closely at Banjo, he felt like he was looking at a rattlesnake who would jump up and strike at any moment.

"You tell that old son of a bitch what he has to do and what is going to happen to him, Sheriff," Mr. Cook ordered. "You tell him so he understands. You're one of his kind."

The Sheriff gave Mr. Cook a dirty look. Rodney tried to stay in the background, but when Banjo saw him he smiled a large toothless grin and waved at him. "How are you gringo?" he called to Rodney.

"I'm fine, Banjo," Rodney called back.

Mr. Cook, seeing the amiable way Banjo and Rodney waved at each other, gave Rodney a go to hell look.

Banjo walked to the Sheriff's car. He looked once again at Mr. Cook and spit, then looked at the Sheriff as innocently as he could. Looking innocent was not an easy task for Banjo who only came off looking like a coyote that had been caught with a chicken in his mouth and would not drop it even though he was cornered.

"Tell him. It's your duty," Mr. Cook ordered.

The Sheriff took a deep breath. "Mr. Cook," he began, "tells me you have cut his fence and are letting your sheep run on his land and drink his water."

Banjo turned his back on the men, walked back, sat down on the porch and started rolling a smoke. After the smoke was rolled and the flame shot out of the end of the cigarette, he smiled at the Sheriff. "I don't know what you are talking about Sheriff. If somebody cut my good neighbor's fence, it was not I."

"That lying son of a bitch," Mr. Cook roared. "We all know he damn well cut the fence. Nobody else would cut it."

Banjo calmly stood up and went into the house. When he came back out, he had his 30/30 in his hand and he levered a cartridge into the chamber but he kept the barrel pointed toward the ground. Mr. Cook jumped behind the squad car and Rodney stepped back several feet.

"Did you call me a son of a bitch?" Banjo hollered at Mr. Cook.

Mr. Cook looked for help from the Sheriff who had neither moved nor gone for his gun. The Sheriff did not want to shoot the old man. If he shot one of his own kind, especially one who had only been cutting the fence of some rich gringo, his name would be mud in the county. This would make him open game for every hotheaded Mexican around. They would find him one day, shot to death in his car, and knowing how tight lipped his kin were, he knew nobody would ever find his killer.

"Mr. Ortega," the Sheriff said calmly. "I know you have been cutting the fence. But there really isn't any proof. But I'm warning you, if you cut the fence and Mr. Cook pursues the matter, you can get in a lot of trouble. My advice to you is to leave the fence alone."

The Sheriff got in the car, not having to tell Mr. Cook to get in.

Rodney was starting to open the door when Banjo called to him. "I like you gringo, you are not like your boss."

Rodney waved to Banjo.

Driving away from the house, Mr. Cook was furious. "You let that old man run you off. You are an officer of the law. He pulled a gun on us. That's against the law."

"Mr. Cook," the Sheriff said, "this state is full of old men like that one back there. Tough old men who would kill a man at the drop of a hat. Before you were here he probably watered his sheep at the river. Probably before you were born he was watering his sheep at that river. Now, if you catch him cutting the fence, you call and we'll handle it. But not unless you see him with your own eyes. If I were you, I'd let him water his sheep."

Mr. Cook glared at the Sheriff and fell into a sulk. Rodney knew he would soon be fixing fence.

Banjo went into the house and walked by Angelena who was stirring a pot of beans. After putting the 30/30 in his room, he sat down at the kitchen table. Being a good wife and knowing the nature of men, she did not chastise her husband. There were different laws living away from town and many times a gun was necessary. Turning from the stove, she noticed Banjo's eyes were shining and he seemed to be in a better mood than he had been lately. His mood was like years ago when he had come back from stealing sheep in Colorado.

"Dinner will not be ready for several hours," she said.

Angelena did not like it when Banjo stayed in the house all day. It seemed they always got along a lot better when they did not see too much of each other. Before he grew old, this was not difficult as he was always out working or stealing. But now that he was old, he seemed to spend half the time under her feet.

Banjo got up, went back to his room, got his 30/30 and left the house. He saddled his horse, put the rifle in the scabbard, and rode toward his sheep. As he rode, a dull pain shot through his chest. He gasped, but ignored it. Ignored it like he ignored the rheumatism in his fingers and the ache in his back.

"You know, horse," he said. "I will go into town and try to get into that movie. I would make a good Mexican bandit in the movies."

The horse plodded along and nipped at a dried piece of grass beside the trail, accepting her fate without worry.

Mr. Cook did not say goodbye to the Sheriff when they got to the ranch house. As the Sheriff drove away, Mr. Cook ordered Rodney, "Go fix the damn fence."

Rodney rode past Karen's house, noticing the curtains were closed. He pictured her standing naked in front of her painting and he smiled.

Gloria was in the front yard wearing a pair of black, skin-tight, leather pants and a dark red, bulky sweater. Her black hair was pulled back into a ponytail. "How are you Rodney?" she said sweetly.

"I'm fine Mrs. Cook," Rodney answered, stopping the horse.

"Why don't you and I go for a ride one morning, Rodney?" Gloria said. "I'd like to learn to ride better and Mr. Cook won't take the time to teach me."

"If it's okay with Mr. Cook, I'll take you anytime you like," Rodney said but did not like the idea.

He wondered if Gloria was part snake or all snake?

"It's fine with Mr. Cook, he really doesn't care what I do. Most of the day he's tied up with the telephone anyway," she answered.

Rodney nudged the horse, feeling Gloria's eyes boring into his back as he rode away.

A prickly heat spread up Gloria's thighs and centered between her breasts. "I bet you can ride a woman better than you ride a horse, cowboy," she thought to herself.

Mr. Cook was sitting in an overstuffed leather chair with a glass of scotch in his hand and glaring out the window. He did not acknowledge Gloria's presence when she came into the room and continued to glare out the window and slurp his scotch. Gloria went into the bedroom, lay on the large bed and turned on the T.V. "Boring," she said.

Rodney began to relax. He thought about Banjo and his 30/30 and wondered if Banjo would have had the nerve to really shoot Mr. Cook. Since Banjo really did not have much to lose, Rodney supposed the old bandit might. He wondered if Banjo had shot Mr. Cook, if some good attorney could beat the charges? In New Mexico calling somebody a son-of-a-bitch might be grounds for killing the offender. He had heard of stranger things happening.

Rodney was not far from the fence when he saw Banjo moving his sheep toward the hole. Rodney rode up to Banjo and Banjo smiled his rattlesnake grin at him. "I saw you coming and I decided I would save you some work," Banjo said.

"You are only going to cut the fence as soon as I leave," Rodney replied.

"Gringo, gringo, you do not trust me," Banjo said.

Rodney did not bother to reply.

They drove the sheep through the hole and Banjo followed the sheep through while Rodney dismounted and took out his fence pliers and small roll of wire. Banjo dismounted with difficulty and sat down on a large rock and began to roll a smoke.

"I don't know who would keep cutting this fence," Banjo said lighting the smoke and dodging the large flame that shot from the end of the cigarette.

"Must be some stubborn old goat who thinks he's being wronged and doesn't really have much power to do anything about it," Rodney said.

"I hate fixing fence," Banjo said and suddenly coughed several times. The pain that shot through his chest was so severe he put his hand over his heart.

"Are you okay?" Rodney asked when Banjo stopped coughing.

"It is nothing. I think I have caught a cold," Banjo said, hiding the pain that still radiated in his chest.

Rodney knew Banjo was lying. "You should go to a doctor," Rodney said.

"Why? So they can tell me that I am old," Banjo smirked.

Banjo watched Rodney work while he finished his smoke. Rodney strung the last wire together and twanged the wire with his hand.

"You do good work," Banjo said, admiring the fence. "Too bad you will have to do it again, gringo."

"I know," Rodney said, mounting his horse. "I imagine the fence won't stay fixed for long."

"I don't think so," Banjo said, standing up. "That new wire they make these days doesn't seem to be very good."

"Nope," Rodney said. "Seems to nick and break really easy."

Rodney waved good-bye to Banjo and started riding back toward the houses. Looking at the sun, he knew it would be dark before he got back and he felt the chill of the evening coming on.

As Rodney rode over the crest of the hill, Banjo took out his wire cutters and cut the fence exactly where Rodney had fixed it. Smiling, he walked back to his horse and carefully mounted.

"It is strange, old horse," he said, riding back toward his house, "but sometimes your enemy is your friend."

Banjo stopped at the top of the hill and watched as his sheep filed back onto the Last Day In Paradise Ranch. "Yes," he said. "I think I would make a good bandit in the movies."

Rodney rode slowly and watched the sun dip below the horizon and turn the hills a pale red. Off in the distance, a coyote yelped and against the horizon, a solitary night hawk began its evening vigil. He patted the horse on the neck. "Only one hundred years too late," he said to the horse. "But it might as well be a thousand."

Banjo was sitting on the porch watching a small black spider try to wrap a fly up in its web. For some reason the spider was having a difficult time of it, but, with calm, deliberate movements, the spider plodded along. Banjo wished he could reach down and help in some way without breaking the spider's web. Angelena was in the kitchen doing something of no interest to Banjo. Banjo, bored with the spider, looked out on his small, dilapidated domain. He looked at the wood pile which was pitifully small. He knew he could not cut enough wood this winter and would have to buy some. He hated to buy wood. Ever since Santa Fe had become the mecca for the elite, firewood cost more than gold. Before, only poor people heated with wood, now all the fancy homes had fireplaces so people could sit in front of them and drink wine and feel primitive.

Banjo knew his artist son would not cut the many truckloads of wood Banjo would need, since it might hurt his delicate hands. Looking away from the firewood, he noticed the spider had finally succeeded in wrapping up the fly and was hiding in a corner of his web waiting for something else to fall into his trap. He wondered if spiders ever got old and tired or if they just lived with the same energy level until they died.

Banjo took a deep breath and he felt tired. More than tired, he felt weary. It was as though his bones did not want too carry flesh anymore and his brain was tired from constantly thinking. With winter coming, he did not look forward to sitting in the house and always feeling cold. It seemed he could never get warm in the winter. No matter how he bundled up or how much wood he put on the fire, his toes and fingers were always cold. Banjo felt winter was God's way of telling people they were all small and insignificant pieces of garbage. He could see no other reason why man should have to spend half his life cold, unless it was a punishment.

Banjo noticed the spider was now busily wrapping a struggling red ant in his web.

Banjo thought about Rodney. He liked the young man, even if he was a gringo. There was something sincere about him, something likeable. He would have been a good man to have had years ago on a sheep stealing ride to Colorado. Banjo wished his son was like Rodney. Rodney and Banjo were both men of the land. Men who knew nothing else and were locked in until the end.

"It is bad I will cause you so much work, Rodney," Banjo said. "But you are on the one side of the fence and I am on the other. Fate is seldom kind."

Thirteen

Mr. Cook did not bother to knock on the back door and came in the kitchen while Rodney was drinking his first morning cup of coffee. Rodney expected Mr. Cook to be in a bad enough mood he was ready to take on the world but Mr. Cook poured himself a cup of coffee and sat down looking like he had just made another million dollars.

"I saw Karen last night through her bedroom window while she was painting," Mr. Cook said. "She paints in the nude."

Rodney, to his amazement, did not get angry over the statement. "She told me that," he said, wondering if Mr. Cook spent his time in Phoenix as a peeping tom.

"Wonder why she paints in the nude?" Mr. Cook said, more to himself than to Rodney.

"I've never asked her," Rodney answered. "Must be something to do with freedom."

"Women," Mr. Cook said, sounding like a perplexed little boy. "In one way you're lucky you've never had to give one a small fortune."

Rodney thought about the statement for a few moments. "I'd like to take a woman out once in my life and be able to spend more than ten dollars on her," he said.

Mr. Cook reached into his back pocket and handed Rodney six one hundred dollar bills. "Your first month is now paid," he said.

Rodney looked at the crisp hundreds, trying not to show his excitement and put them in his shirt pocket.

"I got you a part in the movie. You will even have a few lines," Mr. Cook said.

"What?" Rodney said in amazement.

"It's more than a bit part. You will be playing one of the bandit leaders. You'll get $300 a day and meals and you can hang out with all the stars," Mr. Cook said proudly, making it obvious he had pulled a few strings.

Rodney was flabbergasted. He would make half of a month's salary in one day. If he could work for several weeks he would have a small fortune.

"The construction crew will be out here in a few days and start building the movie set. When they finish, they'll try to shoot the entire movie in a month, before the real bad weather sets in," Mr. Cook said.

"I'll be," Rodney said still in shock, then getting up and refilling their coffee cups.

"Gloria told me she wants you to give her riding lessons," Mr. Cook said.

Rodney had always had a sense of impending trouble, which he did not always follow, but he knew Gloria was big trouble.

"I'm going into town this afternoon and then I'm going to Albuquerque," Mr. Cook continued. "Gloria wants you to start her lessons this afternoon."

Rodney knew it was an order. He tried to keep his voice neutral, "I can show her all I know, but what she does with it is a different question."

"I'll tell her you'll have the horses saddled and ready to go in about an hour," Mr. Cook said as he left.

The shutting door sounded like a jailer had slammed the bars closed. "Dear lord," Rodney said, "riding lessons for a snake."

Rodney drank another cup of coffee and decided to tell Karen the news. He would not tell her Mr. Cook had been looking through her window. He doubted if it would bother her anyway. Looking was quite a bit different than kissing and touching. The possibility of Karen ever letting Mr. Cook touch her was about as far fetched as the Middle East not being at war.

Karen sat at the table wearing skimpy silk underwear and a midriff T-shirt. When Rodney knocked, she did not bother to get up but motioned for him to come in. Karen saw the reaction in Rodney's face over her attire and smiled at him teasingly. "Marry me, you fence fixer, and you can see me like this every morning," she said.

"A second before you pass out," Rodney teased.

"Not nice," Karen said.

"If I married you, I'd never get any work done," Rodney said trying to look nonchalant.

"Work isn't your problem around here, Rodney," Karen said standing up and walking toward the bedroom.

When she came back she had on a pair of faded Levi's with a hole in the knee, the same T shirt and heavy wool socks.

"Better?" she said.

"Much," Rodney said. "But I would like to come over for dinner tonight."

Karen looked at him with her head cocked slightly to the side and raised her right eyebrow. "My calendar doesn't seem to have any cowboys on it this evening, I think we can arrange that. Let's say, about seven, my husband will be gone then and the guy who was going to come over and eat cake with me last night didn't show up so I don't think I'll see him again."

Rodney had forgotten Karen asking him over for cake and ice cream.

Karen laughed a sexy in control laugh. "He doesn't know what he missed."

"I bet he does," Rodney replied.

"What happened with Banjo and the Sheriff?" Karen asked seriously.

"Mr. Cook threw a fit, but Banjo went in the house and got his gun," Rodney answered. "It could be trouble but I don't think Mr. Cook would ever do anything himself. He'll always call the cops."

"Banjo sounds like he's right out of the old west," Karen said.

Rodney shook his head slightly. "Banjo is caught in a time warp. A time warp that he can't get out of."

"I'd like to meet him someday," Karen answered. "I bet he would make a good painting."

"Mr. Cook says he got me a part in the movie," Rodney said.

Karen jumped up and threw her arms around Rodney, then sat down on his lap. She kissed him on the forehead.

"Hell, Boy," she quipped, "you'll meet so many of those sex-starved starlets you won't have any time left for me."

Rodney kissed Karen on the cheek, "Seems I keep finding more and more time for you."

Karen snuggled deeper into his arms.

Rodney found himself lost in Karen's embrace until he remembered the riding lesson. "I have to give Gloria a riding lesson," he said and hurried out the door.

"Riding lessons?" Karen mused, letting her thoughts trail off.

Rodney went to his house and got his coat. He noticed a few clouds on the horizon and guessed the temperature to be around 50. In the stable, he saddled both horses, tied them to the rail and sat down on a hay bale to wait for Gloria. He wondered if Banjo had cut the fence by now? A feeling of nervousness came over him thinking about the movie and if he could do what the director wanted him to when the camera started to roll.

Gloria came in wearing skin-tight Levi's and a bulky dark gray sweater.

"Mr. Cook said you wanted to learn how to ride," Rodney said, trying to ignore the intoxicating perfume cloud that settled around him.

"I figured a real cowboy could teach me better than a man who merely owns a ranch," Gloria said with a bit of sarcasm in her voice.

"Do you want to start from the beginning or go and ride and let me tell you what you are doing wrong?" Rodney asked.

"I can get on, Rodney, let's just go out and ride," she answered, walking over to her horse and leading it out of the stable.

Karen was removing her clothes to start painting when she saw Gloria and Rodney ride by. They were talking and Gloria seemed to hang on his every word. She felt a jolt of anger sweep through her body, mixed with a touch of jealousy. "You told yourself you'd never be jealous over a man," she said apprehensively.

She looked at the backs of Gloria and the man she knew she loved, feeling as though the cowboy was riding off to a part of the world she could never know. A part that the women sharks of the world controlled. She took a deep breath and looked at her painting. She had finished the owl, it was flying proud and free, straight into the viewer's eyes. She wished it were possible to be able to paint the cowboy riding away so the viewer could see both sides of the rider. She would paint him with his eyes closed like he was going through life ignoring the rest of the world—lost to everything but the dream of what was. She looked away from the canvas. "You be careful, Rodney," she said. "You be careful for yourself and for us."

Rodney and Gloria rode for about thirty minutes. Rodney told her how to hold the reins and to slide with the saddle. Gloria listened intently and soon was riding as one with the horse and not fighting its every move.

"Now all you have to do is practice, Mrs. Cook," Rodney said.

They rode to a bluff that overlooked the border fence between Banjo and the Last Day In Paradise. Rodney immediately saw the sheep in the distance. Gloria looked out over the expanse of land, but Rodney did not think she recognized the sheep as being anything out of the ordinary.

Gloria dismounted, tied the horse to a small cedar and sat on a stump. Rodney dismounted, tied his horse a short distance away from Gloria's, and stood by the rump of the horse.

Gloria, without a change of emotion in her voice said, "I want to get you naked Rodney."

Rodney felt as though the sky was closing in on him. "Mrs. Cook. It wouldn't be right," he said.

"Don't worry," Gloria said. "My husband would never know, and that little artist friend of yours would never find out if you didn't tell her."

Gloria walked over to and put her arms around his neck. "I don't think we should do this," Rodney said nervously and stepped out of her grasp.

Gloria looked amused. "Next time I'll bring a blanket," she said, walking back to her horse.

Back at the ranch headquarters and riding by Karen's house Rodney felt guilty.

Gloria winked at Rodney as she left the corral. "Tomorrow at the same time," she said, "and I will have a blanket."

Rodney unsaddled the horses and felt perplexed. "If I had any brains I'd hit the road," he said to the horse. "I've got enough money."

But, he thought about Karen. Even though his feelings for Karen confused him she made him feel whole and warm. There was also the problem with Banjo. If he was not around, the situation might blow out of hand and the old man could end up getting hurt. If this was not enough, now there was the movie. $300.00 a day was a lot of money. He might get a months work out of the movie.

Going back to his house Rodney noticed the temperature had dropped and he felt a chill run up his spine but he did not know if it was from the cold.

Karen watched Rodney walk from the stable to his house and tried to visualize Rodney when he was younger. She wondered if he was wild, if after the war he was crazy? She thought about how differently they had led their lives, suddenly to be thrown together on a ranch in the middle of New Mexico.

"You need me," she said. "I'm about the only woman in the world who wouldn't take advantage of you and leave you punching cows with a broken heart."

At six o'clock Rodney took a shower and put on clean Levi's and his favorite blue Western shirt with white coral buttons. He put a quick shine on his good boots and then wished he had a flower he could take to Karen.

He looked through the kitchen window toward Mr. Cooks house. He saw Gloria silhouetted in a window. She was naked and waved to him. He turned around quickly.

For the next twenty minutes, Rodney paced around his house wishing seven o'clock would come so he could go to Karen's. He tried to think about Karen, but all he could see was Gloria standing naked in the window.

When seven finally came, he almost ran from the house, feeling like he was being released from jail after serving five years of a ten year sentence for something he did not do.

Burning candles were in the kitchen and living room and filled the air with the scent of sandalwood. "My husband's been gone for over an hour. Gave me time to bathe and get ready for you, cowboy," Karen teased.

"Wish you would leave that bum," Rodney said.

"Hon, then you wouldn't want me," Karen giggled. "All the excitement would be gone."

Karen took Rodney by the hand and led him into the living room where a bottle of red wine sat next to a plate of cheese and crackers.

Karen sat and patted the sofa next to her. "Sit down stranger," she said. "We can be as slow and comfortable as we want."

Rodney sat down next to her and smiled warmly. "What if I decide that the feelings I have for you aren't love," he asked Karen in a subdued voice.

"I don't want to think about it," Karen said.

But Rodney knew his question made her sad.

"Are you going to sleep with me tonight?" Karen asked.

Rodney poured two glasses of wine and handed one to Karen. "The other night when you got drunk we would have," Rodney said trying to pick the right words. "I don't know how to explain it, and I don't want to hurt your feelings, but right now Karen I need a friend more than I need a lover."

"Rodney Slugger you are one of a kind," Karen said smiling comfortingly.

"Probably the dumbest cowboy there is on the face of the earth," he said.

"Without a doubt," Karen replied with a contented tone.

Karen raised her glass and they clinked them together. "To good friends," she toasted and then thought to herself, "and love."

Fourteen

Angelena could not remember the last time Banjo was so happy. He had been whistling all day and she even caught him singing an old Mexican love song he used to sing when they were first married.

Angelena was standing on the porch wondering if she should go to the wood pile and tell Banjo he should rest—he had been splitting cedar for the cook stove for over an hour. She decided that bothering Banjo might change his mood back to his old brooding self and she did not want to take the risk. She had no idea what had happened to make him so happy. Perhaps it had been having the run in with the police. "Mother of hope," she thought, "there has to be a place in heaven for bandits."

But, she really did not think it was the police and she knew he could not have a girlfriend, since he never went to town without her—although at one time Banjo did have a girlfriend.

They had been married for over ten years and Banjo began to go to town a lot. The going to town did not bother her, nor the fact he never brought anything back with him. When she started noticing that before he went to town, he always washed and put on clean clothes, she began to grow suspicious.

One afternoon when Banjo started for town on his horse, saying he would be back by noon the next day, she took a butcher knife and saddled a burro they used to haul water from the well with and she followed Banjo. Santa Fe was not a sprawling city of traffic and fake stucco buildings then, but a small, quaint, adobe town with dirt streets and only a few noisy bars and two hotels.

From the shadows of a cottonwood, Angelena watched Banjo tie his horse and slick back his hair before entering an adobe house without knocking. Tying the burro to the cottonwood, she took the large butcher knife and walked calmly toward the house. She did not go to the front door, but sneaked around to the side of the house and peered carefully through a window. Banjo was sitting on a sofa with a pretty lady. Angelena went to the front door, and hiding the butcher knife behind her back, knocked on the door. When the lady answered the door she shoved the lady back, sending her sprawling onto the floor, and ran over and stuck the point of the butcher knife against Banjo's throat. Banjo did not move as the young lady regained her footing and started to cry.

"Do not cry, my pretty," Angelena said, holding her rage. "It is not you I have come after, but this swine who crawls around on his belly and forgets his wife."

Banjo started to speak but Angelena shook her head. "You do not speak to me," she ordered, "you get up and come with me."

Banjo stood while Angelena stepped back, holding the knife only inches from his belly. She turned him with her free hand and pushed him in the back with the knife out the door.

"Ride," she ordered as they emerged from the house.

Banjo started to mount his horse, but Angelena grabbed the reins and pointed with the knife toward her burro. "An ass for an ass," she said and mounted Banjo's horse.

Banjo looked at the burro and once again started to speak, but Angelena waved the butcher knife menacingly in front of his face. Banjo, without further persuasion, got on the burro.

"There is wood that needs splitting," Angelena informed Banjo as they rode down the dirt street.

Many people came out of their houses and watched as Banjo, on the burro, led the way for his wife who was riding proudly on the horse, still clutching the butcher knife in her hand.

Back at the house, Angelena did not fall into a torrent of tears. While eating dinner, she looked at Banjo and said simply, "I love you Mr. Ortega, but if there is ever another lady, I swear by the Virgin Mary, I will cut your throat and spend my death in eternity's fire."

Remembering the day, Angelena smiled and looked once again at Banjo who was now walking toward her carrying an armload of wood.

"You work too long," Angelena said, opening the door for him so he could dump the wood in the wood box.

Banjo dumped the wood, poured himself a cup of coffee and sat down at the table.

"Is there anything else that needs to be done?" Banjo asked, blowing on the steaming coffee.

Angelena took several large tortillas from under a pan on the stove. "Yes," she said, "these have to be eaten."

Banjo smiled at her and poured honey on the warm fluffy tortillas and began eating like he had not eaten in days.

"Is it possible that one who is suddenly filled with energy would have the energy to sleep with his wife this evening?" Angelena asked quietly.

"It is possible God may have given me a few last times," he said, giving Angelena his coyote look and then winking at her.

After eating both tortillas, Banjo headed toward the old truck. He had not started it in over a month and he knew it would take a while to get it to turn over. He dug out a few rusty tools from behind the seat and popped the hood and knocked off a large cobweb from around the carburetor.

Angelena walked out on the porch and tossed scraps to the chickens. Seeing Banjo working on the truck, she wondered if maybe she would have to get out the butcher knife again. She shrugged off the thought.

After twenty minutes, the truck still sat lifeless and Banjo was getting angry. His hands were greasy and he was perspiring, although it was no warmer than 45 degrees outside.

"You always were a piece of junk, even when I bought you." he told the truck. "Not like a horse that can be kicked when it will not act right. You are a heartless piece of white man's garbage that has been sent to plague me."

After another half an hour, the truck blew a large cloud of white smoke out of the exhaust pipe and came to life. Banjo quickly fiddled with the carburetor setting, and, when he had the engine racing, slammed the hood. He got in the truck and drove to the front gate then turned around and drove back. Back at the house, he sat in the truck and gunned the engine, which caused the horse to run around the corral and sent the chickens scurrying for cover under the woodpile. When he was satisfied it would start in the morning, Banjo shut off the engine. He turned the key and smiled as the truck once again started. Shutting it off, he got out and looked at the truck and then kicked the door as hard as he could. "You have to be white," he said, walking toward the corral.

He still had a few hours before dark and wanted to check his sheep and make sure the fence was still cut. While he rode, Banjo thought about the movie. In the morning he would drive to the La Fonda Inn. He had no doubt he would get a job as an extra. Banjo had only been to a few movies in his life, but now he wanted to see himself in a movie. He wanted to sit in a theater with Angelena, a big bag of popcorn between them, and see himself chasing the good guys or robbing a train or a bank. He felt that by being in the movie he would, in some small way, record his life.

When Banjo got to the fence, it was still cut and he wished it was fifty years ago. If it was back then, he could have gotten some of his old friends and they would ride over and burn Mr. Cook out, sending the gringo running back to where ever he came from. But Banjo knew that now there was no way to get away with it. There would only be some other rich man buy the ranch and it would go on and on. There was no victory for Banjo, only the knowledge that he could be a nuisance. A fly that hopefully would not get swatted and could die in his own time.

Banjo turned his horse and started back toward the house. As the horse topped the small hill, a sharp pain swept through his chest making Banjo double over. He clutched his chest and grimaced, tears forming in his eyes. The horse, feeling a jerk on the reins, stopped and bit at a clump of dry and brittle gamma grass. Banjo felt himself slipping from the saddle, but was able to hold on. As he slumped over, the pain slowly went away until he could sit back up and wipe the tears from his eyes.

Banjo thought about an operation he had heard of. An operation where the doctors went in and cleaned out your heart and rearranged things so it worked better. Banjo grunted, operations like that were only for the rich. A poor man suffered with his pain until he died. A rich man went to the hospital and let the doctors fix him.

Banjo nudged the horse. He looked at his 30/30 and wondered if he could kill himself. It would be better to die here surrounded by the rocks and trees and sky than in a hospital pushed off in some corner with nothing but misery all around him and no trace of his life or freedom.

By the time he got back to the house it was late afternoon and his breath formed small swirling clouds around his face. He fed the horse and gave the pig an extra scoop of feed before going to the house.

As he stood in the kitchen, the warmth of the wood stove brought the feeling back into his hands. Angelena had on a clean dress and Banjo knew she had taken a bath as he saw the washtub in the corner. A large pot of hot water steamed on the stove.

"You sleep with me, you take a bath," Angelena smiled.

Banjo remembered his wife's words earlier in the day and went over to her and kissed her gently on the cheek. Angelena pulled the washtub in front of the stove while Banjo went to his room and took off his clothes.

He got into the small tin tub and began to soap himself. While he was bathing, Angelena put a fried chicken on the table with tortillas and green chili stew.

"When I get paid for being in the movie," he said. "I will take you to town and we will eat at the La Fonda. There will be waiters all around the table and we will have the most expensive thing they have on the menu with a bottle of good wine. Afterward I will take you to a movie."

"That would be wonderful," Angelena said.

After rinsing off, Banjo stood up in the tub and Angelena took a large towel out of the oven and draped it over the old, stooped shoulders. He smiled at her and walked quickly to his bedroom where, from a trunk, he took out his good pair of pants and a red wool shirt. From under his bed, he took the pair of slippers Angelena had knitted for him several years earlier and put them on.

Angelena was sitting at the table and there was a bottle of red wine and two glasses.

"Where did you get that?" he asked her in surprise.

"For the resurrection," Angelena smiled.

Banjo sat down and poured the wine and drank his glass without putting it down. He smacked his lips loudly and poured another glass. Then looking at his wife, said, "If not for you, my wife, my life would have been lonely."

Angelena, knowing how men lied, only smiled and sipped her wine.

When Banjo left the house, Angelena was still sleeping. Banjo could not remember the last time he had spent the night making love, he only knew it had been a long time ago. Surprisingly, it had not been as difficult as he had imagined it would be.

When she was young, Angelena had been the most exciting woman Banjo had ever slept with, although his repertoire of women was not extensive. There had been the hooker when he was eighteen and Lazette, which had almost cost him his life. But Angelena had always been very passionate with a much stronger sex drive than Banjo. That fact had always puzzled Banjo—how his wife could be such a tigress in bed and yet be so religious. He supposed there was nothing in the Bible telling a woman she should not have a good time in bed.

To his relief, the truck fired up with the first turn of the key. Today he would become part of the movie.

Angelena heard the truck start, knowing Banjo was going to town to try for a part in the movie. She rolled lazily onto on her stomach, staring at the white linoleum floor with the woven K-Mart rug and thought about the first time she and Banjo had made love.

After daydreaming for awhile, she got out of bed and started a fire in the stove. She sat in the kitchen wearing her heavy bathrobe and prayed Banjo would get the job. If not, she feared he would fall back into his melancholy mood and the fire would once again leave his mind and body. Angelena knew that without the mind, the body was nothing.

It took Banjo more than fifteen minutes to find a place to park his old truck with all the fancy cars in the way. He got out of the truck and walked toward the La Fonda Inn, spitting on a metallic gray Mercedes and a black B.M.W. as he walked past and mumbling, "you must be friends of my son."

In front of the La Fonda Inn, several pretty women in their late twenties were looking at a display of Indian Jewelry and leather clothes. As he walked by, he was pleased when they made faces at each other about him. Their faces reminded him of an Indian dance he had once attended. During the dance, a white man, with many cameras hanging from his neck, was taking photographs of a pretty Indian girl who was the main dancer. A drunk Indian was standing several yards from him. When the man finished taking his photographs, the drunk looked at him and said, "Take a picture of me, I'm an Indian too."

The photographer had given the man a sullen look and walked off. To Banjo, the drunk was the only real Indian at the dance. At least he was not selling fry bread to the tourists.

Inside the hotel, Banjo saw a long line of people along a wall. A small, wiry man with short dark hair and cut off sideburns was walking back and forth nervously telling the people to stay in line. Banjo stepped to the end of the line and the man walked up and handed him a piece of paper.

"Fill this out," he said. "When you go through the door, hand it to the girl on your left and wait for her instructions."

Banjo looked at the paper, then at the man in front of him in line. He was in his early twenties with shoulder length hair and Banjo noticed he had a pen.

"Hombre," Banjo said, "let me use your pen."

"I want it back," the young man said, handing Banjo the pen.

Banjo was going to say, "Did you think I was going to steal it because I am a Mexican?" but he kept his remark to himself.

Banjo filled in his name and for age, he put 73. When it came to acting experience, he did not know what to put down so he scrawled, bandit. After signing his name he tapped the man on the shoulder and handed him back his pen without saying thank you. The young man took the pen, not saying a word.

By now, a pretty girl with long shiny blood hair, wearing Levi's, red boots, and a white western shirt came up behind Banjo. She smiled a sweet, delightful smile and even though she was white, Banjo smiled back. "I'm so excited," she said to Banjo. "Just think, even being an extra would be a thrill. I've always wanted to be a movie star, ever since I was a little girl."

Banjo looked at her but could not think of anything to say. After making love to his wife during the night, a sinister thought entered his mind and he wondered if he could possibly make love to a young beautiful girl. After a few moments, he knew he could not and said to the girl, "I want to be a bandit."

The girl gave him a serious going over. "I think you should be able to," she said, "you look like a bandit."

"Thank you," Banjo answered.

After standing in line for over thirty minutes, Banjo's legs were beginning to get tired. It seemed the line did not move at all, then it would move only a few feet. He wanted a cigarette but had forgotten his tobacco and nobody in line seemed to be smoking, so he could not bum one. The more he thought about smoking, the more the slowness of the line bothered him. He did not want to make a complaint as it might jeopardize his chance of being in the movie.

After another thirty minutes, Banjo was not really paying any attention to anything when he heard his name.

"Banjo," Rodney said. "Can't believe you took time off from cutting the fence to try and get in a movie."

"My wife says I would make a good bandit," Banjo said.

"I'm going to be a bandit," Rodney said. "Because they're going to build the set on the ranch I got the part."

"I am a real bandit," Banjo told Rodney.

The pretty blond next to Banjo gave Rodney a big smile which Banjo did not like.

"Listen," Rodney said, "I'm going to do some shopping in town. I'll meet you in the bar when you're done and buy you a drink if you like."

"Only one," Banjo said.

"It will take you at least another hour," Rodney said, looking at the line. "I'll be back."

As Rodney walked away, Banjo noticed the blond's eyes boring a hole in Rodney and wished he was young.

When it finally came to Banjo's turn, he walked into the room. A short, tired looking, heavy set lady sat at a desk, a pencil stuck behind her ear and several stacks of paper in front of her. She looked at Banjo and held out her hand. "Paper," she said simply.

Banjo handed her the paper and looked around the room. Several men stood in the corner eying him and another man sat in a chair also looking him over. The woman read over the paper quickly and set it down in front of her. "You've never been in a movie?" she asked.

Banjo shook his head no.

"What do you want to do?" she asked.

"Be a bandit," Banjo said.

"What makes you think you can be a bandit?" she asked.

"I've been a bandit my whole life," Banjo said, smiling at her.

"I see," the lady said, looking over at the two men in the corner, broad smiles covering their faces.

"Well, Mr. Ortega, I don't think you are suited for our needs. I'm sorry," the lady said as the men turned away from him and started talking to themselves.

Banjo felt as though the floor had come out from under him. He wanted to say something, but he could think of nothing to say. He looked at the woman and over at the backs of the two men and walked dejectedly out of the office. He saw Rodney standing by the entrance to the bar and as if by remote control walked over to him.

"They won't let me be in the movie," he said as if he had lost his last best friend.

Rodney saw the disappointment on Banjo's face and wanted to reach out and put his arm on his shoulder, but he did not know how Banjo would react. Instead he said, "Sorry, guess they don't know a good bandit when they see one."

Banjo followed Rodney into the dimly lit bar, looking like an old dog following his master. They sat at the bar and Rodney ordered a Coors and Banjo ordered a shot of Bourbon.

Banjo drank the shot in one gulp. "Another one," he ordered, "if the cowboy is buying."

Rodney nodded his approval to the bartender, and the shot glass was filled to the rim.

"Thanks gringo," Banjo said and drank the shot.

"One more," he ordered.

Rodney tipped his cowboy hat back on his head and told the bartender, "As long as he can drink them, set them up."

The bartender looked at Banjo and said, "The way he looks, he could drink all the whiskey in the place."

Banjo reached over the bar and grabbed the young man by his shirt collar. The man tried to pry the hand off with both of his, but found out, to his amazement, he could not break the grip of the old man. "If I was younger, I would bite your nose off," Banjo said, releasing his grip.

The bartender poured the shot without any further remarks and walked away from Rodney and Banjo, leaving the bottle setting on the bar.

Rodney looked at Banjo. "You would have shot Cook, wouldn't you?"

Banjo swallowed the other shot and wiped his lips with the back of his hand. "I've never shot anybody," he answered. "But your boss might be the first."

Rodney finished his beer and waved to the bartender for another one. The bartender sent a young Mexican girl down with the beer. She set the beer down, gave Rodney a dirty look, and smiled at Banjo. Banjo sat turning the empty shot glass in his hand. "I cut your fence again, hombre," he said.

"I figured," Rodney answered.

"I will cut it and cut it and cut it," Banjo said, still rolling the shot glass in his hands.

"They'll toss you in jail, Banjo," Rodney said.

Banjo laughed. "Look at me Rodney, how long would they keep me in there?"

"Hell, Banjo," Rodney pleaded, "you can't beat him. You know it. I know it. He knows it. Let it go."

"Let it go and roll over and die like an old beat Mexican. Die like some white pampered man who has lived in a big home all his life and is afraid of everything. Spend my last days being told what to do like a good dog."

Banjo laughed sarcastically. "I should, but I can't."

Banjo stood up from the bar. "I thank you, senior, for the drinks and the conversation. My wife by now will think I am in town chasing all the women or getting into trouble and my pig needs to be fed and my horse watered," he said and started to walk away.

After a few steps, he turned and looked at Rodney. In a calm, serious voice, he said, "If I shoot, my friend, you be sure and duck."

Rodney watched Banjo shuffle out of the bar. He looked around the room and noticed several couples and a few long hairs in the corner. Without Banjo sitting by him, the bar suddenly seemed like a place where he did not belong. Not bothering to finish his beer, he waved for the check.

The young man who Banjo had grabbed came over and handed him the check saying, "I could have whipped him, you know."

"Son," Rodney said, handing him a twenty, "you might have whipped him, but you would never have beaten him."

In the lobby, Rodney went into a small flower shop and picked out one yellow rose. The young lady working the floral shop did not talk to him as he gave her the three dollars. Walking back to his truck, a cold wind began to blow and Rodney knew tonight might be the first hard frost of the year.

Rodney parked the truck and walked straight to Karen's house, going in without knocking. The sun was setting and the red and purple sunbeams danced off the walls of the house. Karen was naked and working on her painting. She was so absorbed, she did not hear Rodney behind her. Rodney coughed, causing Karen to jump about a foot in the air, trying to cover both her breasts and her thighs at the same time. Seeing Rodney, her face turned red in anger and she was about to yell when he held out the yellow rose for her.

"It reminded me of you," he said, turning and walking out of the house.

Karen held the rose lightly in her hand and smelled it, then she turned and looked at her painting. She was now working on the sky, deep blues crossed with vivid purple. She wondered if somewhere in her painting, she could hide a small yellow rose. Hide it so well very few people would ever see it. Only those that would truly look at her painting.

"Hiding a promise," she thought.

When Banjo left the bar, he no longer felt angry at not getting a part in the movie. He did feel angry at the snide glances of the two men and the lady with the pencil behind her ear—angry that they had belittled him, belittled him because he was old and poor and he had told them the truth about being a bandit, not made it up like they believed.

The truck started, blowing out a large cloud of white smoke. Banjo drove away from Santa Fe and the tinsel town shops and was soon outside the city limits where the pinon trees and cedars lined the highway. As he turned on the dirt road that led to the gate of his small ranch, he stopped and looked down the road at the northern boundary fence of the Last Day In Paradise. He rolled the window down and spit.

He drove slowly down the rutted road and wished he had drank one more shot of bourbon. Another shot could not have hurt him and maybe it would have checked the hollow feeling that was beginning to form in his heart.

Angelena smiled at him when he walked in the house, but she immediately saw the fire was once again out of Banjo's eyes. He was the same old man of yesterday. He did not walk with a slight bounce in his steps and he was not smiling. When he sat down heavily at the table, Angelena sat a cup of coffee in front of him and smelled the liquor on his breath. She wanted to ask him questions, but knew he would not be in the movie so she said nothing.

Banjo drank the coffee without speaking, then went outside to feed the animals. Pouring the pig food into the trough the pig grunted and snorted in happiness. "We are both the same my friend," he said. "We are fed and taken care of only to be slaughtered. But yours is a clean and easy death. Mine is stripped of everything a man holds dear."

Banjo watched the setting sun. A faded orange glow colored the hills. Banjo remembered the words of his uncle, "Beauty is only for the rich."

Seeing the reassuring curl of smoke coming from the stove pipe, Banjo felt better—he was home.

Angelena and Banjo ate dinner in silence. Angelena knew there would be no reason to ask her husband to her bed this evening. Although he needed reassuring, Banjo had always kept his problems to himself, fighting them in silence until he had battled and won. Angelena knew the battles were being lost and there was nothing she could do.

When she finished with the dishes, Angelena patted Banjo on the shoulder and walked to her room and readied for bed. She looked at her crucifix on the wall and crossed herself. Lying down, she picked up her romance novel and started to read, but the words seemed to enter her mind and then vanish. She soon laid the book down, turned off the light, said her prayers and shut her eyes.

Banjo sat in his room with his boots off. He thought about the men who would soon be coming to the Last Day In Paradise to build the small western town that would be the set for the movie. He thought about all the money Mr. Cook would make and how he would be a big shot with all his friends. As he thought, an idea began to form, a preposterous and risky idea. At first a wry smirk crossed his lips, but it soon spread to a large toothless grin, then a few cackles, until it ended with Banjo shaking with laughter.

Angelena, not yet asleep, wondered what Banjo could possibly be laughing at? Looking into the darkness toward her crucifix, she whispered, "Dear God, he is up to something no good, please help him?"

Banjo held his side, took several deep breaths, and wanted a cigarette. He rolled a double large cigarette which shot out a huge flame when he lit it. He took a deep drag and tried to blow a smoke ring. He succeeded in blowing only puffs with no true form. Banjo finished the smoke, turned off the light and went to bed.

"Mr. Cook," he said, "you will wish you had never bought the Last Day In Paradise Ranch. I think I will now become your true enemy."

Fifteen

Rodney was hoping Karen would make him breakfast. But halfway to Karen's, Gloria approached him wearing English riding pants, tall black boots, and a white sweater that fit her like a glove. "Rodney, you forgot my riding lesson yesterday you bad boy," she scolded in a playful manner. "But today will be fine."

"Mrs. Cook," Rodney answered, trying not to show how nervous she made him, "I had to go to Santa Fe yesterday about my part in the movie, I'm sorry I missed our lesson and now Karen is going to fix me breakfast."

"Yesterday is not a problem," Gloria smiled seductively, adding, "you go ahead and eat and I'll meet you down at the corral in an hour."

Rodney felt like a school boy who had received permission to go to the bathroom from his teacher.

"Is Mr. Cook back?" Rodney asked as Gloria started to walk away.

"No, something to do with the contract about the movie set," Gloria said. "An hour, don't forget."

Karen was in the kitchen and watching through the window Gloria do everything but take her clothes off in front of Rodney. Once again she felt herself growing jealous and once again she fought back the feeling. When Rodney knocked on the door, Karen was all smiles and in no way let on she had been watching him.

"You look lovely this morning," Rodney said, sitting down.

"You must want breakfast," Karen said, giving Rodney her little girl smile.

"Are you giving Gloria a riding lesson this morning?" Karen asked, trying not to show any concern.

"After we eat," Rodney replied, adding, to change the subject. "Banjo was in town yesterday. He didn't get a part in the movie."

"That's too bad," Karen replied.

"Yes, it is. I could tell he really wanted in the movie."

As they ate Rodney could tell something was bothering Karen and he hoped it was not because of Gloria.

"You watch out for the big bad wolf," Karen told him as he left.

Headed toward the corral, Rodney knew he was headed for trouble.

Gloria was in the barn. She had saddled both horses and there was a set of saddle bags on Gloria's horse. "Who taught you how to saddle a horse?" Rodney asked.

"I watched you," Gloria said, jumping up and climbing into the saddle like an old pro.

As they rode by Karen's, Karen was standing in the bathroom on her tip-toes peeking through the window at Rodney and Gloria. But instead of being angry or jealous, she had a sinking feeling that started in her stomach and spread through her body.

The morning was warm and a slight breeze barely moved the tops of the pinon trees. Gloria and Rodney rode without speaking and Rodney noticed Gloria was having no trouble riding. She had a graceful move with the horse.

Rodney saw a flock of light blue birds. He did not know their name, but he knew they came out of Canada before winter blew in with full force. When the flock moved and turned, it was like a blue flash of light through the sky.

Gloria stole glimpses of Rodney as they rode. He seemed rugged and yet had a gentle quality about him. A man who could take care of a woman during a crisis and not falter, no matter how tough the situation became.

Gloria stopped her horse by a large cedar tree that had fallen down years earlier. The trunk lay on the ground surrounded by an area of smooth sand. A small pinon grew through the dead branches of the cedar. Gloria dismounted, tied her horse to a nearby tree and carried her saddlebags back to the dead cedar and set them on the ground. Rodney, from the safety of his horse, sat and watched Gloria.

"Come on Rodney, get down. I brought something for us."

She took a tablecloth out of her saddlebags and spread it on the ground.

By the time Rodney had dismounted and tied his horse, Gloria was sitting on the tablecloth opening a thermos. "Sit down Rodney, I brought a thermos of Bloody Mary's to drink," Gloria said, pouring some into a cup.

Rodney sat on the tablecloth as far away from Gloria as the cloth allowed. Gloria smiled to herself thinking how most of the men she knew in Phoenix would be jumping at the chance to get into her pants—jumping so quickly it ruined the game.

Gloria handed Rodney a cup and poured herself one. "To blue sky and horses and fall, and cowboys," Gloria toasted.

Rodney sipped the Bloody Mary. The only other time he had tasted a Bloody Mary was after a heavy New Year's Eve party. They had poured a fifth of vodka into a can of tomato juice and half a container of salt. It had sufficiently soothed everybody's headache so they could at least go through the motions of working. The only thing that saved them was the fact the boss was feeling a little woozy himself.

Gloria did not sip her drink but gulped it down and poured herself another one, offering the thermos to Rodney who had not finished his. "You look like you're about to be thrown in jail," Gloria said, laughing.

Rodney smiled at her feeling the mixed emotions of fear and despair at his situation.

Gloria leaned against the cedar trunk making the fabric of her sweater pull tightly against her breasts. Rodney could not help but look at the protrusions of her nipples which Gloria noticed and liked. "You haven't been with a lot of women have you, Rodney?" Gloria asked.

Rodney finished his Bloody Mary and refilled the cup. "I don't kiss and tell," he answered.

"A man with scruples," Gloria said. "I like that."

That has no sooner left her mouth when Gloria stood up and in one movement pulled the sweater over her head. She looked down at Rodney, pulled off her boots and, in another quick motion, peeled the tight riding britches off her legs. Standing naked and framed by the blue sky. Rodney felt like he could not move but he had never seen a more beautiful woman. Her body was in proportion from head to toe and her bikini lines accentuated her assets.

Gloria stepped over to him and kneeled down with her knees a foot apart. She removed Rodney's cowboy hat and ran her fingers through his hair and leaned over and kissed him lightly. Rodney suddenly stood, making Gloria fall slightly forward. He looked down at her, still mesmerized by her beauty. "Lady," he said, "you're the most beautiful woman I've seen in my life. The kind any man would want to be with. But I can't. I'm sorry."

Rodney walked quickly to his horse. As he rode away, he did not look back.

Riding toward the fence, he wished Karen was with him and wondered why he had never asked her to go for a ride with him.

Gloria dressed quickly trying to quell the rage that was boiling in her—a rage that had taken the passion out of her body. She watched Rodney ride away and knew that if she had a rifle she would shoot him. A shooting she could get away with by telling the authorities he had tried to rape her and she had struggled and killed him.

Riding back toward the house, she kicked the horse into a gallop and did not stop until she was by the corral. She unsaddled the horse and without brushing him down, led him to his pen and stomped away.

Karen was naked in front of her painting when she heard the horse gallop by the house. Looking out the window, she saw Gloria alone and by the look on her face, she immediately knew what had happened. Walking back to her painting, she felt the dark haze vanish that had covered her since Gloria and Rodney had ridden out. She picked out a small spot on her cowboy's leg where she could paint the tiniest of yellow roses. Taking a brush and cutting away most of the bristles, she dipped the remaining few hairs in yellow paint mixed with white, and started to hum, "Your Cheating Heart."

Gloria slammed the bathroom door behind her and filled the bathtub with extremely hot water. She undressed and slipped into the full tub and lay seething. "I'll get you for this," she swore as she began to wash herself with a bar of rose scented soap.

Rodney did not stop his horse until he was on the crest of the hill that looked down upon the fence. He saw Banjo's sheep not more than five hundred yards from where they had been last time, grazing peacefully along the stream. Dismounting, he sat down but held the horse's reins in his hand and tried to quell the pounding of his heart. He knew for sure his days at the Last Day In Paradise were numbered. There was no way he could stay on. He knew Gloria would have a vendetta out for him and try to get back at him in anyway she could. But he did not want to leave Karen. When he had first met Hazel, he thought it was love. It was as though a steamroller had rolled over him and all he could do was think about Hazel. With Karen, there had been no steam roller. But, he found peace with Karen—a rest that he had never experienced before.

Running away from the aftermath of the war, Rodney had lost himself in hard work, long hours and the camaraderie of men around him. It was not a soft life, or a really fulfilling one. It was a life that left a man so tired he did not have time to think about his problems. In that, it was secure. But there was always something missing. Some small element of existence that, when the bunkhouse was dark, yearned in Rodney's heart. With Hazel, that yearning did not leave, but seemed to grow stronger. With Karen, there was no yearning, only a feeling that the world was okay. Being with her and seeing her made the days a little brighter and the hard times a little softer.

Rodney looked at the fence and saw a pair of coyotes slowly moving parallel with the fence, but every step or two looking towards Banjo's sheep, which were unaware of their movement. Rodney looked at his saddle, forgetting he was not in Montana and did not have a rifle with him. A quick shot would have sent the coyotes fleeing. Rodney continued to watch as the coyotes stopped, as though in council, and then split apart. One continued along the fence while the other one turned and started to make a large loop to the south of the unsuspecting sheep. Rodney immediately understood their plan. They would reach a certain point and then creep as close to the sheep as they could and charge, hoping to grab one.

As the coyotes tightened their attack, Rodney remounted and galloped down the hill toward the sheep. The coyotes, hearing the approaching cowboy, raised their heads and taking one look at the rider, ran as fast as they could toward the hills and the safety they provided.

Rodney reined his horse up a hundred yards from the sheep and started to drive them toward the hole in the fence. But as the sheep moved toward the hole, he stopped and trotted his horse back toward the hill. "Screw Cook, screw Banjo, and to hell with those sheep," he swore.

Banjo had ridden out to check his sheep and was about to head down the hill toward the hole in the fence when he saw Rodney riding like a wild man toward his sheep. At first he wondered what he was doing, but then he saw the two coyotes darting away.

When Rodney began to drive the sheep toward the hole in the fence, Banjo hid behind a large cluster of trees. After Rodney rode away, Banjo rode out from behind he trees and scratched his head. "I would have liked to ride with you when I was a boy," Banjo thought. "Ride up to Colorado and steal sheep and drive them back here. You would have enjoyed that. The excitement, the danger. The feeling no man owned you or possessed you and you were not tied to a small part of the earth but a piece of the wild."

Banjo did not bother to ride down to the fence but turned his horse toward his home. There was wood that needed splitting and he hoped to make a decision about whether he was going to butcher the pig or not.

Back at the house, Banjo turned his horse into the corral, but, as it was still early, he did not feed him but walked to the woodpile and began splitting wood. Angelena was sewing in the kitchen and heard the familiar ring of the axe as it stuck into the stump. She looked out the window. When Banjo rode away it always worried her. She was afraid he would fall off his horse or die and she would be unable to go after him. Or even if she could, she would be unable to get him back to the house. Banjo had never taught her to drive the truck and she had not been on a horse in years. She wished he would not go out and look for his sheep. Over the past few days she had wanted to tell him to sell the sheep. The sheep were only a problem anyway. They did not make any money and only caused trouble over the fence. But she knew she could never get it through Banjo's thick skull that selling them would be for the best.

Banjo struggled into the house with a large armful of wood and dropped it into the wood box. He smiled at his wife and noticed she was mending one of his heavy woolen shirts. He looked at her gnarled and twisted fingers and wondered how she could possibly sew?

Banjo went to the pigpen. The pig was laying down as he approached but, hearing Banjo, stood up and began snorting and squealing. Banjo scratched the pig between the ears and the pig's nose curled up as in ecstasy. "You don't yearn for freedom," he said sadly. "Born and raised in this small trap you have no understanding what you are missing. To you, the world is only inches from your nose. But I, I know what is lost."

Banjo went to the shed and filled two pails of pig feed. Soon, if the pig's days were short, he would begin to feed corn to the pig—each day filling a bucket half full with dry corn and the rest with water and letting it swell until it overflowed the bucket. Then, after a few weeks, he would butcher the animal and the meat would be sweet.

Pouring the two pails of pig feed in the trough, the pig seemed to know he was getting a double serving and looked at Banjo in gratitude with his tiny squinting eyes. Banjo watched the pig devouring the food. "I wonder why I do not want to kill you?" he said to the pig.

He watched the pig for several minutes before going to the corral and giving his horse a larger than usual wedge of timothy. The old horse plodded over and began to eat the hay and ignored Banjo. An old horse was like an old wife. There was no longer any need for conversation. The bond had been reinforced and no longer needed to be tested.

Banjo remembered a man that had been a friend of his father's. Desadario was a striking man who owned a black mare. He had a silver inlaid saddle and reins and a red Indian saddle blanket. The horse was called Tijuana. There was a yearly fiesta then and all the small ranchers gathered to race and gamble. Tijuana had not lost a race for several years and many times the man was offered far more money than the horse was worth. But Desadario would not take the money. His life was his horse. Desadario lived alone in a one room shack by the Pecos River and he was a poacher by trade. One year, during the race, Tijuana fell and broke her leg. Desadario, crying like a child, shot his horse in the head. With the help of several of his friends, they cut the bones out of Tijuana and Desadario packed them to the top of a mountain where the wind never stopped blowing and covered the bones with rocks.

Banjo wished once in his life he would have ridden and tried to find the bones. He would have liked to have seen the bones of a horse so special they would make a man cry and spend days packing him to the top of a mountain. "You, my old friend," he said to his eating horse. "I would drag you behind the barn and let the coyotes gnaw on your carcass."

Banjo went into the barn. In the corner was a stack of old sheep hides, dry and brittle with age. Banjo tossed the dusty hides into the other corner until he uncovered a wooden box. Wiping the dirt away, he exposed a skull and crossbones. He took his knife out of his pocket and pried off the top. The box was full of dynamite and a long coil of fuse. Banjo picked up one of the sticks and examined it closely. He looked at the edges of the dynamite and could see no glycerin beads on it. He put the lid back on and haphazardly tossed the hides back on top.

Angelena was frying tacos. The smell of tacos and the warmth of the fire gave Banjo a contented feeling. He went into his room, took the 30/30 from the corner and levered the shells out of the gun onto his bed. Sitting down in his chair, he pulled his rifle cleaning kit from under his bed and began to meticulously work on his rifle. Cleaning his rifle and smelling tacos, he remembered during the war in Europe and how every evening he would sit down and clean his rifle. No matter if it was cold or warm, raining or snowing he cleaned his rifle. "I was an American then," he said to himself in a whisper. "They needed me. It was not until I was back home that I was once again a Mexican."

He put the bullets back into the 30/30, but did not chamber a round, and set it back in the corner.

"Dinner," Angelena called.

Banjo hurried to the table. He loved tacos. They were almost as good as the tortillas.

"Why are you cleaning your rifle?" Angelena asked, fixing Banjo with her look that told him he should not try to lie.

"One never knows," Banjo said, filling his mouth with taco.

"You are up to no good, my husband," Angelena said. "I can see it in your eyes."

"I am an old man, what can I possibly do?"

"Be yourself," Angelena answered, passing Banjo a jar of her hot chili.

Banjo laughed. But even to himself, his laughter seemed hollow and filled with treachery.

Riding by Mr. Cook's house, Rodney hurried the horse along like he was passing a house filled with plague. Gloria, freshly bathed and dressed in her bathrobe, saw him riding by and stood by the window in a provocative pose and tossed Rodney the finger. Rodney pretended he did not see her.

Passing Karen's, she saw him and walked out of the house. "Dinner on me," she called.

Rodney felt like jumping from the horse, running to her and telling her he had barely escaped death from a man-eating tigress. But, he only waved in acknowledgement and rode to the corral and put up his horse.

Rodney was brushing Gloria's horse when Mr. Cook drove in and stopped. "Movie construction crew will arrive tomorrow and start work. They told me the town will be up within two weeks. When they're done, that barren piece of valley over there will hold the best looking, old time, western town in New Mexico. Do you know what this means, Rodney?"

Rodney did not have time to answer as Mr. Cook went on. "This means my ranch can become the center of all western movies made in the country. It could, in time, rival Tucson." He started to roll up the window but stopped half way. "You have any run in with that Mexican?" he asked.

"No," Rodney lied, picturing the sheep on Mr. Cook's ranch.

"I'm going to fly over the fence this evening and that shriveled up piece of brown meat had better not have his sheep on my place," Cook threatened, rolling his window back up and driving toward his house.

Karen was taking a shower. She decided if she was ever famous, she would put a small yellow rose in every picture she painted. It would be her trademark. Kind of like Georgia O'Keefe and her skulls.

Karen greeted Rodney at the door wearing a long blue cotton dress and a blue sweater. Her hair was pulled back into a shimmering pony tail. Rodney noticed how different her beauty was compared to Gloria's. Gloria was made up and classy. While Karen was unmade and fresh—a beauty that did not need lipstick or eyeliner. "As usual, you're lovely," Rodney said.

"As usual, you lie," Karen said before jumping into his arms and hugging him.

Rodney stood somewhat overcome by the sudden show of emotion until the warmth of her and the fresh smell of her perfume found him holding her and shutting his eyes and enjoying the comfort that spread through his body.

"How was the riding lesson?" Karen asked, stepping away from him and going to the stove.

"It was okay," Rodney said.

"I saw Gloria ride back in alone. Did you scare the poor girl?" Karen asked, not really wanting to know, but digging just the same.

"No, she started to feel ill and came back. I decided to check the fence," Rodney only half lied.

"Did Banjo cut it again?" Karen asked.

"Sure did," Rodney said, looking at the way Karen's eyes sparkled.

"You fixed it then," Karen said. She opened the oven door.

"Nope," Rodney said. "I didn't."

She turned and looked concerned. "Mr. Cook is going to have a fit," Karen said.

Rodney laughed halfheartedly, got up and opened the refrigerator. To his surprise, there were three six packs of Coors beer. "I'll be damned," he said. "Do you want one?"

"Sure," Karen said sitting at the table. "A cowboy taught me how to enjoy beer."

"What else did he teach you?" Rodney asked.

Karen looked deep into his eyes and without smiling answered, "How to worry."

Rodney and Karen heard the engines to Mr. Cook's airplane kick over. "The war is about to begin," Rodney said

"The damn sheep and the fence keeping nothing in," Karen said.

"I wish I was Banjo," Rodney said, "I wish I had a few acres somewhere tucked far enough away that the world couldn't touch me."

"You sound like an old hippie," Karen said.

"I almost was a hippie, but I became a cowboy instead," Rodney said. "Not much difference when you get right down to it. Just a bunch of dreamers with no direction."

"If you were Banjo, you'd be out cutting somebody's fence," Karen said. "And hopefully I'd be sitting in an empty living room worrying and wondering why you were such a strong-headed, old goat."

Karen looked at Rodney with a hint of sadness in her eyes at what she had said.

Rodney reached over and held her hand. "If I were Banjo and you were sitting in an empty room waiting for me, I'd be the luckiest man in the world," he said.

"Don't tease me," Karen said squeezing his hand.

"I'm sorry," Rodney said.

"Did Gloria seduce you?" Karen said out of the blue, letting her subconscious rule her lips.

Rodney studied her face and smiled faintly. "She tried," he answered.

Karen felt her heart pounding in her chest and felt relieved. She was also happy she believed him.

"In the real world is love truly enough to get through life?" Rodney asked solemnly.

"I don't know, but it's worth a try," Karen said.

"I don't mean to hurt you," Rodney said.

"Me loving you and you not knowing if you love me isn't hurt, Rodney. It's sadness. But I know you have deep feelings for me," Karen said.

"I'm a mess," Rodney said.

"No. You're stupid," Karen said and smiled and got up and put the food on the table.

While they were eating they heard Mr. Cook landing the plane.

"I bet Mr. Cook is furious over the fact a poor Mexican is not doing his bidding or bowing to his threats," Rodney said.

What Rodney did not know was, besides looking at the fence, Mr. Cook was looking at landmarks as to where to begin his sub-division and that another course of action was already in his mind on how to deal with Banjo.

Sixteen

Banjo woke up with his chest hurting and with great difficulty caught his breath. Angelena's snoring echoed softly through the rooms. "Not now God," he prayed painfully.

He did not want to die in bed and have Angelena find him. Without a phone, she would have to walk for help and walking too far might kill her. "I should have listened to my son and gotten one of those modern telephones with no wires," he muttered.

With great effort Banjo sat up and swung his legs over the side of the bed. He stood feebly, turned on the light and fell into his chair. He was able to put on his boots and jacket to get the chill out of his bones. Banjo grunted, stood up and walked as quietly as he could into the kitchen. Turning on the light, he poked around in the wood box, finding a few small pieces of wood to put in the stove to rekindle the fire. Within a few minutes, the fire kicked in and he put several larger pieces of wood in the firebox. The warmth began to radiate through the room. He inhaled as deeply as he could and savored the aroma of the cedar wood.

Angelena stopped snoring for a moment and Banjo worried she might be getting up. He would not be able to hide the pain and she would force him to go to a doctor. A doctor he could not afford to see.

Thankfully, the snoring continued and Banjo filled the coffee pot with water and dropped in a handful of coffee. Sitting down at the table, he rolled himself a smoke and dodged the flame. The warm smoke filling his lungs seemed to dull the pain and he thought about the bottle of whiskey he had hidden in the barn several years ago. "If I drank a little of the whiskey, it would help. But, it is too dark to go look for it," he said.

Angelena had never cared if Banjo drank, as long as it was not in the house. Years ago, when she found whiskey bottles in the house, she broke them.

Butting the cigarette, Banjo felt wearier than when he had struggled out of bed. Turning off the light, he went back to bed, forgetting the coffee. He put his coat over the covers and held both of them tightly to his chin. He could hear the crackling of the fire mingled with the snoring of his wife and the pain started to subside. Taking a deep breath, he shut his eyes and willed himself back to sleep.

Banjo woke up and to his relief his chest did not hurt. Angelena was singing in the kitchen and the aroma of coffee and frying bacon greeted him. He did not want to move, he wanted to lie quiet in his bed and smell the coffee and the bacon. It was almost heaven to smell bacon and coffee in the morning. "I wonder if I make it to heaven if there is coffee and tortillas," he said. "I know God would surely like Angelena's tortillas."

The sun shone brightly through the window. But, he could see ice crystals on the outside of the windows stubbornly hanging onto their short lives.

Angelena smiled at him but said nothing. Her smile conveyed that she knew something was going on that Banjo had not bothered to tell her. It was a smile he had seem many times in his life.

Setting a plate of thick-cut bacon and a cup of coffee before him, Angelena said, "You do not look well."

Banjo, eating the bacon, ignored his wife's statement. There was nothing more important than eating the still warm bacon and sipping the coffee.

After breakfast, Banjo went to the shed and started tossing years of miscellaneous odds and ends around, looking for his bottle of whiskey. After several minutes, he found the bottle. Wiping off the years of accumulated dirt and dust, he put the bottle in the corner. When it was safe, he would smuggle it into his bedroom and hide it under the bed. And, if during the night he would get the pains, he would have a swallow. Never a lot, he told himself, just enough for the pain.

It was about ten in the morning and the day was warming when Banjo heard a car coming toward the house. "It is probably my no good son," Banjo said.

Angelena gave him a stern look.

When Armondo walked into the house, Angelena hugged him dearly. Armondo kissed his mother and handed her a large sack. "Something for you, mother," he said.

Angelena anxiously opened the sack and gasped audibly as she pulled out a light green dress. She laid it over the back of the chair and took out a green sweater covered with bright yellow daisies. Holding the sweater up to her body, Banjo could not remember when he had seen her eyes filled with so much love. Armondo went back outside and brought back two more boxes. One he handed to Angelena, and looking troubled, handed the other to Banjo. Banjo took the heavy box and tried not to smile even though his heart was filled with joy over the happiness of his wife and the fact he too had a present.

Angelena sat down and opened her box and put her hands to her face in joy. In the box was a new pair of lined, winter boots with zippers on the side and a pair of woolen, night slippers and four packages of Winston's.

"O Armondo," she said. "You must have sold a painting."

"I did, Mother, remember the painting of the old Mexican man standing by the tree with his burro loaded down with red chili? A rich man from back east gave the gallery $5,000 for it."

"I am so proud and happy for you," Angelena said and then told Banjo. "Open your present from your son," Angelena urged.

Banjo, trying with all his effort to not show any excitement, opened the heavy box. His eyes grew wide as he looked at the black boots he had dreamed about his whole life. Cowboy boots with very sharp pointed toes that, when slipped on, were so tall they would come up almost to Banjo's knees. The tops of the boots were made with a hole on each side to put one's fingers through to help pull them on. The high heels were made solely for riding and stitched on each side of the boots in red, white, and blue thread was an eagle with talons reaching out as though he was about to plunge his claws into some frightened prey. Next to the boots were five pairs of heavy wool socks, one pair of lined leather gloves and one unlined pair.

They were the most beautiful boots he had ever seen. He took off his old, worn boots and socks and pulled on a pair of the new wool socks, and then, tugged on each boot. They slid on like they had always been on his feet. He tucked his Levi's into the stove tops of the boots and stood up, looking at his son he held out his hand.

Armondo took his hand warmly and both men looked down at Banjo's feet. "Years ago at the dances, the women would have loved to dance with me," Banjo said.

Angelena laughed, "Years ago the women liked to dance with you, anyway."

Angelena went into her bedroom and put on the new dress and sweater and her new boots. When she walked back into the kitchen, it seemed to Banjo she had grown younger. He whistled softly and Angelena did a small curtsy. Banjo picked up each pair of gloves from the box and tried them on. He had not had a good pair of gloves in years. The leather gloves were more than he could afford so he was reduced to either not wearing any or wearing the cheap yellow cotton gloves that ripped and did nothing to keep his hands warm.

Armondo once again went outside and came back with another box and handed it to his father. Banjo held the box as though it contained eggs. He set the box on the table, took off the lid and picked up an extra large brimmed black felt cowboy hat. Banjo folded the top of the hat into a small crease and bent both the front and back of the brim downward at a slight angle. He put on the hat and looked in the mirror and started to laugh. He laughed so hard that soon his wife and son were laughing. Turning, he hugged his son warmly. "Now," he said, "mui bandito, mui bandito."

Angelena took both men by the hand and led them to the front porch. "You two get out of my way. I will make us some coffee and something to snack on."

Banjo sat down in his chair and put his feet up on the rail and looked at the splendid boots. He cocked the black hat back on his head and took his tobacco out of his pocket and rolled a smoke, being extra careful to make it as round and perfect as he could. A man with boots such as these should only smoke cigarettes rolled with care.

Lighting the cigarette, only a small flame erupted from the end. He took a small drag and then looked once more at his boots. After gathering his thoughts he said to Armondo. "I am a man to whom the white man has never been a friend. I should never have tried to bend you to my will. Your life is your life. I am sorry."

"I am like you, though, father, you could not bend me," Armondo replied softly.

Banjo looked at his boots, touched his hat and took a drag off of the smoke. "Maybe it is good there are no longer many bandits left."

"I love you father," Armondo said. "You are the backbone of your race. The last of the people who withstood all adversity and gave your people the chance to go and become part of the white man's world. Without your courage and work, I would never have had the opportunity to become a painter."

"Nor sleep with pretty white women," Banjo said and winked at his son.

"Or sleep with pretty white women," Armondo agreed, smiling.

"You must promise me one thing, my son," Banjo said seriously, tossing his cigarette butt out into the yard where a chicken ran up and pecked at it. "You must promise me you will not sell the land. Never, not if you are broke, not ever. This small piece of land will stay in our blood until we have no more blood. It is the life of all I have ever known. A place, that if life ever starts to break you down, you will always be able to come back to. It will not make you rich, but it will sustain you."

"I promise you, Father," Armondo said, looking out at the land. He now understood there was a true beauty here. Here was life, real life and toil and strength. If there was a God, he would live here. Here with the simplicity.

"When are you going to butcher the pig?" Armondo asked.

Banjo looked toward the pig. "I don't know," he answered. "Maybe in a few weeks."

"I do not want to sound greedy after the wonderful boots you have given to me but I would like to ask a favor," Banjo said.

"Anything," Armondo replied hiding his surprise. Banjo was never a man to ask for favors.

"I would like to have one of those telephones with no wires. I worry over your mother. It would be nice if she could call you," Banjo said.

"The next time I come out I will bring you one."

"I have cookies and coffee," Angelena said, holding the door open for her husband and son.

Following his son, Banjo stopped and whispered to his wife, "You are as beautiful as the day I first met you."

Angelena smiled and answered, "And you, you are as ugly and mean. But I love you no less.

Karen examined the obsidian arrowhead Rodney gave her and was transfixed by the small delicate point. She wished it could talk to her. She wished she could see the man who had so laboriously worked on the point. And she wished she knew how he came to lose it. Looking at the point and then at her painting, the painting seemed overshadowed by the true life art laying in her hand. Here was something solid that would stand the test of centuries. Her painting was nothing but a flat, one dimensional glimpse of her mind. Something that really did not show life or feel of life. "Maybe I should be a sculptor," she thought.

She set the arrowhead on top of the painting and looked from the arrowhead, to the cowboy riding away, to the owl, to the tiny yellow rose and back to the arrowhead. "There will be a time when the cowboys will be forgotten, but arrowheads will last forever," she said to the painting.

The thought shocked her and she wanted to walk over to Rodney's and hold him close. She wanted to tell him how special cowboys were and how important it was to hang on to what you believed in. Not to give into the modern world. Stay simple, and brave, and alone if need be. If for no other reason than for history and to say, at the end, you made it with your convictions.

Standing back from the painting she wished she could meet one of Rodney's old girlfriends from Montana. She would walk up to her and smile and say, "Hon, you don't know what you're missing."

Walking to the bathroom to brush her hair, Karen thought, "But on the other hand, maybe the old girlfriend did know what she was missing."

Rodney was sitting at his kitchen table, drinking coffee, waiting for Mr. Cook and the outburst he knew was coming.

Ten minutes later Mr. Cook stormed into Rodney's house. His face was a vivid red and the veins in his temples were pulsing. "Ride out and fix that damn fence," he bellowed. "Ride out everyday and fix that fence. I'm going to town and have that Mexican arrested for whatever crime I can."

"Don't you have to catch him first?" Rodney said, putting on his coat.

"You just fix the fence," Mr. Cook ordered.

Rodney headed toward the corral. The frost was completely gone and the temperature had climbed into the forties. The blue sky seemed as though it was painted and there was not a cloud to be seen.

Gloria was standing on her porch as he rode by. Seeing him, she turned abruptly and walked into the house. He could see Mr. Cook through a picture window yelling into the phone.

Rodney did not think about Banjo or Gloria or Mr. Cook or the movie. He thought about Karen. He knew he loved her although it did not change his fear. She was exciting, refined, and unpredictable. He knew she was rich, but how rich he did not know, but her money did not mean anything to him anyway. Having enough was all that was important. But he wondered if he did ask her to marry him and she did, if it would only be doomed? At least being lonely, he knew everyday was lonely. But being married, he might not ever shake the nagging fear that loneliness was only a heartbeat away.

Rodney patted the horse on the neck. "You dumb bastards don't know how lucky you are. You eat and crap and when somebody wants to ride, you plod along and do your bit and then go back to eat and crap."

The horse bent its ears backwards toward Rodney as though he understood.

"When I die, if there is such a thing as reincarnation, I want to come back as a horse," he said.

But he thought about what he had said and decided being a horse was not all that great. What if you did not like whoever was riding you? Life would always be spent with some jerk on your back, kicking you in the sides or smacking you across the face or cinching the saddle too tight or not feeding you or brushing you.

Rodney laughed and pushing his knees tighter against the horse's side, moved the horse into a fast trot. The horse seemed to enjoy the extra speed. He touched the flanks of the horse with his heels and the horse moved into a steady gallop. Rodney felt the cool air sweep across his face. "Get up," he yelled. "Get up."

The horse flared his nostrils and tore off as fast as he could with Rodney yelling and waving his right hand in the air. They galloped along the fence and passed the milling sheep but did not stop. Rodney galloped until he felt the horse was growing tired. Pulling gently on the reins, he slowed the horse steadily until they were once again walking and he turned back toward the sheep.

Gathering the sheep, Rodney looked up and saw a man wearing a large black hat and boots that almost reached his knees. The man resembled Banjo in many ways, but Banjo did not have a black hat. The man rode through the cut in the fence and as he neared, Rodney saw it was Banjo's grizzled face beneath the large drooping brim of the hat.

"That's a nice hat you got there, Banjo," Rodney said.

Then he whistled, seeing the boots with the stitched red, white and blue eagles. "Some kind of boots."

Banjo grinned from ear to ear. "Nice huh, gringo?" he said and added, "and new gloves."

"What did you do, rob a bank?" Rodney asked.

"My son gave them to me," Banjo answered with pride in his voice.

Rodney felt happy for Banjo. "Somebody must have cut the fence again Banjo. Either that or one of those sheep of yours is really smart and has hidden a set of wire cutters somewhere around here."

"Sheep of mine pretty smart," Banjo said. "Especially that old one over there, he has been through a lot."

Both men started the sheep back toward the hole. "Mr. Cook is hopping mad, Banjo. He is calling the cops right now."

Banjo laughed. "Cops won't do anything. They've got drug addicts and killers and murderers and rapists and car thieves to worry about. What do they care about a fence and some rich gringo from out of state?"

"Never thought of that," Rodney confessed, amazed at Banjo's reasoning.

The sheep once again on Banjo's land, Rodney dismounted and tied his horse to a tree. Banjo rode over to his side of the fence, dismounted and walked back to the fence. "I'll help you, gringo," he said, picking up a strand of the cut wire.

"Wish I had me a pair of boots like that," Rodney said, picking up the other end.

"Get married and have a son," Banjo answered him. "There are times in one's life children are worth it."

"Never been married," Rodney said, stretching the wire and taking the other half from Banjo.

"Gringo," Banjo said in a fatherly way. "A man is lonely enough without going through life alone. We are not hawks that mate only once a year. We are creatures that need."

Rodney twisted the piece of wire he had in his hand into a loop and attaching the other wire to it, stretched them and wrapped them together.

"There is a pretty lady that lives at the ranch. So pretty I have heard any man would like to be with her. You should get to know her," Banjo said, sitting down and watching Rodney stretch another wire.

"How did you know about her?" Rodney asked in surprise.

"The news of pretty women is hard to keep quiet," Banjo said. "There has been more than one man make the long drive to ask her out, only to be turned down. I have heard she is a hard nut to crack."

She probably wouldn't like some horse bum like me," Rodney said, smiling to himself after hearing Karen had turned down other men.

"That's true," Banjo said. "You are almost as ugly as I am."

Banjo climbed on his horse. Rodney watched how difficult it was for him. Sitting on the horse, Banjo tipped his large black hat back on his forehead. "I think one of these smart sheep will probably cut that fence again," he said. "If I knew which one it was, I would take him home and have lamb chops. But I do not have the time to sit out here and try to catch him."

Rodney mounted his horse. "I wish you would talk to him and tell him not to cut the fence until tomorrow. I would appreciate it," Rodney said.

Banjo smiled his toothless smile. "I think maybe he is listening."

Rodney started to ride when Banjo started coughing. A severe pain shot through Banjo's chest and he slid out of the saddle. Rodney jumped off the horse, clamored through the fence, and ran to him and held him up. "It is nothing," Banjo said.

"It's more than nothing," Rodney said. "You have to go to the doctor."

"I will die on my land, gringo," Banjo said.

Banjo coughed a few more times and struggled to get up. Rodney helped him into the saddle.

"You will not tell my wife," Banjo ordered.

"Sure wish I had me a pair of boots like that," Rodney said, hiding the concern he felt. "A pair of boots like that must cost two weeks pay."

He tipped the brim of his hat to Banjo.

Banjo nudged his horse and started back up the hillside toward his house. The sheep milling around the fence parted as he rode away. Rodney watched Banjo until he crested the hill. Stopping at the top, Banjo took of his hat and waved to Rodney before disappearing from view.

"Banjo, life isn't worth a damn," Rodney said as he rode away.

Back at the headquarters Mr. Cook's truck was gone and loud country music emitted from Karen's. After unsaddling and taking care of the horse Rodney went to his house. Mr. Cook was sitting in the kitchen, drinking a beer. He scowled at Rodney but didn't seem to be in as bad of a mood as earlier in the morning. "Cops won't come out," Mr. Cook said.

Rodney took off his coat and sat down. He noticed, for the first time, his hands were cold and the tips of his fingers were tingling.

"The movie construction crew is in town and will start work tomorrow. The producers told me they want to start shooting in three weeks—winter or no winter," Mr. Cook said.

Mr. Cook headed for the door but stopped. "I'm going to catch that old goat and, when I do, there will be hell to pay. I almost forgot to tell you, Gloria has taken the truck and gone to the airport to fly back to Phoenix. She said you were a lousy riding instructor." He chuckled slightly, "But I know all she really wanted to do was sleep with you. If you did get her, son, it's okay by me. For as good looking as she is, she really isn't all that great. Those pretty ones get so full of themselves they really don't try as hard. It's those plain ones that really throw one on you. Only problem is, the pretty ones seem to be the ones people like to catch."

After Mr. Cook left, Rodney was amazed by Mr. Cook's words. He wondered what it would be like to be married to a woman and not care if she messed around? But he supposed Mr. Cook had a lot of girlfriends, so it really did not matter.

Rodney opened the refrigerator and looked at his dwindling beer supply. He would have to go to town soon and buy a few supplies.

Mr. Cook was in his den studying the maps spread across the desk. Along his border with Banjo, twenty parcels had been plotted out. Parcels he could sell for enough money to buy another ranch. But he knew he could not get the kind of money he wanted if the parcels bordered a poor Mexican's land—wealthy people were not impressed by poverty. "Your days are numbered Banjo," Mr. Cook thought. "Nobody stands in the way of progress, nobody."

True to his word, Banjo did not cut the fence until the next day. Rising early, he took his time pulling on his new boots and stood looking at them for several minutes before going into the kitchen. Angelena had risen before he did and the coffee was already made. She was wearing her new dress and sweater. She was chipper but, as usual, not talkative as she set his coffee in front of him.

After a second cup of coffee, Banjo left the house and saddled his horse and rode out to the sheep. It only took thirty seconds to cut the fence and watch his sheep scamper toward the river.

As Banjo crested the hill that led down to his house, he could see in the distance, passed where the Cook's houses were, large dust clouds rising in the air and he could make out loads of lumber on the trucks. A school bus, that he knew was filled with workers, followed the trucks. "It is a crew to build the movie set," he said.

Banjo rode toward his house and chuckled as he envisioned bits and pieces of lumber flying through the air. Bits and pieces of the gringo's movie set.

Seventeen

Rodney was checking the Arabian's hooves when three flatbed trucks loaded with building materials rumbled into the headquarters followed by a school bus filled with men. The vehicles stopped in a cloud of dust, but nobody got out. Rodney looked at the men in the school bus and waved and a few gave him half-hearted waves back. "Must be union men," Rodney thought to himself.

Within five minutes, a silver Bronco pulled into the headquarters and Irv Abraham and Saul Heilman got out. Mr. Cook, dressed in Levi's, ostrich cowboy boots and a white cowboy hat, came around the corner of Rodney's house and smiling widely, shook hands with the men. Rodney could not hear what they were saying, but all three of the men seemed to be having the time of their lives. Getting back into the Bronco, the men sped away, followed by the trucks and bus.

Bending over and picking up the back foot of the horse, Rodney felt a twinge of nervousness go through his body. The movie was going to be a real thing and soon he would be in front of a camera. Setting the foot down, Rodney looked over at Karen's house, as if seeing her would give him strength.

Rodney finished cleaning the horse's hooves when Mr. Cook returned. Mr. Cook got out and hurried over to him. "I might have an errand for you to do this afternoon, so stay close. I have Banjo Ortega right where I want him."

Mr. Cook went to his house leaving Rodney with a bad feeling in his stomach.

Karen was starting to take her clothes off and work on her painting when she heard the trucks drive in. She stopped unbuttoning her blouse and watched Mr. Cook get into the Bronco. He reminded her of a banker dressing up like a cowboy for a Halloween party. When the trucks were gone, she finished undressing. She had an idea to paint a large white cloud in the sky in the shape of an arrowhead. It would give her painting a sense of time and lore. It would make the viewer imagine the kinship between the cowboy and the Indian, although enemies dictated by history, in truth, they were brothers in spirit.

Starting the arrowhead cloud she could picture Rodney as an old cowboy—silent and brooding, hardheaded, but independent, free, as free as one could be. Dabbing the purple sky with white paint, Karen shrugged her shoulders and smiled wryly, "My folks have to be right, I am crazy. I divorce a man who is secure and move to the wilderness. And now, I want to be a painter. Dear God, to top it off, I fall in love with a cowboy."

Stepping back, she scrutinized the outline of her arrowhead cloud and was pleased with it. She set her brush down for a moment, picked up the arrowhead and held the dark point up to the light. It seemed to glisten and shimmer like gold, although it was black, and for a moment her happiness vanished. This tiny arrowhead would still exist when she was long gone. All her dreams and hopes and thoughts would vanish, but this arrowhead would remain. Remain to tell the proceeding generations there was a time when a man was part of the earth and not just a living movie.

Rodney was eating a sandwich when Mr. Cook knocked on the back door. Mr. Cook was all smiles. Rodney decided he liked him better when he was mad, then he would not have to talk to him as long. Mr. Cook sat down at the table and gave Rodney a long stare before speaking. "There's a lawyer in town by the name of Spitzer. He's a thief like most of them, but he has a pack of papers for me. I want you to go to town and pick them up. Tell him when you pick them up that money is no matter, I just want the land."

Rodney took a piece of paper from Mr. Cook with an address on it. "When you're done eating is soon enough," Mr. Cook informed him and left.

Rodney knew Mr. Cook was referring to Banjo's land. He finished the sandwich in two large bites. He hurried to the truck, started it and tore away from the houses, not thinking to stop and ask Karen if she needed anything from town, or if she wanted to go along.

Rodney pressed the accelerator and left a good size patch of rubber as he drove onto the pavement. Two young Mexican boys, walking on the other side of road, waved at him as he sped by.

It took Rodney over thirty minutes to find the lawyer's office and another twenty to find a spot to park the truck in the narrow winding roads of Santa Fe. The receptionist was an attractive woman who looked as though she should be in New York and not New Mexico. "I presume you are the man Mr. Cook said was coming to see Mr. Spitzer," she said smiling through perfect teeth. "Have a seat. He will be with you in a moment."

Rodney nodded his head yes and picked up a Time magazine. A few moments later, the lady looked up from her desk, "Would you like a cup of coffee, sir?" she asked, looking much too friendly.

"Yes, ma'am," Rodney answered, feeling like he was sitting in the principal's office knowing he was about to be expelled from school.

"Black?" she said

Rodney nodded.

The lady brought him coffee in a styrofoam cup. Their eyes made direct contact and she smiled.

Sipping the coffee, Rodney thumbed through the Time and a Newsweek and was halfway through People magazine when a thin, wiry man, no more than five foot five, wearing an expensive suit walked into the room. "Mr. Slugger, right this way. I have the papers for Mr. Cook in my office," he said not bothering to shake hands. Mr. Spitzer's office was decorated with bronze statues of cowboys and Indians and eagles. In the corner was a putter and several golf balls. The rug was so thick Rodney felt he was walking on air. Mr. Spitzer's highly polished desk had to weigh a ton and the dark leather chair he sat in made him look like a boy king.

He fiddled around with several stacks of envelopes on his desk and handed several to Rodney. "These are the records he requested and a letter to him," Mr. Spitzer said. "Tell him as far as I can tell, Mr. Ortega has never paid any land taxes, and it would be quite easy to pick up the land by paying all the taxes. The exact amount is in the envelope."

Spitzer did not smile or frown, but seemed like a computer spitting out facts.

"How can somebody live on a place so long and not pay taxes?" Rodney asked.

"Land records in New Mexico are a mess. There was so much Spanish land grant land deeded that half of the land in this state is not even registered," Mr. Spitzer informed Rodney.

Rodney held the envelopes like he had a death warrant and walked out without saying goodbye. Rodney knew, beyond a shadow of doubt, that Banjo would not have the money to pay off his taxes.

Driving back to the ranch, Rodney thought about Banjo sitting at home, drinking coffee or eating a tortilla, oblivious to the fact everything he had done in his life was about to be taken away by a man he did not really know. "True capitalism," Rodney sneered.

Mr. Cook must have heard Rodney drive in because he was waiting by Rodney's front door. Rodney handed him the envelopes, wishing he had tossed them out the window on the way back. "Mr. Spitzer says you can pick it up," Rodney said, feeling like a traitor.

Mr. Cook smiled. "He cut the fence again, Rodney. But don't worry about it. Soon it won't be any big deal."

Rodney went into his house feeling like Judas.

Rodney was sitting in the kitchen so lost his thoughts he did not notice the sun go down. Nor did he hear Karen walk into the house until she turned on the kitchen light and he leaped up out of his chair. "You look like hell," Karen said, appraising him as though she was his mother.

Rodney sat back down. "I feel like hell," he said.

"If you had a dog, I'd say your dog died, but since you don't have a dog, it has to be something else," Karen said, sitting down.

"I've got to go see Banjo," Rodney said. "It's important. But I can't let Mr. Cook know I'm going."

By his voice, Karen knew whatever was bothering Rodney was serious.

"I can get the Cadillac and we can go in it. Mr. Cook would never suspect we were going to see Banjo in my car. And clean yourself up. You look like you've been on a five day drunk and haven't been in bed with a woman in months, neither of which is my fault," she said giving Rodney a coy smile.

Rodney smiled feebly. Karen hurried to her house, put on a down jacket and got her keys.

Rodney was waiting on the porch when Karen drove up and he walked to the Cadillac nonchalantly so that if Mr. Cook saw him, he would not guess he was up to mutiny.

Approaching Banjo's house, Rodney wondered if they should honk. He figured Banjo was not used to having company at night and he did not want to get greeted by a hail of 30/30 bullets while getting out of the car. Karen was amazed at the house and the outbuildings as the headlights of the car swept over them. She felt as though she was in a South American country. "Leave the lights on until I wave at you," Rodney told her, getting out of the car.

He started yelling, "Banjo, Banjo, it's me, Rodney."

Banjo was taking the last bite of a large bean burrito, when he heard a car approaching. He got his rifle and was about to go out on the porch when he heard his name called out and recognized Rodney's voice. "It's my enemy friend, the good gringo," he told Angelena and put his rifle behind the door before he opened it.

Karen saw an old Mexican man, wearing knee high boots, and wished she had a camera to take a photo so she could paint it later. She would call it Late Night Greeting.

Rodney waved at her to come in. Angelena, meeting Karen, smiled and grasped both of Karen's hands. Karen immediately liked the woman. Banjo hurried to his bedroom and brought out another chair for Karen.

Karen looked around the room and could not believe it. She did not know people lived like this anymore. But the house was clean and warm and the two old people seemed to be in good health. As he sat, Banjo left his feet out so Karen would see his new boots with the eagles on them.

Karen felt as if she was in a bandit's lair in the mountains, but, since she was not the law, she would not be harmed.

Banjo glanced at his wife who brought four mismatched cups and filled them with coffee. Karen looked at the coffee and wondered if it would keep her awake for a week?

"You're so pretty," Angelena told Karen.

"That's a pretty sweater you have," Karen said.

Angelena ran her hands lovingly over the sweater. "My son gave it to me," she said proudly.

Banjo, listening to the women talk, was upset. They did not mention anything about his beautiful boots.

"Maybe you and I should go into a different room, Banjo," Rodney said. "I want to talk to you in private."

Banjo snorted and tossed his hands in the air. "I have no secrets from my wife," Banjo said. "We can talk here."

"All men lie," Angelena said to Karen, giving her a 'only women know the truth' look.

Karen laughed and sipped the coffee and found it did not taste as bad as it looked.

Rodney took a deep breath. "Banjo, have you ever paid any land taxes?" he asked somberly.

Banjo gave Rodney a quizzical look. "Taxes on my land. This land has been in my family for three generations. We own this land. There are not taxes on what we own. It was given to us by the King of Spain before their were any gringo's."

"Banjo, every year you have to pay taxes to the state on land that you own," Rodney said. "If not, somebody can pay the back taxes and kick you off your land."

Karen saw a look of worry spread over Angelena's face and she felt sad.

"How can the government do that?" Banjo asked.

"How can the government do anything?" Rodney said.

"I didn't think they taxed poor people," Angelena said, unable to control her worry and looking around the small house as though they would be forced to leave right away.

Karen reached over and patted her on the back of her hands and smiled reassuringly at her.

"Your boss is going to pay the taxes and take my land," Banjo said, figuring it all out in a split second.

Rodney nodded and could not look at Banjo but stared into the depths of the dark coffee.

"I will kill him," Banjo said so icily Karen winced. "You tell your boss, if he comes on my land, I will kill him and everybody that is with him, except you gringo. I will only wound you. I like you."

"Do you have any money Banjo?" Rodney asked.

"Maybe twelve dollars. Do you think it is enough?" he asked with hope.

"I happen to know you owe about $15,000," Rodney said, not telling Banjo he had looked at Mr. Cook's private papers. He did not know if it was a crime, but, he figured with all the laws, it probably was.

Banjo seemed to shrink before Rodney's gaze. "$15,000, $15,000 is more money than I have ever had in my life."

The four people sat around the kitchen and did not speak. Only the sound of the wood crackling in the firebox filled the void. Angelena, after a moment, stood up and put a few more pieces of wood in the stove and sat down quietly.

Rodney looked at Karen. "I guess we should go," he said feeling useless.

Karen hugged Angelena.

"Maybe something will work out, Banjo," Rodney said. "You should try and get a lawyer and see what you can do. Maybe you can set up a system to pay a little at a time and stop Mr. Cook from getting your land."

Banjo and Angelena both knew there was nothing they could do. There was no need to get an attorney, they could not afford one. And, even if they could, there was no money for even small payments. They could not ask their son, that was unthinkable. A man did not go to his son for help.

Driving back to the Last Day In Paradise, Rodney and Karen were lost in their own thoughts. "Do you want to come in Karen?" Rodney asked when they got back to the ranch.

"No, not tonight," Karen said. "I want to go home and take a shower. Somehow breaking the bad news to Banjo makes me feel dirty."

Karen turned the shower on. Soaping up, she thought about Angelena and Banjo living their lives in the small house and how simple their lives had been. She remembered a book she had read several years earlier about the Lewis and Clark expedition and an Indian they had met. The Indian prophesied that the white man would ruin the world when the rivers ran backwards, the crops grew straight out of the earth and mice would have antlers.

"But you won't grow antlers, Mr. Cook," she said, washing the soap off of her body. "I've got a surprise for you."

Banjo and Angelena both knew there was nothing they could do. There was no need to get an attorney, they could not afford one. And, even if they could, there was no money for even small payments. They could not ask their son, that was unthinkable. A man did not go to his son for help.

🐂 🐂 🐂

Angelena lay in bed and picked up her romance novel. She read for a few moments, listening to Banjo as he turned off the kitchen light and went to his room. She heard him groan as he pulled off his boots.

Setting her book down, she looked at the crucifix on her wall and clasping her hands together prayed, "I know all is your will. But do not let the land be taken away until my husband is dead. He is a brave and strong man. To live without his land would be to take his life."

She said three Hail Mary's and an Our Father and went back to her book content to let God's will run its course.

Banjo sat in the dark. He did not feel angry or sad. He only felt hatred. Hatred for a world that would charge a poor man for land he already owned. He lay down on the bed until it started to grow cool in the room, then he covered himself. Warm once again, he wished he was in bed with his wife. He wished he was young and could make love every night. He wished he could get up in the morning and saddle his horse and ride over and kick the hell out of Mr. Cook. But most of all, he wished he had money.

    In the morning, Angelena was smiling as she served Banjo his coffee. They had scrambled eggs with green chili on top of them. Banjo ate and finally said, "There is nothing we can do wife. Only go on with our lives and hope fate is kind."

    "No matter what my husband, we have had a good life," she said and kissed him on the cheek.

Eighteen

Karen was driving ninety miles an hour. She loved the feel of the car as it was going fast. It gave her a sense of freedom, a sense she could outrun the world. Before she got married she wanted to be a race car driver—a fancy she still held in the recesses of her mind. But one that no longer held much importance.

Karen parked in the private parking lot of Attorney Patrick Hamilton. When she walked into the office, the secretary knew her by sight and led Karen to a private waiting room with real cups for coffee and a fully stocked bar. "I'll tell Mr. Hamilton you're here. I'm sure he'll be with you in no time at all," the secretary said.

Karen was halfway through a rum and coke when Mr. Hamilton came into the office with a college, frat rat grin spread across his face. Hamilton reminded Karen of her ex-husband. But, he was an excellent attorney and handled her money matters well.

"Karen," Mr. Hamilton said, "you look lovely as usual."

"Cut the crap, Pat," Karen said. "I need something done fast, real fast."

"What is it you need done, Karen?" Mr. Hamilton asked, putting on his 'I can solve all your problems' look while taking her by the arm and escorting her to his office.

Fifteen minutes later Karen walked out of the office having been told to come back in two hours. Karen did not want to go to the plaza and tour the dress shops. She really did not need any clothes or want any. She decided she would browse a few of the art galleries and see if anything was new. Maybe she would make a few inquiries about getting her painting shown.

After an hour of browsing, Karen's ego had been inflated. Most of the art she saw was not worth the canvas it was painted on. At least her painting had feeling. Although, some of it had been so well done she knew she would never be able to paint as well. But, art was in the eye of the beholder and the investor.
"Mr. Hamilton is waiting for you, you can go right in," the receptionist said.
"I paid them," Mr. Hamilton said. "$15,876."
"In their name from an anonymous source?" Karen asked.
"Yes," Mr. Hamilton said and added, "You can't be everybody's savior, Karen, you know that."
"Hon," Karen said. "This heart might have a few soft spots, but it's no virgin."
Mr. Hamilton laughed and watched Karen walk out of the office, wishing she would once give him a chance to get to first base.
Rodney spent the afternoon moping around the house. All he could think about was Banjo and how he wished he had the money to pay Banjo's back land taxes. If he had it, he would pay them without hesitation. The fact he knew Banjo would never be able to repay him would not make a difference. He hoped if he was ever in such a jam there would be somebody to come to his rescue. But, Rodney had learned in life, there were few things that turned out for the good, and he never knew of a time when a dream came true.

He tried to listen to the radio, but the news only made him more depressed and he turned it off in disgust. In regards to knowledge of the world, Rodney was the proverbial ostrich with his head stuck in the sand.

Rodney was feeding the horses when Karen got back to the ranch. She waved at him and he waved back. He had not known she was gone.

Karen felt good at what she had accomplished. She paced back and forth in her living room, an emerging painting of Banjo in her mind's eye. He was standing in the doorway of an adobe house with his tall boots on, wearing a brace of pearl-handled six shooters, with a sawed-off double barrel shotgun cradled in his left arm. He was neither smiling nor frowning, but stared into the eyes of the viewer with eyes that radiated both humility and a sense of danger. Behind Banjo, in the shadows, was a faint image of a Mexican lady with a long rosary in her hand. You could not see her face clearly as the darkness covered her image.

Feeling an urgency to paint, she took her clothes off and stood in front of her easel. But, each time she picked up a brush, she could not force herself to put brush to canvas. After doing this for over an hour, she opened a bottle of wine and sat on the floor cross legged, drinking the wine straight out of the bottle, and looking at her painting. After the bottle was empty, she stood up woozily and picked up the arrowhead. "That's it," she said out loud.

The old Mexican bandit would have a large arrowhead hanging around his neck from a leather thong. And on the porch of the adobe would be a dead owl, hanging upside down from a weathered exposed vegas, with its wings frozen in a position as though it had died trying to fly.

She went to the living room and lay down on the sofa. She could see Angelena cooking over her stove with the slow graceful movements of one who accepted fate for what fate was. She wondered if she would have been able to go through life as Angelena and still been able to smile and radiate hope after having so little? She shut her eyes and for the first time in years she prayed. "I don't know if you're there, God, but, if you are, people like Angelena should get a break."

Rodney saw Karen's lights on but was still in such a bad mood he knew he would be lousy company and he went to bed.

In the morning, after eating breakfast, Rodney walked over to Karen's. He was still in a morose mood, but there was no reason to be angry. Banjo was out of his control and he would have to learn to live with it. It was no different than the war. What happened had happened and he should not let it make him bitter.

"You didn't come over last night to even say hello," Karen said.

"I was tired," Rodney lied. "Went to bed early," which was not a lie.

Karen felt like telling Rodney she had paid Banjo's taxes, but decided she would not. There really was no reason for anybody to know. She knew all hell would fly when Mr. Cook found out and Rodney might have his suspicions, but she would not tell him. She had already made the mistake telling him she was rich. Although it did not seem to make much difference to Rodney. He had not treated her differently. On the other hand, she wondered if Rodney really knew what being rich was. He might think she had a mere couple of hundred thousand dollars.

"It's another exciting day on the Last Day In Paradise," Karen said. "The only ranch in the world where a cowboy can spend his time fighting being seduced by the owner's wife and spurning the love advances of a lost and wandering woman trying to make a foothold in the art world," Karen said.

"Hell of a note, isn't it?" Rodney said.

Karen looked at him in a pensive way. "You know, since I'm trying to be a painter, maybe you should take a hand at writing. I bet the way you have lived alone your entire life, you would be a good writer."

"You must be kidding," Rodney said. "I haven't written a letter in years. The most I ever wrote my folks before they died was a postcard."

"You never told me your folks were dead, Rodney," Karen said, feeling sad.

"You never asked," Rodney answered. "They were killed in a car wreck in California. Both of them were retired and ready to enjoy life when they were run over by a trucker, wired on bennies and trying to get to L.A. before the rush hour."

"I'm sorry," Karen said.

"At least they didn't suffer or grow old and spend their last days sitting around, looking at each other wondering which one was going to die first," Rodney replied with a distant tone in his voice.

They fell into silence for a few moments. Karen was about to speak when Mr. Cook banged on the door. He did not sit down in the kitchen but said quickly to Rodney. "I'm going into town and I want you to ride out and see how the movie set is coming."

Mr. Cook smiled at Karen, then looked at her from head to foot, before leaving. Rodney felt like jumping up, chasing after Mr. Cook and stomping him in the ground. But, he sat and looked at Karen and said, "Guess Banjo is about to bite the bullet."

"Maybe the old man has a few more bullets left Rodney."

"I doubt it," Rodney replied in a dull tone as he left the house.

Rodney did not go to the corral to saddle a horse but decided to drive to the movie site. He really was not in the mood to do anything, but, he had his orders. And, bad mood or not, they were orders.

Driving away from the houses, Karen stepped out and waved. He waved back and the wave cheered him.

When Rodney arrived at the movie site, he was amazed at how many men were working. The movie set was almost complete—an old western town had materialized in a few days. There was a livery stable on the south side of town, a blacksmith shop, and over a dozen other buildings. Near where he stood, was a hotel and a bar. A board sidewalk in front of the buildings was almost completed. In the center of the street, a crew was working on a gallows. Rodney pushed through the swinging doors to the bar. It looked like an old time saloon complete with tables and chairs and a piano except the back of the room was nothing but a black canvas drop cloth. Rodney sat down in one of the chairs. He expected, at any minute, a man to walk through the swinging door of the bar, wearing two guns, with a scowl on his face. He visualized the bar going silent and the piano player stopping playing.

Rodney suddenly felt cheated. It was all a sham. A sham put together so well one could not tell it was not real. All the anxiety, and fear, and hope, and dreaming he had gone through watching movies as a boy was nothing but a joke on him. And now he was going to be part of the joke. "Dear lord," Rodney muttered.

A deep voice came from the swinging doors. "Lord help all of us," a man said.

Rodney recognized Matt Walker immediately, not from seeing his movies but from several magazine articles he had read. Walker was the biggest western star in the country. Rodney felt in awe. "Name is Matt Walker," the man said as he sat down but did not hold out his hand to shake.

"Rodney Slugger."

"Irv Abraham told me about," Matt said. "You're a real cowboy. Not one of us movie jokes."

"I suppose," Rodney said.

"I always wanted to be a cowboy," Matt said. "Always wanted to ride and brand and rope."

"It's not what it seems," Rodney said, regaining some of his composure.

Matt laughed. "Nothing is."

"You ever been around a movie before?" Matt asked.

Rodney shook his head.

"Hell, I bet you don't even go to movies," Matt said. "Movies are for people who lead boring lives and have to get out to think they are really doing something besides growing old. Real cowboys don't get bored."

"On this ranch they do," Rodney said.

"It's beautiful," Matt said, ignoring Rodney's remark. "All the land and space, the sky stretching in every direction. No cars or smog, no horns or buses, no thousands of people standing on every corner dreaming about ways to rob you. No lawyers, no contracts, no women who only want to go out with you for bragging rights."

"A few women," Rodney said with a grin.

Matt laughed. "Yea, I suppose cowboys hold a certain amount of awe to women."

Matt reached into his jacket pocket and pulled out a silver flask. "Shot," he asked, taking a deep pull on the flask.

Rodney took the flask and tilted it back, not really expecting what poured into his mouth, tequila. He almost choked but managed to swallow the fire. Matt laughed, taking the flask and taking another shot. He again offered it to Rodney but Rodney shook his head. "Keeps me going," Matt said. "Used to be dope, but I kicked that."

Matt stood up. "Well, have a good look around. Not much to see really. See you when we start to shoot."

Rodney explored the movie set for another thirty minutes and driving back to the headquarters he felt as though he had been a part of the illusion for the past hour. A big trick on mankind. But everybody knew movies were nothing but illusion. Knowing this Rodney could not really understand why the thought bothered him. As he neared the headquarters, he grimaced to himself. "Hell, life is an illusion. Everything we say and do is just something to cover up the truth. Maybe love is even an illusion. An illusion to try and convince ourselves our lives are really worth something."

To Rodney's relief, Mr. Cook had not returned while he was at the movie site. He had imagined Mr. Cook's face all screwed up in a big grin gloating over his new acquisition of Banjo's land and telling Rodney to inform the old man and his wife they had thirty days to get off.

Rodney thought about saddling up one of the horses and going for a ride, but nixed the idea with a shrug of his shoulders. He felt anxious and jittery, but there really was not anything he wanted to do. "If I would have stayed in Montana I would never have been on this God forsaken ranch bossed by some little man with a big ego who can't do anything but buy people out. I would never have know what an art town was. I would not have met Karen or Banjo. Lord, two good things out of all this and it keeps me hanging around. Banjo, it's a dog eat dog world and you just happen to be a little dog."

Rodney was about to go inside his house when Mr. Cook's Suburban raced through the gate and skidded to a stop by his house. Mr. Cook slammed the door and stomped over to Rodney. "Go out and fix the damn fence, Rodney," he yelled. "Somehow that son- of-a-bitch paid his taxes."

When Mr. Cook was gone, if Rodney had been a young boy, he would have jumped up and down and run around the house, but being an older half-worn out cowboy he ran to Karen's house and went in without knocking, leaving the door open behind him. Karen came out of her bedroom, stark naked, thinking as she did, "what if it isn't Rodney?" But not really caring.

Rodney ran over to her and picked her up, in the process getting hit across the face with the paintbrush, leaving a large stripe of purple across his forehead. He spun Karen around and, kissed her on the neck. "Banjo paid his taxes, you should see the look on Mr. Cook's face. He looked as though he had lost all his money."

Karen, feigning excitement, threw her arms around Rodney's neck, dripping paint on his shirt and kissed him. "I'm so happy," she said, releasing him.

Rodney stepped back from her and looked from her forehead slowly down her entire body and whistled. "Nice dress," he said. "Whoever your designer is, I'd like to meet him."

Karen turned sideways and put the paintbrush between her teeth and posed. "It's the new fall look for the western housewife, called keep your cowboy at home," she teased.

Rodney started for the door. "Off to fix the fence, lady," he said over his shoulder. "Just thought you'd like to hear the news."

Karen watched him walk away and smiled. Looking at her painting, she wondered if it was possible to put a naked lady somewhere without losing all the meaning she had meticulously brushed into her painting. But, she decided it was impossible.

Riding toward the fence, Rodney felt better than he had in days. The cooling afternoon air was vibrant. A few small grey birds sang as he rode by and what he thought was an eagle soared off to the south. He felt like riding over and asking Banjo how in the world he managed to raise the money so quickly. But, if he did that, he would not get the fence fixed and be back before dark and he had not brought a flashlight. He knew he was getting lax. In Montana, during the winter, when the men rode out, they took matches, dry soup, canteens, and a bedroll in case the weather blew in and they had to spend a night under a tree. Here, with nothing to do, he forgot all the small rules of survival. A mistake he knew could hurt him. There was always a chance the horse would slip or a snow storm would blow in and he would not be able to make it back. He knew of several cowboys who had been found days after leaving headquarters unprepared. They were frozen solid as a rock and had to be tied onto a saddle like a stick of wood. Rodney thought of several Jack London stories he had read as a boy and shivered at his stupidity.

When Rodney got to the hole in the fence, he wished Banjo was there, but there were only the sheep scattered along the river. Rodney drove the sheep back through the hole and fixed the fence.

Rodney heard the engines of the airplane kick over. Soon he heard them rev and the plane start down the runway. The plane rose up over the hill and climbed quickly for altitude and flew straight west. Rodney felt like a dark gloom was leaving the ranch.

The sun was about to set when Rodney rode by Karen's house. Karen was outside, dressed in Levi's and a red and black wool shirt, shaking out a blanket. She had on a pair of cowboy boots and her hair was braided. Rodney stopped the horse and watched her until she noticed him. "I got a friend who used to work here," Rodney said. "He told me about this real good looking woman who was a painter. Seems she liked to paint in the nude and was partial to cowboys. I was wondering if that woman might be you and if you were busy tonight?"

"That friend of yours say the woman was easy?" Karen asked.

"No, he said the woman was caring and loving and wished he could have stayed around," Rodney said.

"Did he tell you that I loved him but that he would never sleep with me," Karen asked.

"He said he would have liked to have slept with you more than anything in the world but he didn't want to unless he was positive he loved you."

"Did he ever say if he loved me?" Karen asked.

"I could tell he did," Rodney said.

"You're probably like him," Karen said. "If I happened, by chance, to not be doing anything this evening, and then by chance happened to fall for you like I did that no good cowboy, you'd be gone with the sunset just like he was."

"Well, ma'am," Rodney said. "I wouldn't want to lie to you, but I also wouldn't want to miss the opportunity of getting to know you either. But you're right, the sun sometimes seems to beckon me and I have to follow it."

"Well, in that case, stranger, I've always had a soft spot in my heart for no account, drifting cowboys so why don't you amble over tonight."

Rodney tipped his hat. "Why thank you," he said. "About an hour or so," and he started to ride toward the barn, which was now covered with a dark purple shadow.

"By the way, stranger," Karen called after him. "Take a bath, this lady doesn't like cowboys who don't bathe."

"I'll sparkle like a baby," Rodney called back.

Karen thought of a sequel to her painting. In the new one, the cowboy would be riding into the darkness, where one could only see the vague outline of him and his horse. In the distance, in a small clearing of trees would be a small fire illuminating a woman, standing with her arms folded across her breasts, gazing into the flame. It would symbolize woman's vigil, her inner strength, and the endless wait and worry over her man.

After showering, Rodney shaved and put on his favorite shirt and good boots. The dark cloud that had been his companion for the last two days was gone, replaced by a feeling of good will and contentment. At the moment, he did not wonder how long the contentment would last. Mr. Cook had probably flown off in his rage to Phoenix, but Rodney had a feeling Mr. Cook was not done with Banjo.

Rodney took special care in combing his hair and splashed on a little extra Old Spice.

Rodney knocked on Karen's door and she answered it and looked at him coyly. She was dressed in a long Levi skirt and a dark blue turtle neck sweater. "At least you knock," she said. "That bum that rode away used to just barge in."

"My friend didn't lie to me," Rodney said. "You're beautiful."

"Flattery will get you everywhere," Karen said and gave Rodney a quizzical look. "And by the way, what is your name?"

"Buck," Rodney answered. "Just call me Buck."

"I suppose you have a deep, dark past," Karen said.

"About as dark as campfire coffee," Rodney said.

"Well Buck, come on in."

Karen had candles lit in the living room, a bottle of wine and two glasses set on a tablecloth on the floor. Two large, overstuffed pillows were by the tablecloth. Rodney sat down slowly, grunting as he did so. "This being a cowboy is getting me old," he explained. "If I was a banker, I could sit in my hot tub each night and think about all the houses and cars I'd repossessed during day and my bones wouldn't hurt."

"You'd dream about riding horses and breaking your bones and being cold," Karen said, pouring the wine.

Karen turned on the radio to a country FM station and sat down.

"I always knew your friend would leave, Buck. I think he liked me more than a lot of women he had been with. But, I guess, I was like all the rest. They couldn't tame that spirit of his. He'd been lonely so long, it was just a part of him. A price he had to pay to be free," Karen said.

"I don't know, I think a man reaches an age where he's tired of being lonely. Having a lady and a home to come back to might be worth losing that freedom. A right partner and there could possibly be more freedom in life than a person alone would ever know."

Karen knew she could spend the rest of her life with Rodney. He could go away for as long as he wanted and she would still love him. He could go away and never write and there would always be a place in her heart for him. She had known him for such a short time to feel like she had always known him. All her life, he had been out there somewhere. A soft breeze with the evening, a cool rain during the summer.

Rodney looked down at his glass of wine and seemed to fall into deep thought. He looked up at Karen and smiled faintly, "I guess I shouldn't tell you this. It might ruin my chances and all. But old Rodney, before he took off for parts unknown, told me he thought he was in love with you. He said you filled a void in his life that had never been filled. I promised him I would never tell you, but I feel like I should. When a person is special to someone, they should know."

Karen felt like the world had stopped. She finally had heard the words she had wanted to hear. Although she knew he still might ride away into the sunset, at least he had let her know her feelings were not hers alone. She leaned over the tablecloth, picked up Rodney's hand and kissed it tenderly. "Thanks for telling me, Buck," she said. "That damn Rodney never was one to talk much."

"Lady," Rodney answered. "I didn't get my name Buck from riding horses or talking."

Karen laughed.

To Rodney, her laughter was the most beautiful thing in the world.

Nineteen

*N*ow, where ever Banjo went he took his 30/30 with him with a bullet in the chamber. Although it was dangerous all he had to do to fire was pull back the hammer and squeeze the trigger.

Angelena was afraid over Banjo's behavior but there was nothing she could really do. She thought about sneaking into his room when he was asleep and taking the rifle, but, she could not force herself to go against the will of her husband. So she prayed. She prayed off and on all day—small prayers her husband would come to his senses. She also prayed no men would come to tell them they must leave the land. She knew her husband would shoot at them and probably be killed. The land was not as important to her as to Banjo. To her, man's only fate rest in the heavens. The land was only a place where man lived out his life. A place where God's beauty could be seen and his will reasoned out. But Angelena knew, to Banjo, this parcel of land was everything.

Angelena was preparing for winter by putting clear plastic over the inside of the windows when she saw Banjo go into the barn. He had his 30/30 in one hand and he reminded her of one of Pancho Villa's soldiers.

Banjo set the 30/30 in the corner and drank a shot of whiskey. He had not been coughing and his chest did not hurt but he was having bad headaches. Tossing the sheep hides off the box of dynamite, Banjo took out one stick and cut a fuse. He hid the whiskey and the dynamite under his jacket so Angelena would not see them.

Banjo picked up his rifle and walked west away from the house. Not more than five hundred yards from the house was an old Indian camp site. When Banjo was a child, he would go and sift the dirt for arrowheads and pieces of pottery. Somewhere in the house, he had a box of shell beads he had found while sifting the dirt. He learned that Indians from California, long before the white man came to New Mexico, had traded shells for obsidian with the Indians of New Mexico.

"What a journey it must have been," Banjo said. "The land would have been teaming with game and danger."

Angelena watched Banjo and he seemed frail. She knew Banjo had not been feeling well lately, although Banjo never said anything to her, she could still tell he was not himself.

After going only a hundred yards from the house Banjo sat down on a rock and wiped the perspiration off of his face with the back of his sleeve. He reached for his tobacco, but did not take it out of his pocket, his hands were shaking too much to roll a smoke.

After a few minutes, he stood up woozily and continued walking. He reached the Indian site and sat down on what had been the outside rock wall, but was now no more than two feet tall. A large cedar tree grew between the walls. He propped his 30/30 against the wall. Once, as a boy, he had spent the night here and during the night he had felt like many eyes were watching him—eyes that looked into his soul and his heart. He had run home and never spent the night here again. To this day, he never visited the site at night. Even though he did not believe in ghosts, the Indians did, and because they did, there might be Indian ghosts—ghosts that did not like Mexicans.

Banjo pulled the bottle of whiskey out of his coat and took a large swallow. The whiskey made his eyes water, but the burn in his mouth and throat felt good. He took another large swallow. Raising the bottle to the air, he toasted the sky and took another swig before corking the bottle and setting it by his feet. The whiskey made him feel better and he stood up and walked around, looking at the ground for arrowheads.

Each season, there would be more pieces of obsidian and pottery shards uncovered by the wind and the snow. It had been years since he had looked for arrowheads. He always seemed to be too busy after he grew up. But now he wondered what could have been so important that he had not taken the time to do something he enjoyed?

Finding nothing, Banjo sat down. He picked up the bottle and held it in both hands. The swallows of whiskey made him feel mellow and he started to reminisce. As a boy, for the few years he did go to school, he liked the stories his teacher told him of the battles during the Civil War. The stories of men charging each other, with no fear of death—men pushed past endurance who still fought on. He did not like the reason the south fought the war. No man should be a slave, unless to himself. But he did sympathize with the southern man whose way of life was taken from him.

With both hands Banjo lifted the bottle of whiskey to his lips and drank deeply. Setting the bottle on the ground, he thought back to his sheep stealing raids. They had not stolen the sheep out of malice or greed. They stole the sheep because they were poor and needed the sheep. And they never stole all of a man's sheep, only a few from many flocks. Now, there were companies who stole millions and millions of dollars after they already had millions and millions of dollars. There were people who went hungry, while governments developed bigger and bigger planes and bombs and ships. "Enemies are but a part of life," Banjo said to the whiskey bottle. "No man can escape them. They seem to come out of the rocks and make one always spend his life on guard and fearful."

He stood up and looked at the crumbled Indian ruin and tried to visualize the family. A man would be chipping out an arrowhead while his wife ground corn. Children would have been running around half naked playing games. But even these people were afraid. Afraid of other Indians who raided them. Afraid of hunger or no rain. Fear was the driving force of all people and love was the dream.

"My Angelena," Banjo cried out, "our house will turn to dust and all the sweat and toil of our forefathers and ours will be like this ruin, only a mystery, only a crumbling wall with trees growing where we once lived."

Banjo walked away from the ruin, leaving his rifle and bottle by the wall. He put the stick of dynamite into a hole in a dead pinon tree and attached the fuse. Taking a stick match out of his pocket, he lit it and held the flame to the fuse. For a few seconds, nothing happened and then the fuse began to burn and Banjo ran as fast as he could and hid behind the rock wall. He lay with his hands over his ears and his eyes tightly closed waiting for the explosion but nothing happened and he felt depressed. The dynamite was no good and it was now impossible to buy dynamite without proper papers.

As Banjo started to get up the dynamite exploded. Pieces of branches and rotten stump flew around him and several hit the whiskey bottle hard enough to make the glass ring. Banjo jumped up and started to do a jig next to the cedar tree. "Gringo bastard," he hollered and laughed, "gringo bastard."

Angelena heard the boom and ran from the house. Looking west, she saw an off white cloud of dust. "Dear Mother of God," she cried, "What is that old fool up to now?"

She feared Banjo was lying in tiny pieces all over the ground and hurried toward the settling dust cloud. After hurrying a little over a hundred yards, she met Banjo. He had a look of deep satisfaction on his face. Angelena, relieved to see him, felt like hugging him but seeing the whiskey bottle she did not. Banjo tried to cover the whiskey bottle with his coat, but it was too late. "Only a little," he mumbled.

Angelena could smell his breath. "A little too much," she said taking the bottle from him.

They walked back toward the house. Banjo reached over and took her hand in his. "If there is a heaven, I wonder if God would let me stay in a place with you that had no gringos?" Banjo said.

"How about your friend, the cowboy from the ranch?" Angelena asked.

Banjo's face screwed up in deep thought and then, smiling a twisted grin, he said. "Rodney must have some Mexican blood in his veins, he is too nice of a man to be all white."

"My husband," Angelena said. "We are but a spot on this land and you try to make of it a battle. You must accept what is and continue to live."

Banjo snorted in contempt of her statement, but his voice was filled with love as he answered, "Yes, my dear Angelena, we are but a spot, but we are life, and life must fight, even if it is just a spot."

Stepping up onto the front porch, Banjo let go of Angelena's hand. Turning away from the porch, he looked in the direction of the Last Day In Paradise. He would have to go on a scouting mission, sneak over to the ranch at night. After dinner, he would go. But first, he would have his fill of tortillas and coffee.

Angelena looked at the far away look in Banjo's eyes and sadly shook her head and decided she did not want to know why he was blowing up dynamite. After putting the whiskey in her room she stirred a pot of beans. "My poor mother, who sits with the angels," she thought, "You always told me a woman needs a good man. But would not life be much easier without men?"

Banjo was sitting at the table fidgeting with a spoon. Angelena brought him a cup of coffee and a tortilla and watched how his eyes lit up. Back at her stove she stirred the beans once again and brought the steaming pot over to the table and sat down. Looking at Banjo greedily scooping the beans out of his bowl and putting them onto his tortilla, she could not help but smile.

Banjo, feeling her gaze on him, looked up to see her smiling. "Why do you smile?" Banjo said.

"Because of you," Angelena replied.

"Why me?" Banjo said, spilling a few beans on the table.

"I don't know," Angelena answered truthfully. "I really don't know."

Banjo took a large bite out of his bean burrito and chewed vigorously. "The beans are good," he said.

After dinner, Banjo wanted to sit out on the porch and smoke, but the air was too chilly to be comfortable so he went to his bedroom and sat in his chair. He was trying to figure out where the movie site was being constructed.

He knew it must be close to the headquarters because he had seen the vehicles. Banjo felt tired but was determined to sneak onto the ranch—tired or not. The main problem that confronted him was Angelena. He could not tell her what he was up to, although she had made no mention of him blowing up a stick of dynamite. She was a tolerant woman, but telling her he wanted to blow up the movie site would be more than she could stand. So, he did not know what to say. He had never been a good liar. A good stretcher of the truth, yes, but not a good liar. When he did try to lie to Angelena she knew even before the words were out of his mouth that he was lying.

As the darkness filled his room, Banjo went back into the kitchen. He put on his warm coat and picked up his new lined gloves and the 30/30. He wished Angelena had not seen the whiskey bottle because he would have taken it too.

Angelena watched him putting on his clothes, making Banjo feel like a rabbit being circled by a hawk and there was no brush to hide in for hundreds of yards. He started to speak, but Angelena waved her hand at him. "I don't even want to know," she said. "Then, when the police come, I can tell them the truth, that I know nothing and my husband is another stupid man whose pride far outweighs his reason."

Banjo put on the large black cowboy hat and set it low on his head. As he started to walk out of the door, Angelena said to him, "Wait," and walked to her room and returned with a grey wool scarf she had knitted which she wrapped around his throat. Banjo patted her gently on the shoulder.

There was no moon in the sky and Banjo felt like going back and getting his flashlight, but he decided against the idea as a light might draw attention. In the old days, he had the best night vision of any man he knew and figured he could ride safely through the gullies on the ranch.

The horse, not used to being bothered at night, bolted when Banjo walked up to her, but recognizing him, settled down. Banjo had difficulty saddling the horse in the dark and still more difficulty making the horse take the bit. "You stubborn glob of glue," Banjo moaned. "You eat my food and when it is time to earn your keep, you protest."

Banjo rode away from the house but not before tying four gunny sacks to his saddle. Banjo rode toward the new fence but closer to where it ended at his fence. When he got to the fence he cut the wires. Banjo had heard how Butch Cassidy had always been able to outrun the law because he kept fresh horses in gullies and cut any fences that might hinder his escape.

As he rode, he looked at the stars. "See, it is safe," Banjo said to the horse. "The stars shine and are happy and the moon does not come out to throw shadows that would send you galloping off into some deep gully or ravine."

The old horse seemed to be enjoying herself after the tussle to be bridled and saddled. She seemed to feel the excitement that Banjo felt.

Banjo crested a hill, stopped the horse by a pinon tree and saw the lights from the ranch headquarters about half mile away. He could make out the dim outline of a large house but noticed that, where the brick home was, there were no lights on. Only the adobe had lights on. "Ah, Rodney," he said. "You find the woman to your liking. Good. A man in love is never conscious of what is going on around him."

Banjo decided to skirt the ranch houses to the north and cut back to the south, then he hoped to stumble onto the movie site.

When Banjo drew even with the houses, he could hear music faintly coming from the adobe. Riding by, he had the urge to go over and knock on the door and have a drink with Rodney and Karen. When Karen had come over with Rodney, she was so caring for his wife, that he wished he could get to know her. Even though it was disconcerting to Banjo that he had met two white people that he liked.

Banjo rode by the houses as planned and then stopped, dismounted, and taking the gunny sacks from the saddle, slit each one and doubled them over and wrapped them around the horse's hooves. It was a trick he had seen in a western movie when he was in Albuquerque. When Banjo started to ride again, he could hear no sound whatsoever coming from the horse's hooves as they struck the ground, although the horse picked his feet up too sharply like a man who had gum on his boots. "It works only in the movies," he said in disgust.

Banjo had ridden for twenty minutes when, off to his right, he heard voices. He turned toward the voices and he soon saw the ghostly shadow of a town. Banjo felt like a bandit who, with the morning sun, would ride into town with his guns blazing and rob the bank—escaping back to the hills through a hail of bullets. He would then make his way back to Mexico, artfully dodging the posse and every attempt at his capture. "Life was life then, my friend," Banjo said to the horse. "There were places to run."

The horse shook its head up and down and tried to bite at the sacks on its front hooves. Banjo saw a light shining above a small trailer not far from the town and several men standing outside. There seemed to be no other activity, but Banjo saw a man with a dog on a leash approach the two other men. All three of the men wore pistols. Banjo had not expected guards, but he supposed the movie people did not want to take any chances. This was still the west and one could not be too careful.

Banjo nudged the horse and rode in a large circle around the town, staying behind rocks and trees as much as possible. If the moon had been out, Banjo knew the men could have spotted him. But halfway around the town, the three men went inside the trailer. Banjo tied his horse to a tree and walked to the back of the town. Keeping in the shadows of the town, he went from building to building counting as he went. Finished, he started to walk back to his horse when a loud voice rang out, "Stop, who goes there? This is private property."

Banjo started to run as fast as he could. But he fell twice before getting to the horse. He was so out of breath he barely managed to get into the saddle. Behind him, he could hear men shouting and a dog barking. He kicked his horse and sensing the danger she broke into a gallop. When he was well away from the movie set, he stopped the horse and could hear nobody pursuing him. "You are a true bandit's horse," he said and patted the horses neck.

Banjo rode around the Last Day In Paradise headquarters. The light was still on in the adobe, but he could not hear any music. "If you are smart, my cowboy friend, you are in her bed and not yours," he said.

He knew the men at the movie site would report there had been an intruder, but he figured they would think it was only kids from Galisteo and would not be alarmed.

Banjo felt more alive than he had in years. The excitement, the chase, the stars overhead, and the horse breathing deeply all blended into his goodwill. "I wish Sanchez was alive, and Lupe, and Ernest. We could give them a show then," Banjo said.

When they were alive, they had always drank together and in times of too much alcohol, they had planned many daring robberies and escapades that would have enabled them to break away from being poor. But, always with the dawn, they had gone back to their small ranches and eked out a living.

Angelena was reading in bed when Banjo got home. She had kept the fire stoked and had wrapped a tortilla in tin foil and kept it in the oven in case he was hungry. "There is food," she called to her husband, not asking him what no good he had been up to.

Banjo took off his jacket and scarf and set the 30/30 in the corner. He piled honey on the tortilla and ate it in large bites. When he was done, he went into his room and sat down and planned. He would need all the sticks of dynamite and a very long fuse system where he could light one and it would, in turn, light all the other fuses. The dynamite would go off in a series, much like an artillery salvo.

Feeling confident Banjo rolled a cigarette, after dodging the flame, Banjo took several deep drags and coughed, which caused his side to hurt and lungs to feel like they were being pierced by tiny sharp splinters of glass. But he continued to smoke the cigarette, only making his puffs smaller.

After finishing the cigarette, Banjo butted it and set it on the window sill and pulled off his boots. He set his boots in the corner and admired them. He realized he still had on his hat and set it by the boots. "I wish my old friends could see my boots," he thought, "and the hat. They would connive to try and get such boots for themselves."

Banjo turned out the light. Lying down, he gazed into the darkness of the ceiling, he could see bright flashes and huge billowing clouds of dirt and rock filled with flying chunks of wood and glass. "It will be better than the fourth of July. Better than the fireworks when we beat the Germans," Banjo said out loud. "Better than the Alamo."

🐂 🐂 🐂

The airplane buzzed the ranch houses and Rodney drove to the airstrip. The last two days had been peaceful without Mr. Cook around. It was as though Rodney was the owner of the ranch. He had cleaned out the big Quonset hut and checked out the movie site several times. All the buildings were up and the crew was doing the final polishing jobs. A worker had told him, the next thing to do was haul in the trailers for the stars and the makeup people and get the food tent set up for the extras. The movie would then be set to roll. The crew treated Rodney with respect after they found out he was going to play one of the bandit leaders in the movie and was the foreman of the ranch. "Hell, son," one of the men told him. "People in L.A. would kill to get a part like you got that gave them a credit, and you're not even an actor."

Mr. Cook shut off the engines to the plane and quickly got into the truck. "I'm late," he informed Rodney. "Have to be in town and meet some movie people and head back to Phoenix right away."

When they got to the houses, Mr. Cook went directly to the Suburban and drove away.

The last two days with Karen had been quiet and comfortable. Karen mentioned Angelena several times and how she wished to go see her again. Rodney had promised her he would take her over today. Rodney had asked to see her painting, but Karen made a face at him and told him flatly, "No, not until it is done."

Rodney did not pursue the matter, although once, when she was in the bathroom, he felt like lifting up the sheet she kept draped over the painting and taking a glance. But he knew, if it was his painting, he would not like somebody looking at it before it was done. He thought maybe it was the fear of rejection that made artists so touchy.

During the ride to Banjo's, Karen was silent and sat looking out the window. Rodney wanted to know how Banjo had raised the money for his taxes and wanted to sit down with Banjo and figure out a way Banjo could cut the fence on certain days, so Rodney would know when to fix it.

When Rodney and Karen arrived at Banjo's, Angelena was washing the laundry in a large wash tub. "Oh, Rodney," Karen said getting out of the truck, "that poor woman."

"She doesn't know she's poor," Rodney managed to say before Karen was hurrying to Angelena, who stopped scrubbing the laundry and was drying her hands on her apron.

Rodney, standing by the truck, did not see Banjo. But the horse was in the corral so he figured he was not out with the sheep.

Banjo was in the shed, sorting his dynamite and connecting the fuses. He was trying to arrange the fuses so he could get the effect he wanted. Hearing the truck stop, he picked up his 30/30, and peeked through a large crack in the wall, fearful it would be the sheriff with papers to evict him from this land. If it was, he would shoot the sheriff first and then whoever else was in the car, hopefully Mr. Cook. But seeing Rodney, he walked out of the barn holding the 30/30.

"Gringo," Banjo said. "Sorry to say it is good to see you."

To Rodney's surprise Banjo stuck out his hand to shake.

"I just came over to say how happy I am you were able to raise the money to pay your taxes," Rodney said.

"What?" Banjo asked looking bewildered.

"The taxes, how did you raise the money?" Rodney repeated slowly.

"I have not paid the taxes," Banjo said, confused. "I have not done anything."

Rodney looked quickly over toward Karen who had taken off her jacket, rolled up her sleeves and was rubbing clothes against the scrub board. "You little vixen," he thought to himself. "You sneaky, wonderful lady."

"I don't know how it happened Banjo, but Mr. Cook came back to the ranch a few days ago ranting and raving somebody had paid the taxes so he couldn't grab your land."

Banjo took off his hat, looked at the top of it and rubbed his chin. "I'll be damned," he said. "I wonder if it was my son?"

Banjo started to walk toward the house quickly. "Follow me gringo," he said. "This calls for a shot of whiskey."

Banjo felt Angelena's eyes boring into the back of his head. Inside the door, Banjo started looking everywhere Angelena might have hidden the whiskey. Rodney watched the old man ferret around, wondering what he was doing, but saying nothing. Coming out of Angelena's bedroom, Banjo had a mischievous grin on his face and was clutching the half-empty bottle. "She hid it in her closet, I didn't think I would find it. But I found it."

Banjo took a quick swallow and handed the bottle to Rodney who tipped it back and took a swallow. Banjo took another swallow, corked the bottle and hid it once more in the closet. Both men sat down at the table. "This is a strange thing," Banjo said. "My son might have a little money, but I know he does not have $15,000. I know you do not have any money. There is nobody who could have done such a thing."

"Whoever it was Mr. Cook is shot out of the saddle," Rodney said.

"It is a mystery," Banjo said. "But I would like to meet the person who did it. I owe them many thanks."

"Maybe they don't want any thanks," Rodney said.

"Even with the good news you brought me I have to tell you that one smart sheep has cut the fence again," Banjo said.

"I figured as much and thought I would go out tomorrow and fix it," Rodney said.

Karen and Angelena walked into the house.

"Rodney came over to congratulate us on being able to pay our taxes on the land," Banjo told Angelena.

Angelena gasped at the news. She started to speak but Banjo cut her off. "I told him we did not pay them. Whoever it was I do not know."

Angelena clasped her hands in front of her like she was praying and Rodney and Karen could see the relief she felt. They did not know it was relief for her husband and not herself.

Angelena served everybody a cup of coffee and they talked about the sheep and the weather and how hard it was to find wood anymore. Finished with the coffee, Rodney and Karen excused themselves. Banjo and Angelena followed them to the truck.

"Whoever paid the taxes, I wonder if they would also buy us a vehicle like that," Banjo said to Rodney, admiring the truck. Angelena elbowed him in the ribs.

Angelena waved at Karen as Rodney drove away.

"That's a hell of a thing you did, Karen," Rodney said.

"What?" Karen said.

"Paid Banjo's taxes," he said.

"I don't know what you're talking about Rodney," Karen replied.

Rodney looked at her and knew, no matter what he said or did, she would never admit to it, so he reached over and patted her on the knee.

"That's how you pat a horse, isn't it?" Karen said.

"Never thought about it, but I guess so," Rodney replied.

Karen smiled, "Maybe I'm gaining some ground if you treat me like a horse."

Banjo watched Karen and Rodney drive away and then looked at his wife. "Did you pay the taxes?" he asked, but immediately knew how stupid his question was.

They both walked into the house and sat down at the table. "Why don't you get the bottle of whiskey and we can both have a shot to celebrate?" Angelena said.

Banjo, not thinking, walked to her room and brought out the bottle. Angelena smiled at him and poured a small shot of whiskey into her coffee cup and poured Banjo an even smaller one. As he watched her pour, he made a sour face. "If you had not already had some with Rodney, I would give you more," Angelena said.

They smiled at each other and drank the whiskey. Angelena took the bottle and put it by the stove. "I will have to hide this again," she said.

"Who paid our taxes?" Banjo asked.

"I don't know," Angelena answered. "But whoever it was, bless them."

Twenty

*M*r. Cook did not think about the movie while flying to Phoenix. He thought about Banjo. He did not know who had paid Banjo's taxes, or how Banjo had discovered they needed to be paid? He had ruled out Rodney, Rodney was a drifting cowboy who did not have enough money to fill his pockets. It was a puzzle Mr. Cook knew he would never answer, but he made up his mind he must take drastic action to get Banjo's land—the old Mexican had to go. Mr. Cook did not take defeat lightly.

Mr. Cook parked his Mercedes in the large driveway to his sprawling southwestern styled home. The Bentley was gone so he knew Gloria was not home. The maid greeted him at the door, but Mr. Cook walked by her like she was not there and went to his office.

His office was immaculate—decorated with original western art and bronze sculptures that really meant nothing to him unless somebody was in the office to admire them. Mr. Cook opened a wall safe and took out a leather bound address book. He jotted down two numbers on a scratch pad and returned the book to the safe. Mixing himself a Tanquera and tonic from the wet bar, he sat in his leather chair and drummed his fingers on his desk. "You Mexican bastard, now I will have you," he said. "The game is over and you will lose."

Mr. Cook was still in his office when Gloria came home. Gloria, looking beautiful as ever, hugged him. Sensing he was in a bad mood she stepped back.

"There's no need to beat around the bush," Mr. Cook said. "My lawyers are going to file for divorce. You will get this house, the condo, the Bentley and some money. Don't try for anymore or you won't be around to enjoy it."

Gloria smiled faintly and walked out of the office. "Not bad, girl, not bad," she said on the way to her room.

Mr. Cook made himself another Tanquera and tonic, drank it in two swallows and put the paper with the two phone numbers in his pocket. He wanted to get his business out of the way. Then he would come home and take a shower and call a flight attendant from American West Airlines that he had met.

Gloria was walking from the master bedroom toward the pool in a very skimpy white bikini and crossed paths with Mr. Cook. She smiled warmly at him and he smiled back.

"We are both rattlesnakes," he said.

"I know," Gloria said. "The only difference between you and me is that I don't strike to kill."

Mr. Cook laughed a deep, boisterous laugh.

Gloria sunbathed by the pool. Now she could lead the life she wanted. There would be no parties with rich, boring men, who only talked about what they owned. No more dodging lecherous hands. No more going to that God forsaken ranch. First, she decided, she would take a six month cruise around the world. She day dreamed about meeting a European man—a dream she could now pursue.

Mr. Cook went to a pay phone in front of a Baskin Robbins Ice Cream store. After dialing, he waited for the beep to the paging machine. He recorded the pay phone number on the machine and hung up and waited less than a minute before the pay phone rang.

"This is James. "I'd like to see somebody in thirty minutes," Mr. Cook said.

"Thirty minutes," the voice answered. "The usual."

The one thing his silent partners understood was efficiency. In many ways, their business dealings were far easier than the normal, above board, cut throat business. At least with them Mr. Cook knew where he stood. In legal business he never knew who was about to try and cut his throat.

Mr. Cook went to a Mexican food restaurant on 17th street. Sitting in a corner booth, lit by a candle even during the day, he ordered another Tanquera and tonic and nachos. He was getting hungry, but he did not want to ruin the good meal he planned to impress the stewardess with. Fine wine and two hundred dollar dinners had a way of convincing young women to be friendly.

Mr. Cook did not have to wait long before a man in a light blue summer suit walked into the restaurant and came and sat down at the table. He did not bother to shake hands or be overly friendly. "The boss sends his regards," the man said motioning for the waitress to come over. "Ice tea please," he ordered.

"What is it you need, Mr. Cook?" the man asked, flicking an imaginary piece of lint off of his suit.

"I need two men to come to New Mexico. There is a certain person who had to be convinced to sell his land to me."

"When?" the man asked.

"Two days. They can drive to Santa Fe and I will meet them at the Hilton Hotel. Have them register under the name Mr. Sampson."

A few minutes later, after Mr. Cook had explained what was going on, the man stood up. "No problem, when the work is done you can contact me again for the fee," he said.

Mr. Cook watched the man walk away and smiled to himself. The waitress came over. "Bring me another drink and the ticket," he told her.

Mr. Cook, seeing a pay phone in the corner, called the stewardess. He felt good. Better than he had in weeks. He would have an enjoyable two days before he went back to Santa Fe.

🐃 🐃 🐃

Mr. Cook parked the truck in the parking lot to the Bull Ring Bar in downtown Santa Fe and went into the lobby. He went to the pay phone and called the Hilton Hotel. The girl who answered the phone sounded like she had been eating and was trying to swallow a bite of sandwich and speak at the same time. "Mr. Sampson's room," Mr. Cook told the girl.

The phone rang twice before it was answered. "Mr. Sampson," a congenial voice answered.

"This is James I'll meet you in the bar in ten minutes."

"OKAY," the man said and hung up.

Mr. Cook quickly walked the three blocks to the Hilton. The bar was filled with people, who Mr. Cook did not realize, were connected with the movie that was going to be filmed on his ranch. He sat at a table by the fireplace and looked nervously around the room. He did not know the man he would meet, but he was sure the man's boss had described him. A young waitress wearing a long, Mexican styled dress, with a blouse that left her shoulders exposed, came over. She seemed bored and out of sorts and spoke with no emotion, "Your order sir?"

"A martini, dry, with olives and a chilled glass," Mr. Cook replied in a demeaning voice.

The waitress gave him a snide look and walked away, scribbling on her order pad.

Mr. Cook was looking into the fire when two men dressed in Levi's, boots, and western shirts stopped by the table. Both men were in their forties and could have been undercover cops. "James," the man nearest to him said.

Mr. Cook, not one to stand up for many men, stood and motioned for the two men to sit down. The men sat down and looked around the bar as though expecting trouble at any minute.

"Let's just say my name is Bob and this is Barney," the man who spoke first said.

Barney nodded his head at Mr. Cook but said nothing. Mr. Cook noticed the man's eyes were lifeless and a creepy feeling spread over his body. The waitress came back with Mr. Cook's martini and waited for the two men to order. "I'd like some coffee," Bob said.

"A draw," Barney said.

Mr. Cook did not pick up his drink until the waitress brought the coffee and the beer back to the table. "You seem to have a problem," Bob said. "All you have to do is tell us how to get to the man's house. Our mutual friend has explained the problem."

"The man's name is Banjo Ortega," Mr. Cook said. "He lives in a run down adobe with his wife. I should tell you guys he is an old Mexican cowboy and you should be careful."

Bob laughed and sipped his coffee. "You let us worry about Mr. Banjo Ortega."

Mr. Cook explained to the men how to get to Banjo's house. "I don't want him killed unless it's necessary," Mr. Cook told them.

Both men stood up at the same time as if they had not heard his last comment. "It's been nice meeting you, James," Bob said. "I'm sure your problems will be solved in a way that will be satisfactory to you and our mutual friend."

Mr. Cook watched the two men walk away and was glad they were gone. He put a ten dollar bill on the table and walked out of the bar, wishing he had the exact change for the bill since the waitress did not deserve a tip.

It was getting close to five and Mr. Cook decided to stop at Marie's for some Mexican food before going back to the ranch. He was not the best of cooks and he really doubted if there was anything besides booze at the ranch anyway. Gloria had never been one to slave over a stove. She might slave over her fingernails and makeup, but she had never excelled at cooking.

Eating, Mr. Cook thought about Banjo. The poor bastard did not know what he had started. It would have been so much easier if whoever had bailed him out of his taxes had stayed the hell out and then none of this would have had to happen.

Driving to the ranch, Mr. Cook thought about Karen. He wondered if Karen would go out with him? He knew she dated Rodney but what the hell was Rodney but some over the hill cow jockey with no potential to be anything. He made up his mind to go see her in the morning. There would be some good parties, once the movie started, and she would make a pretty lady for him to take to the parties. Every lady he had ever known was sucker for a big party with all the right people. It was not until Mr. Cook was almost to his house that he thought about Karen's car. "I wonder how she can afford that Cadillac?" he pondered.

Walking into his house Mr. Cook looked over at Karen's house and remembered seeing her naked through her window. The thought of Karen and the thought of Banjo getting his due made Mr. Cook feel good and he decided to take a Jacuzzi and have a few drinks before going to bed. Things were looking up.

Bob and Barney were in their room drinking and cleaning their nine millimeter pistols. Neither one of them had really discussed their plan. It did not seem all that difficult after all the men they had jacked up in their careers as collectors and strong arm men. What could an old Mexican man possibly do to two tough guys in their prime? Barney took a vial of coke out of his pocket and took a snort through a silver straw. He held the vial out to Bob.

"Nah," Bob said. "I want some sleep. Hopefully we can scare the hell out of this old man in a day or so and get the hell out of here."

Barney put the top back on the coke bottle and lay down on the bed. He felt like he was in the Army again—biding time waiting for the action. This time, little action.

Rodney did not enjoy getting up in the morning since he knew he would have to talk to Mr. Cook. As he drank his coffee, Mr. Cook stuck his head in the door. "You'd better go check the fence, Rodney," he said, sounding friendly. "I forgot to see if the sheep were on the place, but I bet they are."

"Sure thing, Mr. Cook," Rodney answered, glad Mr. Cook was on his way.

Rodney scrambled two eggs and ate a half a can of pork and beans with them before going to the stable. Karen was in the kitchen as he passed and he waved at her, but she did not see him.

After saddling the horse, Rodney rode to his house, went in and put on a set of long underwear as the day was cold and by the clouds, there could be a storm. Rodney stuck a few matches in his pocket and got his scarf.

Riding away from the house, Karen, still in the kitchen, saw him this time and waved. Rodney tipped his hat to her and trotted off. Karen, watching him in his coat and hat and flopping scarf, smiled and said, "You'd make a good Marlboro man."

By the time Rodney got to the crest of the hill that overlooked the fence, a cold, stiff, northern wind was blowing and the clouds were building up on the mountains. He knew it was snowing in the high country and he had no doubt it would be here before the day was over. The cold wind exhilarated the horse and made Rodney alert. The first real snow would be good. The second, not so good, and anything after that, a pain.

As he rode closer to the spot where Banjo always cut the fence, he noticed the sheep were farther away than usual. He would have to talk to Banjo and maybe Banjo could pick out another place to cut the fence so the sheep would not have to be driven as far.

Rodney stopped the horse by the hole. A rock sliding down from Banjo's side of the fence made him jump slightly. Looking up, he saw Banjo riding toward him wearing a large, fleece lined, leather coat, and his hat and new gloves. "You must be psychic," Rodney said as he rode up to him. "You and I have met here twice."

"What does psychic mean?" Banjo asked.

Rodney thought for a moment and could not figure out how to explain what the word meant so he said, "It means strange things happen."

"Oh," Banjo said. "It must be a white man's word."

"It's going to snow," Rodney said.

"Big snow," Banjo said. "I can feel it. Could be one of those that keeps people snowed in a few days. Bet you wouldn't mind that with your pretty girlfriend living right next door."

Rodney liked the idea of sitting in front of a fire with Karen for a few days.

"My son was conceived during a snowstorm," Banjo said proudly.

"More than one of us was conceived during a snowstorm," Rodney said.

Banjo looked in the distance to where his sheep were. "Maybe that smart sheep I have will make a new hole. A hole closer to where the grass is taller."

"I was hoping to find him and tell him that," Rodney said.

"He knows," Banjo smiled. "He is psychic."

Rodney looked at Banjo and started to speak, but Banjo was already riding toward the sheep. Rodney shook his head in disbelief and kicked his horse into a trot to catch up.

By the time Banjo and Rodney had the sheep moving in a group back toward the hole in the fence, the sky was a dull grey and snow was falling in quarter size flakes. When the sheep were once again back on Banjo's land, Rodney started to fix the fence.

Banjo, not dismounting, watched him intently and then said, "One day they will have robots to do work like this. A cowboy will sit in a room with a big screen and push buttons and everything will be done for him. The only thing it will take to be a cowboy is to have a pair of boots and a hat and a Master's degree."

"They will be dumb robots," Rodney said.

Banjo wiped the accumulating snow off of his horse's neck. Removing his gloves, he reached into his coat pocket and took out his tobacco and papers and rolled a cigarette under the brim of his hat. Lighting the cigarette, Rodney noticed the flame shooting out of the end of the cigarette was small.

"You're getting better at rolling your smokes," Rodney said.

"It is the hat. I do not want to catch it on fire," Banjo said.

"Nice things have a way of changing a person," Rodney said.

Banjo took a deep drag on the cigarette and exhaled loudly. "I would like to know who paid my taxes," he said more to the snow than to Rodney.

"I cannot remember anybody in my life, except my wife, doing anything nice for me for no reason."

"Whoever it was, besides having a lot of money, must be a good person," Rodney said.

"If I knew, I could repay them in some way," Banjo said.

"I imagine they know how grateful you are," Rodney said, finishing restringing the wire and standing back and looking at the many patched strands.

Banjo looked at the fence and grinned. "Gringo, if I was young, you and I would make a good pair of outlaws. We could ride up to Colorado and steal some sheep and maybe hit the bank in Durango. Then we could take all our money and go to Mexico and buy a ranchetto the size of this whole damn state. That would have been the life."

"If I was young and you were young, Banjo, we would probably try to rob a bank and end up breaking rock somewhere for twenty years. By the time we got out, things would have changed so much we would be doing what I am now. Working for wages on somebody else's place," Rodney said, looking at the sky and noticing the snow was building up quickly on the ground.

"You are probably right," Banjo said. "I guess a poor man now would have been a poor man then. It would not make much difference. But there is always the thought."

Rodney mounted his horse and settled into the cold wet saddle, wishing he had the slicker he had given away in Montana. "I like you Banjo," he said. "Something about you reminds me of myself."

"I like you, gringo," Banjo said. "You keep going even knowing this life we lead is doomed. Maybe when you are my age you will not be able to die out on the land. Maybe then, all the city people will have nothing but condos dotting all the open places. Or people like your boss will own all the land and the only thing left of the west will be places where they make movies that lie about what was."

"Maybe it was the movies that killed us all," Rodney said. "The myth that good always wins."

Banjo turned his horse back toward his house. "Maybe so, maybe not. Tell your boss hello for me, gringo. Tell him I am still here by luck and luck alone."

Rodney tipped his hat at Banjo. "Tell that sheep of yours with the wire cutters to wait until the snow is over before he wants another drink."

"I will," Banjo said. "He does what I want him to. He knows if he does not, I will be eating mutton."

Banjo let the horse pick its way up the hillside. He felt good. The first snow of the season was special. For now, the winter did not bother him. For now, it was quiet and beautiful. And the world seemed the way it should be.

Rodney moved his horse into a fast walk. The way the snow was coming down it did not look like it would let up for the rest of the day. He followed the fence further north than he usually did before cutting back toward the ranch houses. He wanted to avoid the hill, with the way the snow was falling, and cut across a flat plain—it was a little longer but had no sink holes or gullies. Covered by the snow, the land was treacherous and he could hurt himself and the horse.

About to turn toward the headquarters, he saw two sets of foot prints in the snow that came from the direction of Banjo's house, crossed the fence and followed the fence north toward Banjo's front gate. He felt like he should follow the prints as they made him feel uneasy, but the way the snow was coming down he knew he had better get home.

He hurried his horse back to the stable, rubbed her down well and gave both horses a can of grain and a wedge of timothy. Finished, he did not go to his house but took the truck and drove to the highway and took the dirt road that bordered the ranch. Stopping at Banjo's gate, he saw where a vehicle had parked and looked at the two sets of tracks crossing the fence to get to it. "It must not have been snowing when they arrived," he said. "But it caught them."

Judging by the tracks, they were walking quickly and they were wearing tennis shoes which were the wrong type of shoes to be out in bad weather. He could think of no good reason two men would walk down the fence and cut over to Banjo's house. No good reason at all. But he did not want to go tell Banjo and maybe scare him for no reason. After all, the people were gone.

Rodney drove back to the ranch house and once inside, realized his feet were cold. He stood by the porch window and looked over at Karen's house. The brown adobe was blanketed by the snow. A fire was going and the smoke rising into the grey sky made Rodney feel peaceful. In the kitchen, he removed his wet boots, turned on the oven and pulling up a chair, sat with his feet on the open oven door.

🐄 🐄 🐄

Mr. Cook, after telling Rodney to go fix the fence, went back to his house and took a shower. He put on a light pair of tan pants and ostrich boots and a handmade western shirt.

When Karen heard the knock on the door, she knew it was not Rodney. She had waved at him as he rode by. But answering it, she was surprised to see Mr. Cook trying to look like a cowboy. "Come on in, Mr. Cook," she said playing the subservient renter.

Mr. Cook walked in and Karen changed her mind. He looked more like a car salesman from Dallas, only Mr. Cook could not be as obnoxious. "I haven't had much time lately and thought I'd come over and say hello," Mr. Cook said, sitting down without being invited.

Karen, who had been about to take her clothes off to paint, did not want any company but said, "Would you like some coffee or tea?"

"Coffee would be good," Mr. Cook answered, eying Karen from head to toe and making her feel like she was a horse about to be auctioned.

Karen put a pot of water on to boil and sat down at the table. "I saw Rodney go by," she said.

"I sent him out to fix the fence," Mr. Cook said. "That Mexican still cuts it every time he gets a chance."

"Wish he would cut your throat," Karen thought.

"I'll have that land of his one day," Mr. Cook said, trying to sound like everything he wanted he got—which in most cases, was true.

Mr. Cook reminded Karen of all the big whigs she had grown up around back east. They all sat and talked about their stocks and bonds and boats and where they were going to take a vacation. They never seemed to realize life had to have more worth than what one could buy. But she was away from it now and it really did not matter. To her old circle, she would be considered one of those who dressed down and tried to be like common people—a task she knew she could never really do. She had money and the money brought her security and the chance to think about more than surviving. Surviving, she had discovered, was about all most people could think about. Living her life without money, she knew, would be entirely different.

"I never see you out on the ranch," Mr. Cook said. "There are some very beautiful places here."

"I've been keeping busy," Karen replied. "Seems there is always something to do."

The water started to boil and Karen made two cups of instant coffee. Ever since Rodney, she had tried to develop a taste for the mud. At times it was not bad, but most of the time, she ended up pouring it down the drain.

"You wouldn't happen to have any brandy, would you?" Mr. Cook asked.

"No," Karen said, "sorry."

"That's okay," Mr. Cook replied, smiling at Karen over the edge of his cup.

Karen knew what Mr. Cook had come over for and felt disgusted. She wondered what it was about moneyed men thinking every woman in the world would rip their clothes off and jump in bed with them.

Mr. Cook opened his play with, "I've noticed you ever since the day you moved in."

"How is your wife?" Karen parried, smiling slightly.

"She and I are separated while my attorneys draw up the paperwork for our divorce," Mr. Cook said with no sign of remorse. "I'm sure she will be satisfied with the settlement."

"I'm sure she had better be," Karen thought.

"There is a party for all the main stars of the movie in a few days and I was wondering if you would like to go with me?" Mr. Cook asked.

"Mr. Cook, you may not know it, but Rodney and I have been seeing each other. Maybe, if that were not the case, I would go. But, as of now, I feel we are sufficiently involved to at least try and maintain trust," Karen said.

"Well, if you change your mind, you know where I live," Mr. Cook said, sounding disappointed but standing to leave.

Karen was relieved. She stood and walked toward the door to open it. As she passed Mr. Cook, he reached out and patted her on the butt. Karen spun around and started to slap him but caught herself. Mr. Cook, winked at her and said, "I have more to offer than any dumb cowboy who doesn't have a pot to piss in."

Karen glared at the door while the rage built inside of her. She could not remember being patted on the butt since high school. Even the jerks back east had more class than that. Their favorite ploy was "would you like to come sit in my hot tub and have a glass of wine", or "how about a ride in my new Corvette or Mercedes?"

While Mr. Cook walked to his house it started to snow. He knew Karen was interested. They all liked expensive presents, even if they did not like the men who gave them. But for now, he would let the issue die. He figured she would not tell Rodney in fear he would fire the cowboy. There were cowboys all over the place looking for a place to stay and a few dollars in their pocket. Rodney would be as easy to replace as buying another horse. In fact, the cowboy would be cheaper and not take as much money as a horse.

Thinking about the horses, Mr. Cook thought he might sell his soon to be ex-wife's horse. One hay burner was enough when there was not much to do around the place.

Karen stood in her bedroom and closed the curtains. She undressed slowly and wished she had the nerve to go over to Mr. Cook's house and hit him in the head with a ball bat. She picked up the arrowhead and once again marveled at its beauty and simplicity and remembered a saying she had heard somewhere concerning the Indians, "Once there was no crime and no police and then the white man came to make things better."

Putting the arrowhead down, she looked at her nearly completed painting. She felt sad. She felt that when she made the final stroke on her canvas her life would pass on to a new phase. She felt a kinship with the painting as she felt a kinship with Rodney. It was as though the painting had become a part of her. The cowboy, the heart, the owl and the yellow rose were all important aspects of her life. Soon it would be done and she would feel hollow again—hollow and alone and searching.

Moving the curtain back slightly, she watched the snow, and wished Rodney was with her—if only sitting in the other room drinking a beer. "Rodney, you dumb cowboy," she said to the falling snow. "Capturing you is about as hard as hanging a snowflake on a wall."

Banjo took his time riding back to the house after leaving Rodney. With his new gloves, for the first time in many winters, his hands were warm. And the large oversized brim of his hat kept the snow from falling down his neck. Although his feet were cold in his new boots, wearing such grand boots made a little discomfort worth it.

Banjo remembered when he was a boy and his father and uncles would wait until the first snow and go deer hunting. It was not an occasion like he had read in a magazine where father and son shared the moment of the hunt. Deer were important food, and, they shot any deer they saw. The hide was tanned and made into slippers and tie downs and the antlers were made into buttons and knife handles. Banjo could see the skinny dogs standing outside the shed as his father and uncle cleaned the deer. As they worked, they tossed scrapes of meat and fat to the shivering, hungry dogs. Banjo had never enjoyed the actual killing of the deer, but he did like being with his father and uncles when they drank and told stories of other hunts, and when they thought he was asleep, of other women.

Banjo was deep in thought when he unsaddled the horse and wiped her down carefully. He gave her extra grass and taking his rifle walked toward the house. About to step up on the porch, Banjo stopped. "The pig," he said. "If I feed it now, I will not have to go back outside for the rest of the evening."

He left his rifle on the porch and went back to the shed and filled two cans of pig feed and headed toward the pig pen. He started to pour the feed in the trough when he stepped back as though he was about to step on a rattlesnake. The pig was dead, half covered with snow. Warm red blood still oozed from its throat, which had been slashed. There was an envelope on top of the pig. Banjo opened the envelope and took out a sheet of paper. In large red letters, it read—LEAVE OR DIE.

There were two sets of footprints in the snow going away from the pig pen and toward the fence.

Banjo ran to the house, stuffing the note into his pocket as he did, picked up his rifle from the porch and stormed into the house. "My Angelena," he called. "Angelena."

Angelena was sitting at the table, drinking a cup of coffee and smoking a cigarette. Banjo took a deep breath of relief.

"What is wrong, Banjo?" Angelena said anxiously.

"Nothing," Banjo said, removing his hat and shaking the snow off it onto the floor.

Banjo started to put his hat down, then put it back on. "I am going to shoot the pig," he said. "It is time. The snow will make it easier to clean."

"He will be a good pig," Angelena said, visualizing pork chops sizzling on the stove.

Banjo shot the dead pig in the head. Using the horse and a rope he pulled the pig to the barn and hung it up from an extending rafter. The work made him tired, but he hurried because if he did not hurry, the tracks of whoever had killed the pig would soon be covered with snow. Banjo cut the stomach open and the insides fell out on the snow. Leaving them in a pile, he took his rifle and went back to the pig pen and started to follow the tracks. He followed them to the fence with the Last Day In Paradise, Banjo knew the men had followed the fence in from his gate and crossed over to his house. The snow had caught them. He also knew who was responsible.

He went back to the shed and shoveled the entrails behind the shed where the coyotes would sneak in and make quick work of them. Banjo took a stick and stuck it between the rib cage of the pig so air would circulate inside the pig and cool the meat. In the morning, he would cut it up. In the old days, they would render the lard, but now that was too much work for Banjo. Besides his son had told Angelena about cholesterol and Angelena did not use lard anymore. When they went to town, she insisted on buying vegetable oil, which Banjo did not like, but he did not cook so had little choice in the matter.

The pig splayed and hanging, Banjo stood back sadly and looked at the carcass. "I am sorry you had to go this way, my friend," he said. "I might have let you live and turned you loose to terrorize coyotes and chickens, but I guess we will never know. But I know whoever did this to you will be back and when they come, your blood will be revenged. You are only a pig, but you were my friend."

In the fading light of the day, Banjo walked to the house. Placing the rifle on the porch he brought several large armfuls of wood and put them on the porch. Then he brought another armful inside and put it by the stove. He put the rifle in his room, laying it on his bed instead of standing it in the corner.

Angelena was singing an old Mexican song as Banjo sat down in his chair. He listened to the soft, sweet voice of his wife. The song was a eulogy for his murdered pig.

Twenty-one

*I*t was five a.m. and Rodney was drinking a cup of coffee. He looked over at Karen's house and to his surprise her light was on. Rodney put on his coat and walked through the foot deep snow to Karen's house. The snow was still falling, but only slightly. Rodney knocked on the door. In a few moments, Karen's face peered through the door window and she let him in.

"Your wife out of town?" Karen said.

"She took off with a banker, stole my limo and my credit cards," Rodney said.

"What are you doing over here so early, Rodney?" Karen asked.

"I needed a smile," Rodney said.

Karen grinned at him. "I missed you last night," she said. "The snow was falling, the fire was burning, and I was all alone with nothing but a bottle of wine and a warm blanket."

"Why didn't you come over?" Rodney asked.

"You're supposed to come over here. I can't be running around chasing you all the time. After all, I chased you first, remember?" Karen said.

"I thought about it," Rodney said, remembering what Karen told him about being too stupid to know when opportunity strikes.

"We can make up for it today though," Rodney said. "The way the snow is, nobody will try to get in here. And if the sun comes out and melts a little, nobody is going to get out of here for a few days unless they have a mud mobile."

"I'll have to think about it," Karen said. "I may not be in the same mood when the sun comes up."

Rodney laughed. "Well, while you're thinking about it, why don't you make me a cup of coffee?"

"Now I know why you really came over," Karen said. "You ran out of coffee."

Rodney looked hurt and started to say something but Karen cut in. "I'm glad you came over. I was lost in my painting and not getting anywhere."

Rodney ran his hand through his hair and felt lost or confused, he did not know for sure which one.

When the sun began to rise, Rodney and Karen were standing by the kitchen door looking directly at it. The clouds were parting on the horizon and the golden darts of light filtered through the snow and ice covered branches of the cottonwood tree. The tree seemed to be coated with millions of diamonds. The glare was so bright, Rodney and Karen had to squint. "It's so beautiful," Karen said. "So alive and lonely at the same time. But, I suppose most of life is lonely, isn't it, Rodney?"

"Sometimes more than others," Rodney answered.

Karen hugged him.

"Do you think Mr. Cook would do anything to physically harm Banjo?" Rodney asked, hoping to hear an answer to quell his fears.

Karen had to choke back what she wanted to tell Rodney. She wanted to say Mr. Cook had come over and treated her like a cheap tart. But she did not. "Mr. Cook is a powerful man used to getting his way. I wouldn't put anything past him," Karen answered. "Why?"

"I saw footprints of two men in the snow that crossed into Banjo's land yesterday," Rodney said. "It doesn't seem right, is all."

Karen looked worried. "I wonder if Mr. Cook knows any hoods. Phoenix is full of them."

"I was wondering the same thing?" Rodney said. "Since Banjo's taxes were paid, he might have some people come in and try to scare Banjo away."

"For some reason, I don't think Banjo would need much help," Karen said.

"I thought the same thing yesterday but he's an old man. What could an old man do against a couple of tough guys?" Rodney asked.

"It's his home, Rodney. What wouldn't he do?" Karen answered.

The ice on the roof began to melt and Rodney knew the white wonderland would soon be a muddy, sloppy bog. "This will slow up their movie," Rodney said.

"Do you care?" Karen asked.

Rodney kissed Karen on the forehead. "Not really. Being around one fake guy this long is more than enough. Being around a bunch of actors really doesn't seem to turn me on."

"Get out of here and let me get back to my painting." Karen scolded.

Rodney looked west toward Banjo's house and then at Mr. Cook's mansion. "If anything happens to that old man, Mr. Cook," he swore, "you are mine."

There was a note on Rodney's kitchen table from Mr. Cook. "Movie producers will be here to see you this morning concerning your part."

It was close to noon when a Land Rover slid to a stop in front of the house. Irv Abraham, Saul Heilman and a blond lady who looked like Marilyn Monroe, got out. Rodney had heard the vehicle approaching and was standing on the porch. They took their shoes off on the porch and went inside.

Rodney led them to the kitchen and put on a fresh pot of coffee. The blond looked at Rodney and liked what she saw. "He'll be great," she said. "One hell of an outlaw."

"This is Rosemary. She's in charge of casting and wardrobe and wanted to take a look at you. But watch out, she only likes men for their bodies," Irv Abraham said smiling at Rosemary.

Rosemary stuck her tongue out at Abraham and smiled a big toothy grin at Rodney. "What they say is all true," she said to Rodney.

Rodney poured them a cup of coffee but did not pour himself one. Rosemary patted Rodney on the back. "Damn, you're a good looking man," she said. "I bet every lady in town loves you."

"I wish," Rodney said.

"After this movie, you'll do more than wish," Rosemary said.

"Why don't you tell him what he's going to do so we can leave?," Heilman said.

Rosemary sipped her coffee and looked at Rodney, the joking tone out of her voice. "You will need to report to makeup every morning you are due to shoot, at 3:30 A.M. They will have the outfits set out for you. You won't be with the other extras since you're playing one of the main outlaws. You'll have your own trailer. I want you to grow your beard, don't cut your hair. You can ride a horse, I presume?"

Rodney did not have time to answer as Rosemary went on. "You will have a few lines, nothing major, but a few. Then you'll get killed and you can get back to your normal routine," Rosemary said matter-of-factly.

"And I get $300 a day for that," Rodney said.

"The boy's learning," Abraham laughed.

"$300 a day and meals. I imagine you'll work a week or so." Rosemary said. "But if I were you, I'd get into a casting agency, have a few photo's made and try to get in more westerns. I certainly would recommend you if this one goes well. You have that down home, bad guy look. Westerns might be coming back into vogue. This movie will tell."

"If the weather clears up, we should start in about a week," Heilman said.

Rosemary, after putting her boots back on, looked at Rodney. "Would you like some company some night?" she asked, not bashful at all.

"Sorry," Rodney said. "Full up at the moment."

"Oh, well," Rosemary said, blowing him a kiss. "Things change daily in this modern world. I'll take a number and wait."

Rodney watched them slosh to their Land Rover and wondered just what in the hell he was doing? And for some strange reason he felt like a traitor.

🐖 🐖 🐖

Banjo did not sleep well. His chest hurt all night and it was not until early morning he was able to catch his breath. When the sun started to peak through his window, he put on his boots, jacket and hat and taking his rifle went to the barn. Banjo stuffed as many sticks of dynamite in his pockets as he could and taking the fuses with him, walked back to the house.

Banjo hid the dynamite under his bed and put the fuses in a small box in the corner of the room. Going to the kitchen, he got a handful of matches and put them in his pocket. He then laid back down in bed and fell asleep.

When he woke again, it was past eight and he could hear the ice and snow melting off the roof. Angelena was not in the kitchen and he picked up his rifle and went outside, trying not to show how worried he was. He saw her footprints through the slushy snow heading toward the shed. Angelena was cutting up the pig and tossing pieces of meat into a wash pan. "I would have done that," Banjo said.

"You must have been tired and I had nothing better to do," Angelena said, cutting out a ham.

Banjo sat on a stump by the barn. "I have to tell you something," he said, trying not to speak in a way that would make his wife afraid. "I found footprints along our fence. I think they are men who have been hired by Mr. Cook to run us out."

Angelena did not stop cutting up the pig. "Why do you say that?" she asked.

Banjo coughed and a sharp pain swept through his side. He grimaced and Angelena saw him. She stepped over to him quickly, but he tried to keep her away. "It is nothing, nothing," he protested.

"I have seen you lately, Banjo," Angelena said more concerned than her voice conveyed. "You cannot lie to me, I see the pain all over your face. Come, you are going to lie down."

Banjo got up slowly and Angelena steadied him as they walked back to the house. Lying down in bed, Banjo turned on his side as Angelena went to the kitchen to put on a pot of tea.

She came back to the bedroom and Banjo had broken out in a sweat.

"If we had a phone, I would call a doctor," Angelena said, hurrying to the kitchen and bringing back a towel soaked in cold water and placing it on Banjo's head.

"We cannot leave here today anyway, so a phone makes no difference. The road will be nothing but mud and our truck will not get up the hill. Besides, it is nothing, it will pass. It always has," Banjo said weakly.

Angelena brought Banjo a cup of hot tea. "You stay in bed and drink this," she ordered. "I will finish the pig and then make you some pork chops."

Banjo lay in bed and dreamed about pork chops. He had not eaten pork chops since the last pig was butchered. Pork chops with a thick brown gravy all over them and then the gravy sopped up with a warm tortilla. Thinking about the pork chops he did not notice the slight, dull, throbbing pain in his side. But he was aware of his rifle setting in the corner. And the dynamite under his bed.

Angelena finished cutting up the pig and it took four trips for her to carry the meat to the house. Banjo could discard the carcass when he wanted. But not today, today he would rest. As to the strangers on the land, Angelena had no feelings what so ever about them. It was a man's problem to protect his land and his wife. But if they tried to do something while Banjo was ill, she would kill them as sure as the ground was muddy.

When Angelena finished wrapping the meat and putting it in the freezer, she went in and checked on Banjo, he was asleep. She looked at his old and worn face with the shallow cheeks and the sunken eyes and he was as handsome now as he had been when he was young. "Oh Banjo," Angelena prayed, "your life has been one of strife and toil and unfulfilled dreams. But you have weathered them well and stood tall with dignity, even with your dreams of being a bandit. Surely God loves the bandits of the world. You are one like your sheep. Fenced off from what is good and easy, made to dream for the one day it will all change."

She looked at his boots and smiled. He was proud of his boots. Proud his son had given them to him and proud of his hat that was so large it made him seem thinner than he really was. Angelena picked up the wet towel which had fallen to the floor, wiped Banjo's face and went back to the kitchen.

Angelena saw a small brown sparrow light on the window sill and appear to look at her. He chirped several times and pecked at the window. Angelena's mother would have thought the sparrow was a spirit trying to enter the house and bring goodwill. But Angelena only saw the bird as a small, tiny, defenseless creature who sought the warmth of the house, not unlike all mankind in their endless quest for peace and tranquility.

Angelena heard Banjo coughing and looked in on him. He was sitting up in bed rolling a smoke—something she knew he should not do. But who was she to tell a man, who had been alive for over 80 years, what to do? It really did not make any difference now. Banjo lit the cigarette, dodged the flame, and then jumped out of bed and grabbing Angelena by the hand, pulled her into the kitchen.

"What is wrong with you, Banjo?" Angelena scolded.

Banjo sat down heavily, "Nothing, nothing," he mumbled, not wanting to tell her he had not remembered the dynamite under his bed until after lighting his cigarette.

When the smoke was finished, Banjo looked much better. Color had come back to his face and his chest did not hurt. He kept looking over at the stove, as if by magic, the stove would suddenly have pork chops on it. Angelena, seeing his impatience, put the pork chops in a frying pan and started to cook them. Banjo breathed the scent deeply. "Do Catholics believe there are pork chops in heaven?" Banjo asked seriously.

"People don't have to eat in heaven, Banjo," Angelena said as if talking to a child. "Nothing from this earth that chains us will be there."

"Doesn't sound like a good place to go to me," Banjo said.

"I wouldn't worry about it if I was you, Banjo," Angelena responded.

Banjo ate four pork chops and three tortillas soaked in gravy and had three cups of tea. Finished, he sat back in his chair and started to roll a smoke when Angelena said, "Wait."

Banjo was still holding the rolling papers in his hand when Angelena brought out two tailor made cigarettes and handed him one. Banjo lit the cigarette, took a deep drag, exhaled loudly and looked at the smooth, even roll of the cigarette. It seemed perfect, perfectly round, perfectly cut, perfect when burned. "This is the perfect smoke," Banjo said.

Angelena wondered to herself what made him say some of the things he did.

Finished with the smoke, Banjo stood up and went to his room. He put on his coat and hat and picked up his rifle and put the sticks of dynamite in his jacket pockets.

Angelena started to tell Banjo he could not go outside but the look in Banjo's eye told her it would do no good. Instead, she stood up and buttoned the top button of his coat. Banjo squirmed around like a little boy. Safely away from the house, he unbuttoned the top button and smiled in satisfaction.

Banjo went behind the barn where for years he had tossed cans into a small arroyo. He rummaged around until he found several to his liking. Then he went to the shed and got his hammer and a handful of rusty nails.

Banjo studied his house, and shed, and corral and pigpen and the scattered trees. There were only a few places where people could hide and not be seen. Banjo went first to the pigpen. He nailed a can to the side of the pen and stuck a piece of dynamite into it. He then did the same thing to the outhouse and then on the edge of the shed that would give a person a good view of the house. Satisfied with his work, he decided he needed more and went to the shed and got several more sticks of dynamite.

He put a stick in a can and set it against the woodpile and then put a can next to the road leaving the house. Finished, he went and sat on the porch and looked to see if he could see all the cans, which he could. He stood in the kitchen, where he could see half the cans. From his room, he could see the edge of the woodpile and the can by the outhouse.

Taking off his coat, Banjo felt short of breath and weak and could hear his heart racing in his ears. It sounded like a kettle drum being beaten much too fast—so fast Banjo lay down on the bed. He felt chilled and pulled the blanket up over himself. Angelena came into the room and looked at him and came back with another cup of tea. She set the tea where he could reach it and put her hand on his forehead. "I told you not to go outside," she said. "And I bet you unbuttoned your coat."

Banjo was shivering and did not answer. Angelena brought him two aspirins and made Banjo take them. He hated medicine of any kind, feeling whiskey could remedy everything. The more serious the illness, the more the need for whiskey. "What are all the cans for?" she asked Banjo anxiously.

"There is dynamite in them," Banjo answered, not feeling well enough to try and think up a lie that would only be found out anyway.

Angelena did not want to pursue the question any further. Why Banjo would want to put dynamite in cans all around the area was something only Banjo could figure out. "You will stay in bed the rest of the day and all night and tomorrow, if the roads are dry enough, we are going to the doctor," Angelena said.

Banjo looked at her determined face, listened to his heart race and did not protest. "I will go," he said.

It was an answer Angelena did not want to hear.

After two warm days and freezing nights the mud was almost gone. Rodney had been doing what he considered nothing jobs around the ranch. He swept out the stable, cleaned out the stalls and fixed a few things. But mostly he worried about Banjo. He had wanted to go over and see the old man, but he did not want to go over and offend Banjo's pride.

Rodney had only seen Karen once. She was busy with her painting and did not want to be bothered—artistic license was a phrase he added to his vocabulary. Before knowing an artist, he would have called it being stuck up and antisocial. But now he knew there was a difference.

Mr. Cook had not come out of his house in the two days. Whatever he was up to, he did not confide in Rodney, which suited him fine. The more he was not around Mr. Cook, the better he felt. There had been no word from the movie people, but he had spent one afternoon pulling several trucks out of the mud that tried to make it to the movie site too soon. Now he would have to take the blade and smooth out the huge ruts they left in the road. Being from the city, they did not know people do not drive on country roads after a snow storm until the roads were either frozen at night or completely dry. Maintaining a ranch road was an art unto itself. Rutting a road for no reason, in some parts of the west, could be a killing offense and a good, old western judge would surely let the killer go free.

Rodney finished his lunch and washed the dishes. It was close to one o'clock and would be dark by five. Rodney hated the winter. It seemed, no sooner was he awake then it was dark. He wondered how people in Alaska handled the long, cold winters and the endless darkness. He went outside and an airplane, that was not Mr. Cook's, was flying in the area where Banjo's land bordered Mr. Cook's. The plane was flying as slow as it could. When the plane reached the far end of the ranch, it turned and flew back on the same line. The plane did this three times before it climbed for altitude and headed back in the direction of Santa Fe. Rodney could not take it anymore and he decided he would ride over and see how Banjo was. He could pretend it was a social visit and snoop around and maybe discover something to substantiate his fears concerning the footprints in the snow.

He went back to the house and put on his coat and hat and stuck his gloves in his back pocket and headed for the stable to saddle a horse. Halfway to the stable, he wished he had a rifle or a pistol.

Karen was standing by the window. She watched Rodney as he headed toward the stables. She had been thinking about Rodney a lot the past two days. But thinking about him as though he had already ridden out of her life. It had started as she was about to finish her painting.

In the far upper left corner of her painting was an inch square of bare canvas. All she had to do was color it in with the rest of the sky and her painting would be done. But she could not force herself to complete the painting. One entire day, she sat cross legged on the floor, with the painting in front of her. Here, in red and purple, and flying owls and cowboys, was all the dreams and hopes she had held over the past weeks. Here, in her own form of hieroglyphics, was her heart. And try as she may, she could not complete it. She felt if she finished the painting Rodney would surely ride away.

At one point, she felt like taking her large brush, dipping it in black paint and painting over the entire canvas. Then, only she would know what lay underneath the black. She would call her painting, Vanishing Dreams, and instead of trying to sell it, she would hang it in her living room. It would be everything to her, but, to everybody else it would be nothing but black.

As Rodney rode by, Karen wanted to run out and pull him from his horse and yell at him. "See what you have done to me. See, you no good, cowboy bastard. I was alone and coming to grips with my aloneness and you came along and made me want again. You made me love you, and want you, and enjoy you. Now I'm confused, thinking about being hurt and lonely again. You jerk."

But watching him ride away, she sighed and turned once more to her painting. After a few moments she decided she would make a nice dinner for two. "I am such a push-over," she said.

Turning once more to the window, she could barely see Rodney on the hillside. He seemed so distant and so alone. But she knew alone was part of him. A part she would never be able to touch. The land, the trees, the cactus and the horses were probably more dear to him than any woman could be. A woman was something who could take him away from the land for only brief moments. "It's a hell of a deal," she said.

Rodney was half way to the fence when he remembered there were no gates in the fence and he felt like an idiot.

Banjo was sitting on the porch watching the sparrows dart in and around the woodpile. The 30/30 was leaning up against the porch within easy reach. After the ground had dried up Angelena was ready to go to town and the doctor, but Banjo had refused to go. Angelena had not talked to him since and his tortillas were flat and salty. Salty enough that Banjo was contemplating going to the doctor so he could have good tortillas again. But, now that she had made it a battle of wills, it would take at least a few days of thinking to decide if giving in was worth the delicious tortillas. Banjo knew the tortillas would win in the end.

Banjo had been on the lookout for anything unusual but there had been nothing, until today, and even the plane going back and forth along the fence was probably the rich bastard gringo who owned the ranch. When the plane flew directly over the house he could see two people in the plane, but he could not make them out. If it had kept circling the house, Banjo decided he would shoot at it. There had to be a law against people flying over his property. He had heard about noise pollution in California. Maybe he could get off by having a defense of noise pollution.

Angelena walked out of the house and tossed a pan of potato peels into the yard. They were immediately attacked by the chickens and a small flock of sparrows. Walking back into the house, Angelena stuck her tongue out at Banjo and slammed the door. Banjo only sat impassive. Being impassive was about the only thing he could think about doing. He knew he was in the wrong. He said he would go.

"It is a good thing I can only make love once a year," Banjo said to the scratching and milling chickens. "I wouldn't be getting any for a long time."

Banjo was thinking about getting up and splitting some wood when he heard a noise some distance behind the shed. He picked up his rifle and walked as fast as he could to the shed and snuck around the corner. He could only see a man's legs through the trees and he crouched down. As Rodney walked out of the trees, Banjo stepped from behind the barn with his rifle up to his shoulder. Rodney jumped. "What the hell, Banjo?" Rodney said, hearing his heart pounding in his ears.

"Dumb gringo," Banjo said lowering the rifle. "Don't you know to whistle?"

"I didn't know there was a war going on," Rodney said, "plus if there was a gate in the damn fence I wouldn't have had to walk."

"Maybe there is war and maybe there isn't," Banjo said. "But there is something going on."

"I saw the footprints, Banjo," Rodney said.

"Somebody killed my pig and left me a note. It is not good," he said and dug the note out of his pocket and handed it to Rodney.

"That no good son of a bitch," Rodney muttered after reading the note.

"He is a bastard and the son of a bastard," Banjo said.

"Maybe I should stay over here with you, Banjo," Rodney offered.

Banjo's face lit up in a twisted smile. "No, but if you hear me, you come running, okay?" he said.

"I don't like the way you said that," Rodney said. "How will I hear you?"

Banjo laughed. "Gringo, I have a few tricks. Enough tricks to catch a rat. Now come to the house. Angelena is mad at me but maybe with company, she will make some food that is fit to eat."

"What did you do, Banjo, get caught chasing women?" Rodney joked.

"No," Banjo answered simply, not telling Rodney about the hospital.

"Where is Karen?" Angelena asked Rodney when he walked into the kitchen.

"She is painting," Rodney answered, removing his hat.

"Such a nice lady," Angelena said. "She likes you too much."

Rodney did not know what to say.

"Sit, sit, Angelena will make us something to eat," Banjo said with a big grin on his face.

"For Rodney, I will make something to eat," Angelena said defiantly. "For you, I will make nothing until dinner time."

The smile on Banjo's face disappeared and he frowned at Rodney who gave him a 'that's how it goes' look.

Banjo watched Rodney eat the beans with the thick tortilla and tried to imagine how good it was. Several times, he wanted to reach over when Angelena was not looking and steal Rodney's tortilla and put it in his pocket for tonight when he would be in his room. He noticed Angelena had several nice tortillas on the stove in a pan and maybe he would be able to sneak out after she was in bed and get one.

When Rodney finished eating and had drunk several cups of coffee, he stood up. "Have to get back, thank you for the food Angelena," he said and added, "you'd better feed this old coot, he might wither up and blow away."

Angelena smiled at Rodney and gave Banjo another dirty look, "Then at least I would not have to worry about someone who does not worry about himself," she said.

Banjo walked with Rodney to his horse. As Rodney started to ride away Banjo asked, "Was the tortilla salty, gringo?"

"No Banjo, it was the best tortilla I ever ate in my life," Rodney said.

"That's what I thought," Banjo answered sadly.

Riding back toward the Last Day In Paradise, Rodney lost all his mirth. He knew there was going to be trouble and he also knew, although Banjo did not seem afraid, that whoever had killed the pig were serious people.

After feeding the horses, Rodney saw the envelope tacked to his door. There was a little heart drawn in the corner and it read, "Dinner for two, my place, come as you are."

Even though Rodney was worried about Banjo he smiled.

Twenty-two

*I*t was almost bed time and Banjo was sitting in his room feeling strangely uneasy. He had had this same feeling only twice in his life. Once, when he and several of his bandit friends were high up on a ridge in Colorado, watching one man herd several hundred sheep. His friends wanted to split up and ride in from different directions and scatter the sheep and drive off with as many as they could. But, Banjo talked the men into waiting awhile longer. About an hour later eight armed riders came out of the trees around the flock of sheep. It had been a trap. The second time was when the German's thought they were attacking Banjo's squad by surprise, but they were waiting for them.

Banjo knew the next day would bring trouble. What the trouble would be or who would cause it, he did not know. But there would be trouble. Banjo looked at his 30/30 leaning in the corner. He did not feel too formidable. Nor did he feel confident about being able to handle the situation. "Maybe I should have taken the gringo up on his offer for help," he said.

But, asking for help would be worse than begging for money—two things Banjo had never done.

Angelena turned off the light in the kitchen and Banjo heard her go to her room. He heard her lie down in bed and pick up her book. He hoped she would not read for long and fall asleep so he could sneak into the kitchen and get a few tortillas.

Hoping to fool Angelena, Banjo removed his boots and set them down loudly in the corner. Turning off the light, he lay down on the bed. But he did not try to fall asleep. He lay and worried about the next day, not so much for him but for Angelena. "Old man," he muttered, "at least you will go out with a fight and not be sitting in some house in the city watching T.V."

Banjo had dozed off. Waking, he held his breath, breathing might wake Angelena. Angelena was snoring loudly. Creeping into the kitchen, Banjo felt his way to the stove and silently took two tortillas. Sitting on the bed in the dark he took a large bite of tortilla and shut his eyes, savoring the flavor. It was a tortilla like Angelena could make, not salty or thin. But thick and moist and almost melting in his mouth. Taking another bite, he heard Angelena's voice ring through the darkened house. "You have not won, my husband."

Banjo smiled and swallowed and took another bite and called back. "Even without your tortillas, Angelena, I still love you." "If you do not go to the hospital I will have nobody to love," Angelena replied.

After eating both tortillas, Banjo lay down and fell into a deep, dreamless sleep, a sleep undisturbed until 4 a.m. when he awoke and immediately got out of bed. He put on two pair of socks before putting on his boots, two shirts and a sweater before putting his coat on. He put on his black hat and then pulled a scarf over the top of it and tied it under his chin. He put on his insulated gloves, picked up his 30/30 and walked as quietly as he could out of the house.

Angelena, deep in sleep, did not hear him leave.

Banjo looked at the stars mirrored in the frost and decided he would hide behind a stand of trees not far from the pig pen. From there, he could see all his cans and have a good view of the house. The ground was frozen solid and he wished he had brought a blanket with him to sit on. But he did not go back into the house. Sitting down behind the branches of a large pinon, he made himself as comfortable as possible. He cradled the rifle in his arms after making sure it was off safety and chambered.

Banjo remembered when he was deer hunting as a boy. One snowy, winter morning he left the house with his father and walked several miles.

When the sun rose they saw the tracks of a large deer. All day they followed the tracks, but never saw the deer. Banjo thought he knew where the deer was heading. The next morning, while it was still dark, he went to a saddle between two rolling hills and sat down beside a tree and waited. In a short time his hands, ears and feet were so cold they hurt. But he forced himself too wait. When the sun rose, he knew at any moment the big buck would come between the two hills. As the sun rose higher and higher, the deer still had not come. Banjo, out of patience and shivering from the cold, stood up and the large deer bounded away, not more than fifteen yards from the tree. "If I would have sat still for another minute, the deer would have been mine," Banjo said, still remembering the day like it was yesterday and visualizing the large majestic rack of the deer.

"Patience, patience, you old goat," Banjo said. "You have set the trap, now have the patience."

Banjo knew the sun would be up within an hour and he was beginning to get stiff, but, because of all the clothes he was not cold. In fact it had been enjoyable sitting under the tree. The stars were bright and clear and off to his right, an unseen bird had chirped to the darkness. He also heard the scurrying of mice, the hoot of an owl, and in the distance the call of several coyotes beginning to go back to their den.

Bob and Barney left the hotel at 4 a.m.. They drove north toward Espanola for several miles and then did a U turn and drove back through Santa Fe. Driving toward Galisteo, they stopped several times and waited for over ten minutes, each time carefully checking behind them. They did not speak.

They left Banjo's gate open after they drove through and continued down the road until they knew it would only take them about ten minutes to reach the house. Their plan was to be at the house about sun up and catch the old man when he came out of the house. They did not want to hurt the old lady unless they had to. Bob figured it would only take a few slaps to get the Mexican to leave anyway. That, and the fear his wife might be hurt.

When the sun started to rise, they got out of the car and walked toward the house.

Banjo heard the faint sound of an approaching car. Noise traveled far in the cold, early morning air. He heard the engine stop and knew the car was not far from the house. Now he was no longer old, he was a man with no age whose senses were as the night. "Patience, patience," he told himself.

As the eastern horizon started to turn silver, Banjo heard the faint sound of feet crunching the frozen ground. He saw a figure silhouetted against the skyline and then dash behind the wood pile. Another figure snuck around behind the shed causing the mare to bolt to the end of her corral. Banjo carefully looked down the barrel of his rifle to see if he could aim in the dim light. "Patience, patience," he told himself once again.

When the sun cleared the horizon, Banjo immediately felt the warmth from the sun's rays coming through the branches of the trees. He could see Angelena moving around in the kitchen and saw the puff of smoke from the stovepipe as she stoked the stove.

Bob, crouched behind the woodpile, was freezing. He had not worn enough clothes and did not have on gloves. Being from Phoenix, the cold was beginning to get unbearable and he wished he and Barney had not split up. He was for rushing the house, dragging the old couple outside and telling them to get the hell off the land or the next time they came back they would kill them.

Barney, behind the barn, was beginning to wonder if the old man was home. He was able to see the old woman moving around in the kitchen, but he had not seen the old man. Maybe they were sitting out in the cold for nothing?

Unable to take it anymore, Barney stepped from behind the barn and ran toward the house. Banjo saw a pistol in his hand. His partner, also with a pistol, joined him. Neither man said anything but looked at each other and Banjo could tell they had not enjoyed the sunrise.

Banjo could shoot them now, but he watched. Perhaps they would leave when they discovered he was not home. One of the men stood in the yard and kicked at several chickens running by him while the other went to the door and knocked loudly. Banjo saw the curtain part and Angelena look out. When she answered the door, she did not open the screen. "Banjo! Banjo!" the man yelled. "I want to talk to you, Banjo!"

Angelena shrugged her shoulders. "No habley, no comprendo," she said with no fear in her voice.

"Banjo!" the man hollered.

"No habley, no comprendo," Angelena said again.

The man reached for the door and started to yank it open and Banjo fired. Angelena slammed the door shut and picked up a cast iron pan. Bob spun sideways as the slug ripped into his shoulder. At first, he did not know what had happened. But seeing his arm bleeding limply at his side, he ran from the porch. Barney, with the sound of the shot, started backing toward the wood pile. He did not know where the shot had come from. The two men crouched behind the wood pile. Banjo rested the sights on the tin can and squeezed off a shot. With an earth shattering boom the woodpile disintegrated and both men disappeared in a cloud of splintered wood and dirt. Banjo did not move or lower his rifle while the debris settled. When it settled enough, he could see both men laying on the ground. He got up and walked cautiously toward them, holding the rifle ready to fire. Angelena ran out on the porch after hearing the explosion and Banjo yelled, "Get back in the house!"

Angelena immediately obeyed, went back inside and started praying. Banjo nudged one of the men with his boot. A piece of pinon wood was imbedded in his head and blood was oozing around the hole. Banjo did not have to make sure the other man was dead. The top of his head had been blown away by the blast. "It is too bad you died so quickly," Banjo said to the men. "Men like you should have to suffer."

Banjo looked at his demolished wood pile. "Damn," he said. "Now I will have to get much wood."

Putting the rifle on the porch, Banjo dragged each man to the barn and covered them with sheep hides. He would have to decide what to do with them. He knew he could not bury them as the ground was frozen.

Angelena fell into his arms when he entered the house. She kissed him warmly and Banjo could see she had been crying. "It is okay, my love," he said, holding her.

Banjo sat at the table and Angelena poured him a cup of coffee. "Why did you pretend you could not speak English?" he asked Angelena.

"I suppose I am a bandit's wife," she replied no longer crying.

Banjo sipped the coffee and tried to roll a smoke, but his hands began to shake. Angelena, seeing his hands, rolled two cigarettes and lit one and handed it to him. She went to her room and brought out the bottle of whiskey from where she had hidden it. Opening it, she took a large swallow and handed it to Banjo. "For their souls," she said.

"For their souls," Banjo said, taking a large swallow and then holding the bottle up, looking at the few remaining shots left. "And for us," he said, taking another one.

Angelena took the bottle from him and finished it, saying, "and for me."

Rodney was watching through the window the sky turn from purple to bright blue when he heard the dull thud of an explosion coming from the direction of Banjo's. It sounded like the thud of a five hundred pound bomb exploding in the distance. Karen got to the truck at the same time Rodney did. "I heard it, too," she said.

"You can't go," Rodney ordered.

"You don't tell me what I can do," Karen said as she got in.

Rodney took the corners so quickly, the rear end of the truck fishtailed behind them. Driving around one corner, he almost hit a bus load of workers heading to the movie site. The bus swerved and the driver honked the horn, but Rodney did not slow down. Karen quickly fastened her seat belt and hung onto the door handle with both hands.

Rodney took the corner into Banjo's, barely missing the gate post. He was doing close to fifty over the gutted road when he saw a car in the road. He slammed on the brakes, yanked the wheel and the truck swerved off the road, coming to rest with the rear axle several feet off the ground, hung up on a large rock. Rodney ran down the road with Karen several yards behind him. When he ran into Banjo's front yard, the first thing he saw was the woodpile blown everywhere and Angelena picking up pieces of smaller wood to take into the house. Seeing Rodney, she looked amazed, but when Karen ran up to her, she smiled warmly and said, "It has been an exciting morning."

"Where is Banjo?" Rodney asked Angelena, still fearing for the old man.

"He is inside eating," Angelena answered, bending over to pick up another piece of wood.

Rodney ran to the house and without knocking, stormed in. Banjo was sitting at the table eating with his hat on and the rifle beside his leg. "Gringo," he said, "did I wake you?"

"Jesus Christ, Banjo," Rodney said. "Did you blow up your woodpile on purpose? I thought somebody might have dynamited your house."

Banjo stood, picked up the rifle and walked past Rodney. Karen and Angelena were walking toward the house, both with an armload of wood. Rodney followed Banjo to the shed. Without ceremony, Banjo tossed the sheep hides off the two bodies. "Now there is real trouble," Banjo said. "I didn't mean to kill them, but they started to harm my wife."

"My God," Rodney said, having not seen bodies since the war and never really thinking he would ever see twisted and torn men again. "Mr. Cook must have sent them, Banjo."

"I know," Banjo answered, sitting down on a wooden crate. "But there is no way to prove it. I have killed the only people who would know for sure."

"Looks like you did a good job of it," Rodney said, sitting down and turning away from the bodies.

"I guess you should call the police," Rodney said after a few moments.

"No," Banjo replied. "I will not call the police. I have never called the police in my life. The police are for cowards and people too afraid to defend themselves and it would be a big hassle. The way the laws are now I might go to jail for defending myself."

"What are you going to do then?" Rodney asked.

Banjo rubbed his stubble beard and shrugged his shoulders. "I don't know," he replied. "But you, being white, might have a good answer."

For some reason, Rodney laughed. "I'm glad you're okay, you old coot," he said.

"Me, too," Banjo replied. "But I am not a duck."

Rodney went through the men's pockets and found no identification. He did find the keys to the car and 800 dollars in cash. He handed the money to Banjo, who looked at it for a moment, looked at Rodney, tossed some thought around in his head, and then stuffed the money in his pocket.

"Do you think Angelena has told Karen what happened?" Rodney asked.

"She is a bandit's wife. She does not talk about what I do," Banjo said.

Rodney was relieved. "We could bring their car down here, put them in the trunk and go park the car in a parking lot in Santa Fe and leave it. I'm sure there would be no trace back here. As long as we don't leave any fingerprints on the car," Rodney said.

"I like it," Banjo replied. "It is what to do."

"Let me use your gloves," Rodney said.

"I want them back," Banjo said, handing Rodney the gloves.

Rodney put the gloves on while running to the men's car. He backed the car as close to the shed door as possible, which also made it impossible for Angelena or Karen to see what they were doing.

Banjo was sitting on a box with the men's pistols and the money laid out in two piles in front of him on another box. "Here, you should take one," he said, looking at the money.

"I don't want it," Rodney replied.

Banjo did not protest but put both piles back together and put the money in his pocket.

Rodney opened the trunk and he and Banjo quickly stuffed the men in it. "I wonder how many people they have done this to?" Rodney asked.

"It does not matter now," Banjo said.

Rodney wiped off the two pistols, tossed them in the trunk and closed it.

Rodney put his arm around Banjo's shoulder. "You could be a book, Banjo," he said. "If somebody wrote a book about this, people would think it was fiction."

"Tell people the truth and they think you are lying," Banjo said. "That's why I lie all the time, then people think I am telling them the truth."

"We should go to the house before we go to town," Banjo said.

Banjo and Rodney drank several cups of coffee and listened to Angelena and Karen talk about kids and weather and how to make tortillas. Rodney cut in on their conversation. "Banjo and I are going to get the truck unstuck and then I'm going to run him into town for supplies. We won't be gone long."

By Karen's reaction she did not care if he was gone for a year.

They left the house and walked to the truck.

"I stuck my truck once, just as winter was starting. It snowed so hard I did not get it out until spring," Banjo said.

It did not take Rodney long to get the truck off the rock and back on to the road. Riding back to the house, Banjo looked at the dash of the new truck and shook his head. "This is a nice truck, gringo, a real nice truck."

"It's Mr. Cook's," Rodney said.

"It is a lousy truck," Banjo said. "A real lousy truck."

Banjo drove the truck and followed Rodney toward Santa Fe.

Driving the new truck Banjo felt like a wealthy man. He wished he had a tailor made cigarette to smoke while he drove, then he would really feel rich.

Rodney took the back road into Santa Fe. Driving past the penitentiary he marveled how distant and yet so close the arm of the law could be.

Rodney parked the car behind the Sears store in the Villa Linda Shopping Mall. Even though he was wearing Banjo's gloves he wiped off the steering wheel and left the keys in the ignition. Banjo waited behind him, with the truck still running.

Banjo pulled away from the car. "Maybe I should feel bad," he said. "But I do not. People like that should be dead."

Rodney thought about the statement. He did not feel bad either. In fact, he did not feel anything, one way or other. He knew there was no evidence the authorities could link to Banjo. The two men were sure to have records. To the police, it would be another killing of hoods by other hoods.

"If I had a truck like this, I could take Angelena to town whenever she wanted to go," Banjo said.

But, in a moment he added, "If I had a truck like this, I would not have the gas to take it to town so it would sit and rust like my other one."

Rodney had Banjo stop at a convenience store and he bought two six packs of Budweiser. In the truck, he opened two cans and handed one to Banjo. Before they pulled out of the parking lot, they had finished their beers and opened another one. A police car pulled up next to them and Banjo waved. The white policeman nodded menacingly and went into the store.

Banjo drove slowly back to the house, wanting to enjoy driving while he could. There was deep satisfaction in driving Mr. Cook's truck. A satisfaction that seemed to have more meaning than killing his henchmen.

After five beers a piece, both men were feeling the effect. "Do you think there will be more men?" Banjo asked, opening the last beer.

"No," Rodney answered. "I think this will do it. Mr. Cook might find himself in trouble with the people who supplied the men. At least, it will be a big embarrassment."

"I don't know if I could keep doing this," Banjo said. "You know, in time your luck runs out."

Karen and Angelena were washing dishes when they got back. Keeping warm on the stove were tacos, a pot of beans and tortillas. Banjo smiled at his wife who grinned back at him with a hand-rolled cigarette hanging out of her mouth and wondered if she could tell he had been drinking. Karen walked over and kissed Rodney on the cheek. "I told you before, Rodney, she likes you too much," Angelena said.

"Nothing like home and a warm stove and good food," Banjo said, sitting down at the table.

After they ate, Rodney and Karen drove back to the Last Day In Paradise. It was late afternoon, but there still was at least an hour of sun left. Both of them were quiet during the drive. Karen was thinking about her afternoon with Angelena and how she enjoyed the lady.

"Why did Banjo blow up his woodpile?" Karen asked as they neared the headquarters to the ranch.

"He told me it was full of rats and he wanted to kill them," Rodney replied.

"Seems like a pretty radical way to do it," Karen said.

"They were big rats," Rodney said. "Really big rats."

Banjo saddled his horse and rode to check his sheep. He found them scattered along the fence, nibbling at semi-frozen blades of dark brown grass. Along the river on the Last Day In Paradise, a small swath of green grass still remained. Getting off the horse, Banjo started cutting the wire several posts down from where it had been fixed the last time. His sheep, knowing what he was doing, milled around him until the last wire fell out of the way and they darted toward the fresh water and grass. "Sorry, gringo," Banjo said, remounting his horse, "but it seems after all the problems in life, there are always problems that remain."

Riding toward the house, Banjo looked in the direction of the movie site and smiled.

When Banjo got back from cutting the fence, he went to work putting what wood was not disintegrated, back into a pile. Angelena, seeing him working, came out and helped. By the time it was dark, the wood was again in a pile and they went to the house. Angelena noticed Banjo looked very tired and grew worried. "I am happy the men did not hurt you," she said.

"I worried about you," Banjo said. "I do not know what I would do without you."

Angelena laughed. "You would go to town and chase all the pretty old women, and take them drinking and dancing like you never have me."

Banjo embraced Angelena. He held her for several minutes without speaking and then stepped back and looked into her eyes and smiled sadly.

There was no way he could tell her how he felt about her. No way he could take all the years and form them into words that would come anywhere close to what he wanted to say. Angelena reached over and touched his lips with her finger and then turned to her stove.

After dinner, Angelena rolled them two cigarettes and they sat smoking. Then she went to her room, put on her nightgown and slipped into bed. Banjo heard her pick up her book as he turned out the kitchen light and went to his room. Removing his boots, he looked around the small room and for the first time in weeks, he looked at the crucifix and remembered he had not been saying his prayers. But, he could not think of a prayer to say so he looked away from the crucifix. Turning off his light, he could see the wood pile exploding.

"I can still shoot," he thought proudly. "My father would be happy. He always thought I was a lousy shot."

Then he saw the light from Angelena's room filtering into his room. "Angelena," he called out. "Would you like some company?"

For a few moments there was no response, then Angelena called back, "I thought you would never ask."

Banjo left his rifle in the corner and walked to his wife's room. For now, there was no need for the rifle. For now, there was only the need for the warmth a blanket could not bring.

Twenty-three

*K*aren, having slept well, was filled with artistic juices, not bothering to get dressed she went to work on her painting. Within a few minutes, she had the sky finished and stepped back contemplating her first completed painting. After worrying over finishing the painting, now that the painting was done, it was like a child who had been born, grown, reached maturity and was now out in the world living their own life. "I like you," she said. "You will record forever an important aspect of my life."

Looking at the cowboy riding away, she felt sad for a brief instant. Then she shrugged her shoulders and said with determination, "If you leave, you leave, there is nothing I can do but go on."

Taking the painting from the stand, she set it on her dresser and put a blank canvas on the stand. She went to the kitchen and made a cup of jasmine tea and went back to the bedroom. Sitting on the floor, she looked at the empty canvas and formed paintings in her mind that would cover it. She did not know what the completed canvas would be, but she knew there would be an old Mexican woman, smoking a hand rolled cigarette, wearing a dark green cotton dress, a green sweater and men's shoes. In her face would be strength and time and endurance with a hint of sadness in her eyes—sadness, not for her, but for what she saw.

Rodney drank his morning coffee and he had the urge to go over to

Mr. Cook's house and beat the hell out of him and tell him his two goons were dead. But he knew Mr. Cook would know soon enough.

Rodney started thinking about Montana and how he would love to show Karen the wide open grasslands of Montana and the towering mountains. He wished he and Karen were in a log cabin back in the hills with the snow so deep they could not get out for the winter. Karen would have a room for her painting and he would have a room where he could sit and work on his saddles and bridles, and maybe, like Karen said, try his hand at writing. He figured, if nothing else, he could write about cowboys. But then Rodney felt sad. He knew he had to leave. And he had to leave Karen behind. He was no good for her. Rodney looked out the window at Karen's house. "I will have to tell you," he said. "I will have to tell you I am leaving and you are too much of a lady for me. Somewhere there will be a man for you. Rich and refined, gentle and caring, not caught up in a world that has passed him by. But I hope you won't forget me. I love you, Karen. Not out of lust, or for your money, but for your smile and the warmth you have given me. You have asked nothing of me but who I am. I can't deceive myself any longer. I have tried but it would not be fair to you."

The familiar loneliness Rodney carried with him for so many years covered him once again. A loneliness he knew and understood. A loneliness filled with no responsibilities, no chances of hurting or being hurt. He thought of Montana and the night stars and the coyotes and the elk. He thought about the first calf he ever roped, the singing of cowboys in the bunk house, and the way the fire in the pot-bellied stove danced with the silence of the night.

Mr. Cook was watching T.V. when a news bulletin came on. A car was found in the parking lot of the Villa Linda Mall with two bodies in the trunk. Seeing the faces of the men Mr. Cook was afraid and he knew that the people in Phoenix would want more than an explanation.

Rodney heard the airplane engines start. He had heard the news on the radio about the men being found and knew why Mr. Cook was leaving.

🐂 🐂 🐂

It was a nice day and Banjo was feeling better. Maybe it had been gas that was making him weak, or a bad stomach. As to the events of the previous day, they were past and nothing to think about.

Banjo sat in the shed and looked at his dynamite. "Gringo, I am sorry," he said. "You might have been a great movie star. But for all my people, and people like you, I must do what I am going to do. Life is not a movie, my friend."

Banjo went to work cutting and twisting fuses.

🐂 🐂 🐂

Hearing a knock on the door Rodney had a momentary fear it was the police and he was going to be arrested for accessory to murder. But going to the door, he saw Rosemary, the wardrobe lady. She was holding several hangers with clothes on them in one hand and boots and a dark hat in the other. When he opened the door, she walked in quickly. "About time you opened the door," she said. "It's cold as hell out here. I don't know why these idiots didn't want to film this western in California."

Rosemary was wearing a tiger-striped leotard tucked into white cowboy boots and a white, waist length, fur coat. Walking past Rodney, she went into the living room and tossed the clothes onto the sofa. "Here's your new identity, Rodney," she said. "I came to see you in your duds."

Rodney did not know what to say and stood looking at Rosemary feeling like an idiot.

"Yeah, I know, I make all men speechless." Rosemary said. "Why don't you take these clothes into your bedroom, put them on and come out and let me see how they fit. I think I have the right size."

Rodney did what he was told and took the clothes into his bedroom. He put on a heavy pair of black wool pants with light grey stripes and a double breasted dark blue shirt with brass buttons. There was a floppy, extra large, red bandanna that looked like it had been through the war and a grey cloth vest, worn with age. The black hat was almost as big as Banjo's and the boot tops almost hit him at the knees.

Seeing Rodney, Rosemary whistled. "You could have been making a decent living your whole life playing bandits in westerns instead of working your ass off as a real cowboy."

"So this is it," Rodney said.

"You'll have three outfits exactly like this one. Each morning you'll be told which one to wear, okay?" Rosemary said.

Rosemary walked around Rodney, pulled on his pants and shirt and rearranged the bandanna. "Perfect, just perfect. Shooting starts in two days, wear this, be at the set at 3:30 a.m. Report to me. I have a trailer that says WARDROBE on it."

With that, Rosemary pinched Rodney on the butt. Rodney was shocked. "Wish I had more time, hon," she grinned heading for the door. "I never had a real cowboy. I've had everything else though—stuntmen, producers, Jewish directors—but never a real cowboy."

Rodney was looking at himself in the mirror when Karen came in. "When do we rob the bank, Jesse?" she asked and added, "you look great."

"It's fake," Rodney said in a sullen voice.

"Aren't we in a good mood?" Karen said.

Rodney started pacing around the room. Karen watched him for as long as she could and finally said, "Why don't you tell me what's wrong? Watching you walk holes in the floor isn't exactly exciting. Besides, I only came over to see if you dumped me for an L.A. hooker," she said referring to Rosemary.

"I feel like a sham," he blurted. "I guess I don't want to perpetuate the myth."

"Lord Rodney," Karen said. "People don't really care about what's real and what isn't. Do you think people care for the land like you do or being their own man. People don't care. We spend fortunes going to movies and fantasizing about what life could be. And after the movie, we go back to being our own boring useless lives. It doesn't matter. There is no cowboy crusade."

"It matters to Banjo and me. Damn it, it's freedom Karen. It's like every time we go to a movie, we're giving up more of our freedom," Rodney said.

"Oh Rodney," Karen said softly, "There are no winners. Don't you see, we've destroyed all the winners."

Karen kissed Rodney on the forehead and ran her hand through his hair. "Cowboy, they stole freedom, only the myth is worth it now."

Karen was sad as she left the house. She gazed at the blue forever sky of New Mexico through the leafless branches of the cottonwood tree. The tree seemed a stark reality of hope and death.

Rodney took off the cowboy clothes and hung them in the closet. He wanted to go see Banjo and sit with the old man and talk about sheep and cattle and bandits and time. But instead, he went to the kitchen and opened a beer and tried not to think. But try as he might, all he could see was Karen—Karen who he must leave behind.

Twenty-four

When Angelena saw Armondo's car she was excited. But Armondo had a lady with him and the lady was white. For a moment, she feared what Banjo would say to the young woman, but, if Banjo started to get out of hand, she would shut him up. Since Armondo brought the lady with him, then he must really like her.

Angelena opened the door and Banjo stood up. When a tall, thin, very pretty white girl with long dark wavy hair came in first, Angelena was looking straight at Banjo. Banjo did not even flinch as the girl looked nervously around the kitchen. Armondo looked anxiously at his father. Angelena took their coats and put them in her bedroom and came back. "This is Vanessa," Armondo introduced the girl.

Vanessa smiled shyly.

"This is my father, Banjo and this is my mother, Angelena. I love them both dearly," Armondo said.

Banjo stood and put his arm around Vanessa's shoulder. "I know I am ugly and mean looking, but there is no need to be afraid little one," he said soothingly.

Angelena pulled out a chair for Vanessa to sit and the girl sat, seemingly relieved. "She is pretty, Armondo," Angelena said, hugging her son.

"He knows how to pick out beautiful women, like his father," Banjo said, smiling at Angelena.

Angelena went to Banjo's room and brought out his chair and sat down.

"Your father wants you to bring him a painting so he can put it on the wall," Angelena said to Armondo.

Armondo looked at his father, slightly confused. "I will," he said. "One I know you will like."

"Any painting my son does I will like," Banjo said.

"Vanessa is a dancer," Armondo said. "Right now, she is in a show that is performing at the Armory for the Arts."

"I have never been to a dance," Angelena said. "It must be very beautiful."

"I can get you tickets," Vanessa said, starting to feel relaxed.

"I would come pick you and mother up," Armondo said. "You should come." And then he added quickly, "Vanessa and I are getting married."

Angelena stood and put Vanessa's face between her hands and started to cry. Banjo looked at his wife, slobbering over the poor, white girl, and then looked at Armondo and stood and held out his hand to shake with his son. Armondo took his hand warmly and then hugged his father. "It is a different world father. In many ways, a better one than you knew," Armondo said.

Banjo sat down. "Yes, it is a different world," he said.
But, in truth, he did not know if it was better.

Banjo thought back to when he was young, and if a white woman would have gone with a Mexican, there would have been hell to pay from both families. The races lived side by side, but they were different. Although the Mexicans were never really true slaves they had been treated like slaves—drawing poor wages and never being able to afford what the white people had. But there had also been the powerful Mexican families who had inherited large tracts of land from the King of Spain. They treated their own people worse than the whites. The whites only thought they were superior. The rich Mexicans thought they were gods.

"I do hope you will grow to like me, Mr. Ortega," Vanessa said.

"He has never liked anything in his life except tortillas and this land we live on. If you can cook, he will like you. But if you can not cook, he will only tolerate you," Angelena said.

Banjo gave Angelena a hurt look.

"Your boots are quite beautiful, Mr. Ortega," Vanessa said.

"They are the most beautiful boots in the world," Banjo said with pride.

"Before I forget," Armondo said.

He took out of his pocket a cellular phone and handed it to Banjo. "You dial it like a regular phone. I will bring the bill out once a month."

Banjo gave it to Angelena. "Look, it is one of those phones that does not need wires. I asked Armondo to bring us one."

Angelena looked at the phone like it was a precious jewel.

Vanessa listened to Armondo and his parents talk about small things around the ranch. She had never been in a house so primitive in her life. It was a culture shock. But a shock she enjoyed. Armondo's parents seemed warm and loving. Her family was solid middle class with Midwest views and she knew it might not be as easy for her to bring a Mexican to meet her parents. But, if they did not accept him, she would still marry Armondo.

Banjo wanted to talk to his son alone so he stood up and motioned for Armondo to come with him.

Banjo sat on his bed and rolled a smoke while Armondo sat on the nightstand. "I am sorry I treated you as I did for so many years," Banjo started. "But I didn't make of my life as you and maybe, in some way, I have been jealous. I have known nothing but this land and nothing else was important to me. At times, it has been more important than you or your mother. But now I know I was wrong. Your life is your life. It is all you have."

"I know that father," Armondo said. "But living out here wasn't for me, that's all. I wasn't made to be like you. My paintings are to me what this land has been to you."

"If your mother was white, I might have been killed," Banjo said.

"Maybe one day nobody will care what color anybody is," Armondo said.

Banjo shook his head, "No, there will always be somebody who has to hate. Nothing will change that."

Banjo lit the cigarette and dodged the flame when a sharp pain shot through his chest and he lurched forward and gasped. Armondo grabbed Banjo as he fell to the floor. All the color drained from Banjo's face and his eyes rolled back in his head. "Mother! Mother!" Armondo cried out.

Angelena rushed into the room with Vanessa behind her and helped lay Banjo on the bed. Banjo started to cough and looked up at his wife and son. "It must have been..." but his words trailed off.

"You old goat," Angelena said, "now you will go to the doctor."

"Get him to my car," Armondo said urgently.

Angelena put Banjo's warm coat on him while Armondo went and started the car. Armondo and Angelena got Banjo into the front seat and then Angelena and Vanessa got in the back. Armondo drove as fast as he could, looking over at his father as they hit the bumps in the road. Banjo was sagging down in the seat but was still awake. Angelena started to pray and Vanessa put her arm around Angelena's shoulders.

Armondo came to a screeching halt in front of the emergency room of St. Francis Hospital. He ran inside, and within seconds, a team of nurses had Banjo on a stretcher and inside the hospital. Vanessa took Angelena to the waiting room while Armondo gave the head nurse all the necessary information. When he was finished, he went and parked the car and came back in. Vanessa sat with her arm around Angelena. Armondo was struck by how out-of-place his mother looked in the sparkling white hospital. She seemed to look older than time itself. He realized how sad his life would seem when they were gone. They were more than his parents—they were the end of a way of life.

About an hour later, a young intern walked to the waiting room. "Mrs. Ortega, your husband has a very bad heart. Although he is cussing and arguing with us that he feels fine, we know he isn't. There is nothing we can really do for him, it is only a matter of time. I'll give you a prescription for some pills our pharmacy can give you tonight and you can take him home. He must not exert himself. He needs rest, lots of rest."

Angelena got up and stood proudly before the young intern. "I understand," she said. "I understand."

Armondo filled the prescription. When he returned, Banjo was sitting with Angelena. He looked at Banjo in his fancy boots with their eagles and was filled with pride. This old man with nothing had raised him. Raised him on sheep and goats and pigs and hard work. Raised him with the outdoors to where, at an early age, he knew what he wanted and had the strength to go after it.

Vanessa and Armondo helped Banjo to the car while Angelena followed quietly behind. "It is like a dance," Vanessa thought to herself. "A dance of life, played out to man's music."

Banjo sat in the front seat slumped slightly forward. He felt weary. Although the pain was gone, his chest felt warm and sore. He remembered taking a few pills and it now seemed like he was floating. It was as though he was sitting on the roof of the car watching his son and wife and Vanessa below him. He could hear everything they said, but could not speak or be seen. He was invisible and the world could not touch him.

At the house, they lay him on his bed and Angelena removed his boots and coat and covered him with his blanket. Going to her room, she returned with another blanket and tucked it tightly around him. She set his head in the middle of the pillow and smoothed his disarrayed hair.

Armondo had filled the stove in the kitchen and he and Vanessa were sitting at the table. "You two go now," Angelena told them.

Armondo started to protest, but Angelena shook her head and he was silent.

By the door, Angelena kissed them both and as Armondo opened the door to his car, she called out, "Don't forget the painting, my son."

Angelena turned off the light in the kitchen, took a candle from the cupboard, lit it, and carried it into Banjo's room. She set it on the table by the bed and went to her room and put on her green sweater. Returning to Banjo's room, she sat down in his chair and looked at the old withered face illuminated by the candle. She was not afraid, nor was she sad. A feeling of contentment and warmth filled her. A feeling she had done her duty in life by sticking with this man, who, without her would have probably spent his life in jail. A man who had hated the white man his entire life and had never truly embraced her God. But also a man who had a good heart and was kind and loving. She knew Banjo prayed at times. But she had put the crucifix on his wall, not Banjo.

Banjo's head rolled to the side and his eyes opened momentarily and looked at Angelena sitting in his chair. A small, dry smile creased his lips and he tried to speak but nothing came from his mouth. "It is okay," Angelena soothed. "You are home and it is okay."

Banjo's eyes closed and he lay unmoving, with only the sound of his shallow breathing filling the room. But his mind did not stop. In his mind, he was young and riding a horse after hundreds of sheep. He was wearing a red shirt and yelling. Behind him, there was the crack of gunfire and the sound of a bullet singing overhead and he laughed—laughed so hard it hurt his sides.

Now he was in Santa Fe stacking wood beside an expensive adobe house. A white man stood in the doorway and watched him as he quietly stacked the wood so the rain and snow would not soak into it and make it hard to burn. The man said nothing. But Banjo knew the man felt superior. Mexicans were only second class people who trimmed hedges and hauled wood and knifed each other at parties. Banjo felt anger, a deep anger. Anger he could not have a large home. Anger at the looks he received. Anger at the wages he was doled out, as though his keepers were doing him a favor.

And then Banjo saw Rodney. But Rodney was not young and strong. Rodney was old and was riding beside a fence and he was crying. Crying because there was no way he could get around the fence. The fence went on forever and forever, passed all the mountains on the face of the earth and through all the rivers. Endlessly, around and around went the fence. Holding in all the people and all the animals and all thought.

Banjo moaned and Angelena got up from the chair and put her hand on his forehead. He did not feel overly warm, but she tucked the blankets tighter around him.

Banjo opened his eyes and again smiled at Angelena. "You are beautiful," he said softly before shutting his eyes.

Then Banjo saw before him the looming outline of the movie set. The fake buildings held up with two by fours and people walking up and down the street while cameras rolled and people shouted directions. He saw men wearing cowboy boots and hats who were not cowboys. And he saw thousands and thousands of people crowding around the movie set, touching it and pointing at it and making a god of it. And he wanted to shout, "It is nothing, it is a thief, it steals all that is true and proper."

When Angelena knew Banjo was sleeping, she got up and walked to her room and put on her nightgown. Lying down in bed, she looked at the crucifix and prayed, "Dear God, in all your compassion and love of man, you have been good to us in your simple and true way. For your love I thank you."

When Banjo woke up it was dark. The candle had burned itself out. His wife's snores echoed softly through the house. He felt weak and his side hurt, but he slowly sat up in bed. Moving around the room quietly, he put on his boots and coat and taking his hat and gloves, he tiptoed out of his room and through the kitchen. He left the door slightly ajar and went to the barn and got the dynamite and fuses. It was cold, but Banjo did not notice it. With the dynamite stuffed into his pockets, Banjo, with great difficulty, managed to saddle his horse. He quietly led it away from the corral before mounting, groaning as he did so.

Banjo nudged the horse lightly. "We ride, old friend," he said, "one last time, we ride."

Banjo felt he was part of the stars that glistened over head. He felt he was one with the shadowed trees. Stopping, Banjo looked back at the vague, dark outline of his house and smiled.

After awhile, Banjo could see the night light shining brightly above the headquarters to the Last Day In Paradise. When he was a boy, there was nothing there but a small pocket of oak trees. Riding on, he thought about his sheep sleeping along the small river several miles away and wondered who would get them. "What would my life have been without sheep?" he thought.

Banjo rode slowly. There was no hurry. It was though he knew, even if the sun had been up, nobody would see him or care. He was an old man on an old horse and it no longer mattered. He was not good for anything—a few faded dreams, a few heartaches, and a few wishes. It was as though his molecules were already slipping into the air, being absorbed by the trees and land around him. He was becoming part of the rocks and the sand.

Riding past the headquarters to the Last Day In Paradise, Banjo wanted to stop and see Rodney. He wanted to say, "Boy, it is because of you that I no longer hate you gringo bastards."

But, he rode on and looked at the darkened house and wished he could tell Rodney to go with the young lady. The pretty one who did not laugh at or ridicule his wife. "She loves you, cowboy," he said to the darkness.

Banjo stopped on the crest of a hill and looked down at the silhouetted buildings of the movie set. There were no lights on in the trailer the guards had been in the last time he was here. But, there were many trailers and several large tents that were not there before.

Banjo circled south and came in behind the movie set. He left the horse tied to a cedar tree and walked toward the back of the fake buildings on the east side of the street. Taking his time, he tied the fuses to the sticks of dynamite and placed them behind the buildings. When it was done, he took his last piece of fuse, which was over twenty feet long, and tied it to the last fuse. Then he sat down and with more care than he had ever taken in his life he rolled a smoke.

He lit the cigarette and a flame did not shoot from the end. "It is the best cigarette I have ever rolled in my life," he said with pride.

Shortly before sunrise, he heard a vehicle approaching and saw a school bus filled with people coming up the road that led to the site. A man got out of the bus with a bullhorn and proceeded to direct the people to the largest tent, which now was lit up. "All the extras go to the tent," he hollered. "There is coffee and donuts."

Banjo watched as fifty or sixty people, all dressed as though it were the mid 1800's, walked to the tent. There were a few scattered laughs and some loud coughing, but most still seemed asleep. Smiling, Banjo stood up and lit the fuse. The fuse sputtered to life and Banjo ran as quickly as he could to his horse. Mounting the horse, his side began to ache and tears formed in his eyes. But, he sat straight in the saddle and kicked the horse, who, to his surprise broke into a fast trot. He had not ridden more than one hundred yards when the first explosion rocked the fake western town. Within seconds, there was another explosion and then another, and another, and another and the entire movie set was engulfed in fire. He stopped the horse, looked at the flames and listened to another explosion and another. He heard the bullhorn man shouting something he could not understand. "I and my kind are not a movie," he hollered. "I am not a movie. I am a man."

By the fourth explosion, Rodney was out of bed and hurriedly getting dressed.

Karen, sleeping soundly, did not hear a thing.

Rodney drove to the movie site. When he arrived, all that remained of the movie set were smoldering clouds of white and black smoke. The extras were in the tent drinking as much coffee as they could and fighting over the last donuts. Rodney saw Rosemary and a group of men standing in the middle of what had been the town. Rodney ran to them. "I saw the man who did this, he was over there, on the hill, sitting on a horse and watching the whole thing," Rosemary said.

"What did he look like?" Rodney asked, already knowing what he would be told.

"Some guy with tall boots and a dark floppy hat. I couldn't see his face. The cops will have his ass," Rosemary snapped.

"I don't think so," Rodney said. "I really don't think so."

Rodney drove back to the ranch and made himself a cup of coffee. Drinking it, he sat and looked out the window and smiled a deep warm understanding smile.

He poured himself another cup of coffee and drank it quickly. Rodney went to the stable, saddled a horse and started riding toward the fence. He nudged the horse into a gallop and pulled his hat tightly down on his head.

Banjo rode his horse as quickly as he could. He felt himself slipping several times and had to hold onto the saddle horn with both hands. "The sheep, horse," he said. "The sheep."

When Banjo arrived at the river, he looked and could see his sheep in a small cluster by the water and he grinned. He rode down to them and looked at them and then rode to the hole in the fence and onto his own property. He slid wearily out of the saddle and tied the horse to a small cedar tree and sat down with his back against a sandstone rock. He took out his tobacco and tried to roll a cigarette but his hands were shaking so badly he could not. He set the tobacco tin on the ground. He looked at the fence and remembered when it had not been there and then shutting his eyes, he could see the little river when it was springtime. Tiny yellow and blue flowers would blossom along it. He could see himself, as a boy, trying to catch frogs and dragonflies that lived by the stream and then herding the sheep back toward the house where his father liked them at night. He opened his eyes and muttered, "Angelena."

Rodney saw the sheep and saw the hole in the fence. He saw Banjo, with his black hat and tall boots, sitting with his back against the rock. It seemed like the eagles on Banjo's boots were trying to fly. Banjo waved at Rodney and grinned his devilish grin.

Rodney dismounted, tied his horse to a fencepost and sat down by the old man. He saw Banjo's tobacco laying on the ground and noticed that Banjo's face had lost all it's color. "You should have seen it, gringo," Banjo said gasping for breath between each word. "The explosion, the flames, the smoke. You should have seen it."

"I bet it was beautiful," Rodney said.

Banjo coughed. "I did it for all the people like you and me, gringo."

"There's going to be big trouble, Banjo," Rodney said, picking up a small twig and putting it in his mouth.

"I know," Banjo answered. "But I do not care."

"I didn't think you would," Rodney said, staring at the hole in the fence.

Banjo felt his chest tighten but tried not to show it. "I don't think the sheep will cut the fence anymore, gringo," he said. "I think the sheep is tired."

"I doubt it," Rodney said. "I think the sheep will always cut the fence, as long as there is a fence, he will cut it."

"It would be nice if you would roll me a smoke and then light it," Banjo said. "My fingers are tired."

He handed Rodney two stick matches.

Rodney rolled a cigarette and started to hand it to Banjo when Banjo's head sagged and the black hat rolled to the ground. Rodney knew Banjo was dead.

He picked up the black hat, brushed it off and put it on Banjo's head and looked out past the fence and the sheep to the mountains. "You died with your boots on," he said to Banjo and brushed a tear from his eye.

Rodney stuck the cigarette in his mouth and lit it. A large flame shot out of the end of the cigarette. He smoked the cigarette half way, butted it, and put the butt in Banjo's pocket.

He got Banjo's horse and picking up the frail body lay him over the saddle. He mounted his own horse and holding onto Banjo's reins led Banjo home.

Rodney looked at the pinon trees and the cedar trees, gnarled and twisted from the New Mexico weather. He watched two mountain jays dart between the trees, waiting for spring to fly back to the mountains.

Angelena was about to go in the house with an arm full of wood. Seeing Rodney she dropped the wood. She did not cry as Rodney carried Banjo into the house and lay him on his bed. Rodney pulled Banjo's boots off and placed them in the corner and put his black hat on top of them. Rodney wanted to say something to Angelena but nothing seemed adequate.

Angelena knelt down beside Banjo. "Our Father, who art in heaven, hallowed be Thy name....."

Rodney put Banjo's horse in the corral, fed it, and checked its water. He went to the shed and found Banjo's wire cutters.

Rodney rode to the fence. He walked for hours and cut each strand of wire between each fence post that paralleled Banjo's land. When he finished, the sun was beginning to set and he tossed the wire cutters to the ground and said, "They'll never fence you in again, Banjo."

Back at the ranch, Rodney unsaddled the horse, but he did not put him in his stall. Opening the door for the other horse, it bolted out. The two horses galloped into the vast, dark expanse of the ranch.

Rodney packed his suitcase and tied his sleeping bag to it. Leaving the house, he did not shut the door. He looked at the large mansion, the empty corrals and the stalls and felt like he was in the middle of a void.

Karen was in the kitchen when Rodney walked in without knocking. She started to speak but she saw his suitcase. Her heart felt like it suddenly turned old. Rodney did not smile. Setting the suitcase down, he pursed his lips, removed his hat, looked her straight in the eyes and said, "Do you want to go to Montana?"

"When?" Karen asked almost in a whisper.

"Right now," Rodney answered.

"Do you love me?" she asked.

"I love you, Karen, more than anything in the world," Rodney answered.

"How will we get there?" Karen asked.

"Your car," Rodney answered.

"Okay," Karen said and went to her bedroom.

She packed two suitcases and brought them to the kitchen. "We're not coming back, are we?" she asked.

"Never in a million years," Rodney vowed.

Karen went back to the bedroom and put the obsidian arrowhead in her pocket before picking up the painting. She looked at the cowboy riding away, the owl flying toward her, the arrowhead cloud, the hidden yellow rose, and smiled.

She put the painting in the fire place, poured starter fluid on the canvas, and tossed a match. The painting burst into multi-colored flames. Karen watched the painting until it was only ashes.

"What did you burn?" Rodney asked as he picked up her suitcases.

"An ending," Karen said.

Printed in the United States
49314LVS00005B/1-51